By Love Divided

The Lydiard Chronicles | 1630 - 1646

ELIZABETH ST.JOHN

Published by Falcon Historical Press 2017
ISBN: 978-0-9993944-1-0

Other books by Elizabeth St.John

The Lydiard Chronicles | 1603 – 1630
The Lady of the Tower
A Novel
Counterpoint: Theo, Earl of Suffolk
A Novelette

Praise for The Lady of the Tower
BRAG Medallion Honoree

"Elizabeth St.John has brought the early Stuart Court in the years before the
English Civil War vividly to life."
Historical Novel Society

"The Lady of the Tower is a beautifully produced novel with a well-crafted
story that will keep you both engaged and entertained."
Writers Digest 24th Annual Book Awards

" Elizabeth St John brings these years of Stuart England to the fore, bringing the
known facts of her ancestor's life together with richly imagined scenes creating in the
process a believable heroine, an intriguing plot and an enjoyable novel. "
Discovering Diamonds

Author's Note

The quotes, letters, and poetry featured at each chapter heading are extracts from Lucy Apsley Hutchinson's own work, *Memoirs of the Life of Colonel Hutchinson*, edited by N.H. Keeble; and *Order and Disorder*, edited by David Norbrook. For reader clarity, I have changed Lucy Hutchinson's use of third person point of view into first person.

Writing is said to be a lonely profession, but researching certainly isn't. My sincere thanks to the many people who threw their time and energy into reading various drafts and answering my incessant questions. This includes the online writing community at Scribophile.com, my alpha reading group Reading Between the Wines, Deborah and Sally for fine beta draft insights, and the landlords of pubs from Exmoor to Nottingham who invited me into hidden rooms and secret tunnels.

I'd also like to thank the enthusiastic staff and volunteers at libraries, council offices, churches, cathedrals and archives across England, including those of Barnstaple, Exeter, Nottingham, and Essex, along with the National Archives, who supplied priceless original documents and esoteric chats. Much appreciation to members of various societies, including the Sealed Knot, who helpfully described the sounds of a 17th Century battle and guided me through the lost gardens of Owthorpe.

Huge thanks to my extraordinary editors Jenny Quinlan and Emma Craft, who rescued me from plotholes and pluperfect.

Finally, my heartfelt gratitude to my family and friends who have traveled with me from obscure battlegrounds to ancient churches and ruined castles, cheered me on through the dragons of doubt, and lovingly guided me back into the 21st century when I would have rather stayed in the 1600s.

A word on Lydiard

The St.John family home of Lydiard Park and House, along with St. Mary's Church, is located just west of Swindon, England. Set in more than 200 acres of beautiful parkland, the house is open to the public, and contains many portraits of the St.John family featured in The Lydiard Chronicles. St. Mary's Church, one of the finest small churches in England, is full of extraordinary monuments, including The Golden Cavalier, Sir John St.John's life-size tribute to his favorite son, Edward.

The Friends of Lydiard Park is an independent charity dedicated to supporting the conservation and continued enhancement of Lydiard House and Park

www.LydiardPark.org.uk
www.FriendsofLydiardPark.org.uk
www.stmaryslydiardtregoze.co.uk

Selected Family Trees

❧

Sir Oliver St.John, Viscount Grandison b. 1559 (m) Joan Royden
- *No issue*

Sir John St.John b. 1552 (m) Lucy Hungerford
- *Sir John St.John b. 1586 (m) Anne Leighton*
    - *John b.1616*
    - *William b.1617*
    - *Edward b.1618*
    - *Walter b.1622*

- *Eleanor St.John b. 1587 (m) Sir William St.John*
    - *Huw b. 1612*

- *Barbara St.John b. 1588 (m) Sir Edward Villiers b. 1585*
    - *William, Viscount Grandison b. 1614*
    - *Anne, Lady Dalkeith b. 1610*

- *Lucy St.John b.1589 (m) Sir Allen Apsley b. 1573*
    - *Allen b.1617*
    - *James b. 1618*
    - *Luce b. 1620*
    - *Barbara b. 1623*

- *Sir Thomas Hutchinson b. 1589*
    - *John b. 1615*
    - *George b. 1618*

- *Sir Leventhorpe Francke b. 1584*
    - *Mary b. 1620*

- *Sir John Petre*
    - *Frances Petre b.1624*

Map

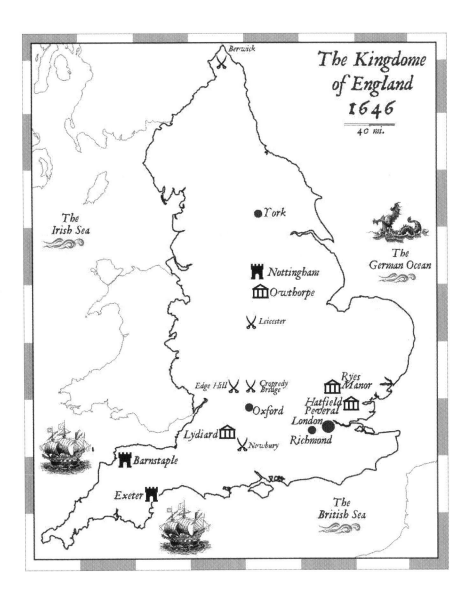

The Kingdome of England 1646

40 mi.

Berwick

The Irish Sea

York

Nottingham

Owthorpe

Leicester

The German Ocean

Edge Hill

Cropredy Bridge

Ryes Manor

Hatfield Peveral

Oxford

London

Lydiard

Richmond

Newbury

Barnstaple

Exeter

The British Sea

Prologue

The fire is most fervent in a frosty season.

Luce

21st August, 1642

These were the times in which Lucy Apsley questioned if God had deserted her.

Around the table, her children gathered. When had they grown into men and women? Where went the innocent Allen, the child in Luce? These young people talked recklessly tonight.

Lucy shook the ghosts of yesteryear from her thoughts.

Be grateful for the hour at hand, the joy shared in this pleasing home.

Still, the doubts chattered in her mind. The past crept close tonight, the door ajar between dead and living.

This dinner was a happy occasion, a celebration of Allen's knighthood. A fresh carp caught in their own fishponds graced the table. Elegant clothes were unpacked from trunks, dried lavender shaken from the skirts. Even Luce, always careless with her dress, wore a fine gown of blue watered silk, dotted with moonstones.

And then, as unpredictable as a summer storm, a lightning exchange heralded dispute.

For the king. Against the king. Favored by Villiers. Betrayed by Parliament.

Those old arguments restored her husband's memory, twelve years departed from this life. And now, their past disputes echoed in her children.

"Where lies your loyalty, Allen?" demanded Luce. "Your family deserves the truth."

He shrugged, his broad shoulders strong under the fine holland shirt, the beautifully cut doublet. Court was good to her son.

"Why, Luce," he replied, "As God is my witness, I am loyal to His Majesty and faithful to the Parliament. My heart lies with the men of this country, and their wish for peace."

1

"By forming armed bands of Cavaliers?" cried Luce, her voice rising. "My heart is loyal and faithful too—loyal to the Parliament who represent the rights of men, faithful to the tradition of monarchy. Consider your own world order, not mine."

Allen stood too, his soldier's physique suddenly charging the atmosphere. His color rose. "The king is as a father to the people of this nation. He knows what is best for them."

"Is that why he commandeers our ammunition, leaves our towns defenseless, our woman and children vulnerable to any band of armed men?"

"Keep to your writing and notebooks, Sister, and leave the business of government to men."

Lucy prayed for the storm to subside. Thus always ranged their arguments, until one caught the other's eye, and a shared smile would appear, contagious and healing.

Please, God, let this night be no different.

"Tomorrow, we ride to Nottingham to attend King Charles," she said. "He speaks to unite our country, to stand down the armies. Tonight, let not differences divide us."

A mother knows what is best for her children. And still, they seek out their own destinies. Perhaps, once more, she could protect her children with a lie.

God save us. For again, the fate of my family and of England lies within this deceitful king's hands. And if he cannot have his way, he will destroy us all.

1

Our uncle Lord Grandison was married to a lady so jealous of him, and so ill-natured in her jealous fits to anything that was related to him, that her cruelties to my mother exceeded the stories of stepmothers.

Luce Apsley

16th January, 1631

Leaving sweet Chelsea for the Battersey shore, Lucy was ferried to the underworld, where Cerberus guarded the gates to Hades. Only this hell was her childhood home, and the sentinel, Aunt Joan.

"Hold tight to the side, my Lady Apsley." The Thames boatman, etched black against the lowering January sky, stood and plied his oar. "The current runs strong upon the shallows."

Lucy already gripped the weathered wood, for she knew this treacherous river of old. On the southern bank appeared St. Mary's spire, an obelisk marking the family crypt. There, her uncle would reside, laid beneath the chancel, where the flesh would fall from his bones and his spirit be exalted to the heavens.

Lord Oliver St.John, Viscount Grandison, no longer of this world. Another funeral, when her husband's death still shrouded her heart.

Would she ever be free of the melancholy? A tear stung her eye— surely from the hostile wind, unfurling silvery banners all the way from the Tower and the cold northern sea beyond.

"Do not despair, Mother. You have me to care for you," murmured her son, Allen's namesake, fourteen and caught between youth and manhood. Her eldest boy, a witness to more in the Tower than any child ought.

He huddled close to her on the rough plank bench, his threadbare cloak pulled tight across his chest. Those final years in the Tower afforded no new clothes, for the departing prisoners left but shabby pickings. At least she'd salvaged mourning silks, payment obligatory for their keeper duties.

Lucy sighed. Her husband had been so proud of his appointment. Sir Allen Apsley. Keeper and Lieutenant of the Tower of London, with all the fees and privileges that accompanied the position. Three thousand pounds he'd paid for that perquisite, moving them into the Tower to administer the prison. And so little income, after the Duke of Buckingham's death ended his favors. All had turned to dust in their last years of residence.

Her son nudged her, breaking her thoughts. Those clear glass-gray eyes. Lucy's heart clenched at the youthful reflection of her husband, before the ruinous debts and the devastating consumption had drained the life from him. Death came as a relief, his Calvinist soul content with its destiny. Who was she to challenge the doctrine that sustained her through her darkest hours? Sir Allen Apsley's time was done.

Lucy smiled and took his cold-reddened hand. "Boon—"

"Allen," he corrected her.

"Allen," she continued. So, his childhood nickname departed also. "No mother could ask more of her son, and the example you set for your brother and sisters. In these difficult times, you are still our boon."

He flushed, his young skin translucent, the down on his chin almost stubble. "Father would have wished this so. He instructed me to protect our family upon his death. My training with the Yeoman Warders will serve me well."

The wind gusted bitter at the river's center, pushing their craft upstream as the boatman struggled to steer a straight course. A fragment of muddy ice floated by, and as they approached the bulrushes, more appeared. How deep the winter gnawed.

"Eleanor is waiting for us." Lucy's heart quickened. Her beloved sister stood on the snow-covered landing, bundled in black furs and a deep hood. As the boat edged closer, Eleanor's delicate face reflected the brittle light, framed by the glossy beaver skins.

"My darlings," she called. "Praise God, you arrive safely."

Lucy stepped from the rocking boat and stumbled into Eleanor's arms.

"I have missed you sorely," she whispered.

"Sweet Lucy, your life has transformed since leaving the protection of the Tower. I am heartbroken at your suffering," responded her sister softly. Her tone lightened, "Ah, Allen, look at you—how much you have grown!"

She held her hands out to Allen as he clambered to the landing. The boatman handed up their packs and tipped his hat in thanks as Eleanor paid him.

Lucy stood silently on the dock, memories surfacing. This riverbank once was her haven, until she'd discovered the plague man, dead in the reeds. Then came the summer of change, when Uncle Oliver returned from the Irish wars, bringing with him her cousin William.

"How is Will?" she asked. "You wrote he is at sea?"

Eleanor nodded, her eyes softening. "My husband is happiest when on his ship, Lucy; you know that." She shrugged under the heavy furs, making light of her feelings as only Eleanor could. "He sails regularly to the Americas. And yet, the commerce is still not forthcoming."

Lucy glanced through the black lacework of twisted apple trees to the manor. Unrecognizable since her time here, what with Aunt Joan's vulgar adornments of turrets and a false front. Beneath, the old house she knew still rested, ancient bones settling into the ground, decay concealed behind its rendered face. Best get this over soonest.

Lucy reached for the comfort of Allen's hand. "Should we go? This cold bites to the bone."

"And even more so inside. Joan has not changed her frugal ways, despite her title." Eleanor led the way along the frosty path, her boots squeaking on the gravel. "She will expect to see you tonight at the funeral, not before. She has kept to her rooms since Oliver's death."

"And Barbara?" Lucy's voice hung with the mist of her breath in the frigid air.

"She arrives later this evening."

So Barbara attends. Of course. She was Joan's favorite. My sister. My enemy.

As they entered the great hall, Lucy paused, unable to take a step farther until catching her breath. They haunted still, events from so long ago. The cruelties of Aunt Joan lingered like a canker in her soul.

Now, the room was draped in full mourning. Black velvet canopied the walls, covering the mirrors and windows, swathed from the curving banisters, and shrouded the portraits. Even the visitors' bowl of water on the board was covered by a dark wool cloth.

"She commands all this?" Lucy asked Eleanor. "Joan keeps to the old ways. There is no reflection anywhere."

"She fears the spirits. Her conscience is not clear. She does not want to keep him earthbound."

"Where is Oliver?" At her side, Allen drew himself up taller.

"In his library. His favorite room." Eleanor paused. "You wish to see him? You can wait and rest."

"No. I prefer now," replied Lucy.

In the dim chamber, surrounded by pillars of candles in tall sconces, a coffin lay on a long table. The cloying smell of wax masked a sweet, sickly odor and mingled with the pungent essence of rosemary crushed beneath their feet. The carved cedar-paneled walls closed in as they entered, and the tang of ink and vellum from a thousand books disguised the scent of death.

Lucy walked slowly forward, Allen at her side. As they approached the coffin, the strong features of her uncle appeared, illuminated by the flickering candles. A faint glint on his armor reflected the tiny flames. Allen did not falter, but stood respectfully at the coffin's edge.

She reached out and calmly touched the dark painted elm where the wood met the black silk lining. There was no expense spared in the construct of the coffin. Oliver's face was slackly smooth and already presented as an effigy. She recognized his visage, but he was not there.

Thank you, she thought, not trusting herself to speak aloud. *Thank you for bringing me to your home when I was orphaned and no one wanted me. Thank you for your love, although you were absent. You did the best for me as you knew how. We were all victims of the Villiers' ambition, you as much as any of us.*

Lucy leaned over the coffin and kissed his brow, unyielding as stone.

"Good-bye, Uncle," she whispered. "Good-bye."

Eleanor took Lucy's arm and led the way to a front chamber. The chill wreathed around them, a meager fire quivering in the grate, helpless to dispel the cold. More black hangings draped the window frames and a mirror. A pitcher of water and a platter of bread and cheese stood on a table.

They sat on a bench by the window, Eleanor lighting a lamp in the waning afternoon light. Wavering shadows stretched across the sparsely furnished chamber. "How fare you, Lucy?"

"Our life has been difficult since leaving the protection of the Tower," Lucy admitted. "In the last days of his illness, Allen could do little except try to fight off the creditors. Even the king refused to acknowledge his letters or make good on his warrants. Thank you for the cart to take us to the manor at Newington. I had one less expense to worry about. But the house is derelict, and we cannot remain."

"Have you heard nothing from Lord Goring?" Eleanor tucked a portion of her fur over Lucy and huddled closer. "He should be active in your probate. Six months have passed since Allen's death."

Lucy shook her head. "No. And I have written many times. He does not acknowledge my letters."

"What will you do? Can your brother-in-law Apsley help? And what of Allen's other children—Peter and Jocasta? Are they not mentioned in the will? Can their mother's family come to your assistance? She was well connected."

Lucy shook her head at Eleanor's rush of questions.

"John Apsley is a simple country man. Allen named him as the other executor only to appease him. But he has no experience when it comes to court and petitioning the king. As for Peter and Jocasta, I hear little. Peter is on the Continent, fighting for the Dutch." Lucy stared at the small flame struggling in the fireplace. "He always was a hothead. And Jocasta has her life with the Blounts. She and her husband have little contact with me." She rubbed her eyes. "Eleanor, I must travel to the palace at Whitehall while I am here, to confront Lord Goring. I have to know what he is doing to hasten the probate. Our money runs low, for all was tied to Allen's position as Keeper."

Eleanor nodded. "I think that may be best, Lucy. And can John assist?"

"John?" Lucy's voice raised, and she quickly muted her tone again. "Our brother made it very clear to me that I should not rely on him to help untangle my husband's debts. He still congratulates himself on avoiding the fall of Buckingham and the scandal. John plays squire in the country with his new wife, and has no interest in shouldering Lord Goring's responsibilities."

"What about . . ." Eleanor's voice trailed off.

"Barbara? You cannot mean that." Lucy laughed, but with no mirth. "She would rather die than help by influencing the judges at Chancery Court. And I would rather die than ask her."

In the silence that followed, the old house creaked around them. A door slammed, and a woman's sobbing echoed loud, then faded. Lucy glanced at Allen. He paid no heed. They'd lived with far worse in their last years in the Tower. They may have lodged in the official residence of the Keeper and his family, but they had still been surrounded by prisons.

"You will see her tonight. Time has passed." Eleanor took Lucy's hand.

"Three years."

"Three years since you last met. Perchance her humor has mellowed."

Lucy sighed. "I think not, Eleanor. We exchanged such words that could never be forgotten. She hates me, and always will."

"But she won Theo. And at the end of it all, she has a title, riches, a lover at court."

"There is no cure for envy of the spirit, Eleanor. And in her jealous mind, Theo chose me first."

Eleanor reached across and smoothed the wrinkle from Lucy's brow.

"Yes, he did, Lucy. He loved you, despite Barbara's deceptions. You are fortunate to have been loved by two men."

"And lost them both," replied Lucy. "You are fortunate to have been loved by one and still keep him close, Sister." A tear brimmed from her eye, and she brushed it away impatiently. "This talk of the past will get us nowhere. I must look to my future and that of my children. God has a plan for us; he has a destiny mapped since our birth. All I can do is trust in his mercy."

"And your head and heart too." Eleanor kissed her cheek, and the familiar warmth of her sister's love comforted Lucy. "Do what you think is best, sweet sister, and you will find the way forward out of these troubles. Barbara's malice will not deter you from your course."

Shouts from outside penetrated the melancholy room. Lucy turned to the window and pushed aside the heavy drape, scratching at the frost-etched glass with her fingernail. A cavalcade of riders circled the yard in front of the manor, breaking the stillness. The riders wore black, mounted on great chargers. She counted four men with fine Spanish riding boots and coats of heavy leather—her brother, and three of his sons.

Allen appeared at her side, drawn by the commotion.

"They look like the king's troop," he breathed. "Their stallions are the most handsome I have ever seen."

"John rides so to honor our uncle," replied Lucy. "Oliver was an exceptional army commander. My brother and his sons are paying their respects the way they know best."

A cortege of a dozen matched black Belgian horses came into view, pulling a draped wagon. On its sides were wooden tablets painted with Oliver's heraldic shields. A half-dozen or so men—hired pallbearers, Lucy assumed—brought up the rear of the procession. Now, the stable lads lit torches around the drive, and orange flames leapt in the cold air as night's dark velvet curtain enfolded them.

"We should leave." Eleanor interrupted her thoughts.

Lucy started. Her mind was back at St. Peter's, the Tower's own chapel and her husband's final resting place. At least he had been given that honor. His funeral had been a hurried affair, scant funds left to pay for the mourners or the pallbearers. In truth, she recalled little of the day, as she'd tended the children's well-being, paying scant attention to her own grief.

She gathered herself. She had faced worse. "Come, Allen. Don your cloak and hat. The temperatures will be woefully cold in the church."

To Eleanor, she murmured, "A very plain funeral. No other mourners, and just our family attending?"

"'Twas his request," Eleanor replied. "Barbara wanted to give him a full burial ceremony according to his rank, but it was not his decree."

They walked through the great hall. An awkward procession was slowly negotiating the staircase, led by a tiny figure swathed in black, half-carried by two burly footmen. Two maids trod behind. Aunt Joan.

Lucy curtsied deeply, as did Eleanor. Allen bowed. The old woman flicked a glance from her rheumy eyes, but did not acknowledge them. Staring ahead, her prominent nose white against the blackness of the hall, she clutched the hands of the footmen. Her gnarled fingers were ringless, great loops of jet necklaces her only jewels.

She was a cadaverous shell of a woman. Lucy exhaled. Loss claimed its own vengeance on her stepmother. Now, she knew the suffering that accompanied death's grasp. And from thence came retribution for those evils done so long ago. There was nothing left to fear in this empty vessel.

9

"Where is Barbara?" Joan's voice, surprisingly strong for her frail appearance, brought back a flood of memories.

Outside, the crunch of wheels on gravel. A large coach, by the sound of the rumbling.

"She arrives now, Aunt Joan," replied Eleanor.

"Very well. Eleanor, she will take us to the church in her carriage." Joan held out her arm, turning her back on Lucy. "The rest will follow on foot."

No surprise in the exclusion. And no matter. Lucy was not staying long. The pallbearers carried the coffin from the house. Time she left, too.

A toll of the bell—six for a man, and a further threescore and ten for his age—rang the news of Oliver's burial. The creaking and cracking of the ice from the river punctuated their steps as they followed the cortege along the snowbound lane.

Allen gripped Lucy's arm. "Aunt Barbara did not invite us to ride with her in the carriage?" His question was offhand, almost a statement.

"I did not expect her to. Do not lower yourself to her pettiness by mentioning this again," Lucy replied.

At the church door, they paused as the coffin was removed from the cart, the thick-cloaked pallbearers struggling on the icy path.

Lucy refused to be relegated to the rear of the procession. She guided Allen through the open door, nodding briefly to the clergyman before walking down the aisle. The space was bare, echoing. In the family pew, the veiled figures of Joan, Eleanor, and presumably Barbara were facing the chancel. They did not stir as her footsteps echoed on the tile. John turned and nodded solemnly as he caught sight of Lucy. His younger son, Edward, turned as well, and broke into a smile. At her side, Allen relaxed a little. At least his favorite cousin was close by.

A yawning hole in the chancel floor revealed the St. John family crypt, and a fetid odor greeted her as she drew near. The huge stone slab lay to the side, the tomb ready to receive Oliver. Funeral hatchments hung from poles lining the walls. Clusters of pillar candles lit the chancel, but did not penetrate the damp darkness below.

The shuffling of the pallbearers heralded Oliver's funeral procession, and Allen turned to watch the coffin carried down the aisle. In a moment, it passed them, and in another, the casket reached the crypt. Within minutes, after the clergyman recited the Lord's Prayer, the pallbearers lowered the coffin into the floor. No hymn was sung, no sermon preached.

True to his wishes, Oliver's remains were interred with the sparseness his soldier's character commanded. Joan did not move, even as her beloved husband's remains were delivered to God.

The clergyman motioned for the family to depart from the church. Lucy held her arm across Allen, keeping them standing still. For the first time, Lucy looked upon Barbara's face as her sister walked up the aisle. Framed by a black hood and a high black ruff, her face was immobile, her perfect features as if carved from alabaster. She paused.

"Ah. The prodigal niece." Barbara lifted an eyebrow and nodded slightly. "I assume all else has failed."

Before Lucy could respond, her sister walked past. John stood at the vault, his sons at his side. The three boys were joined by another: William, Barbara's son, the new Viscount Grandison. Of course the Duke of Buckingham reached from beyond the grave to favor his nephew with Oliver's title. Allen slipped from the pew and reunited with his cousins.

The family gathered. Now, to return to the manor and the reading of Oliver's will. And face the woman who'd once betrayed all she held dear.

2.

My mother was by the most judgments preferred before all her elder sisters, who, something envious at it, used her unkindly.

Luce Apsley

17th January, 1631

Lucy's hands clenched in her lap as the clergyman read the list of bequests to the men of the parish, friends, clerks, and servants.

"*And to John St. John, the second son of my nephew Sir John St. John, all my goods and chattels in the realm of Ireland . . .*

"*And finally, to Richard Little, John Bird, Elizabeth Marsh . . .*"

The reading concluded.

"You appear to have nothing, Lucy." Barbara stood and smoothed the watered silk of her skirts. "My son, of course, inherited the title, Viscount Grandison, and all the benefits. Oliver even remembered his servants—twenty pounds each."

"That's enough, Barbara." John stood. His boys rose to their feet too. "This is neither the place nor time to talk of these matters."

"I disagree." Barbara approached Lucy. String upon string of jet and priceless black pearls encircled her white throat and draped across her exquisitely fitted velvet bodice. Black diamonds dangled from her ears; ebony combs held her delicately curled hair. Barbara fared well.

"He left you nothing because you deserve nothing, Lucy," she continued. "Your husband was a profligate debtor and nearly brought our family down with his schemes—"

"That is not true." Color burned in Lucy's cheeks. "Your brother-in-law, the Duke of Buckingham, devastated our family—"

"—while we struggled to regain our political capital," Barbara continued as if Lucy had not spoken. "Oliver left his riches to those who would be the rightful custodians of the titles, the land, the heritage for future generations. You have no claim, my dear, as your past indicates."

John's voice cut across them again. "Barbara," he warned.

Lucy froze. She should never have come, never have considered she could enter this world again.

"So, what did your Victualler leave you, Lucy?" Barbara continued. The room was quiet. "What do you have . . . four children? Let me see if I can remember. Of course, there's Allen . . ." She nodded to the young man standing tall with his cousins. "Luce, her father's little prodigy, James . . . and my namesake, Barbara."

"Leave my children from your conversation, Sister," Lucy warned. "They are no concern of yours."

"Ah, little Barbara. Babs. Of course—you nearly died birthing her, didn't you? If not for your husband urgently sending to me at court for the king's physicians, you wouldn't be here today." Barbara's voice was silk in the muted chamber. "So much for his faith in Calvinism, Sister. He ran straight to the Villiers when he encountered a crisis. Your beloved, grateful husband, naming her after me. How charming."

"Only once, Barbara, and never again did he call on Villiers for help. And that, Sister, is my children's most important inheritance. They are free of the Villiers' taint and all that come alongside." Lucy's temper boiled over. "Yours are not. For you mortgaged their future by marrying them to Theo's heirs. Along with securing yourself a place in hell reserved for procurers."

"That's enough." John stepped between them and, as he had so many times before, separated them. "Barbara, you have gained much this evening with Oliver's death. Leave the past behind."

Lucy sipped her wine. Her fingers shook slightly, but none would see. She had not crumbled in front of Barbara; her dignity remained intact. John avoided her eye. God forbid any controversy would disturb his peaceful existence. Barbara took her leave of Aunt Joan, kissing the old woman's wizened cheek. Her carriage no doubt stood ready to return her to Whitehall and her lover, Theophilus Howard, the Earl of Suffolk.

Lucy turned to the boys. "Edward, take Allen, ask the cook for a hot meal. You must be hungry. He does not need to attend me."

"Mother, I can stay—"

"No, I insist." Lucy kissed her son's cheek. "I will be retiring shortly. Tomorrow, we ride to court to visit Lord Goring."

"Lord Goring?" John's voice made her turn on her heel. "Why do you seek him out, Lucy?"

So now he was interested, that she called upon a highly-ranked courtier. "Probate is delayed, John. I am begging him to plead with the Chancery judges to review Allen's will, to pursue the warrants the king owes in payment to us."

"You are settled in Newington Manor. Why the haste? Do not upset Lord Goring with your troubles."

"My troubles happen to be his responsibility as executor." She was so tired. Surely for once he could understand her predicament, listen to her side. "And Newington Manor is uninhabitable, John. We cannot stay there any longer."

She searched his face, looking for compassion in his blue eyes, urging him to remember their youthful closeness. Once, he'd brought all the sisters back together again, given them a home. Was that memory really forgotten?

After an eternity, John nodded.

"For Anne's sake, I cannot let you suffer." He held his arms out to her, but she could not yet return his embrace. "My late wife loved you as her dearest sister." John cleared his throat. "I regret that I was absent when Allen died. My duties at Lydiard occupied me."

Lucy hesitated, for the memories of her beloved sister-in-law constricted her voice. She did not completely believe John's excuse. And yet, time for this vicious circle of bickering to end. John took her hands, gripping them tightly. She stared at the satin ribbons entwined in his velvet doublet, the delicate stitching, the black Frenchwork in his fashionable square lace collar.

"Lucy, if you need shelter, you and your children should stay at our manor in Essex, at Hatfield Peveral. The house is accommodating, and you are not far from London for when you are called to attend Chancery."

"Your new wife would not consider this an intrusion, John?"

"She does not visit Essex, preferring to remain at Lydiard." John held his arms out again. "Take my offer, Lucy, and fetch the children to Hatfield until you sell Newington Manor and your hearing date in Chancery is set."

John's home would be a respite, bringing the children into healthier surroundings. Still, she hesitated, remembering their old conflicts, her pride preventing her from agreeing with his plan.

"I will arrange for Edward to stay there too," he continued. "Along with his tutors."

Lucy nodded. One less worry, for truly Allen and Luce must continue their education. She made up her mind.

"Thank you, John. I will stay, but only for as long as we must." She smiled at him and leaned forward to kiss his cheek. "And I will still travel to seek out Lord Goring at court tomorrow. He must expedite our case, and I am not afraid to demand such of him."

Time had passed, but Whitehall was once her palace, too.

In Oliver's library, Allen's cousins sprawled on chairs dragged close to the fireplace. Now the coffin was no longer in residence, the room returned to a welcoming, masculine ambience. Outside, the wild winter closed in around the manor, but within the luxury of the book-lined room, Allen could imagine that he was back in the Queen's House. Their official lodging within the Tower was once magnificent—until the troubles came.

The other boys shared their loot. William had found his way to the kitchen and returned with roast chickens, bread, and a great wheel of cheese. Henry and Jack, who knew the manor of old, had raided the buttery and came armed bearing eight flagons of Rhenish, two under each arm, laughing at their find. And Edward, always the practical one, had rounded up a pile of logs that would last them well into the night.

They were good men, Allen thought as he drained his fourth glass of wine. He knew them well after all those summers spent together at Lydiard and Hatfield Peveral. They were brothers to him. William was perhaps a little aloof. The new Viscount Grandison should remember the conflict of their mothers was not of the sons. Allen shrugged. Plenty of other good company in the room.

"Must say, that was quite a show in the parlor," said Jack, his glass full, a heel of bread clenched in his fist. "Your mother, Apsley, is not one to shy from confrontation."

"She is a good 'un, Jack," Allen replied, taking another large swig of his wine. The room dipped a little, and the chicken appeared to have three legs. He burst into laughter, pointing, unable to speak, tears running down his cheeks. Edward joined in, and soon the room was full of laughter.

"What lies ahead for you, Allen?" Jack asked. "Do you attend Oxford?"

"I do," replied Allen. "My father considered our schooling most important. Along with swordplay and horsemanship, of course. Which I consider more important." He waved his hand around at the hundreds of books in Oliver's library. "Glad the old bugger didn't leave me these. Gives me a big headache. But he did reserve a place for me at Trinity College before he died."

"Luce has a lot more use for this library than you ever will, Allen." Edward raised his goblet. "A toast to your sister, long may she run rings around you."

"You are simply jealous, Coz. She runs rings around our tutors, too."

"And yet she dances admirably, writes verse like an angel, and is a tolerable musician," Edward continued. "She is more suited to court than you ever will be."

Allen threw a pillow at Edward, missing him but knocking over the flagon. They both scrambled to save the precious wine.

"My name is down for Oxford, too." Edward grimaced at his brother. "Now that Jack has received Uncle Oliver's inheritance, there is little left for me. I must earn my living. We shall attend university together, Coz."

"That sounds like trouble," Henry commented. "Look out for each other, boys. I don't want to be hauling you out of messes as I did when you were children." He grunted as Edward punched him in the stomach, and a brief fight ensued, which Edward—the larger of the two—won.

Allen gulped his wine, wondering if Oliver had left any tobacco in his study. Ever since Raleigh had taught his father the pleasures of a pipe, he enjoyed a puff. He needed to get some practice in. If he and Edward were going to enjoy themselves at Oxford, they may as well take advantage of all men's vices during their stay. Education should not interfere with life.

The next day, his head and stomach did not love anything. Allen slept soundly in the dormitory under the eaves of the manor, awoken by a nervous maid with a jug of water and a washcloth. He looked around the room, his cousins bumps under the coverlets, snores rasping in various pitches from their beds. Why was he the one awoken early?

And now, his mother was making him put on a clean cambric shirt under his black silk doublet, when the one he wore yesterday would have done perfectly well. He groaned. The mere act of bending to pull on his boots made the room tilt alarmingly, and his mouth tasted like a whore's armpit. He rolled the phrase around a little, pleased with his creativity.

"Allen."

He winced. Even his mother's musical voice made the back of his eyes hurt.

"Allen, I know you and your cousins stayed late last night, and I know you enjoyed the hospitality of Oliver's Rhenish. But you must hurry. If we are to catch the tide to Whitehall, we leave within the hour."

Edward, Jack, and Henry would sleep till noon, he swore. No doubt William was already at his desk, reading up on the protocols and proprieties of being a viscount. He'd softened a little last night, matching drink for drink with the rest of the cousins. Perhaps he wasn't so arrogant after all. They did not speak of the tension between their families. No need to put into words what men silently understood.

A tremor of excitement replaced the biliousness of stale wine. Now he remembered. The Palace of Whitehall.

"I'm ready, Mother," he announced as he gave his points a final tug to ensure they were laced tightly. It was not every day he went to court. Buckling on his sword, he touched the falcon for luck. Time to do his father proud. Time to find Lord Goring and insist that probate be commenced. After all, he stood to inherit more than Henry and Edward combined, once the warrants were paid.

His mother looked the part, he must admit. Very elegant. Holding his arms out, he swept her a deep court bow, one taught by his tutors in the Tower. Those dance and etiquette lessons stood him well. At least he knew how to behave in respectable company. And the contents of his stomach stayed down.

She kissed his cheek, smelling faintly of roses and jasmine, a familiar scent from days gone by.

"You are wearing father's favorite perfume," he said.

"For remembrance," she responded. "This will be the first time at Whitehall without your father in many years. I keep his spirit close for courage to obtain Lord Goring's attention and commitment."

"I will ensure that he does so." Allen would not let his mother down. "If I could stand with Father, fighting off the creditors at the Tower, I can certainly address our concerns with his appointed executor."

17

"I hope affairs will not come to that, Allen." Lucy took his arm and paused in the hall. "Your Uncle John has offered Hatfield Peveral at our disposal, and we move there as soon as we return."

"I will be ready, Mother, to do what is necessary to complete Father's probate."

"At least your education will continue," replied Lucy. "John is providing tutors for you and Luce while we stay there." She turned and smiled at him. "And Edward will be joining us."

Ah how sweet a life lay ahead. Whitehall, Lord Goring's patronage, and a return to the standards to which he should be living, with his cousins. No more would he taste the disgrace of his father's debts.

3

My father, being a godly man, was severe in the regulating of his family, especially would not endure the least immodest behaviour or dress in any woman under his roof.

Luce Apsley
19th January 1631

Whitehall Palace Privy Stairs. Lucy recalled when court was as much a part of her life as poverty dwelled with her now. All the times she'd visited, sumptuously dressed, her thoughts filled with the anticipation of court happenings. The ceremony conveying her brother's baronetcy, elegant gatherings at the apartments of the Earl of Suffolk. And then those dreadful interludes—Frances Howard's witchcraft, Barbara's betrayal at Theo's masque.

Those memories held no pain for her now, for all washed away in life's tides. Within the Tower, she'd overseen her own world, had no need to pretend to enjoy the vapid courtiers and their drama and intrigue. Her marriage to Allen was blessed. Even then, his sober demeanor suited her more than the superficial court manners. Only when he was commanded back to Whitehall to serve Buckingham and the disastrous expeditions did she return to the palace again. And that was when the troubles hit hard.

"Where will we find Lord Goring?" asked Allen.

"Let us walk through to the Stone Gallery," replied Lucy. "Everyone promenades there during the day; the royal party will not be far. They could be at the tennis court or the tiltyard, the privy garden, on a sunny day such as today."

"And then—"

"And then, we will demand to speak to Lord Goring and share our tribulations."

Lucy stepped easily from the barge and walked confidently along the wooden jetty, disregarding the bustle of noblemen and their retainers, and the cries of the bargemen as they arrived and departed. Colored pennants hung limply from the masts of the moored barges in the cold morning air.

From the riverside, the palace appeared as a city within itself. This entrance, reserved for nobility and members of the court, was Lucy's old path.

"All this does not make you nervous?" Allen took their packs from the bargeman and ran a little to keep up with her.

She whirled around, oblivious to those who impatiently stepped around her.

"Do not ever be anxious in this company, my son," she replied. "Your veins run blue with the blood of royalty; remember your ancestress Margaret Beauchamp was the grandmother of Henry Tudor. You have as much right to be here as any of these court caterpillars, and own a great deal more integrity."

Allen blinked. Lucy softened her tone.

"Allen, your father brought you up to be a strong, honorable man. His traits for honesty and plain speaking are ones that will stand you in good stead. Today, you will witness many things—some good, some absurd. Never lose your sense of integrity in these circles, and, above all, never feel you do not deserve to be here."

Lucy turned and strode the rest of the way along the wharf, Allen at her side, and entered a tall iron gate where guards let her pass without question. She knew this palace of old, the secret hallways, the long galleries and hidden chambers. She knew the games that were played by sycophants, the fake smiles and false flattery. Time now her son learned to navigate these waters.

One only had to listen wherefrom the greatest laughter originated, Lucy thought, and George would be found in the middle of the merriment. Leaving the Stone Gallery and entering the Privy Garden, they spied the king's party gathered around the sundial, flamboyant coats and feathered hats bright spots of color in the winter-bare landscape. A guessing game was in progress, and, of course, Lord Goring was the master of ceremony. Lucy beckoned a page and gave him her message.

Moments later, Lord Goring broke away from the game. His florid face glistened in the sunlight, despite the wintry day. Bundled in layers of fox and beaver, he resembled a Southwark bear at the pits as he ambled toward them.

"My Lady Apsley," he bellowed, raising his hat as he walked. "What a pleasure to see you here, and certainly the sun shines brighter now you have gifted us with your presence." He took a large linen square and mopped his forehead where a bead of sweat glinted. "'Struth, I had not thought this a warm day until the king asked me to read his sundial. Now, I sweat with the anxiety that I may have called twelve of the clock instead of eleven, so muddled are my calculations."

"Did you make provision for the winter solstice, sir?" asked Allen.

"Eh? What?" Lord Goring peered at Allen and broke into another smile. "Ah, clever lad, clever lad. And a chip from the old block, for I see Apsley in that face, as plain as day."

He turned to the guard and pushed his pike to one side.

"Come, come, walk with me. Tell me what brings you to Whitehall. Can you stay for an amusement tonight? There is a masque put on by Jones, always good fun."

Lucy took his arm, and they strolled along the stone path together with Allen following closely behind. Ahead was the avenue of lime trees, bare now, marking the boundary of the bowling green. And if she turned her head just a little, there lay the gate to the tiltyard, where her husband had once drilled his horses.

Enough of the memories. To the matter at hand.

"Dear Lord Goring, you are too kind," she replied. "But I have just a short time here. We are no longer at the Tower, and we have a ride of more than an hour to reach our home."

"Ah, yes. Understood." Lord Goring looked abashed. "Look, sad business about Allen's death, sad business. Buckingham wasn't able to procure money from the king before he died, either. Must say, he left us all in a bit of a predicament."

Lucy stopped. The unforgiving January sun emphasized the self-indulgence in the earl's face, the love of fine things apparent in his heavy jowls and high color. Shrieks of laughter from the women in the king's party drifted across the dormant rose beds. Lord Goring's bloodshot eyes flickered in their direction.

"That's why I have come to see you, Lord Goring," she said. "You are named an executor of Allen's will—"

"Proud to help an old friend," Lord Goring interjected. "Anything I can do to provide assistance, I will."

"We need probate. And you are the one who can expedite this through the courts." Lucy drew Allen close to her side. "I must think of my future, my children's prospects. They must complete their education and gain a means to live according to their station. My husband was not able to secure this for us before he died, for the warrants remain unpaid by the king, and the creditors fight over every asset we own. You have the king's attention and the influence to help us. I implore you to fulfill my husband's faith in you."

There. So stated. And words could not be clearer.

Lord Goring mopped his forehead again and looked around the Privy Garden. The king's party was calling and beckoning to him, and he waved back at them. Some eyed Lucy curiously and whispered to each other. She thought perhaps she glimpsed Barbara, but if her sister was there, she made no attempt to step forward.

Lucy wrapped dignity around her like a cloak. There was nothing those courtiers could say that would disturb her poise. Before his last voyage to La Rochelle, her husband had met frequently with the king, counseled him on his military campaigns, drew maps and charts for his foreign wars. She'd been there. She'd stood in Buckingham's treasure-filled apartment as the fleet was readied. And now? Now, the king was as distant as the moon. Lucy could no more go to him than she could meet with God. Although he would claim there was no difference.

"Bid the sun stay still until I return," Goring called. "The king governs by divine rule. He can command the firmament!"

He clasped Lucy's hands in a large, damp grip.

"I will make securing your husband's money my first priority, Lady Apsley," he promised. "Chancery returns to Hilary term this week. I shall send a messenger to ensure that probate is activated." Bending low and kissing Lucy's hand, Lord Goring bowed. "So sad you cannot stay."

"And will you send us confirmation of such, sir?" Allen asked, his voice clear. "We shall be lodged with my uncle, Sir John St.John, at his estate in Essex. He is taking a great personal interest in expediting these hearings and securing justice."

"What?" Lord Goring turned from his path to the king and stared at Allen. "You doubt me and feel a need to mention your uncle's attentiveness?"

Lucy stepped in smoothly. "Of course not, Lord Goring. Allen only wishes to follow the progress of the suit. He has an interest in the law himself."

"Ah, quite right, quite right. I will send confirmation, Allen, within a month. I have a son myself. I know how eager these young men are to receive their allowances. Funding is always on their minds. As it is on mine, on mine. Farewell."

Lord Goring bowed again and hurried off. As his heavy figure trod along the path, several women of the party stepped forward to greet him. Allen stood on tiptoe, craning his neck to see if he could see the king.

"Please do not stare." Lucy looked to the sky. "We need to be on our way. We can hire horses from the Three Daggers on Cannon Row." She took one more glance after Lord Goring and sighed. "There is no more to be done today."

"A lively life, I think, being part of the king's court," Allen replied, his voice wistful. "I suppose that is what William will enjoy as Viscount Grandison."

Lucy gripped him by the shoulders.

"This life may seem carefree and fun, but there is an underbelly to this world that you are not seeing today. These courtiers have little to do except surround the king with fawning and flattery. They exist on credit and preferences, perquisites and favoritism."

"My father made his fortune at court. Why shouldn't I?"

"In his youth, your father also lost his fortune, when he took an affection to gambling. If he hadn't left with the Earl of Essex for Cadiz and distinguished himself, Queen Elizabeth would not have rewarded him so. Do not think the monarch is always so free with their favors."

How difficult this age was—no longer a boy, not yet a man. And last night's interlude with his cousins whetted his appetite for fresh pastures.

"They seem to be enjoying themselves."

"Until that life turns on you, Allen. Until your credit runs out and you are no longer a favorite. Or you are betrayed by your family so they may gain advantages that you have no interest in."

"Is that what happened to you? Is that why Aunt Barbara was so rude to you at the funeral?"

Lucy walked on, pulling the thin wool cloak tightly over her black satin. She was not yet ready to tell Allen the story of Barbara. *Keep him innocent a while longer, before the taint of this palace and its inhabitants hasten him to manhood.*

"Come. 'Tis time to return home. There is much to be done, for John will be sending the carriage for us in a week, and we must secure the house before we travel to Hatfield Peveral. We have done all we can here."

"Can we not stay? Lord Goring invited us to sup with him."

Turning Allen back to face the king's party, she forced him to look at the group of courtiers. She wanted him to see if Lord Goring watched them leave the garden or sent a page to secure their passage home. He did neither.

"Lord Goring has already forgotten us. We are no use to him, only a liability. And that, my darling, is the way of the court."

4

By the time I was four years old I read English perfectly, and having a great memory, I was carried to sermons ; and while I was very young could remember and repeat them exactly.

Luce Apsley
4 th May 1631

In the gloaming, John's substantial timbered manor house settled comfortably into the gentle landscape, with candles in the windows and lanterns lit by the door, radiating an air of prosperity and permanence. The Essex estate of her brother did not compare in grandeur to the mansion at Lydiard, but this house was well built and charmingly situated with a copse of trees at its back and lawns stretching in front. Lucy recalled her father talking about his love for this home, and took comfort in the distant memory.

When April's showers melded into the softness of May, and all the world was green, Lucy had taken to strolling in the twilight evenings. The grounds of the estate stretched far, and the walks were pleasing and soothed her restless temperament. She was ready to settle what was owed to her and begin her life as a respectable and educated widow. If only her future could be secured, perhaps in a manor such as this.

Uncertainty plagued her.

Lord Goring still did not write.

What did arrive was news of Joan's death, a letter from Eleanor outlining the last months of the old viscountess's life, alone and bitter in the mansion Lucy once called home. Although she did not dwell on the past, there came upon her a sense of freedom, as if the child who had been so tormented by her jealous aunt was no longer captive to the hurt.

Now, the emptiness which troubled Lucy grew stronger. A flight of crows settled on the church tower across the field; their cawing resembled those of the ravens on Tower Green. *London.* She desperately missed the sermons and lectures that she'd attended with such frequency in the city.

Her spirit craved the stimulation that such humanists and philosophers brought to her world.

Lucy pulled from her sleeve a small piece of paper and smoothed the creases. Someone left it on the sill in the small parish church last Sunday, and her eye had been caught by the name on the bill. Thomas Hooker. A preacher of such repute, and a clergyman of such controversy, that even Archbishop Laud threatened to imprison him for his sweeping political statements.

"What are you reading?" her daughter's voice broke across her thoughts. "You did not hear me approach, so deep are you in your study."

"Luce." She looked at her girl, bright-eyed and flushed from the walk across the footpath. "Are you done with your lessons?"

"The tutor would not let me sit inside anymore. He shooed me out as if I were a chicken."

Lucy concealed a smile. This one would study until she wore out her eyes, if she was allowed. It was good to hear that the tutor followed direction and applied restraint. Luce's fierce intellect drove a thirst for knowledge like none she had witnessed. A pity this thinking did not manifest in her brothers.

Lucy handed her daughter the paper. She read the bill quickly and looked up, eyes dancing.

"Reverend Hooker. He is preaching nearby?"

Nodding, Lucy took the bill back. "At one point, the king threatened him with the Tower, you know. It would have been a tragedy if we were appointed his captors."

"Did you and Father hear him speak often?"

"Me more than your father. Although he countenanced my attending the sermons, he did not accompany me often."

"And you would hear him speak again, even though he was banned for his rhetoric?" An eager note crept into Luce's voice.

"He spoke on behalf of many when he preached against the queen's Catholic household." Lucy smiled at her daughter, now twelve and more studious and serious than ever. Her father would have been so proud of her accomplishments.

Lucy looked again at the paper. "He leaves for the Continent, and then on to the New World. Men can speak freely there, across the ocean, free from the king's ear. He is to preach one more sermon, illicitly, and yet with his full congregation at St. Mary's in Chelmsford."

"You must go," replied Luce.

"And you shall accompany me." Lucy loved to see her daughter's face light up. "You will not have this opportunity to hear such a magnificent orator again."

Lucy tucked the pamphlet back in her sleeve.

"But don't tell Allen we go to hear him. Your brother does not approve of these preachers. Tell him we just attend church."

Luce took her place on a narrow wooden bench below the chancel arches of St. Mary's Church. A muted light settled upon the stone floor, and she was thankful for the dusty sunshine. Joining the other transcribers, she steadied her writing box on her lap. Under a vaulted roof, the cavernous meeting space echoed with the sound of several hundred footsteps as it gradually filled. Her mother stood close to the pulpit, lost in a crowd of somberly dressed parishioners.

The gathering was hushed, an air of expectation obvious. This opportunity to hear Reverend Hooker before he left for the Massachusetts Bay Colony would never be repeated. You must capture the words accurately, Luce's mother said, so they might reread his sermon over and over.

A girl of Luce's age slipped onto the bench next to her, carrying a large wooden writing box. Unlike Luce's, which gleamed with inlaid mother-of-pearl, hers was unadorned oak.

She smiled shyly as she carefully placed the box beside her. "Do your parents worship here? I have not seen you before." The whisper was clear, conspiratorial in the expanse of the building.

"My mother and I worship in Hatfield Peveral at my Uncle Sir John St.John's church. My father is dead," Luce said. The girl seemed pleasant, although quite provincial and dressed in a dark brown serge gown with a white hood. Definitely a Puritan. "My mother, Lady Apsley, wanted to hear Reverend Hooker preach before he left for the New World. And she has charged me with writing down his sermon so we may bring it back to our church and repeat it."

"My father asked me to do the same. Have you transcribed sermons before?"

"Yes," replied Luce. "I have been well-schooled. I used to take notes when we lived in London and attended the sermons. My mother would then write them out in long-hand, and we would have discussions over the meanings."

The girl fiddled with the sheaf of rough parchment in her box, her expression worried. "My father asks much of me. I am not sure I will be able to fulfil his expectations."

Luce dragged her attention away from the nave, where the crowd was thickest. A man was climbing into the pulpit and held out his arms to silence his audience.

"Surely he will understand if you do not write every word correctly. There are plenty of clerks who are also recording Reverend Hooker's words." Luce caught a glimpse of her mother standing with a group of women, all more soberly dressed than her. The Puritan influence was strong in this part of the county. In London, all manner of folk made up the congregation. Here, not as much.

"He expects me to follow in the path of my older sisters. They have all recorded the sermons with great accuracy." The girl pushed her hair back under her hood and sighed. "What's your name?"

"Luce Apsley. And yours?"

"Mary Francke. My father is Sir Leventhorpe Francke of Hatfield Broad Oak."

The girl seemed most nervous and kept her eyes downcast.

"Well, Mary Francke, Reverend Hooker is starting his sermon. Let us do the best we can to take notes and then compare at the finish." Luce touched her arm lightly. She was sorry to see Mary's distress. "Do not be concerned; I help my brother Allen with his lessons all the time. We will make sure you have all your words in place before returning to your father."

Mary smiled gratefully and started to scribble notes as the preacher began his sermon.

As Luce's pen flowed swiftly, dipping with easy regularity into her traveling inkwell and leaning on the lid of her writing box, she slipped into the welcoming comfort of words and phrases that had colored so much of her childhood. Her father had been especially proud of her accomplishments, and he'd found great amusement in her excelling over Allen when their tutor set tasks. Listening to the rolling cadence of the preacher as he lectured against the queen's Catholic influence over the king and the restriction of freedom of worship for the people, she felt great pride that her mother entrusted her with this important task.

After the preacher's final words, Luce's mother walked to the chancel. Luce held out her notebook to show her the neat notes, and her mother nodded approvingly. She stood up and was about to leave when she heard a heavy sigh come from Mary. Remembering her promise, Luce turned to her new friend and quickly saw she needed help.

"Mother, this is Mary Francke. Her father has tasked her to record the sermon, and it is the first time she has done so. I promised her I would aid her. May we stay for a moment?"

Her mother smiled. "Of course. That was kind of you, Luce. We are in no hurry to leave, if Mary needs your help."

Luce opened her writing box again and sat next to Mary, rapidly reading the sermon back from her notes and stopping where Mary needed help.

"Daughter, are you done with your work?" Melodic, with the rich cadence of a preacher, a man's voice interrupted their hurried work.

Mary kept her head bowed, hastily scratching the last sentence.

"Yes, Father, I am ready." Mary held a fistful of hurriedly collated papers to the man who now stood before them. He was as tall and slender as a reed, gray hair cropped short under a broad-brimmed hat.

"Your work needs much attention, Mary. There are a lot of corrections within the text. Did you do this on your own?" He returned the sheaf to her and stepped back, concealing Luce's mother.

"My friend helped me," replied Mary. "This is Luce Apsley."

"My thanks, Mistress Apsley. I hope you were not put upon by my daughter's inadequacy." He bowed slightly and beckoned for Mary to follow him. "And now, we must go."

"Her uncle is Sir John St.John of Hatfield Peveral," Mary continued.

Sir Leventhorpe stopped. "Sir John St.John?"

Luce's mother stepped around the tall Puritan.

"My brother, sir." She held out her gloved hand for him to bend over, which he did after a moment's hesitation. "Your daughter has a beautiful hand. Her penmanship is to be much commended."

Sir Leventhorpe swallowed. He looked quite uncomfortable, and Luce knew her mother's words were designed to soften the harshness of his tone. As they stood in silence for a moment, two other girls joined them, and Luce could see their resemblance to Mary.

He nodded. "Sir Leventhorpe Francke of Ryes Manor. My daughters, Susannah and Frances," he acknowledged. "And your name, madam . . ."

"Lucy, Lady Apsley. And your wife, Sir Leventhorpe?" Lucy smiled at the girls.

"Alas, I am a widower." His voice did not sound so sorrowful. But with those melodic tones, perhaps all his words were musical. "You are recently moved here, Lady Apsley?"

"Yes. We are temporarily staying with my brother." Lucy motioned to Luce to shut her writing box. "Come, Luce. Time for us to leave."

Sir Leventhorpe cleared his throat. "Did you enjoy the sermon, Lady Apsley? I thought Reverend Hooker spoke with great erudition of the queen's Catholic influence on the king's character and his capacity to govern wisely. Many of us here in Essex are greatly concerned."

Lucy paused. "I thought his argument raised strong points. I would have liked to have heard more of his sermons. But I understand this was his last before he leaves for the New World."

The older of the sisters nodded. She must have been in her early twenties, Luce thought, a respectable Puritan housewife. "The last that he is preaching in person, Lady Apsley. But there are a series of talks planned in his honor over the coming weeks where other preachers will be reading his words from previous lectures. They will be held every Sunday after morning service, and after the reading, we encourage discourse between the parishioners as we debate his teachings. Perhaps you and your daughter would care to join us."

Luce looked at Mary and saw a spark of hope in her eyes. She wanted to see her new friend again. "Please, Mother, I would be most interested to hear more of his words."

Her mother nodded. "This is good to know. Thank you, Mistress Francke. Sir Leventhorpe." She took Luce's hand, and together they made their way out of the dark church and into the sunny graveyard. Luce felt a lightness in her mother's being.

"Did you enjoy the sermon, Mother?"

"I did, sweeting. Although your father and I did not embrace the Puritan cause, there are many tenets of their beliefs we strongly support. When I was not much older than you, I was boarded with a French Huguenot minister in Jersey; there I first became acquainted with the Geneva doctrine. I am most heartened to find free thinkers again."

Luce looked up at her mother. There was a glow in her eyes that she had not seen for a long time. "May we come again, then?"

"Yes, I think we will. It is important you understand the various principles that are being expressed in our times."

"Will you bring Allen?"

Her mother paused. "I would like to, but I am afraid his mind is quite closed against opinions other than those that support the king's position. I don't want to cause a breach between us. Perhaps best just to let him follow his views, and we ours."

After a summer where lessons were never-ending and swordplay was relegated to practice on Sundays, Allen was desperate to escape the boredom of the country. His mother and Luce were firmly embedded in their social calendar, frequenting lectures two or three times a week, sometimes as far afield as Chelmsford and beyond. Why they found joy in listening to repeated lamenting about the king and queen, Allen had no idea. Besides, what learning came from John Donne and the like when the real power was at court?

The sooner he could return to Whitehall, the better. He and Edward planned their move together, for neither could contemplate securing a position without the other. And since their cousin William was the conduit for their ambitions, they would follow his fortune.

In September, Goring's personal messenger arrived at the manor, bringing with him the news that Allen had been waiting for. Finally, forward movement. Lord Goring was a man of his word. He knew so. No matter communication came after six months, rather than the one he'd promised.

"We must heed his advice," Allen pleaded with his mother as he and Luce sat at supper with her that evening. Their younger brother and sister were abed, and he had been waiting impatiently for this moment. Surely she could see that action would best serve them after almost a year of delay. "He recommends the probate is best heard with us as witnesses. I trust his judgment, for Father appointed him his executor to guide us in these decisions."

His mother looked at him, her eyes worried. "That means returning to London, Allen. Selling Newington Manor, for I cannot afford rent without doing so. And bringing you and Luce into this mayhem of false accusations and ill feeling from the creditors. Is that what you want?"

"If this means we settle the claims of those to whom our father pledged his credit, and the king will restore our money, yes, it is." Allen pushed Goring's missive to his sister. She would support his argument. Surely this was the fresh wind to blow good fortune their way.

"Lord Goring thinks we have an opportunity to settle with some of Father's creditors and retrieve the warrants," Luce said carefully as she reread his letter. "They wish to call us as witnesses to the time we spent in the Tower and our life there. How difficult could that be? We lived a simple existence with you and Father. There is little to tell, even less to be worried over."

Their mother sighed. "You are but children. How can they ask you to appear before judges in Chancery?"

"We are no longer babes. And with the education you and Father have provided for us, we can present ourselves well. I think it only an administrative hearing, Mother," replied Allen. "If Lord Goring thinks this is our best way forward, and Father trusted him to be his executor, then we should follow his wishes."

"When are the court appearances set?" His mother read the document that accompanied Lord Goring's letter. "You may be right, my son. If this would set things right, give you money to attend Oxford, make provision for Luce, James, and Babs to continue their education, then we should accept Lord Goring's advice."

"Court dates are not until Hilary term, next spring." Allen looked at Luce. "That means we have six months to write our statements, to sell Newington Manor, to find a home in London."

"You could return to Merchant Taylors' School, Allen, and prepare for entry to Oxford," Luce added. "And, Mother, we could go to the readings at St. Dunstan's, with the legacy of John Donne's sermons. The

Francke family attends lectures there frequently when they are in London, and Mary tells me the parish is most welcoming."

"Please." Allen leaned forward and took both of his mother's hands. "Please, Father would want us to do this. Our time here is done, Mother. We should return to London, to fight for my future, our future. Father appointed Lord Goring to be the executor because he trusted him, and we must honor that trust."

His mother sat still at the head of the table, a myriad of emotions flying across her face.

Allen looked at Luce and nodded. He could rely on her to support him. She knew where their future lay. And it wasn't in this backwater.

"Father would have wanted this," his sister repeated. "Time to return to London."

ſ.

My mother showed as much humility and patience, under that great change,
as moderation and bounty in her more plentiful and prosperous condition

Luce Apsley
21ˢᵗ March 1633

Lucy picked up a golden hairpin from within her strongbox and cradled the trinket in her hands. The little robin, with its enameled red breast and emerald eye, so familiar to her touch. She blinked through her tears and placed it carefully back on the velvet. Not this jewel, the last Twelfth Night gift from her husband.

Her hand hovered over the meagre selection, and settled on a curious brooch, a woman's hand dangling a bracelet of pearls. The bauble carried little significance, a careless token from the Duke of Buckingham while dancing one night. The goldsmiths of the City would pay something for this.

After a year, despite her thriftiness, the cash from the sale of Newington was gone.

All that was left were a few pieces of plate and three good gowns, a pair of court slippers and a fan, and the gloves requisite when she went to the palace. All were still in decent repair. By God's fortune, she hoped to gain a good penny for them, for they were her last reserve.

Their rented rooms in the parish of St. Dunstan's were cramped and not of the best quality. But the town house was convenient to an area she knew, Blackfriars being just to the southeast, and Westminster a mile west. The other tenants were, without doubt, questionable and anxious gentry who had fallen on hard times, and this preyed on her mind. They were so close to the brink themselves.

She hid the strongbox away again. Now that Allen studied at Oxford, she felt the responsibility of her youngest children even more. James and Babs needed education, clothing, a good start in their lives. Please God things would improve.

Tomorrow, probate opened, and the court sat in session.

Tomorrow, Luce and Babs would be called as witnesses to their life in the Tower.

Lucy placed a worn leather-bound copy of John Donne's last sermon at St. Dunstan's on the small table beside her. The apprehension in the girls' hearts must be allayed, and she knew of no preacher better than Mr. Donne to bring solace to a troubled soul. 'Twas her deep sorrow that he had died shortly before they moved to the parish, but she found great consolation in the preaching of others who preserved his words. The Francke family had a particularly large collection of his sermons, and she enjoyed the Sunday meetings where they would all sit together and discuss Donne's teachings.

She called for Luce and Babs. Time to practice their testimony again. After a year of delays, she must ensure the girls were word perfect.

God grant them courage, and may these troubles soon be over.

Fear ruled in Chancery Court, tapping at the cobwebbed high windows, undeterred by the flimsy partition walls, settling on the piles of pleadings heaped on the clerk's table. Quills on parchment scratched like fingernails on a tabor, and a clerk's hacking wet cough punctuated the expectant silence.

Luce gripped the worn railing that constrained both her and Babs, and attended to the interrogator. It would not do for him to see her tremble, and the witness box proved useful to conceal anxiety. Besides, how else could she impart her younger sister courage but to meet accusation with brevity? She murmured the comforting words from John Donne's sermon. The lawyer continued his questioning.

"My client, the plaintiff, claims there exists many riches in your mother's house, acquired from the time she lived in the Tower. The prisoners were generous to your parents, according them more than the customary payments to provide for their upkeep. And yet, in the three years since your father's death, still your mother avoids his creditors. Before probate is granted, you must satisfy the debts. What say you, Mistress Apsley?"

Now the questioning turned to Babs. Tall for her ten years of age, she lifted her chin and spoke clearly, as Luce had practiced with her the previous evening under their mother's watchful eye. Banned as she was by the judge—fear of tainting their responses, he said—her mother had schooled them in readiness. As if they would be contradicting Mother when speaking the truth of Father's deeds. Besides, at fourteen, Luce was old enough to recognize twisted words.

"My father was generous to his prisoners. Mother said that he treated them as if they were his own family." Babs's voice wavered. "He was loved by all men who came under his care."

Luce caught her sister's hand and squeezed it reassuringly. She nodded toward the stone statues of the royal deer, standing sentry at the Chancery Court within Westminster Hall. Watching over them, she'd whispered to Babs when they'd first arrived—ancient white harts with magical properties, guarding them from the lawyers. For herself, the wooden angels flying with the buttresses gave her courage. Lord knew they needed it.

"To the extent that they gave him clothes, jewelry, furniture, plate, while those to whom he owed money starved?" The interrogator picked up a well-thumbed broadsheet pleading, its circular red wax seal dangling by a green ribbon. "Item, one tawny velvet court gown with pearl buttons. Item, a pair of Italian leather gloves, worked curiously with gold thread. Item—"

"These were gifts . . ."

"And your mother refuses to sell any of these to settle his debts?" The chamber waited expectantly as Babs struggled to respond.

A second interrogator approached the dais. His stooped back and inked fingers spoke of decades spent in the Westminster courtrooms.

"Have you no feelings for the hundreds of men your father bankrupted in his schemes to support the Duke of Buckingham, deceiving honest citizens into extending him credit while he promised he had the king's assurance?" The lawyer squinted at the papers, one eye half-closed by a ripening stye.

He should rub a black tomcat's tail on the lid to keep it from swelling more. Luce pulled her thoughts back from the satisfying distraction of her book of curatives and answered instead of Babs.

"My father was loyal to the king and his council, and served his country with a faithful heart. While he was in the duke's service relieving the siege at La Rochelle he caught the fever that caused his death. Even until his dying, he worked to repay the debts he incurred on behalf of the king. And in the three years since his death, we have responded to every suit, every pleading with honesty and integrity." Luce placed an arm around her sister's waist, drawing her close. "The gifts are all we have left. If King Charles would honor the warrants, my mother can honor our debts. You have no truck with Barbara. I can answer your questions. I was there. My sister is too young to remember those days in the Tower."

"I can speak, Luce. 'Tis not your burden to bear alone."

"Babs, they will twist your words and force you to speak ill of our father." Luce turned to the lawyers sitting on the bench across the dim room, perched as Tower ravens in their black gowns. "You have done enough to ruin my family with your endless delays and insinuations. Put your accusations to me and leave my sister alone."

"It is not for you to say who answers to this court." The oldest lawyer stood and approached the girls, fat belly spilling over stained velvet breeches. He looked like the bullfrog that lurked under the well cover in the herb garden at the Tower. "Your father knowingly bankrupted good citizens of England with his empty promises and talk of the rewards of supporting the duke. Your mother was complicit in removing the treasures from your home in the Tower when he died. Your brother thinks himself safe studying at Oxford, taking refuge behind its walls, aping the young nobles."

He leaned forward, jabbing a finger at Luce. The other justices shuffled on their perch above the chamber, adjusting the long sleeves of their robes, eager for carrion.

"Mistress Apsley, do not think to hide behind your precocious education and your distinguished family connections. Lord Goring has little influence here, for his debts are worse than your family's. I am telling you now, and you may convey to your mother, that I shall pursue you all to repay your creditors until there is nothing left and you are as destitute as those whom your father deceived."

Anger flared in Luce's heart, and, predictably, her tongue ran away with her.

"I have been a scholar in English and rhetoric for the past ten years, sir. Since I was four years of age, our parents employed tutors who taught us Latin, languages, arithmetic, logic. My brother studies at Oxford to restore our family's fortune. He will train in the law to defend us from these suits and your relentless pursuit of us—"

A rapping from the judge's bench drowned Luce's words and echoed from the ceiling vaults. The white harts stood as cold and motionless as the stone they were carved from. The angels flew overhead and did not look down.

"You speak out of turn, Mistress Apsley. Your brother has no more chance of saving your family than you do. Respect this court and hold your tongue, else we shall hold you in contempt." The judge gestured to the bench. "Continue with the inventory."

The lawyer shuffled to the table and pulled a crumpled folio from the pile.

"Item, a jeweled box with a red velvet interior and a gold clasp wrought in the shape of a dolphin. Item, a pair of French heels with silver tassels. Item . . ."

Leaving the partitioned chamber and descending the broad stairs into the echoing expanse of Westminster Hall, Luce and Babs briskly crossed the flagstone floor, wooden heels clicking. Groups of clerks huddled under the arched windows, using the diffused light to proof their work, while lawyers steered their clients to recessed embrasures for private conversations. Although tempted to stay and peruse the stacks of tomes at the booksellers' stalls, Luce had no interest in the bloodsucking lawyers standing in the hall, preying on their troubled victims. Even if her mother's purse permitted legal counsel to guide them through the maze of interrogatories, she would not have trusted these corrupt lawyers with their defense.

"You were so composed, Luce." Babs looked up at her. "How do you keep calm?"

"They are simply men and answer to the same God as I. He will be their judge as much as they are mine. And He sees all." Pushing a strand of hair back under her starched white hood and adjusting her cuffed sleeves, Luce carefully straightened the decorative small bows. She must remember to sponge a clean set for tomorrow. The courtroom dust clung to the linen like a shroud.

"Our parents did nothing wrong, did they, Luce? That is a long list of items they accuse us of stealing." Babs stopped still, her blue eyes filled with tears.

"Our father was the king's man. His only crime was that of blind loyalty to a corrupt court and a foolish monarch who considers himself divine."

"Hush, Luce, you cannot speak this way." Babs looked around. "You sound like a Puritan. Remember Allen's warning. Do not voice your opinions aloud."

Luce ignored her, for she needed to spill the words denied airing before the judge.

"And you think it is right that our family lives in penury, our mother is dragged into lawsuits, our brother exiled behind the walls of his university to evade the interrogators, all because the king commanded our father to finance the Duke of Buckingham's ill-planned French war?"

She steered Babs around a cluster of weathered country folk huddled around an extravagantly beaver-robed justice.

"Where is King Charles when his citizens are held hostage by a rough justice that no longer cares for the common man?" Luce waved her hand around Westminster Hall, disgusted at the sights and sounds of men's grievances dissected before corrupt magistrates.

"Look around you, Babs, for this is what England has come to. You are not too young to learn." Unspoken thoughts plagued Luce's mind. "This day in Chancery Court has brought a new awareness, and your innocence is eroding in this knowledge."

Luce dropped her voice. She cared not if Babs understood her words or not. This was the rhetoric she learned from the sermons she attended with her mother. The preachers did not hold back their anger. Why should she?

"Take heed, Babs. This is the new world. I say there is something terribly wrong when an honest citizen has no say in their life or liberty, and the king and his servants mete justice unchecked by Parliament."

"Allen told me he will plead before the Privy Council when he reaches his majority. He'll remind the king himself of the promises he made in person to our father." Babs put her hand on her sister's arm. "Luce, please be careful with your words. Mother cautions the king has ears everywhere."

They crossed the threshold of Westminster Hall's towering wooden doors and stepped through into the spring sunshine, leaving despair behind them for another day. Luce blinked away the shadows of the courtroom and inhaled joyfully of the gardens outside the hall, grateful for their refreshing scent of forsythia and jasmine. She let the cacophony of the palace lanes wash over them with a reassuring clatter and looked around for the Francke family's groom.

"Mistress Apsley. Are you ready to return home?" He stood close by, as promised when they left him early that morning. Sir Leventhorpe was kind to lend them a guard.

"Yes, please, Matthew. We must make haste to reach St. Dunstan's by dusk." Luce took Babs's sweete bag, safely stowing it away from purse-pickers under her cloak. "Mother is waiting for us. We should hurry."

By God, Oxford was a merry town. As he stumbled into the Sunne Inn, no more than ten paces from Trinity College's gates, Allen took a deep breath of the delightfully warm and yeasty fug. His friends were waiting, and he was ready to enjoy their company.

"Allen, come, sing us 'A Messe of Good Fellowes.'"

"Aye, Allen, sing us a ballad to season our wine—"

"—and warm up the maids, for I'm working a thirst—"

Allen swayed and almost spilled the precious Rhenish a friend placed in his hand as he bowed to his fellow students. Fortunately, his footwork was still nimble, and he would challenge any in Oxford to out-dance him, even with his belly full of the Sunne's best wine. He raised his goblet and poured the contents down his throat, not pausing till the dregs trickled down the sides of his mouth and dripped from his chin. Damnation, another collar for the Trinity College laundress—and more expenditure from his meager allowance. He slammed the empty vessel down on the bar, and the landlord filled it again from a large pitcher.

"Your credit's nearing its end this week, Master Apsley. Just one more."

"And don't forget a little extra for me." The whore was buxom, her face smooth, her teeth present. One of Oxford's better doxies, and a treat Allen was saving coin for later this night.

He pulled a broadsheet of his favorite drinking songs from the wall. Obligingly, Edward held the parchment in front of him, raising a smoking tallow dip to illuminate the words. Allen raised the cup to his cousin while keeping hold of the whore in the other hand. Her plump bosom was just too tasty to leave go.

"To the king's health, long may he live. To my friends, long may they give. And to my doxies, long may they swive . . ."

He was warmed by the laughter of his friends as they joined the chorus.

"Another, another, and a round for all my friends! To drink the health of the king is to drink to the health of our country!" The room swayed a little, but the whore propped him up, and Edward stood at his side.

"'Tis the end of your credit, Master Apsley." The landlord folded his muscled forearms and stood solid at his kegs.

"Now, my good host, just one more for the king." Allen held his gaze.

"Not in my tavern. Your father, good friend that he was, left his debt here when I gave him money for Buckingham's voyage, and two years passed till I could recover my loan from you."

"Aye. Well, Newington Manor was a fine, if derelict, property. We sold it to the upstart cheese maker to increase his standing and put coin in my mother's purse, more fool him." Allen squeezed the whore's breast, and she giggled and leaned closer. "Now, I feel my own standing increasing . . ."

"Not 'ere, Master. I've got me own place down in St. Anne's Alley. I'll take good care of ye there." The whore pushed his hand farther into her bodice and gave the tavern keeper a wink. "We can settle up there, me love."

"Your own place, eh? We have privacy? Who else do you share rooms with?"

"Oh, just me sisters. Me father is dead at La Rochelle with that sod Buckingham. Me mum got thrown off our farm and died of melancholy, I say. A girl's got to eat and pay rent, ain't she?"

Allen looked down at her and shook his head. She wavered, wraith-like, in and out of his vision.

"You have sisters, too? And this is how you make a living?"

The whore turned and kissed him wetly, her hands grasping his hair and pulling him closer to her. Allen could no longer enjoy the moment, lust departing as quickly as it had arrived. The wine turned sour in his throat as he pushed her away.

"No more for me tonight. 'Tis time to drink the health of the king and leave." He threw back the last of the wine and extended a hand to the landlord.

"Master Bowen, I shall take my leave. I will see you next when my purse is a little fatter." Allen spoke quietly, for fear his friends would hear that his coin was depleted.

"On your father's cognizance, you are always welcome, Master Apsley. Good night and good health to you." He shook Allen's hand with an older man's firm grasp. The kindness in his words brought a lump to Allen's throat.

Pulling his shabby leather coat from a peg by the fireplace Allen drew the last groat from his pocket and tossed the coin to the whore. He swayed into his cousin, who, as always, was standing by.

Edward threw his arm around Allen's shoulders and steered them toward the door. "Come, Allen, I will keep you company tonight. Family must stay together."

"I think I've had one too many, Edward."

"And not for the first time have we ended up in these circumstances, Coz. Come, let's go home."

Falling into step with his cousin, Allen picked his way through the crooked alley to the gateway marking the entry to their college. An east wind gusted brutish cold, causing him to shiver and draw his coat closer.

"I remember that wind from our days at the Tower, Edward. Those last years in the Queen's House when my father was so ill cost us much." Allen paused under the stone arch and looked up across the rooftops at the scurrying clouds lit by a distant moon, the chill air sobering him. "That doxy, Edward. She was the same age as Luce." He took a great shuddering breath. "I tried my best, Edward. I tried to protect my sisters, my mother, from the creditors and their demands. I tried and failed. There was no shelter behind those ruined walls, for fate found us wherever we huddled. And now they face the challenge of the courts at Westminster, alone."

"They are in good hands with Goring looking over them. And those days of the Tower are gone, Cousin. You have your own life to enjoy in recompense for those difficult times. You are no longer confined to your father's ambitions."

"Or his broken dreams." Allen pulled open the narrow door of the passageway to their rooms and nodded to the sleepy serjeant perched in the antechamber. "Edward, you are always one to look out for me. My mother and your father are not close, but by God I am grateful that you and I are bound to each other."

"And so we shall remain, Allen. Friends for all time, and brothers in arms."

6

The care of the worship and service of God, both in her soul, and her house, and the education of her children, is my mother's principal care. She frequents week-day lectures, and is a great lover and encourager of good ministers, and most diligent in her private reading and devotions.

Luce Apsley
31ˢᵗ March 1633

That wind, that east wind, buffeting the ramparts, whistling through every crack in the stones, drowning the cries of the seagulls seeking shelter in St. Dunstan's yards and gardens. When they were children, Allen and Luce would quiet their chatter, subdued by the wailing of the wind in the chimneys, echoing the shrieks of the prisoners in the Bloody Tower. This time of year, the March winds always returned Lucy to the Queen's House. Did she ever think she would rue the day she left the Tower?

She buttoned her cloak and stepped into Magpye Alley, into the teeth of the gale that had sprung up the night before. Hurtling from the Essex marshes, rocking the barges clustered at Greenwich Palace, and screeching through the narrow streets of the city, proud Aeolus spared none in its path. For a moment, Lucy doubted the wisdom of attending morning service. But the Lord did not let the elements stand in his way, and neither should she. Besides, with Luce and Babs in court again today, she must pray to Him to guide them through the horrendous labyrinth of interrogatories.

Picking her way along the edge of Fleet Street, she avoided the running channel in the middle of the muddy lane. Overhead, the elaborately gilded wooden signs swung and creaked to such an extent, their clatter drowned the whistle of the gale. Lucy carefully stepped around the planks under the Eagle and Child sign, which was known to not be well maintained by the parsimonious innkeeper. Only last winter, a resident of the tenement adjoining was killed when the sign fell on her, and her body had lain for a day until removed by the watch. This was not a fate Lucy wished for herself.

Lucy returned the calls of the storekeepers as they opened their shutters and greeted her with the familiarity of old friends.

"Good morrow, Lady Apsley."

"A bright morning to you, m'lady."

"An ill wind today, Lady Apsley."

After living within the parish for almost a year, she felt at home.

The crowds thickened around her as she reached the steps of St. Dunstan's Church. Still buffeted by the wind, Lucy turned quickly into the churchyard sheltered by the ancient yew, a remnant of an old convent garden growing twisted into the street. She ran, full tilt, into a brown-garbed Puritan standing on the steps.

"Madam." He stepped back as quickly as if bitten when she landed in his arms, almost tripping over the last step. "Ah, 'tis you, Lady Apsley."

"Sir Leventhorpe. My apologies. The wind knocked me." The man seemed to always be at St. Dunstan's now. He evidently preferred his London home to his country estate.

"No apologies, my lady. I consider this most fortuitous that the good Lord placed me in your path. If I had not been here, you may have tumbled."

She smiled at his earnestness. He always found a reason for God to govern his actions, and in the discussions after the sermons, he was not afraid to bring God on his side to prove a point. Lucy sometimes wished she shared his conviction.

"The Lord works in mysterious ways, Sir Leventhorpe." She attempted to detach herself from his grip. "Especially for one as pious as you."

Sir Leventhorpe Francke folded his reedy frame in half and bent over her hand, which he still gripped firmly.

"It was the Lord's providence that brought you to our parish in St. Dunstan's, madam."

"It was John Donne's legacy, Sir Leventhorpe. His sermons were of great comfort to me." Lucy took a deep breath and tasted the brine in the air, a gift from the Essex seashore borne on the wind. When she opened them again, Sir Leventhorpe Francke still stood before her, his gooseberry-green eyes zealous.

45

"Ah, a tragic loss to our cause, and yet, in his death, his words remain to inspire us." Sir Leventhorpe struck a dramatic pose, one fist clenched before him. He was particularly fond of his voice, resonant as it was. She suspected he wished to stand in the pulpit himself, so often did he quote Donne. "No man is an island, entire of itself—"

A summoning peal from St. Dunstan's rang out.

"—never send to know for whom the bell tolls, it tolls for thee," Lucy finished adroitly. "I am glad you find his words inspiring, for his writings are a great solace to me."

Sir Leventhorpe dropped his hand and bowed again. His slender physique reminded her of a diseased elm, sickly and yet quivering with a desire to remain upright.

"I could offer consolation, too, madam." He licked his chapped lips and swallowed several times. "Lady Apsley, I am not unaware that you have encountered great adversity. Since our families have become acquainted, I have noticed that your struggle to secure satisfaction in the courts continues. It is common knowledge that your circumstances force you to dwell in a humble leasehold in this parish. I have heard the stories of your late husband's debts and witnessed with my own eyes the deprivation in which you are forced to live."

Lucy looked about, for the steps now teemed with parishioners attending the morning service. "Sir Leventhorpe, perhaps this is not the occasion on which to discuss my personal business."

"Quite right, quite right." He coughed and cleared his throat. "Lady Apsley, with your permission, I have a proposition for you. I will call on you on Thursday afternoon at four of the clock." He bowed again, quickly departing the yard and into the church without a backward glance, deaf to her words tossed by a spiteful wind.

"Sir Leventhorpe, I do not wish—"

But he was gone. Alone on the ancient steps of St. Dunstan's, the parishioners now sheltered with their families inside their church, Lucy gazed after him. The wind scattered a small pile of leaves with a dry rustling sound, reminiscent of the fallen sassafras leaves on the cobblestones outside her home in the Tower. She pulled her worn cloak around her more closely as the cold fingers of fear tightened their grip around her heart again.

46

"Mother, I cannot say how much longer we will be able to bear this inquisition." Luce removed her gloves as she entered their parlor. "Babs is not sleeping for worry, and today, poor Sarah broke down in tears in front of the interrogator."

Lucy looked up from the letter she was reading and gathered Luce into her arms. Her chest was so constricted that she could hardly muster breath. But this was not the time to fall victim to her own fears.

Smoothing her brave daughter's hair, Lucy steadied her voice. "That they should separate us during the hearings and put you and our maid through this dreadful ordeal is beyond human belief." She took a deep, shuddering mouthful of air. This news was going to be the hardest of all to deliver. She blinked back tears and cleared her throat. "Luce, I'm afraid this has all been a terrible ordeal. But it is over."

Luce pulled away, her face brightening. "We won our case? They will process the warrants? Surely this is God's will."

Her heart breaking, Lucy shook her head slowly. "This was the last day for you to appear in court. I have received notice that Lord Goring and your father's uncle have resigned their places on your father's probate. They will not support our pleadings to the king to pay the warrants. There is nothing left to fight for."

"What does that mean? Why is there nothing?" Luce's face crumpled in rare tears. "Why? Why are they deserting us?"

"Your father's affairs were left so tangled that none will touch them further. The first day of interrogatories gave an indication of all that lies ahead. Lord Goring has declined the trouble to pursue any further action on our behalf. We must prepare ourselves to move again—"

"—but we must fight to preserve our name, our reputation!" Luce burst out, sobbing. "I am never going to let the king's debts ruin our family. All that Allen is working for at university. He will take up our cause with the Privy Council."

"We have no choice, Luce. I have written to your Aunt Eleanor. She will take you, James, and Babs to stay with her until I can sort us cheaper lodging. My sister has rooms leased in Holborn from the small purse Joan left her. She will care for you until I find a way for us to prevail."

Luce looked around the cramped room, and through her eyes, Lucy could see again its mean contents and lowering ceiling. The few pieces of cheap furniture did little to improve the air of poverty.

"Where, Mother? Where will we live next? A stew in St. Dunstan's in the East?"

"I just need time, Luce. I had to decide swiftly to preserve our family and escape our creditors. There is little we can do now we are no longer under the protection of the executors."

"And Allen? Our plan for me to write the pleadings, my brother to stand in court? You know we have the skill; we just need the time."

"You are but fourteen, Luce. And Allen three years from his legal majority. We have no more time." Lucy could not break her heart by telling her that no court would listen to them, no justice prevail.

"Take Sarah and help Babs and James gather your clothes. Our valuables are in a chest for Aunt Eleanor to keep safely. She will send the cart in the morning to collect you while I secure a new home for us."

Lucy's heart broke as she said these words, for it summoned such a history of her own unfortunate circumstances that she could not fathom how she had reached this position.

"So, you send us to live with our relatives." Her daughter turned to Lucy, her face white with hurt. "I would have thought you would remember your own childhood clearly enough not to repeat the mistakes of the past."

Luce's anger hid fear. Lucy understood the passion with which her daughter spoke. This was the way she always responded: a fierceness on the surface that belied the anxiety beneath. Lucy tried to smooth her cheek, but Luce pushed her hand away.

"I have no choice, my darling. We have nothing left. Until your father's name is cleared, no money will be released from his estate. We are now just a breath away from debtors' prison."

"Your brother, John, could help. Where is my dear uncle in all this? He was quick to let us stay at Hatfield when it served his purpose."

Luce's intuition shocked Lucy. It was true, for when Lord Goring was their patron, John was all-accommodating. Now he had resigned, John's commitment to stand by them dissolved. John. A lifetime of contention, fighting as only brother and sister could. She would not let Luce see the grief that even he deserted them at this time of trouble.

48

"He has tried, Luce. But it is not convenient for him to constantly be attending Chancery. He has his own position in Wiltshire to maintain and the estates in Essex and at Lydiard to run."

"Another Royalist excuse. God forbid he would challenge the monarch." Luce opened the door and paused on the threshold. Her words ran on, the emotion of all she had endured over the past months igniting her spirit. "I despise all that has happened to us. I will write to Allen and Edward to seek their counsel, for I fear greatly for our future."

She choked back a sob and left abruptly. Lucy listened for her familiar step as she ran up the stairs, the walls so thin that every word could be heard.

"Babs, James, come. We go to Aunt Eleanor's. And you have the king to thank for all our hardship."

The bell of St. Dunstan's pealed the four o'clock hour, and a sharp rapping sounded on the door, startling Lucy as she sat alone by the dying fire. So many ghosts crowded around her while she mourned the impending loss of her home, the dispersal of her children. Could she have done more to prevent history repeating itself? Lucy's only consolation was that Eleanor was no Joan, and would not visit on her children the crimes of her own aunt.

She jumped up, her heart skipping a beat, thinking the bailiffs knocked again. Then, she remembered the Puritan's words. Thursday had come.

"Sir Leventhorpe." Lucy opened the door, and he strode in, immediately filling the space in the cramped room, stooping to avoid knocking his head on the low ceiling.

"Lady Apsley. I thank you for your kindness in accepting my visit this afternoon." He removed his wide-brimmed hat and bowed deeply. "I have attempted many times over the past year to bring myself to call upon you, but God did not place the opportunity in my path."

"And today is different?"

"You agreed that our respect for John Donne and his sermons were a common interest between us—"

"Yes, but—"

"And our daughters are of an age, are they not?" He stepped farther into the parlor.

Lucy nodded, wrapping her shawl closer.

"So, I would ask you to consider a deeper commitment, Lady Apsley." Leventhorpe Francke twisted the brim of his hat between his thin fingers. "It has not escaped my attention that you have found yourself in rather difficult circumstances after the death of your husband."

"As do many widows in my position." Lucy was not going to accept his singling out of her unfortunate condition. There had been enough gossip, and she did not care to hear of more.

"And yet yours are perhaps encumbered by the lawyers and suits that are pressed upon you and your family as a result of your husband's profligate spending."

Lucy's pulse quickened. What right did this man have to decry her husband's decisions? "He did not intend harm. He was charged by the king to seek funding for the French War. He spent over forty thousand pounds of his own money to provision the fleet."

Sir Leventhorpe thrust his head forward, his eyes widening.

"Forty thousand? I had not heard you were owed so large a sum. And how much is to be recovered, Lady Apsley?" He swallowed several times, his large Adam's apple bobbing above his plain linen collar.

"All of it. The king and the Duke of Buckingham issued warrants to cover all of it. But when the duke was assassinated and the king dissolved Parliament, there were no means to pursue payment."

"And you seek no further compensation?"

Sir Leventhorpe's tone rang discordant. What really was his concern here?

Lucy shook her head. "I have no capital to defend against the creditors and entreat the king to pay."

Leventhorpe flung himself onto his knees, narrowly missing a small side table.

"I will defend you!" His exclamation reverberated within the cramped quarters, filling the room with emotion.

Lucy shrank back, her hands involuntarily crossing her breast.

"I need no help with my defense, for I am innocent, Sir Leventhorpe. My son and I simply need time to plan our approach to the Privy Council." His presence perturbed her, and she wished him gone.

"I will take you under my protection, Lady Apsley. I have a fine house, a yearly income of eight hundred pounds, my daughters are compatible to yours, I have no creditors . . . to speak of."

Dear God, where was this man's speech leading? "Sir Leventhorpe, I don't think—"

"And I will fight the king and his corrupt justices for every penny that is owed to us—you." He shuffled awkwardly on his knees, and a bone cracked in the silence. "I have discussed this with your brother."

"My brother? You have spoken to John?" It was as though the east wind had blown her over, so surprised was she to hear of this.

"He was at Hatfield Peveral when I was last at my country property. I called upon him to ask his advice. He freely gave his permission for me to pursue my proposal."

Lucy turned aside and stared out to the tumbledown tenement that formed the other side of the alley. The buildings crowded in, and even the sky was leaden, sinking over the broken-tiled roofs as if filled with a thousand unshed tears.

"Lady Apsley, if you will do me the honor of becoming my wife, we can jointly approach the justices, and I can retrieve what is rightfully yours. You have no power as a widow. Your son is in his minority, a mere stripling, with no influence at court. As the wife of a respected citizen," he stood up with a grunt, "I will bring you the credibility and authority you need for the king to make good on the warrants. I will carry out the wishes of your dead husband and restore your fortune."

She could not turn and face Sir Leventhorpe—not yet, not with the memory of her husband's voice with its soft Irish lilt ringing clear in her mind.

Never was a man beholden to a woman more than I to you, Lucy.

"If you do not fight now, Lady Apsley, your children will suffer greatly. Your son will no longer be able to stay at Oxford, and his future schooling in law at Lincoln's Inn will be in jeopardy. You cannot care for your children if you are in debtors' prison."

She continued to stare through the window, the filthy street outside now blurred through tears.

Lucy, my love, my wife. You are the most loving mother toward our children. And I desire all the world to know how virtuous you are. For my sake, you have endured so many sorrows.

"Forty thousand pounds is a great deal of money, my dear. Under my name, we can approach the Privy Council and pursue settlement immediately."

How did this come to be? What choice was left?

"Do not wait years for your son to mature. He has not the means to fight, and alone, you will never be heard."

7

The large estate my father reaped by his happy industry, he did many times over as freely resign again to the king's service, till he left the greatest part of it at his death in the king's hands

Luce Apsley
2nd April 1633

"You cannot mean to marry that . . . that . . . Puritan?" Allen instinctively reached for his sword. The embossed silver hilt felt as familiar as the clasp of his father's hand—restraining, a gentle touch. *Think first, less haste.* "He is only interested to lay claim on the money owed to us." His anger rose, a rush of blood heating his face. The chamber he shared with Edward at Trinity closed in on him, and he wanted to shout aloud, to leave this stifling room and wrap his fingers around Francke's neck. *Steady, my son . . . steady.*

"Allen, we have no money, only debts. I have no resources, only useless warrants. The bailiffs bang on my door daily. I have nowhere to turn." His mother sat on the cushioned bench, her traveling cloak still wrapped around her, her hands clasped in her lap. Even in his anger, Allen wanted to cry as he saw the worn purse twisted between her reddened fingers.

"Listen to what Aunt Lucy is telling you, Allen. She is acting out of love for you." Across the chamber, Edward stood by the carved desk, his tall figure framed by the large diamond-paned casement window overlooking the quadrangle. He picked up a cut-glass Italian ink bottle and turned it over and over in his hands, examining the piece closely, as if seeing it for the first time.

Allen snatched the bottle from Edward and flung it at the fireplace.

"Damn it, Edward! And I hold her best interests in my heart. I will pursue our money, take on the justices. I plan to study the law to that end. This is my battle to fight. My father charged me so on his very deathbed." He turned to his mother and flung himself on his knees in front of her. "I will honor his wish to protect you and my sisters."

53

She covered her face, rubbing her eyes. "Allen, please think calmly. You have no standing, my darling. You are not yet a lawyer. There is no time left for us."

"I cannot have you marry that odious man."

"And I cannot refuse him." She took a deep breath and pulled Allen toward her.

He resisted, for to accept her comfort was to be the boy she thought him, not a man.

"Allen, a woman alone has no choice in this world." She accepted his defiance and held him at arm's length. "Your father cleared my reputation when he died, but he left me encumbered with his debts. Lord Goring has resigned the executorship to manage his own disastrous affairs. My brother cannot find it in himself to intervene. And he gave his blessing on this union. Sir Leventhorpe will provide for me, for us. He gave me the fare to travel here to Oxford, to tell you personally of my decision. He cares for my well-being."

Allen searched her face for a sign there was honor in this life she was choosing. But her expression was blank, smooth, no emotion showing.

"But everything our father stood for, he refutes. How can you betray his memory so, Mother? The king, the monarchy, a belief in the natural hierarchy of life. All this that our father fought for, these Puritans wish to trample." Allen cursed, for his voice broke on these last words.

"We do not speak of politics, Allen. We talk of lectures, of sermons, of philosophies. Our discussions these past years at Chelmsford and St. Dunstan's have been enjoyable. There are no clear lines of discourse, only a common desire to live the best life we can in the pursuit of God's rewards in heaven." She took a deep breath. "I came to tell you that I have sent your brother and sisters to Aunt Eleanor's, for the bailiffs leave me no choice, and I have departed the house in St. Dunstan's. Sir Leventhorpe will help me reclaim our money and reunite our family."

"Dear God!" Allen broke free from his mother and paced to the window to stand by Edward, who placed a hand on his shoulder. He impatiently shook it off. "Dear God! And you believe him? You believe that this man will not use our money to further the Puritan cause in Essex, will not cause more sermons against the king to be preached, more sedition to be raised in these rural communities where one man's oratory can sway a village, a town?"

"Allen, enough of your protests. You speak out of turn." His mother gestured to the comfortable chamber, the venerable buildings visible through the clear paned window. "Save your arguments for your lectures, for you can stay here at Oxford with Edward, thanks to this Puritan's purse that you despise so much. I have made up my mind. God has shown me my destiny, and your father, of all people, would have understood my obedience to fate. I will marry Leventhorpe Francke. I remove to Essex next week after our wedding."

Edward turned to Lucy and embraced her. "My father agrees to this match?"

"He gave his blessing. Leventhorpe paid him a visit before he spoke with me."

"Then, Aunt, it is surely the best course to follow."

Allen stared from the window. Oxford, his future studying law at Lincoln's Inn, his promise to his father . . . all turned to dust in his mouth.

"And my life? All is for naught? This plan you undertake considers nothing of my oath to my father to restore our wealth, to recover our place?" He fought back the hot tears that threatened to spill, furious that his emotions betrayed his green youth.

His mother stood. "All in good time, my love. Your father would think nothing less of you, for you have tried your best. We cannot survive on our own, and you are not yet a man by the law that governs these matters."

"You have trampled my heart, Mother, and usurped my vow to my father. I bid you good-bye." Allen turned away before his tears overflowed, and gazed across the prosperous buildings of Trinity College, the promise of these ancient halls of learning no longer a beacon to light his future. His hand rested again on his sword hilt, gently caressing the carved silver falcon. His thumb rubbed the smooth head of the bird, seeking assurance as he had done so many times before. If he was not of an age to use words to fight for his family, he was well schooled in swordplay.

Luce looked up from her notebook, her pen poised in mid-air.

"Leventhorpe Francke? He asked you to marry him? What consideration do you give this, Mother?"

"You know he is a respectable member of our parish, well known for his piety and godliness." Her mother's voice was quiet, controlled. Surely she did not mean these words?

"Does he like the poetry my father loved? Does he dance the galliard with the grace of my father? Does he laugh aloud at your jokes? Does he share his purse with those who are destitute?" Luce swallowed the tears that burned her throat. "And his daughters? Does he love them with a father's true heart that knows no boundaries?"

Her mother's mouth trembled before she ran her hand over her forehead and pushed her hair back. Luce caught a glimpse of a few silver strands and realized gray had not been there before.

"There will never be another man in my life such as your father, Luce," her mother said gently. "But those times are past. A woman needs a husband to survive, for I cannot fight this alone. Allen is not of age. Sir Leventhorpe is prepared to shelter us, protect us, and fight at our side to reclaim our money."

"Allen could do the same, if you just believed in him. I could help write the pleadings. You know my skill with words." Luce swallowed her emotions as Father had taught her, and caught Mother's hands. "Father believed in me, my mind, my aptitude. Let me fight with you. I have held my own in these hearings. Allen and I can win this battle, I know we can. Do not yet give yourself in marriage. There must be other solutions."

"Luce, there is no more time left for these dreams you have. Today, the bailiffs sealed the door of our home. I managed to retrieve the last of our possessions, and I leave them here with you and Eleanor for safekeeping." Her mother righted the stool and turned to her. "Ryes Manor is not far from Hatfield Peveral. You shall join me as soon as I am settled. And then we can bring Babs and James too."

"You are not staying here now?"

"I marry this afternoon—"

"How can you arrive afore noon and tell me you marry in an hour?"

"We have arranged a Fleet marriage within the Savoy. It will be convenient and fast. Leventhorpe wants what is best." Her mother lifted her head, her face expressionless.

"A Fleet marriage is chosen by those pursued for their debts. So no one stands for you, no witnesses, no family nor friends? And this is his idea? What haste motivates him?" Luce paced in Eleanor's small parlor, three steps one direction, three the other.

"Now that we have made our decision, we are eager to begin our lives together. We are marrying at the chapel within the Liberty of the Savoy. This is neither illicit nor illegal. We are simply marrying in a privileged place exempt from the usual jurisdiction."

"Exempt from the reaches of the bailiff, Mother. Debtors marry in the Liberty of the Savoy. It is no better than the Fleet Prison. It just has the appearance of propriety because it's within the old palace and not the prison. Does this not tell you anything?" Luce's voice rose in anguish. "I will get my cloak. At the very least, I must stand with you."

Her mother continued as if she had not heard.

"And then we leave for Leventhorpe's house in Essex. I will send for you shortly. Please stay with Babs and James; look to their needs and continue with their education. They will benefit most from the routine they are used to." She gathered Luce into her arms and kissed her brow fiercely. Luce stood stiff-backed. "I do not betray your father's memory, my darling, I honor it. For if I did not take this action, all would be lost— Allen's future legal training, yours and Babs's education, James's opportunities. I have made my choice."

The drizzle turned to a heavy rain as Lucy threaded her away through the alleys around Smithfield and the site of St. Bartholomew's Fair. Walking up Ludgate Hill and crossing the Fleet Bridge, she could see far ahead to the Strand maypole. *Papa, look at me, I wear my May ribbons.* Luce had always been so excited for May Day, and the last, just weeks before her father died, lingered in Lucy's mind. The cold raindrops mingled with the tears on her cheeks. As she walked through the familiar streets, each step taking her nearer to her destiny, turmoil churned her thoughts, interrogating her decision.

Her wits betrayed her, casting back to memories of her wedding day with Allen. The happy procession through the streets of Blackfriars, her family's joyful reception—even Barbara congratulating her, standing at the church with gifts. She brushed the tears from her face, and with them, the prospect of retreat. There was nowhere else to hide, no protection for her children except that offered by this man she was to marry. Around her reverberated the cries of the street sellers, the rumble of carts, and the barking dogs; all the familiar noises washed over her, but could not penetrate the wall that enveloped her. Numbness cloaked her, and she knew not what moved her feet forward except the fear that chased her.

Slipping through the Small Savoy Gate, Lucy walked through the narrow passage between the houses and the distillery, the light at the end of the alley beckoning her forward. The air was dank in the passage, a stink of urine and vomit catching at the back of her throat. No doubt this was also a handy stopping place for the drunks from the Savoy Arms Inn. Ironic she saw the prison first, for the church of St. Mary's was hidden. In her present mood, she was more suited to being committed to jail than to marriage. Or, perhaps, one was the same as the other.

The Chapel Royal of the Savoy stood small, stone-hewn, with a steeple offset to the rest of the building. Surrounded by remnants of the old palace, now a hospital, it was dwarfed by the sheer walls that blocked the river view. Lucy took courage. This ancient royal church had endured so many masters, richly endowed under Catholic Queen Mary, cloaked and penitent under Protestant Edward and Elizabeth. Now, worship thrived here again, with Henrietta Maria as queen, commanding biddable King Charles. A masquerade. Familiar ground. She, too, could change her guise to survive.

As she walked out to the burying ground, the rain flowed again. Through the sheets of gray, Leventhorpe Francke stood in front of the chapel, his large-brimmed hat shadowing his face. He stepped forward to meet her from the shelter of the porch.

Lucy took Francke's extended hand, pushing back the hood of her traveling cloak, lifting her face to the falling rain. She closed her eyes and let the rain trickle across her lips, standing as still as the carved angel on the headstone beside her.

"My dear," Francke commanded her to turn her attention to him. "Are you ready to accompany me?"

Lucy brushed the raindrops from her cheeks. Her bridegroom reached out a cold finger and blotted one that lingered near her mouth, and she blanched. A thrush warbled a refrain from the graveyard wall, and a watery sunbeam slipped across the flagstone, lighting the path before them. Lucy glanced back over her shoulder, tilting her head. Was that a distant whisper? Francke peered into the drizzle. She hesitated and looked around her with searching eyes. Still, she did not move.

"Ah, 'tis a fortunate omen, my dear," he whispered. "Lighting our way forward. Today, you are joined to me, and my name will ensure your suit judged and the monies restored. I pledge that you will not regret this decision, and that you will find ample reward in our new station in life."

Lucy bowed her head and accompanied Francke through the ancient wooden doors to where the clergyman was standing.

8

When I was about seven years of age, I remember I had at one time eight tutors including dancing and needlework, but my mind was averse to all but my book.

Luce Apsley
6ᵗʰ May 1634

In the two months since she had joined her mother at Ryes Manor, if not for her compositions, Luce would be completely and utterly mad, and committed to Bedlam upon her return to London. Thank God James and Babs remained with Aunt Eleanor, for this was no place for them.

Luce hurriedly concealed her journal under a silk shawl as the chamber door creaked open. The ink might smudge, but she would rather a blot than relinquish her truest companion to a demand from her stepfather, who detested all scribbling.

'Twas her mother, not Leventhorpe Francke filling this miserable room with his even more miserable presence. With relief she calmed herself, steadying her trembling fingers. In truth, his character was as lugubrious as a bloodhound, his nose perpetually raised in the air, sniffing out insolence, scenting prey. And who but she was the quarry? His wife's radically educated daughter, forced upon him with no if-you-please, and contrary with it. Even his daughter Mary was nowhere evident, being sent to stay with her older sister. Luce suspected her stepfather did not want the emotional or financial burden of any of his own children under his roof. What chameleon had her mother married, that his character varied with every day that passed?

"Luce? Have you heard anything I said? Or do your thoughts linger with your poetry?" Her mother's voice contained its usual blend of vexation and amusement, but considerate that Luce's imagination created far more interesting worlds to inhabit than the circumstance that dictated their cheerless days.

"You were saying something about a sermon?" Luce hazarded a likely subject. Her mother now attended three or four sermons a week in addition to their mandatory Sunday church service. Some of the speakers repeated John Donne's speeches, and Luce knew these brought her great comfort.

"I was. We are taking the coach to Bishop's Stortford. A Calvinist clergyman is delivering a sermon at St. Michael's Church, and today is market day. I will have an opportunity to visit the apothecary, for we need provisions. Leventhorpe does not keep much to hand." Her mother drew on her gloves as she spoke, the very ones of Italian leather which caused Luce such aggravation in her last Chancery appearance.

"Your gloves are a mismatch to your gown, Mother." Luce eyed her mother's demure black silk dress with its soft gray petticoat and falling white linen collar that embraced her shoulders as a shawl. The gloves' cuffs, embroidered with buttercups and bees, glinting gold and verdant green, belied the Puritan decorum that she was used to seeing her mother display.

"My taste is not always that of Sir Leventhorpe's. He may require that I assume the dress of a Puritan wife, but there are certain standards to maintain." Her mother's voice was defiant.

"And your husband? Where is the Puritan today?" Luce could not resist using the defamatory name. The small subversion gave her great secret pleasure.

Her mother rolled her eyes and shook her head, gently chiding.

"He is visiting Sir Thomas Barrington. A messenger came early. Apparently, there is an important business matter that requires his attention." She smiled, the weary lines on her face softening, her blue eyes sparkling. "Come, sweetheart. Hide your journal and bring your shawl. We have a day of freedom."

Luce caught her sudden lightheartedness and smiled back. "Then let us make haste while the sun shines, for summer storms are always just beyond the horizon."

The rough-hewn wooden coach was little better than an enclosed hayrick, and Luce doubted the conveyance made any swifter time. If they had just the freedom to ride their horses, she would have felt a cooling breeze on her cheeks and gulped the sweet fragrance of the wild roses that clambered across the hedgerows. She could have imagined the cloud shapes as dragons and griffins as they sped across the cerulean sky and soared with the hawks in the hayfields, hunting for mice displaced in the reaping.

Instead, they were imprisoned in this noisome carriage, reeking of dead mice and dung, stored as it was in Francke's derelict barn. His insistence on discretion and concealment within the contraption was just another restriction he imposed on them.

The constant rumbling encouraged abstraction, and as Luce gazed from the makeshift window sawn from the splintered planks, she wondered again where Edward and Allen were. Would today be the day they would ride into Ryes Manor and announce her freedom? Edward, his long hair pulled back by a ribbon, his fine horse prancing as he cantered into the courtyard, cream linen shirt damp from the summer heat. Luce frowned as she caught herself daydreaming.

"Are you sleeping, Luce?" her mother's soft voice broke her thoughts. "How did you like Donne's Devotions? Do you find his meditations helpful?"

Luce blinked away the notion of Edward.

"They are quite beautiful, Mother. I can see why you love his writing."

"As I thought Leventhorpe did, too." Her mother's words were whispered. Luce could barely catch them.

"He said he studied Donne. He certainly attended the same sermons you did. Why do you only think so now, Mother?" Francke was a subject that her mother avoided, and this again showed him in a new light.

"He did. He quoted him extensively. When we attended the meetings at St. Dunstan's, he seemed so familiar with many of my favorite sermons."

"And yet?"

Her mother sat in silence for such a long while that Luce thought she dozed in the shadowy interior. She could barely make out her face in the gloom, so dazzling was the day contrasted through the small window.

"And yet, he feigned knowledge, playacting his learnedness. He knows little, and thinks even less. I should have known better, Luce. I should have listened to my doubts." Her mother leaned forward to catch her hands across the cramped space between the benches. The cart rumbled on, its wooden wheels shuddering over deep ruts baked into the track by the summer sun. In a hushed voice, she continued.

"I acted from fear, Luce. Fear that I would lose you and Allen, and Babs and James. That I would be sent to debtors' prison."

"But why did you think you had no choice? Why not take us to Lydiard?"

"We were tainted, Luce. Still are. Your father's debts and the lawsuits have haunted us since his death. The rest of the family are terrified that they too will be embroiled in the litigation. Your Aunt Katherine went mad with grief when her husband was found guilty of corruption and banished from the kingdom. My sister Eleanor, destitute. Even Barbara, compromised and trapped by her position in the king's Catholic household. All are victims of the duke's poisonous legacy."

Luce shrank back against the bench, pulling her hands back from her mother, aghast.

"You are telling me this now? These tales of my aunts are surely not true?"

"I am telling you because you are old enough to hear. And because there is no escape from the evil influence of the Duke of Buckingham and all that he did to us in the king's name."

"And so you thought by marrying a Puritan—"

"I would avoid the duke's curse upon our name and the justices would see fit to release us from the creditors," finished her mother. "But it seems all I did was bring another affliction upon us."

"Does Allen know of this?" Luce demanded. "His loyalty is with the king; you've heard him say as much."

Her mother nodded slowly.

"Yes. He looks at this very differently. His eyes are those of your father's, whose loyalty was always first to his lord and king. Allen stood side-by-side with the royal guard and defended us against the creditors that were starting to hound us, even when we were still living in the Tower. He believes that the king will be fair and honor his word in memory of the duke."

"And you?" Luce continued the questioning while her mother was still in the mood to speak.

"You know my belief. This king rules with no balance, no representation from our citizens. He believes he rules by divine will. And he is beholden to no one. He is not accountable to us or our family for any of this money." She paused, her eyes luminous in the shadows, watching the trees as the carriage rolled through dense woodland. "Leventhorpe said he would bring this to justice. And so he might. But his idea of justice is to put the money in the hands of the Puritan cause, not to feed and educate my children."

"And you, Mother? What do you expect of all this?"

"I just want what is rightfully ours, Luce. Your father pledged his money, and that of hundreds of others, carrying out his orders to provision the navy and support the king and the duke in the war against the French Catholics. He died from that mission. And our family is tainted because the king refuses to pay on the warrants he issued." She plucked off and pulled on the Italian gloves until Luce laid a calming hand over her mother's.

"We will find a way, Mother. And we will not let Leventhorpe Francke win this case in court only to fund his own private agenda. With Allen and Edward, we will find a way. I promise."

The sermon concluded at St. Michaels, Lucy and her daughter crossed the crest of Windhill to make their way down the broad street to the apothecary. Beyond the confines of Bishop's Stortford, the countryside shimmered in the afternoon sun, folding quilt-like over the slumbering land. A small breeze softly played across their faces, and the dry, dusty scent of ripening wheat caught in Lucy's throat. For the first time in many days, she inhaled deeply, eagerly drinking the fresh air, thinking that it had been a long time since she had felt relaxed enough to breathe deeply.

As they walked down into the High Street, the crowd thickened, for many were visiting for market day. Approaching the square, the noise of the penned animals fused with the cries of the stall holders, creating a deafening cacophony that mingled with the stench of manure and blood from the butchers. The scene was lively, and one that Lucy felt completely at home in.

"Before you were born, you know we lived in the Victualler's Yard, just outside the Tower walls." A plump merchant's wife berated a baker, accusing him of short-selling a penny loaf. Lucy held her daughter's arm tightly as they negotiated around them. "Our lives revolved around the gardens and bakeries, the provisioning and counting office. My time there was happy, Luce, and one that I thought would be my life's destiny."

"And then you moved into the Tower." Luce almost tripped as a couple of small street urchins dodged in front of her.

"Mind your purse. Yes. We moved into the Tower." Lucy folded her lips, and a faint frown appeared on her forehead, brooking no further questions.

She stopped in front of a small stall that was tucked away in a corner of the market, close by the apothecary's shop and curiously decorated with a purple-and-gold velvet cloth with many embroidered symbols. A Persian carpet was draped across the trestle table, where there were displayed numerous dried plants and flowers, withered claws and paws, and small phials of unguents and colored liquids. Picking up a bottle and reading the faded label, Lucy looked sharply at the stallholder, a wizened, gray-bearded man with lively black eyes.

"Where do you hail from?" she asked. "Not from around these parts, I'd warrant. These medicines are far from common in England's cottage gardens."

He grinned and bowed, flashing a gold tooth.

"Is there something that catches your fancy, my lady?" His eyes widened as they appraised Lucy's gloves. "Methinks you are not from here, either. Those are more suited to Whitehall than a country market."

Lucy smiled and picked up a green glass bottle with a cork stopper in it. She pulled the cork and sniffed the pungent liquid, passing it to Luce for her to smell also.

"Aqua vitae. And calamus root adjacent." She placed the flask on the carpet and ran her fingers through a bowl of dried red berries as wrinkled as the ancient man standing in front of her. "And junipers, for protection against —"

"Witches." The voice boomed behind Lucy and made her jump. She turned swiftly. A fat man in an unadorned black jacket, plain white collar, and a tall felt hat was standing close, too close to her. She gathered Luce to her side.

"You seem to know much about these alien curatives, madam." His accent was Essex country, and he gripped a tall cane in beefy red hands.

"No more than any goodwife," responded Lucy. "It is my duty to see to the welfare of my household."

"May I ask, then, why you do not purchase your cordials from Master Joseph over at the corner of Sworder's Alley? He has been trading here for twenty years and is a reliable and responsible shopkeeper." The Puritan was joined by several other men, all dressed similarly and with the same stern expressions. "I fail to see why you would purchase such magics from a foreigner."

"These are precious herbs and spices, sir. There is nothing wrong or harmful about his wares." Her cheeks burning, Lucy's anger rose that the Puritan should slander this innocent stallholder.

"There may be nothing harmful in your eyes, my lady. But to me, it appears that you are interested in purchases well beyond the normal goodwife's curatives." There was a murmuring from the growing crowd. Luce trembled slightly at her side. "You are not from around these parts either, are you? Do you have your papers of residence?"

"I am married to Sir Leventhorpe Francke of Ryes Manor at Hatfield. He will vouch for my security."

"Prove your words, madam." The Puritan was implacable, and as he stood there, one of his companions took his cane and brushed across the merchant's carefully laid-out wares, sending costly bottles crashing onto the cobbles and tipping over baskets of dried petals. The men drew closer to Lucy, and she edged back from the stall, her arm still protectively around her daughter.

"Let her be." A commanding voice rang out across the square, and the Puritans turned in unison at the shout.

"Let her be. Damn it, Latimer, what the devil do you think you are doing?" A noble in verdant green velvet, with a full retinue of men in the Earl of Suffolk's livery, strode up to the stall. Under his plumed hat, auburn hair curled to his elaborately laced collar. His embroidered doublet was fashionably picked in silver thread and slashed to reveal a fine lawn undershirt.

Lucy looked up with a gasp, and simultaneously the man pushed back the brim of his hat and looked full into her face.

"Dear God, Lucy?"

"Theo?"

The Puritans stood solidly behind her. The leader stepped forward.

"My lord, we were simply doing our duty. This lady seemed very conversant with the ingredients on this foreigner's stall, of which could be drawn the assumption that she was familiar with the recipes that witches are known to—"

"Shut up, you fool." The Earl of Suffolk raised his hand, and the leader of his retinue stepped forward. "You take things too far, even in this Essex backwater. You will not engage in your witch-hunting activities while I am in residence at Audley End."

The Puritan swallowed. "Lord Howard, we are commanded by the Lord to find evil in men's hearts and to discover those who cast spells and ill on their fellow citizens. This is God's work."

"Not my God." The earl gestured to his man. "Escort Goodman Latimer to his home, and see that his friends accompany him."

The servant bowed and, summoning six guards, they quickly surrounded the Puritans and marched them away from the town square. With nothing more to see, the crowd dissipated, and Lucy and her daughter were left alone with the earl, the remainder of his retinue standing a respectful distance away.

Theo looked at her quizzically, a familiar smile on his lips.

"Once more that I encounter you at a market stall. The first time, at Charlton Park, you were lost. This time, I think I have found you again."

Lucy said nothing. The black dress clung to her in the warm afternoon sun. Despite her maturity, she still trembled as a young girl in her heart. Beside her, Luce fidgeted with the ribbons on her cuff, a habit when she was anxious.

"Thank you for your intervention, my lord." Lucy kept her thanks tight, formal. "I recall your estate at Audley End is but a few miles from here. A fortunate coincidence of fate." She reached for Luce's hand. "I must be on my way. My carriage is waiting for me."

Theo put his hand on her arm, and she looked down, as if seeing it for the first time.

"You are well, Lucy?" he spoke softly, his voice hesitating. "Barbara told me of your husband's death."

"Of course she did. And I'm sure she told you of my circumstances."

"No."

Lucy lifted her head and stared straight into the earl's hazel eyes. She recognized in them the same longing from twenty years before, the same desire that had almost ruined her reputation. She also noted the marks of dissipation, the slackness around his jaw, the lines of disconsolation drawing down his once-generous mouth.

"Your mistress does not confide in you, then. But then, my sister never was interested in much beyond herself." Lucy removed his hand from her arm.

The earl inclined his head. "Barbara has experienced a difficult time. She struggles to recover from Buckingham's ventures, her husband's debts. Being a widow at court is not an easy task."

"She seems to have done well enough as lady-in-waiting to the queen. And you kept the bargain to marry your children to hers." Lucy looked at him contemptuously. "As for the rest of your deal with the devil—only you can judge if you have lived the life you deserve with her."

She curtsied and, drawing Luce with her, turned and left the earl standing in the square.

"Mother?" Luce tugged at her sleeve. "Mother? That was the Earl of Suffolk? You seemed to know him well. And what business does my Aunt Barbara have with him? What mean you by calling her his mistress? Could she not help us obtain influence at court?"

Lucy shook her head. "You know that my sister Barbara and I do not talk. She refused aid before, when your father was dying. I am not going to her now, under any circumstances. Besides, she is in London with the court. That life is no longer mine."

"Why have you ignored the help those people could afford you? Even your own sister?"

"Because, my love, those golden opportunities turned to base lead when the need arose and brought our family to its lowest. I have no use for the shallow courtiers, the prancing lords and immoral ladies, the sycophants around the king. And my sister Barbara is dead to me."

Lucy leaned back against the crackled leather of the carriage bench and closed her eyes, permitting the memories to flood back. Charlton Park, a summer's night. A midsummer's night. And not much older than Luce was now.

Luce's questioning gaze fell upon her and she refused to respond. Not until she had arranged the thoughts that Theo stirred like a stone tossed into a millpond. Two more hours before they arrived home. That would be enough to return her emotions to the casket within which they belonged.

Theo's handsome face on that mystic night shimmered before her, and she allowed a series of pictures to flash before her mind's eye. The play, the fair, the magic of the most beautiful house in Wiltshire illuminated by a golden harvest moon. Her mouth moved slightly as her thoughts drifted to the kiss, her first, the heat of the summer night, Theo's lips on hers. And his gaze as she'd departed with her sisters for Lydiard, their stay concluded, the party over. *You've stolen my heart, Titania,* he'd called after her, while Barbara had looked on enviously.

The memories arrived quickly now, unleashed from the grave. Letters full of longing, the jealous treachery by Barbara, the ultimate betrayal by Theo, marrying another after she'd compromised her honor. And then, the wilderness. Years of loneliness while her sisters found love and married. The decision to exile herself from all that harkened of her lost love. And finally, the day Allen had strode into her life, her husband—although she was yet to know it—the father of the children she cherished so much. Vanquishing the sad memories, restoring her to life.

A jolt as the carriage hit a deep rut shook her from her dreams, and she opened her eyes a little to peep at her daughter. Good. Dozing. She needed the time to gather her thoughts.

How had her life come to this moment? She'd never intended to see Theo again. And certainly not to talk to Barbara, who had betrayed her over and over. Destroying her love for Theo, tricking him into marrying another, and then herself marrying Edward Villiers, Buckingham's brother, and bringing chaos upon their family. Best Barbara stay where Lucy had banished her—out of her heart and mind, serving the queen at court and Theo in his bed. The incident at Oliver's funeral served only to confirm the wisdom of her decision.

Time to share these memories with her daughter. Time to explain the reasons she rejected court and all it represented. She leaned forward and gently shook Luce by the arm.

"Wake up, sweetheart. There is something I need to tell you. It might help you understand why I could not turn to my family."

An hour later, as the carriage pulled into the yard, Lucy carefully removed her gloves and folded them into her purse. Looking up, she met her daughter's eyes, watching her, soft with unshed tears. Such a sweet girl by nature, so tenderhearted. And yet so fiercely protective of her mother. She smiled ruefully at her precious child.

"It wouldn't do to anger Leventhorpe more. We are far later than we ought to be, and he will have words to say."

"Will you always have to hide, Mother? Is this how your life will be measured—by not even wearing the gloves you wish, by a past you care not to acknowledge?"

"It is the life I chose." The topic was closed.

9

In my mother's youth, one suitor of greater name, estate and reputation than the rest happened to fall deeply in love with her, and to manage it so discreetly, that my mother could not but entertain him.

Luce Apsley

11th June 1635

Although the tug of lust had long disappeared, Lucy was reminded again of how hideous her arrangement was with Francke. The encounter with Theo unsettled more than she cared to acknowledge. Lucy could not describe her marriage any other way than transactional, when it was obvious that her husband considered their bond so. A financial arrangement. No more. There was no love between them, not even affection.

And, after the first night, he shunned her company, gazing at her from a distance with hot eyes, but refusing to return to her bed.

Perchance he had never lost control in such a way before. And so he treated her as if she were poison, avoiding all contact. Which suited her well, for his rank breath caused her gorge to rise.

Truly, this was isolation. She sat in the miserably furnished parlor, distracting herself with her sewing, and yet unable to quiet her mind. Thankful that Luce kept herself to her room, out of the way of Francke and his dictates, Lucy's troubled thoughts spun round and round. What next? What next?

The door banged open, and Leventhorpe strode into the room, bringing with him a swirl of cold air and a stench of farmyard.

"More news from London." He flung a foul look at her. "Peter Apsley. The boy your husband brought to your marriage."

Peter? She had not heard of him for a while. He was serving in the army on the Continent.

"Well, madam, your husband's firstborn son has returned to your old home—involuntarily. He is incarcerated in the Tower of London. Disgraced. Severely fined. And denied a Christian burial, should he die before being pardoned." As was his wont, Leventhorpe trembled in his wrath, his face skeletal, the skin white over his bony cheeks. "What say you now, Lucy, of your dead husband's spawn, who challenged the Earl of Northumberland in front of the king himself? Bringing disgrace upon himself and all who are associated with him."

"Northumberland? What could Peter have done to insult him? He knew him well when we lived within the Tower. They practiced swordplay together."

Leventhorpe shook the letter at her, spittle flecking his thin lips. "This is not play, madam."

Ah, Peter. You always were a lodestone for trouble.

Leventhorpe continued, stoking his anger like bellows to a fire. "Your late husband's brat. A man you told me yourself was like a son unto you."

"My husband was no beggar, so do not insult his son so. I cannot believe—"

"Believe, for I have evidence here." His voice rose as he read further. "And the worst of it? He has lost the office at court that you have an interest in. Another financial forfeiture to cause me yet more pain, Wife."

"Peter's wit is contrary to his character, Leventhorpe. He does not always think before he acts. His father's death left him much sorrowful."

"There you go, making another excuse for your husband's errant son. You have no grounds to defend him, when he has caused us so much embarrassment and loss."

"I will write to the earl. I cared for his father while he was imprisoned in the Tower. He holds a place in his heart for me. He will listen to my reasoning about Peter." All those times she had spent with the old Wizard Earl, funding his alchemy experiments, bringing him to Sir Walter Raleigh's rooms for late night philosophizing, dosing him with her medicinals when he fell ill.

"You will do nothing of the sort. We have enough problems defending your late husband's debts without you being accused of bribing the lords to free his criminal son." Leventhorpe threw the letter at Lucy and turned to the door. He tossed the remainder of his words over his rigid back. "It is a fair burden I bear, now I have brought your viper's brood into my bosom. If I had known then what I know now, I would have considered more carefully my proposal."

"Your proposal was based on financial merit, Husband, not on familial. I seem to recollect that you paid scant attention to my children's interests when you were summarizing the warrants owed to us."

"Enough! Hold your tongue, mistress, else I will report you for the shrew you are and have you wear the scold's bridle." He slammed the door behind him, leaving Lucy shaking and alone.

She sank onto the window seat and leaned her forehead against the cold glass, her breath fogging and adding to the mist of unshed tears. How could this marriage have deteriorated so? Any word of her children enraged Leventhorpe to a fury, and any deed beyond her control brought his wrath crashing on her head. She rubbed a clear spot on the grimy pane and looked out, seeking to calm her nerves and steady her thoughts, but the pitiable yard gave no comfort.

The barn was derelict and the fencing broken. How bleak the prospect. No garden or trees softened the angular walls, and the plaster flaked in many places to reveal the wattle below. Great damp stains spread from the ragged thatch to the deeply embedded shuttered window holes. Dirty cattle stood ankle-deep in mire and filth in an enclosure that had not been mucked all winter, and a few scrawny hens picked at the earth, seeking remnants of seeds left from a distant harvest.

Lucy closed her eyes and thought of her long-ago home in the Victualler's Yard, where she had walked hand in hand with her love through the orchards and allotments, the bakehouses had delivered a fragrance of fresh bread, and the fat pigs had glowed pink with cleanliness, scrubbed weekly by the herder. How long ago. What a distant life. Days so routine, so unremarkable, now precious and forever vanished.

Lucy turned again to thoughts of Allen's son, just eleven when he first came into her life. She recalled Peter at lessons, his fidgeting and drumming of fingers, anxious to be outside at the butts and learning swordplay, not numbers. How he'd knelt by his father's bedside, weeping, broken-hearted that his own debts caused the dying man such affliction. Thank God her own son, Allen, was not a profligate. Thank God Allen—

Lucy sat up straight suddenly as riders trotted into the yard. There was something so familiar about them, and yet—

Rubbing the glass again, she caught her breath, for here was Allen. And with him Edward, John's boy, who was never far from his side.

She jumped from the seat and brushed her dusty skirts, wishing the hem was not filthy with farmyard mud. Calling to Luce and smoothing her hair, she ran to the front door and out into the yard.

"Mother!" Allen's voice rang so clear, and she embraced him as if she would never let him go. In the year they'd spent apart, his physique had filled out rapidly, as young men do.

"My darlings." She turned to Edward, gathered him in her arms too, and they three stood in the muck of Francke's farmyard, reunited in their joy. Allen smelled fragrantly of sandalwood and polished leather, and Lucy buried her face in his soft velvet doublet, the fur trim on his cloak brushing across her cheek. The door slammed as Luce ran into the yard and, with a cry, threw herself into her brother's embrace.

"We came as soon as we learned the news of Peter," Allen said urgently. "You have heard?"

Lucy nodded. "Leventhorpe told me this morning. He does not think I should write to Northumberland. He cautions me not to be seen asking for favors from the lords while our case is still under consideration."

"Mother, our half-brother is in the Tower. Is that asking for favors, or simply ensuring his safety?" Allen had grown strong in his words as well as in his physique.

Lucy glanced quickly over her shoulder. The commotion had brought Leventhorpe to the door of the manor, and he stood watching them, arms folded. It would have been appropriate for him to welcome her son, but evidently he was not going to extend himself.

"We will talk later, my darlings. Now, come, you must be exhausted. Did you ride straight through?"

"No, we stopped at the King's Head in North Weald last night." Edward rubbed his horse's neck, smoothing the sweat-darkened chestnut coat. "My father's credit provided us shelter."

"Provided us shelter, but little protection from the hostility of the locals." Allen threw the reins of his horse over to the stable boy and frowned as the mud squelched over his boots. "It appears there is much Puritan sedition here in Essex, and the inn that was once friendly to our family is one of its breeding grounds."

"Allen, you must be cautious with your words." Lucy viewed her son and his cousin through Leventhorpe's eyes. They were the epitome of the young nobles of university, handsomely attired in lace and plumed hats and a careless elegance that came of their breeding.

"Cautious? In my own mother's home? What has come of this?"

"I am just saying that there are people here that may not share your views, Allen. You must respect that. Life is different here in the country. People are not so intimate with the court and the king."

"Perhaps they only wish to express concerns for their well-being without fear of the king's spies reporting their words." Luce spoke succinctly and Lucy smiled at her sharp-witted daughter. She always grasped the intellectual arguments more so than Allen, who led with his heart rather than his head.

Allen glanced over at Leventhorpe.

"Well, let's see what your husband thinks of these concerns. Will he welcome us into your home, or is he going to stand like a dog at the gates of hell and watch us approach?"

Luce giggled and took Allen's arm.

"Come, let us challenge the guard dog, Allen. He does not bring fear to my heart."

Lucy shook her head. Beautiful, brave, bright children. How she loved to see them together again. How she feared for their future.

"You keep a careful table, Sir Leventhorpe."

Lucy glanced up from her food. Allen reached for the flagon to pour another goblet of wine and shook out the few remaining drops.

"I must commend you on your parsimony. However, I would hope that this does not extend to your plans for what is due to my mother when the warrants are made good."

Luce stifled a giggle, clearing her throat. Lucy lowered her eyes, suppressing a smile.

Allen continued, "But in the meantime, we should discuss what is to be done about Peter and the fine to release him."

Leventhorpe ignored Allen's jibe.

"Nothing is to be done. I have no obligation or intention to intervene on his behalf. Your brother has been accused of a criminal act. He should pay for his indiscretion."

"He is in the Tower of London under trumped-up charges—"

"He is in prison for a crime." Leventhorpe beckoned wordlessly to the maid, who cleared the remains from the table. Lucy noticed that Luce had barely touched her food, leaving the gristly scraps on the side of her trencher.

"Leventhorpe, I can at least ask the Earl of Northumberland to pardon Peter, in memory of former times." Lucy put her hand on his arm, and he jerked away as if burned, almost knocking over his empty goblet. The wine long gone; he did not order the flagon replenished.

"That corrupt courtier? He belongs to your infamous past under the Duke of Buckingham's reckless patronage, madam. There is not a cause on this earth that would make me go begging to that jackanapes."

"Are you saying our father was dishonorable, sir?" Allen was quick to respond, and Lucy saw his temper rising. She tried to catch his eye, to warn him that this was not the way to deal with Leventhorpe.

"Perhaps we could write an apology?" Luce's soft voice broke the silence. "It seems that a word to our former friend would go a long way to help Peter's situation." Lucy looked at her gratefully. She was the peacemaker, the logical one of the two.

"Perhaps you could leave the guidance of this family to me," Leventhorpe retorted. "You are both minors, and you have no say in this or any other matter." He looked at Allen pointedly. "Especially how I manage the financial aspects of this household. What I do with my money—and your mother's money is my money—is my prerogative."

"You forget, sir, I was charged by my father with his dying breath to take care of my mother and my younger brothers and sisters."

"And a fine job you have done, with the bailiffs evicting her and her children scattered."

"Leventhorpe," Lucy reached out to him again, wanting to diffuse the anger smoldering between her husband and her son. "Allen was just a young man when his father died. He could do no more."

"Then I will caution him to do even less, now. He is not welcome with his demands and his arrogance. Our case together, as Sir Leventhorpe and Lady Francke, is prepared to submit to court. Do not meddle, Wife, for I have told you it is not your place to question me."

Allen slowly stood and put his hand on his sword hilt, staring unswervingly at Leventhorpe, his gray eyes alight with disgust. He had such a look of his father.

Leventhorpe leapt to his feet, scraping the chair on the bare flagstones, jarring the deathly quiet. Edward rose too, and only Lucy and Luce remained seated, frozen in place.

"You would dare challenge me?" Leventhorpe said the words in a quiet hiss, pausing between each.

This anger was deeper than any Lucy had witnessed before.

"I will defend my mother against your abuse."

"Allen. Please sit. This is no way to solve anything." Lucy's voice trembled and betrayed her fright. She so dreaded the confrontation that threatened to rip her carefully designed existence into shreds.

"No. Do not sit. You are not welcome at my table." Leventhorpe placed both his hands on the board and leaned toward Allen, his face contorted with fury. "Leave. Leave now, and do not return."

Lucy watched, helpless, as her son and her husband faced each other until Allen finally shrugged and dropped his hand from his sword.

"Come, Edward, let us ride to your father's. Luce, please remain. Mother needs family with her, for it is apparent that she has none that have her interest at heart."

"Of course, Allen." Luce covered Lucy's hand with hers and held it still, hiding the trembling that had set in at the explosion of anger.

"Luce, send for me if you need to. I shall be here in a day." Edward came around the table and, leaning over, kissed Luce's cheek. He laid his hands on her shoulders, and she looked up, a tiny smile illuminating her face.

Allen strode to Lucy's side and hugged her. For a moment, she clung to Allen, her heart breaking as she gripped his waist, dreading his departure. She wanted him to feel the vigor of her embrace, signifying her love and her strength.

"Be strong," he whispered against her hair, his hand soothing her back as she had once pacified him. "Be strong, and I will return."

10

England was not an idle spectator of the great contest between the papist and protestant.

Luce Apsley
31st July 1635

Footpads, highwaymen, cutthroats—all may have been prowling abroad, but swift horses carried them unharmed to their destination. Allen's anger veiled the twenty-mile journey from Ryes Manor to Hatfield Peveral, and he noticed little of their ride. Surely cottages or a humble village marked the way, but he recalled nothing, preoccupied with the image of his mother's circumstance and Francke's wrath.

As they cantered through the gates of Hatfield Peveral, he paid scant attention to the peevish cry of the gatekeeper, roused from his hearth by urgent hoof beats.

Allen lamented the contrast to Ryes Manor. Hatfield's lime-washed walls glowed cream in the gathering darkness, and a solid, neatly clipped hedge indicated a garden stretching to the woods beyond. A breath of wood smoke hung in the still air, a welcome assurance that the fires were lit, even on this mild summer evening. This was the home Allen imagined for his mother, not the miserable wreck of Francke's smallholding. What was his uncle thinking, that he allowed such a marriage to go forward?

As the cousins reined up in front of the house, the dogs set to a furious barking. The door opened, and Uncle John strode out, tugging on his jacket as he walked. He looked up, surprise on his face.

"What in God's name brings you here?" he asked abruptly. "Edward? Allen? Should you not be at your studies?"

"We have a few days' release from our lectures, Father," replied Edward. "And so we chose to ride to Hatfield and spend some time with you." He was always the diplomat, placing John as the priority, not his aunt's troubles.

"And what else? Short of money? In trouble with the serjeant again?" John whistled to his dogs, instantly evoking in Allen a memory of his father calling to the Irish wolfhounds as they bounded on Tower Green.

Allen cleared his throat. "I wished to see my mother—and you, of course. There is something we request to discuss with you." He caught Edward's smile and approving nod. He had spoken wisely, with restraint.

They dismounted. A couple of stable boys ran to take the reins and walk the horses to the stable block. The yard was empty, silent except for the panting dogs.

John glanced at them and then over to the stables. "I have a mare in foal. Hurry up, then."

"Uncle John —"

"Father —"

As John shrugged and walked past them, Edward quickly continued.

"Father, we need to talk about Aunt Lucy. Someone must see reason."

John paused and raised an eyebrow at his favorite son. He did not look encouraging, but he did not continue walking.

"Father, you see, it's been a difficult time for Luce and Allen. Sir Leventhorpe does not hurry to resume action in Chancery—for all his promises, he appears reluctant to appear in front of a judge. After Luce was dragged before Chancery for interrogations, they have heard nothing, and Allen is distracted with worry, which doesn't benefit his studies, and I know that you can help us." Edward gave his most charming smile, one that had extricated the cousins from more scrapes than Allen could count when they were younger. "And so, we rode to seek your advice."

John remained silent. Across the garden, a commotion in the rookery stirred in Allen distant memories of the Tower ramparts, where crows and ravens competed for carrion. So often he had walked with his father in the ceremony of the keys, securing the Tower for the night. Now, the family well-being rested with him. His responsibility was to secure them. A twilight mist drifted across the yard, mingling with wood smoke and carrying the scent of water from a hidden stream.

John pulled them both by the arm into the shelter of the wooden porch that fronted the old house. "There's nothing you can do. She made her choice. And good fortune go with her. Settling the warrants is Sir Leventhorpe's problem now, not mine."

"Sir, what mean you? Have you seen what he is doing to her? Are you prepared to just stand by? When did you last visit her at Ryes?" Allen's prepared speech disappeared in his anguish, along with his plan to broach John over a fine dinner and good wine.

Leaning down and patting the dog at his side, John's face was obscured. "And you rode all this way to complain about your mother's decision? I think you should mount your horses and return to your studies. Sir Leventhorpe Francke asked my permission and presented his credentials with all circumspect. Sir Thomas Barrington vouched for him, and he is a respected landowner in these parts. I received a letter from her after her wedding. She seemed content with her choice. I have no further say, for she is her husband's responsibility."

"But the conditions under which she is living—"

"It was her decision. As Lady Francke, the Puritan's wife, she decided to go her own way. You know your mother and I do not often agree."

"Father, please, listen to us." Edward stepped forward and caught John's arm. The dog wagged its tail furiously but stayed at John's side, obedient to his master. "We have just ridden from Ryes Manor. Aunt Lucy is unaided, neglected in that miserable house. And Luce is in no position to help."

"Damn it, Edward, do not interfere where you do not belong."

"I belong in fairness and kindness, Father, as you have taught me. And Leventhorpe Francke displays neither. He runs a severe household, he is ill-mannered to my dear aunt, and I think he is after her money to sustain the Puritan cause here in Essex, not for the benefit of my cousins, as their father wished it."

Finally, Allen saw a response from John, as shock flitted across his uncle's stern face.

"What mean you? Francke may be a Puritan—many are here in Essex—but he does not run a seditious household." John glanced around him and drew Edward closer.

Allen wished this conversation would continue indoors. He just wanted to feel at home, with family.

"His household may not harbor rebels, Father, but he has no intention of helping Peter Apsley, nor does he welcome us into his home. It is almost as though he were looking for a reason to expel us." Edward's voice became steely. "The lawsuits against my uncle have brought enough strain to this family without Leventhorpe Francke intending to fund sermons against the king and his bishops."

Allen could see that John struggled with his emotions, torn between believing his son and wishing not to be involved with his sister's troubles. Edward won.

"Come inside, both of you, and tell me more. And you had better have some evidence to support your claims."

Allen stepped into the home he had once shared with Edward, blinking back sudden tears. The day had been exhausting, and he was overwrought, weary from expended emotion. A fire flickered in the broad hearth, and the smell of roasting meat made his stomach grumble with hunger. He was ravenous.

John led them to several large chairs placed close to the chimney and ordered ale and food. After eating their fill, John lit his pipe and leaned back in his chair.

"So, you did not find Lucy well? Is she not cared for?" John blew a stream of fragrant tobacco smoke into the air. "What prompted these accusations? And, Edward, you answer me. I trust your level head more than Allen's hasty response."

Edward leaned forward, his hands clasped between his knees. By the firelight, Allen studied the affection between father and son.

"It is apparent that Sir Leventhorpe has little means and even less inclination to spend them, Father. His household is meager, and the farm is poorly managed."

"And yet when he first approached me with his proposal to marry Allen's mother, he pledged Sir Thomas Barrington as a character reference," John responded. "Sir Thomas and I have known each other for decades, and his position as magistrate in the county is not one where I would question his integrity to vouch for another."

"I fear that may have been a deceit, Father. Sir Leventhorpe was not expecting us to arrive at his door, for we came unannounced. The household is impoverished. Worse, this man treats my aunt with great disrespect, and she is not the woman I know. She appears afraid to even speak within her own home."

Despair clenched Allen's heart from Edward's words. He had let everyone down. His father, his mother. Everyone.

John drew deeply on the clay pipe and exhaled. A wreath of smoke curled around his head.

"If, as you say, Francke is planning to use Lucy's recovered funds to right his own affairs and finance the Puritan cause here in Essex, then that is a serious accusation." John's voice was low, measured.

"And one that I feel in my heart is true, Uncle John." Allen couldn't restrain his thoughts any longer. "He is against the king, he runs a strict Puritan household, and under the thin guise of a charity school education he has tricked my mother into thinking that he is an intellectual. He is nothing but a subversive, miserly Puritan, and my mother is trapped."

"Luce as well," Edward said softly. "I fear for her, too."

"My sister's wit and her tongue will keep her out of trouble."

"She is not as resilient as you think, Allen." Edward always did have a soft spot for Luce. "She needs protection."

Exasperated, Allen stood up and leaned on the mantel. The heat warmed him, and the strong ale fired his belly. "I believe we should ride tomorrow and rescue my mother from her husband's grasp. She was not in her right mind when she married him, being fearful of the debtors' prison. We will set her free." He waved his arm to rally his family, missed his footing, and caught hold of the fire irons to steady himself.

"You will rest tonight, and we will talk in the morning." John beckoned forward his steward, standing in the shadows. "You both make grave accusations that cannot be acted upon lightly. I need to think with a clear head. In the meantime, Lucy and your sister are in no immediate peril."

Two days later, they were dining with Sir Thomas Barrington at Barrington Hall, just a few miles from Ryes Manor.

Allen glanced around the paneled dining room, evaluating the carved chairs, the dresser full of pewter that stretched from floor to ceiling, and a freshly woven tapestry adorning the wall. Daylight streamed through the large glass windows. Uncle John may consider Sir Thomas Barrington to be a Puritan, but his hospitality rivaled that of a duke, and his elaborate dinner table groaned with the weight of roast meats, a full pike baked in wine, and numerous flagons of ale. The cousins availed themselves of his board, for their rations at Oxford were not plentiful, and they were perpetually hungry.

"Bad business, this." Sir Thomas wiped his mouth with a large linen napkin and pulled a plump lamb leg from the carcass in front of him. "Seemed like a good idea at the time, St.John, despite Francke's reputation. Thought he'd repented when he embraced the cause."

"You talk of a cause, sir, discussed in Essex for the past thirty years. This has been a long discourse, this talk of men's rights and Parliament." John spoke confidently from his end of the table. "Even though the ship money situation angered those who favor Parliament, the king's men at the coast support it."

"What exactly is his reputation, Sir Thomas?" Allen noticed the baronet's statement and leaned forward in his anxiety to hear more. "Because of your endorsement, my uncle gave his permission willingly to my mother's marriage. Is there more he should have known? What do you consider he should have repented?"

Sir Thomas busied himself with the tender meat, gnawing on the bone until the bloody juice dripped from his chin onto his collar, staining the white lace brown.

"Thought he'd righted himself, I did. When your uncle asked for my opinion, I wanted to be fair to the man. He is a faithful and devout follower."

Sir John stopped eating, his knife held in his hand, poised over his plate. "Stop dithering, man. What didn't you tell me, Barrington?"

"He had some...trouble...in his earlier days." The baronet continued to chew complacently on the lamb, and Allen almost snatched it from his fat fist.

"What? What?" he demanded until a look from his uncle silenced him.

There was a quiet moment, broken only by Sir Thomas's chomping. He swallowed and took a gulp of his wine. A clock struck the hour, a sudden and unexpected peal.

"Sir Leventhorpe was accused of breaking into his neighbor's home, forcing open their chests, and stealing their gold—"

"Oh, dear God," Allen burst out.

"He claimed the gold was his, that he was recovering his rightful possession. After all, he had enough debts pressing to cause any man to act on impulse. But he could offer no proof of original ownership." Sir Thomas busied himself with cutting another hunk of meat.

John dropped his knife with a clatter. "And was he prosecuted?"

"I sat on the bench. 'Scused him this time. After all, he donated most of it to the cause. He was most repentant that he did not pursue his recovery under the law. Seemed a likely mistake."

"And so, you let him free. And encouraged me to agree to my sister marrying a known criminal, a debtor, a thief?" John's voice echoed around the silent room.

"Mistakes are made. Men can change," responded Sir Thomas.

Allen banged his fist on the table "This one obviously hasn't."

Barrington paused mid-chew and blinked.

"And now he is married to my mother and will have access to thousands of pounds' worth of the king's warrants that are due to her, which are meant for us." Allen pushed back his chair, the heavy furniture scraping on the polished oak floorboards. "I thank you for your clarity, Sir Thomas. And for your hospitality. But do not expect us to be sympathetic to your cause. I see it is founded on dishonesty, and fraudulently preys on the souls of the innocent."

Allen beckoned to Edward and John. He could not bear to sit with this hypocrite. Nodding, Sir John and Edward stood with him, their chairs echoing in the hall. Barrington was left sitting at the laden table, surrounded by the debris of the banquet, his mouth gaping open, the grease glistening on his lips.

"You have not heard the last of this, Barrington," said John. "You have deceived me into contracting my sister into a loveless marriage that is not only fraudulent, but threatens to fund sedition in the county to incite men against the king and all I hold dear."

"We will take action," added Allen. "There will be no corrupt justice to excuse Sir Leventhorpe's criminal actions this time."

John nodded, and leaned toward Sir Thomas, raising his finger and pointing directly at him.

"I have the king's ear. My nephew leaves for Whitehall Palace immediately. My sister Lady Villiers will ensure that justice is served. You will not remain a magistrate with a record such as yours, Sir Thomas." John paused. "I suggest you visit your lackey Sir Leventhorpe Francke with the utmost haste and inform him of our actions. And you had better start thinking how you will right this wrong, for right it you will."

Reaching over and grabbing a chicken leg from the platter, Allen grinned. "Thank you for your hospitality, Sir Thomas. And for your revelations. Both were equally appreciated."

Allen led the St.Johns from the banquet hall, their great cloaks swinging as they strode from the suddenly insufferable company of their neighbor.

"Heed yourselves, my friends," Barrington shouted at their departing backs. "You might consider yourselves above all of us, with your court connections and the king's warrants in your pockets. But mark my words. The people's voices are being heard, and being heard loud. Do not think you are above change, for change is coming."

A brief stop at his Aunt Eleanor's to rummage in one of their trunks, and he was suitably attired. Fortuitously, the Earl of Northumberland had seen fit to leave some of his clothes behind when he'd vacated the Tower, for Allen had grown into just his size. His mother's parsimony in saving all such items served him well upon this occasion, his first solo visit to court.

Allen retied his hair in the cream silk ribbon for the third time as he paced outside the queen's privy chamber at Whitehall. He smoothed his cuffs, straightened his white French lace drop collar and brushed an imaginary speck of dust from the burgundy velvet sleeve laced to Northumberland's doublet.

Catching a page watching him with a curling lip, Allen frowned and turned his back on the knave. He glared at the paintings that obscured the walls of the antechamber. A vibrant portrait of a fashionable courtier hung just to the right of the door, and Allen stepped forward to examine the painting closer. Luminous eyes gazed from beneath straight brows while curling dark hair fell to his collar. A generous mouth was framed by a groomed beard. He was striking. A bit of a gallant, perhaps, certainly sure of his appeal.

"Handsome, wasn't he?" A woman's husky voice broke his reverie, and Allen jumped, embarrassed by gawking at the portrait. "The queen hates it hung here, but the king insists. If he must visit the queen, then the least he can do is visit Buckingham, too."

"This is the duke, George Villiers?" Allen turned to the portrait again, staring at the man responsible for his family's devastation. The mouth turned petulant, the gaze sly.

"My dead husband's brother. And yes, considered the most handsome man on earth. The old king called him Steenie, after St. Stephen. And Prince Charles adored him. Still does, in his own kingship. He remains faithful to his memory, and fortunately to our family, who survived his death." Barbara Villiers held out a delicate hand, bejeweled with many rings and perfectly manicured. "You have grown, Nephew. You have a look of your father about you that is unmistakable."

Allen brushed her hand with his lips, catching a musky scent. From his position, he could clearly see her formal court dress, exquisitely embroidered in gold-threaded falcons and studded with pearl drops.

"Aunt Barbara." The encounter in Battersey at Oliver's funeral seemed a distant memory. How curious to visit his mother's sister, here at court. They resembled each other greatly, for the voice was the same, although their hands were so very different. "You are truly as beautiful as they say you are."

"How charming you have become, Allen." She beckoned for him to join her in a window seat, the late afternoon sun streaming in and lighting a face full of beauty, despite the fine lines etched on her forehead. Her hair glistened with diamond drops laced within a small cap, and her dress revealed a full bosom, modestly covered with Flemish lace that hinted at smooth skin beneath.

Allen dragged his attention back to the matter at hand and plunged into his prepared speech.

"I know not what lies between you and my mother." He paused, considering her face for any clue, but her expression was inscrutable, a courtier's mask. "But for the sake of all you held dear in your late husband and his love for my father, I have come to ask your help."

"Your mother and I do not speak." Barbara touched the jewel at her throat and lowered her eyes. "Shall we say, we once fought over the same interest. I won."

Allen coughed into his hand and grew more uncomfortable.

"If my mother knew I was here, she would never forgive me. But Uncle John considered this an approach worth risking her ire, for we have nowhere else to turn. He recently discovered a circumstance that makes this a most urgent matter. And he commanded me to hurry to Whitehall to ask for your assistance."

"My brother is a fool. He has no sense of politics. Why should I lift a finger to help someone who swore me to hell? You were there at Battersey. You see how it is." Barbara's voice was silky soft, vibrant. Allen was fascinated that the timbre should so resemble that of his mother's, and yet the cadence was so very different. This is what court could do to a person.

"Think of this as helping me, Aunt Barbara." Allen turned to his aunt and fell on one knee, folding her hands in his. When he'd practiced this with Edward the night before, they had both thought his actions carried sufficient drama, with a touch of despair. "For the sake of your husband, the duke, and my tormented father." He clasped her hand to his chest, encouraging her to feel his heart beating beneath the fine lawn of Northumberland's shirt. "They are all dead now, Aunt. But their spirits live on in me, your children, and the Villiers heirs. For the sake of our future, one word from you and the king will notify Chancery that our debts must be honored. Uncle John has secured a hearing next week on my late father's annuity. I implore that you help me."

"And you would wish what, then?"

"I would wish for my brother and sisters to continue with their education. To join their cousins and serve at court. To be loyal monarchists—faithful citizens of the king and the three kingdoms."

"And if I don't intervene?"

"If you don't, we will all likely land in debtors' prison."

"Harsh times, indeed." Barbara appeared to consider Allen's plea. "But what of your mother?" Her voice turned harsh.

"She has remarried."

Barbara gave a start. "I had not heard."

"It was a Fleet marriage. He is a Puritan. There were reasons."

"Ha. I am sure there were." Her laugh was mirthless. "A Puritan. He will have no influence in Chancery. And you wish to use the funds to bring your brother and sisters to court. Surely that would disturb her greatly?"

"She had little choice, Aunt Barbara. It is not a happy situation."

"Good."

She stood abruptly, and Allen looked up at her, still on his knees.

"I like you. I think you may have more than your share of your father's spirit in you. I always enjoyed that about him. And your mother's beauty. I'll not begrudge her that. You'll do well at court. While she prays with her Puritan for redemption." Barbara turned, the audience over. She paused and faced him, and he recognized a steel will hidden under the veil of her cosmetics. "Tell my brother I will see what I can do. You will have your day before Chancery. But no promises. And there will be conditions. Many conditions. After all, this is your mother you are asking me to save."

Allen stood and watched as his aunt disappeared through a door in the wall, invisible until she pressed on the paneling. Barbara Villiers did not look back.

11

My mother, endeavouring to vindicate injured innocence, was not well treated by my uncle.

Luce Apsley

11th January 1636

Lucy shook her cloak to hang on the peg by the door before entering her parlor. She grimaced. That was a lie. Ryes would never be her home. She paused, steeling her nerves for yet another tirade.

"I am sorry I am so late, Leventhorpe. Goodwife Johnson is not well at all. I hurried from her side as soon as I received your message." Lucy stopped as she opened the door, surprised by many candles, the golden glow of which made the mean chamber almost hospitable. "Are you expecting company?"

Leventhorpe stood by the casement, his thin back outlined by the last of the fading twilight. A thrush called its evensong. Something was about to change, and in the moment of suspended time, Lucy almost wished not to hear it, for she knew not where this was heading.

"I am here." John's voice cut the silence. Her brother sat by the empty fireplace in the only upholstered chair in the room, Leventhorpe's own. The silver buttons on his doublet gleamed, his highly polished boots reflecting the candle luster.

"John? Why are you here?" Lucy stood still, discomfited in the company of her brother, reluctant to show relief or any other emotion. "Is there trouble? Allen?"

"Nay, nothing to be concerned about. Allen is well—very well, in fact." John turned to Leventhorpe. "Would you like to tell Lucy the news, or shall I?"

"What news? Why is my brother here?" Lucy approached her husband. "What information do you have to share with me, Leventhorpe?"

Leventhorpe started to speak, and all but a croak issued from his mouth. He cleared his throat several times and scratched his head.

"Oh, for heaven's sake, man, out with it," John said impatiently.

89

"With what, Leventhorpe? What do you have to tell me?" Lucy looked from John to her husband, trying to hazard the news.

"My dear." Leventhorpe bared his teeth in an approximation of a smile. "We are returning to London. Your son and brother have found a loophole in the pleadings that may allow us to prevail in one of the cases."

"A loophole? London? John, what means this?"

John got up from the chair and crossed the room, taking Lucy's hand.

"This means that you are returning to Chancery to appear before the judges in Michaelmas term. Allen solicited the support of your husband's old friends from court to raise the visibility of your case. The judges are willing to reexamine the warrants and their legality."

"What friends, John? Who steps forward now, when all ran before?"

"Powerful friends, Lucy. Those who supported Buckingham and now look to his son and his allies as the heir to his legacy."

"And Leventhorpe?"

"He will accompany you. It is important that you appear jointly. As your husband, he is responsible for you and the distribution of these funds when you prevail. This is one of the conditions of the hearing." John took his sister into his arms, and she stood silently, her mind whirling with the information. "It is the first step, Lucy, and an important one. If we can set a precedent with this case, then others will fall into place behind it."

Lucy drew John out of her husband's earshot, murmuring, "And the proceeds if we win? Leventhorpe will choose where these are distributed. How can I be assured—?"

"That your children are taken care of?" John spoke boldly and turned Lucy to face Francke.

Leventhorpe cleared his throat, his thin shoulders hunched. "I commit all funds recovered from these lawsuits will be placed in trust for the education and maintenance of your children." He said the words almost by rote, as if they had been hammered into him.

"Exactly." John turned away from his brother-in-law with a look of disgust. "Leave the distribution to me, Lucy. Leventhorpe has pledged his compliance, and I know he will keep his word. Sir Thomas Barrington and I have come to an agreement whereby he will stand proxy for Leventhorpe in the event your husband defaults on this commitment."

His rigid back making it clear that he had nothing further to say, Leventhorpe left his parlor.

Later, Lucy sat by the open casement long after Leventhorpe had retired. After sending food to Luce and sipping on a little wine, she let the night wash over her as the tallow candles guttered in their holders, smoke drifting in the evening breeze. She did not even care about extinguishing the wicks to save for another night. Change roamed abroad, and although opportune, a goose walked over her grave. Any light was welcome.

"John?"

"Yes, Lucy?" He looked up from where he was reading a pouch full of papers spread across the table.

"Where does this lead us? Has Allen made arrangements that we cannot keep? Who is he speaking with at court? Who did he seek out? And what agreement do you have in place with Leventhorpe? Does your arrangement with Sir Thomas Barrington ensure the funds will go to my children?"

"This leads to resolution, Lucy." John joined her at the window, and his hand rested on her shoulder. "There is nothing you need to worry about. You have had more than your share of tribulation, and I have been hasty to wash my hands of these affairs. The executors were doing their business, but when they resigned, I should have stepped in."

These words and pledge came late from her brother. Lucy prayed for forgiveness that resentment was her first reaction. In the velvet summer night, a barn owl hooted, his call answered by a partner across the pasture. The stars shimmered through the haze of her tears.

"We are redeemed? I can bring Babs and James from Eleanor's?"

"When you return to London, yes." John squeezed her shoulder and patted it comfortingly. "You will go back to St. Dunstan's with Leventhorpe and wait there while we take this case before the judges. Allen and Edward are preparing the brief, and I have every confidence we will prevail. If we can win this first warrant, others will follow."

"And then I return here?" Again the owl hooted, its lonely call piercing the black night, calling the spirits of the dead.

"Your home is with your husband, Lucy. But perhaps these new circumstances will allow for more civility in your marriage."

She sat as still as stone, the dark country just beyond her window as oppressive as the Tower walls, now. What other door of the past was opening?

"Theo is in Essex. I saw him."

John's hand tightened on her shoulder.

"What? Where?"

"In the market. At Bishop's Stortford." John's tension transmitted through her body. "It was only a matter of time, John."

"Was Barbara—?"

"With him? No, of course not. He was paying a visit to his estate at Audley End. He left his mistress at court."

"Did you speak to him?"

"He intervened when some Puritans were being overzealous in their patrol of the market's stallholders. I don't think he knew it was me until he had already spoken."

"And?"

"And I thanked him and left."

"You did not engage with him? You did not encourage his advances as you did of old, when Whitehall was your playground and the court your company? I do not need the attention of the Earl of Suffolk. He is a secret Catholic. It is enough that Barbara consorts with him." John's words rushed at Lucy, sudden as a summer storm.

"No, I did not engage with him." Lucy's temper rose as she caught the selfish anxiety in John's tone. "Barbara betrayed me a long time ago, and when you chose to believe her over me, only Anne's love saved us. Your wife was like a sister to me, and I will never forget the friendship she gave when all others deserted me."

John released Lucy's shoulder, and she felt him withdraw from her, a palpable retraction, animosity between them again.

"Anne's dead. And those days remain a tribulation to me."

Lucy winced, for the scar of Anne's death was one that could still be gouged open. "You must not hold on to those timeworn grudges, John. I beg you, do not compound my difficulties now with painful memories."

"Do not let me down again, Sister. I have invested considerable time into this arrangement with Francke and expended copious energy on treating with Sir Thomas to be certain it is upheld. I do not need your reputation—or mine—challenged again because your long-lost love has returned."

Lucy rose abruptly and stood within inches of her brother, as in the old days when Anne intervened to part them as their anger flared.

"And you, Brother, can maintain your precious relationships intact in this miserable county and at court. I thank you for your assistance, but I see again you think only to protect your own interests. Do not fear that I would sully your reputation in Essex. My hope is that once our funds are released, I will not be required to spend any more time here than I absolutely have to. And I certainly do not intend to encounter the Earl of Suffolk again."

Within the week, they traveled to London. Lucy watched the path framed by her mare's pricked ears as she traversed through the beech woods of Epping Forest. The way was treacherous, curving over the uneven ground, slippery with the mulch of autumn's dying leaves. Tree roots threatened to trip them, but the mare was careful, picking her way around those she could, hopping over the ones that barred progress. The pattering rain only served to further muddy the single track, hampering their progress even more.

Ahead, Leventhorpe sat rigid on a gray gelding, disdain obvious in every stiff joint and his unyielding spine. Behind, Luce quietly hummed to herself as she did when she was happy. And she? She did not know her feelings, for in truth her future with Leventhorpe still presented a dismal prospect.

"We should hurry, Leventhorpe," she called. "Can you ride a little faster? Else we will not reach St. Dunstan's before nightfall."

He refused to acknowledge her, and she swore he even slowed down. His only joy appeared to be perverting her wishes. She was dry-eyed and aching from a restless sleep at the King's Head the night before. Her dreams had been full of the cold welcome from the men in the taproom and their obvious hostility toward her, with her fine Italian riding gloves and the educated accent she refused to hide.

The strict Puritans in London melded with the common citizens, but in an Essex country inn, they were in their own domain and had no reason to temper their attitudes. She shivered. There was a bleakness about them that damped her spirit, and she was anxious to return to the city. At least at St. Dunstan's she could attend lectures and exchange views freely with learned clergy who were not zealots and bigots.

She turned on her horse and smiled at Luce, whose heart-shaped face glowed with the health of youth, her golden-brown hair curling damply around her face from under the dark hood. Luce's face lit up.

"Free," she mouthed, her eyes dancing. "We're free."

Lucy nodded and smiled wider, her spirits lifting. Perhaps there was hope in her future. She would be back in London, her spiritual home, where she could take the cloak of respectability that Leventhorpe provided and cast it into a weapon. She would wield it fiercely and fight for what was due to her and her children.

The woods opened to a rain-soaked heath, and Lucy kicked her mare into a canter, forging ahead of Leventhorpe. She caught a glimpse of his shocked face and knew he would berate her later for her defiance. But for the freedom she briefly tasted, his anger would be well worth it.

12.

At Richmond, where the Prince's court resided, there was very good company and recreations.

Luce Apsley
1st June 1636

Allen stepped forward into a rare pool of winter sunlight. The carved wooden angels stared down at him from the rafters. The Apsleys had returned to Westminster Hall again. *Let us see if the brother fares any better than his sisters.* He addressed the old men, barely visible under their heavy beaver-skin robes and hats, hunched on Chancery's bench.

"And so, my lords, I would respectfully request the warrant issued to my father be fully and completely ratified and the annuity of one hundred pounds for the remainder of its sixteen-year term be immediately paid for the care and education of my younger brother and sisters." Allen took a deep breath and continued with the closing remarks he'd rehearsed with Edward until midnight in their rooms. "This plea, lodged last Michaelmas term, has dragged out for almost a year. My younger brother and sisters are destitute and living with relatives. Some six years after my father's death, probate is yet to be heard."

A sudden commotion in the courtroom interrupted Allen's oratory. What now? He was just readying for the grand closing argument, one that Edward said was irrefutable, the best plea ever written.

A whisper ran through the cramped space, a breath that sloughed the sleep from the eyes of the judges, dozing in their musty furs in the dark chamber.

"The king's messenger. The king has sent his messenger." The murmur grew louder as a liveried man approached the bench, his spurs striking the flagstones. He tossed a scroll on the clerk's desk. Allen's heart leaped. God's Mercy. It was here.

"I come on behalf of His Majesty, King Charles, to ratify the pleas of the petitioners, Allen Apsley and his uncle, Sir John St.John." Without waiting for a response, he turned on his heel and stalked out, parting the crowd before him.

Allen sat down, his breath tight. Had Aunt Barbara secured the king's ear? Had his father's friends and allies at court finally rallied around his cause?

The clerk broke the scarlet royal seal on the rolled, beribboned parchment and perused it, his fingers trembling and face reddening as he digested the content.

He turned and faced the bench.

"My lords." The room hushed. Allen's heart beat faster, the blood drumming in his ears. "My lords, the king recognizes Sir Allen Apsley's position, having approved with the Signet and the Great Seal authorization of the accounts—"

A great sigh escaped from Allen. Edward punched his arm joyfully.

"You did it, Coz!"

"—of the accounts of Sir Allen Apsley, the late husband of the Lady Lucy Francke. Dame Francke and her husband, Sir Leventhorpe Francke, may pursue settlement along with the other creditors."

"What?" Allen jumped to his feet. "They must not appear together. We are requesting that my mother be considered sole, for her husband is not to be trusted."

"Silence, sir." A judge peered at Allen. "You have influential friends, Mr. Apsley. I do not often see the king's Signet and Great Seal appear on documents before me." He nodded to the clerk. "The annuity is awarded to you, Mr. Apsley, for the education of your younger brother and sisters. Command Dame Lucy Francke and Sir Leventhorpe Francke to appear before us tomorrow, where we might ratify this agreement." He waved a dismissive hand at Allen. "You have done well, for your youth. And the king's intervention was timely."

With the hearing over, the common onlookers filed out, gossiping of seeing the king's messenger, the swift change of events because of royal patronage.

Allen sat dejected, staring down at the uneven flagstones, intently watching a beetle navigate the rough mortar. He was determined not to let slip the hot tears that brimmed so full.

"Allen, you must not despair. You have a won a battle today." Edward placed a reassuring hand under his arm.

"But not the war," Allen muttered. No doubt Barbara was gleeful that she had tied his mother to her wretched husband for as long as the lawsuits continued. "My mother must return here. I have failed her."

"And return she will, Allen, with honor. You have given her an opening to fight for her due, for what rightfully belongs to her. The annuity is restored, so your brother and sisters may continue their education. You went to the palace and appealed to your father's allies. You won justice."

The beetle flipped on its back, helpless to right itself. If he did not move it, it would die.

"I did not go to my father's allies." Allen stood up. "I went to Barbara Villiers. Our aunt intervened with the king on my behalf. And, already, her influence has bound my mother to Sir Leventhorpe to pursue the rest of the money." His face contorted. "I wanted this to be over, for my mother never to know that her sister was the one that interceded." He crushed the beetle with his boot. "But I fear truth will out."

A gusty wind from the river cleared Allen's thoughts as he walked back along the Strand to Leventhorpe Francke's home in St. Dunstan's. He scowled at the fine waterfront palaces on his right, the contrast between his rightful inheritance and Francke's mean dwelling darkening his mood even more. For the thousandth time, Allen imagined his life had his father not lost a fortune supporting Buckingham. It was only right that the duke's sister-in-law, his own aunt, should aid them now. His mother would understand.

"Well?" Leventhorpe Francke pounced on Allen the moment he entered the dreary house. "What news today, from my lawyer?"

Allen brushed past Francke and threw his hat onto a bench.

"I would talk to my mother. Where is she?"

"Visiting Eleanor," Francke responded. "What news? If you accomplished anything. I realize you work for no fee, for I would not pay you for any of your clerking."

Allen turned and placed himself within reach of Francke. He realized, suddenly, that he was as tall as the older man, and a lot stronger.

"No, you are not paying me. I am pleading this case because no one else will, and because I am all you have left." He moved closer, and Francke stepped back, pinning himself against the bench. "Or will you dip into your malnourished purse and spend coin on a lawyer from Gray's Inn or Temple, Sir Leventhorpe?"

"I am not paying another shilling on this case." Francke sidled away from Allen and stood by the empty fireplace.

"You have not paid a penny yet," retorted Allen. "The annuity is restored. I am now in charge of my brother's and sisters' education." He must at least establish that point. "As it turns out, you will be heard. The king has authorized the case to continue. You and my mother will appear before the bench tomorrow."

"Your mother and I?" Leventhorpe's face grew red. "Your mother has no position before Chancery. I speak for her, and I accept the outcome, whatever it is."

"You only want one outcome, Sir Leventhorpe. And that is to line your own pocket with the money that is due to my family." Allen touched the hilt of his sword, pleased as he watched Francke's eyes flicker to his hand. "I will remind you of your pledge. Do one thing to divert this money from my family to your own use, and I will reveal every wicked and fraudulent act you have committed."

"You have no proof."

"Do not think to renege now. I have the word of Sir Thomas Barrington, a powerful man in your county. That is enough."

The front door slammed, and both men looked sharply toward the noise, swiftly moving apart to stand on opposite sides of the small chamber.

"Allen. How wonderful to see you. How did you fare today, my darling?" His mother embraced him, standing on tiptoe to kiss his cheek. She glanced at Francke and nodded her head. "Husband." Francke acknowledged her with his own slight bow.

"Well, Mother, well." Allen took her hands in his. "We have overcome the court's reluctance. We have a continuation of the hearing tomorrow. And the annuity is restored."

"How, Allen? How did you manage to appeal to the king? The Lord Chancellor holds all pleas hostage."

Allen looked down at his mother's fingers. They were still reddened and roughened. No longer those of a lady. His anger rose again.

"No matter. Suffice to say that the hearing proceeds. You and Sir Leventhorpe will appear, and the claim heard. We will prevail."

"Leventhorpe? He stands with me?"

"Mother, the king has authorized this hearing. But you must act with your husband."

"His name has been added to the paperwork. That is enough."

Allen looked from his mother to Leventhorpe's averted profile. He sighed.

"You cannot act as though you are sole. You must appear with your husband."

Leventhorpe slammed his fist onto the fireplace mantel, clearly frustrated.

"Woman, is it not enough that I have given you my name, a roof over your head, and now the legal grounds to reclaim our—your—money?"

Allen rounded on him.

"Whose money, sir? I think not yours, but ours. What right have you to attach to my father's funds?"

"The right of the husband, sir. And I will ask you not to challenge my authority."

"And so this is your plan? You seek to reclaim this money for yourself?"

"Allen, please stop." Lucy stepped in front of Allen, her eyes pleading.

"It is none of your business. Your mother is married to me. She is my responsibility." Leventhorpe turned his back on Allen.

"And my younger brother and sisters are mine." Allen grabbed Leventhorpe's arm and forcibly twisted him around. "You will not take what is rightfully ours to settle your own debts."

Leventhorpe pulled himself free and shoved Allen back against the wall.

"Do not ever challenge the rights I have. When your mother married me, the law gave me the authority to decide what is best. She has made adequate arrangements for the rest of her brood, and they are with her family, where they belong."

Lucy gasped. "Leventhorpe—you cannot mean this—"

"Mother, he does. We have proof that he is in great debt and has resorted to common thievery to assuage his creditors. He is going to use Father's money to pay off his—"

"Silence!" roared Leventhorpe. "I will not have you defame me under my roof. Get you gone!"

Allen pulled his sword and stepped forward to Francke, his heart hammering. His father's cautionary words had flown, and all that was left was a burning desire to plunge his weapon into Francke's bony chest and end his life, there and then.

"Allen, desist!" His mother's voice cut through the red mist before his eyes. "On the name of all you hold dear, do not do this."

No one moved. Allen felt his mother's eye upon him, warning him and yet not stopping him.

"Plead truth, sir. Tell my mother your history and your intent." Allen still had his sword unsheathed, and although the tip pointed to the ground, he made no attempt to encase it.

"I refute all that you say. You have no proof."

Allen raised his sword slightly.

"I have the word of Sir Thomas Barrington. He revealed to me just exactly what your condition is, Sir Leventhorpe. And it is monstrous."

"I deny what he says. He does not know my circumstance. I am innocent of any charges." Leventhorpe's voice shook, whether with rage or fear, Allen could not tell.

"He is the magistrate in your county, sir. He knows exactly your circumstance. And I would call this collusion and a thwarting of justice that he ignored the previous claimant's case that you stole money from them."

"It is not true."

"I have witnesses."

"Who?" Leventhorpe's tone was defiant.

"My uncle. Sir John was with me when Barrington exposed you as a common thief. Only by his intervention were you saved from debtors' prison, or worse."

Lucy clung to Allen's arm, her face shocked.

"What is all this, Allen? What knows my brother of this? What are you saying?"

Allen raised his sword again, and Leventhorpe took another step back. He slumped against the wall and clamped his mouth shut.

"Admitting your guilt, Sir Leventhorpe? How plead you now to my mother?"

Francke looked down and said nothing.

"Guilty, by the sin of omission," Allen stated. "Let me tell you how this is to be, Sir Leventhorpe." The phrases rolled off his tongue with a fluidity that emerged from a hidden well. "Item, you will not pursue this case any further for your own benefit. Item, you will authorize the funds be made over to me for the benefit of my younger brother and sisters. Item, you will return to your miserable county and take up residence there. And item, you will not trouble my mother for her money, her time, nor her presence. You will not act jointly, you will not pursue her wealth, and you will never claim marital rights on her again."

"Madam, you intermeddleth with this case as if you were sole. You are married and under the protection of Sir Leventhorpe. Does your husband not speak for you?" The judge picked up a document from a stack of papers and squinted at it. "The annuity has been released by the king to your son. Where stands your husband in this?"

Lucy gripped the wooden railing. "Sir Leventhorpe is a generous man and realizes the need for care for my children." The words stuck in her craw, but she spewed them out, as part of the condition that Leventhorpe demanded.

"And what say you?" The judge turned to Francke, standing at Lucy's side. Suppressed anger vibrated from him like an over-tightened lute string.

"I agree, my lord." The words were surly, the tone blank.

"A curious case." Pushing the papers around his desk, the judge appeared reluctant to issue a decision. "I cannot see the wood for the trees, and there is more to this than I will know." He drew a deep sigh. "But the king has commanded I release these funds, and in this case, the creditors must deal with their loss. Confirm the annuity to Allen Apsley, to be used for the housing, education, and comfort of his younger brother, James, and sisters, Luce and Barbara. And let the king's warrants stand for settlement of Sir Allen Apsley's debts."

Lucy turned to her children, grouped together in the public seating, and smiled. Allen nodded back reassuringly while James broke into his broad grin, carefree at sixteen that he was going to be living again with his adored older brother. Luce was gazing up at the roof, at what Lucy knew not, while Babs stared at the white hart statues flanking the chamber.

In the shadows, by the wooden partition that served to give them some privacy from the expanse of the great hall, Lucy caught a movement. A woman, cloaked and masked to maintain her privacy, was swiftly leaving the chamber. Her maid kept close and concealed her from Lucy's sight, but even so, there was something familiar in her walk that she could not place. The sight niggled in her mind, but was chased away as Allen took her into his arms and squeezed the breath from her.

"We succeeded, Mother. We prevailed. Our family is whole again."

Lucy relaxed into his strong embrace and then reached out her arms, drawing her other children into the circle.

"We are together. And we will stay together. I promise you. No more separation, ever." She paused. "But there is one more thing I must do. Please go to the main door of the hall and wait for me there. And yes, Luce, you may purchase a book on the way."

Lucy's children left the courtroom together, and a tiny bud of happiness bloomed in her heart. But there was still unfinished business.

She walked across the aisle to where Leventhorpe was gathering his hat and cloak. Eventually, he must pass her to leave the courtroom. After a while, when everyone else had left, he turned and made as if to step around her. Lucy placed her hand on his sleeve to detain him, and he stopped dead, refusing to meet her eyes.

"Leventhorpe." She took a deep breath and started again. "Leventhorpe, this was not how I wanted our marriage to be."

"You planned this from the beginning, madam." His tone was surly. How could such a melodious voice spit such sour words? "I see you now for the harlot you are. You identified me as the party who could bring credibility to your husband's criminal acts, and you hunted me with the vigor of a jade pursuing her mark."

"I. . .I cannot believe you are accusing me thus."

"I cannot believe you would think otherwise." Leventhorpe dragged his gaze up to hers, and Lucy flinched at the hatred in his eyes. "I, madam, am an innocent. You, madam—and your entire family—are nothing more than an unholy alliance with the Catholic king and his debauched court. You have no interest in the pure ways of a reformed God. Your son went to his father's cronies at court to obtain your judgment, and that is no different than the buying of powers that your corrupt husband instigated to start this mess."

"Leventhorpe, I will not accept you saying such things. Allen simply appealed to my husband's old friends. My family saved me from continuing this unholy alliance with you, for you are the one that tricked me into marrying you to line your own purse and make good on your debts."

"No, madam. I fear you are wrong, very wrong. And I fear for your soul. For when change comes upon this country—and change will come—you and your kind will see the wickedness of your ways. You will see that the king and his kind cannot overturn men's wishes and subvert the power of the court. And you and your son will be left standing alone with your old ways and old allegiances that will be disappeared and gone. Gone. Gone."

His voice almost incoherent, trembling, Francke lifted his hand as if in benediction, but instead, made the sign to ward off the evil eye.

"You are dead to me." He pushed past her, and Lucy stumbled slightly. "Do not contact me. Do not expect me to sign any more documents, or help you with any more suits. And when the money runs out—and it will—do not think to crawl back to me. From this day forth, you will no longer be under my protection. Go to your precious family and have the king and his sycophants plea for you again. If they will listen. If they still have the power."

The Mitre Inn on the Strand was bustling, its noisy patrons and the aroma of roasting meat a welcome contrast to the cavernous chill of Westminster Hall.

"I have sent word to free Peter from the Tower." Allen sat with Luce and James at the far end of the trestle table, his hands wrapped around a foaming tankard of ale. The art of making decisions lay well upon him, and he was in the mood to continue. "'Tis just a matter of paying the fine, and there was more than enough in our first installment to take care of the penalty."

James leaned forward, his fair hair flopping across his face. "Does he come to live with us? I would welcome learning from his swordplay skills, for mine are out of practice."

Allen shook his head. "No, James, that would not be wise." He smiled at his younger brother, already grown to his height, but yet to fill out. "Peter is on the next ship back to The Hague. No doubt he is anxious to return to his soldiering in Europe." He raised his hand to summon the barmaid, his appetite still not sated.

"He is an adventurer," responded James. "And he knows how to make a good living as a soldier."

As she approached the table, the girl bobbed a curtsy, a blush on her cheeks. Allen grinned at her. "More oysters, sweeting, and quickly."

Luce laughed. "Allen, you will have all the tavern wenches in love with you before the end of dinner." She finished her cider and shook her head, declining more. "The judge did award you care of our father's children. You take the matter most seriously. The army is the right place for Peter. He needs the discipline."

"You could put send me to train under Peter. In Holland. Where the best swordsmen are." James' tone was sulky. "Instead, I am stuck here, with my sisters. This is no place for a man."

Allen shrugged. "One day, James, when you are old enough, you can make your own decisions. Until now, you are under my care. Please, join our mother and tend to her needs."

James scowled and left Allen's side, jarring the table as he did so.

Allen glanced down the table at his mother, who was sitting with Babs, watching her eat. She did not appear to be dining much herself, having no dish in front of her.

"I fear for our mother, Luce. The time spent with Francke weighs heavily on her."

Luce followed his gaze. The muted light that crept through the windowpanes served only to emphasize the shadows under their mother's eyes.

"He was an unforgiving and unyielding man, Allen. She thought she was doing the right thing by marrying him and taking his name to fight for us. But I fear it has taken its toll on her. This is a decision she must live with, for the rest of her life."

"That marriage is over. And I will ensure that she is not castigated for Francke's deception." Allen pushed his tankard away and stood, stretching. "We will rest tonight. I leave early tomorrow morning to secure our new home. Uncle John has recommended me to a landlord who has property near the court. I will not see her back in St. Dunstan's, and Lydiard is too far away for all of us."

"We go to Whitehall?" asked Luce. "I am not convinced Mother would settle there, Allen."

"We go to Richmond," Allen responded. "The princes' court is established at the palace, and there will be opportunity for tutoring and expanding our connections. We cannot exist long on the annuity payments, and I will need to launch us within the court circles in order to take advantage of our future patrons."

"Not court, Allen. The king and his courtiers are not a good influence for James and Babs." Luce glanced again at their mother. "We only wish for peace, and that is not found with this king and his Catholic French wife."

"Don't preach, Luce. My options are limited right now. The living is cheaper in Richmond, and opportunities abound. The further I can remove our mother from the memories of St. Dunstan's and the past few years, the better for her."

"We know no one in Richmond, or at court. Only those friends of our father, such as Goring, who have done nothing to come to our aid in recent years. I am still surprised that you were able to convince any of them to intercede now." Luce pushed her chair back too, and stood in front of Allen, meeting his eye purposefully. "Allen, what ambition takes you to court?"

It was no good; he had never hidden anything from his sister, so close they were in spirit, although so different in temperament.

"I made a promise. A pledge, of sorts."

Luce looked surprised. "What kind of pledge? And to whom?"

Allen threw back his shoulders and placed one hand on his hip. It was a similar pose that he recalled from the painting of Buckingham. He caught the eye of the barmaid and winked at her as she set the oysters on the table, causing her to giggle.

"To bring us all to court and follow the king and the royal family."

"Why? Why, when you know it is an abomination to our mother and me to be around the very courtiers that were responsible for our father's fall, and who live an ungodly way of life?"

"Don't be such a Puritan, Sister. The time has come for us to regain our place in society, to reconcile our family. To bring our mother close to her own sister, who can help her in so many ways."

"I don't understand . . ."

"To Aunt Barbara. She was the one who intervened with the king on our behalf. She has offered to introduce James and me to court and help establish us. We are on our way back, Luce. It was our father's wish, I believe, that we build our lives again at court and honor his memory."

Luce swayed and caught the table behind her.

"Oh, Allen, what have you done? What have you committed us to?"

"Our future, Luce. Secure with the king, the court, and the friends and family who will help us rise again."

As he leaned over and grabbed a fresh oyster, he looked at James and Babs, who were now his responsibility. Francke and that whole unpleasant Puritan incident were gone, to be seen no more. Now, they could move on with the life their father had intended.

"Allen," Luce dropped her voice to a whisper, glancing over at their mother. "Do you know what happened between Aunt Barbara and our mother? Do you know why she left court?'

"Old gossip, Luce. And stories that are long forgotten." Allen caught his mother's eye upon them and gathered up his gloves. "Take her home to Eleanor's, and keep my plans to yourself. There is no need to cause her further anxiety. Wait for my summons, which will be in just a day or two. And don't tell her how Chancery's decision came about. Ever."

Allen kissed his sister swiftly and hugged his mother and younger siblings. He had arranged things without a hitch, and he intended to continue his expert management of their affairs. After placing some coin on the table for the barmaid, he left the inn, touching the smooth head of the falcon on his sword. There was much to do, and it was a three-hour ride to Richmond Palace—home of the royal family, the court, and his future.

13

As for music and dancing, I profited very little in them, and would never practise my lute or harpsichord but when my masters were with me.

Luce Apsley

17th June 1637

"And Mr. Coleman . . . thinks that my lute . . . work shows great . . . promise, Luce."

Luce glanced at her sister—pink-faced as she trotted along beside her—and slowed her pace. She was always accused of walking too fast, and in Richmond, where the streets were wide and the city crowds absent, she could tread with abandon, great strides that spoke of freedom. Luce clasped Babs's hand, swinging it in rhythm to her pace. She was so happy to see her carefree, glowing. In the three months since moving to Richmond, her sister had flourished.

"You love music, don't you, Babs?"

Her sister beamed. "Yes. And poetry, and dancing and etiquette and—"

Luce laughed, throwing back her head. The summer sun warmed her cheeks.

"Mother is so happy that one of us enjoys these frivolous things. It certainly isn't me."

"But no one can translate their Latin as fast as you, Luce. Not Allen, nor Edward, nor any of the other scholars."

"Well, that will come in handy one day, I'm sure. Perchance I'll marry an ancient philosopher who has traveled to our time to study the strange creatures we have become, and we'll talk nothing but Latin and Greek to anyone."

"And they will consider you so learned and invite you to the court to converse with the wisest councilors in the land." Babs joined in the game. "Meanwhile, I will marry a handsome gentleman who loves to laugh and dance and sing and enjoys good company and pleasant pursuits—"

"And clothes. He must enjoy dressing well and present a handsome face, for you will not be happy with an ugly visage."

"Ah, Luce, and you will only have to dress in fur robes and togas, which is a blessing, considering how little care you put into your appearance."

Luce joined Babs's laughter. Together, they rounded the corner from the Palace Yard to the Green, and strolled hand in hand along the row of fashionable homes overlooking the verdant parkland. Mr. Coleman's house was but ten minutes to theirs, and Luce enjoyed meeting Babs after her lute lessons at the king's musician's home and walking her back. She loved the open spaces of Richmond, the charming village by the Thames, where old Sheen Palace dominated the skyline, and the court lodgings huddled under its shadow like chicks to a hen.

Across the meadow, she spied a group of young men and women she knew vaguely from Mr. Coleman's picnicking under the chestnut trees, their summer clothes bright in the dappled shade. Strains of music drifted over the breeze. The scent of fresh-scythed grass mingled with the heady fragrance of wild purple buddleia that waved over the garden walls. A great sense of well-being flowed over her. She may be helpless at her music, and her needlework resembled that of a three-year-old, but she could welcome the beauty of the moment, the flooding of all her senses.

They turned into a well-kept home at the end of the row, where honeysuckle clambered around the arbor-framed path, and a scarlet climbing rose nodded at the deep green door. In the garden, young raspberry canes were laid out in an orderly fashion, serving as a backdrop to the rows of vegetables that were thriving in the rich soil. Pausing to crush a lavender sprig from the hedge that bordered the medicinal garden, Luce sniffed deeply, enjoying the pungent aromas released by the warm sun.

My mother's pride and joy. A place where they both loved to spend time, working together to cultivate the essential plants for curatives and physicks.

"Will you come back to Mr. Coleman's with me this evening, Luce? The princes' consort is practicing for the masque, and we have been invited to listen. And Susan Coleman wants me to be there with her." Babs paused on the stone step. "Perchance we could persuade Mother to come with us. She should spend more time in company."

"I will come with you, for I know how much you enjoy these evenings and your friends. But I doubt that Mother will join us. She is not inclined to spend time with the court, even if it is the princes' and not the king's."

"The princes' court is so much fun, Luce. There are always games and play and laughter. The two princes are adored, and it's a happy place to be. There's not even the formality Mother says she dreads. Well, not if the queen is absent."

"It may not resemble the court she attended, but even so, she did not enjoy that life."

"She hides like a hermit in a cave from all that is happening at the palace." Babs dropped her voice as they walked across the threshold into the cool hallway. A pewter jug of damask roses on a chest glowed in the shadows, and from the rear of the house they could hear the cheerful sounds of food being prepared.

"She has her reasons, Babs. Don't question her." Luce placed her books onto the chest and walked ahead of Babs to the kitchen. "Mother, we're home. And hungry. The walk has given us an appetite."

"Come, my darlings, we're ready to eat," their mother's voice called. "We'll take our meal in the garden, for the weather is too hot to eat indoors. We've made a picnic to enjoy outside, and then, this afternoon, let us go and feed the swans on the river."

Memories of Lydiard suddenly flooded into Luce's mind. A poignant twinge twisted her heart as she recalled a distant summer when her father was alive. She smiled to think of those golden days and realized that for the first time in a long time, she was not burdened with the cares of their living. No longer did she worry about the next day's hearing, or sit tensely anticipating the bailiff's hammering. She lived as a child again—carefree, neither aware of the future, nor dwelling in the past.

"Coming, Mother," she replied. "Coming."

Mr. Coleman's house sat within the confines of the palace grounds, close by the royal mews and next to the maids of honor's housing. *Fortunate location*, noted Allen, spending most of his afternoon as he did with the freshest maid appointed to the princes' court. These newly arrived country girls grew bored quickly, as they were only needed when Queen Henrietta

Maria was in residence. And that was rarely, with King Charles not liking the air at Richmond much. So what was a poor lonely maid at court to do but allow the attention from one of the band of young and attractive—he self-consciously smoothed back his hair—young and attractive courtiers.

"Ah, Allen. You've surfaced. And look as though you might need a drink, man." William Villiers broke into his musings and handed him a large goblet of wine with a smile. "Did you leave the girl intact, or do we now have another Maid of Dishonor at court?"

Allen laughed at his cousin's joke and threw back the wine in one gulp, holding his goblet out for a refill from the servant. Coleman's house could always be relied upon to have a good supply of French wine and a generous table of food. Part of the perks of being the King's Own Musicians.

"Well, it was a challenging enterprise, but someone needed to make the proper introduction to court. And I'm only too happy to volunteer to extend a warm welcome."

"I don't think that's the only thing you extended. You've certainly caught up with the rest of us since you've been here, my friend."

"In conquests, perhaps, but I still have a ways to go to match your splendor, Cousin."

Rubbing his cousin's elegant red velvet sleeve between his finger and thumb, Allen whistled as he felt the quality of the fabric.

"Now that is quite a doublet. I sense the gold thread monopoly still has its value."

"My mother ensures that our income is sufficient for our means." William eyed Allen's burgundy jacket. "That's a little out of fashion, Coz. Where did you find that relic? My tailor can bring some life into it. There is quality still in the material, even if the cut is antique."

Allen felt a flush at the back of his neck. He knew William's offer was not intended to demean, but damn it, he always felt he was inferior to his cousin.

"And so who is your latest passion, William?" Changing the subject to romance would always distract a Villiers.

The chamber started to fill with other young courtiers, and a babble of laughter broke out in a corner where a cluster of young men surrounded a beautiful young woman.

William nodded toward her. "Mary Bayning, Viscount Bayning's girl."

Allen followed his gaze. "She's popular."

"And a catch." William took his own goblet from a passing servant and took a measured sip as he eyed her. "My mother is starting to negotiate a settlement."

"A settlement?"

"She should bring with her at least a thousand pounds a year. We could use it."

"And Aunt Barbara is negotiating?"

"My father cannot from the grave, Allen. Besides, there's no one like my mother to structure a settlement. Look what she has done to restore my poor father's debts and estate." William turned to his cousin, his eyes settling on a darn in Allen's shirt. He raised an eyebrow. "And yours, I hear."

William's attention was distracted by a movement at the door, and the cousins watched Luce and Babs enter. They paused at the threshold, arm in arm, looking around the room. Luce caught sight of Allen, and her face broke into a smile, her luminous blue eyes shining as she moved into the candlelight.

"Now that's a pretty sight," remarked William. "Your sisters are beauties, Allen. And the older—she's a catch. No inheritance, but a face to die for, and I fancy a fire beneath—"

Allen turned to him, his quick temper rising.

"That's my sister you're talking about, William."

"Yes, and my cousin. Is she of marriageable age?"

"Luce turns eighteen come January."

"Better get her contracted soon, Apsley. Get someone to take her off your hands. She's caused some gossip here at Coleman's." He threw back his drink and adjusted the silver-tipped points on his elegant doublet. "I heard she's a tough one to talk to. Only wants to address her studies and refuses to join in the fun. She may be a beauty, but she'll be a challenge to marry off. And you don't want an old maid to care for at this time in your life."

William left Allen's side and walked toward Mary Bayning, cutting his way through the young men that surrounded her. He leaned over her hand with a flourish. She simpered and fluttered her fan, and Allen watched as the Villiers charm went to work again. His gaze returned to Luce and Babs as they crossed the crowded room to him, and he tried to view them from William's perspective.

His sisters were well formed, their figures full, their stature graceful. Babs was the more elegantly dressed of the two, her sleeves matching her bodice, her hair dressed in the latest fashion. But Luce had a careless grace about her that drew eyes. She did not appear to worry about her looks or manners, but walked with an air that ignored those around her. Allen smiled. This unconcerned attitude made her intriguing.

"Sisters." He held out his arms as they approached. "My darlings. And how was your day?"

"More industrious than yours, Allen," retorted Luce as she eyed the empty goblet. "At least I can say I actually did something today. The Lucretius text is proving most vexing, but I think I have found a way to explain the purpose of his narrative."

"Oh, Luce, not again," Babs groaned. "You have plagued me with this since we left home. I cannot stand another word."

Luce looked astonished and then smiled. "You tease me, Sister." She smoothed her skirts, dislodging stray cat hairs. "Oh well, if I have to be social, then lead me to slaughter."

"Actually, my day has been very industrious, Sis. I think I have found a way to explain the purpose of male and female narrative within society." Allen looked over Luce's shoulder to William and Mary, who formed a couple and were standing close together. There was a look about Mary's face that told Allen she was completely intrigued with William.

Allen took his sisters by their arms and escorted them to a row of gilt-armed chairs placed in front of the consort. "Now, let us enjoy Mr. Coleman's music. I am looking forward to the masque next month, and we are most fortunate to have a little advance taste of what the future may hold." He thought of Aunt Barbara and her plans for her son. Marriage prospects. Well, if it was his duty to next see his sister made a good match, so be it. "I feel we will all benefit from the outcome of this evening's events."

Lucy stood in the gracious drawing room of their rented home, holding her brother's astonishing letter to the light from the bay window. No matter this was the third time she had perused the forceful hand and that no clues lay between the lines as to the motivation behind the missive.

Come to Lydiard with Luce, John wrote. *Our Hungerford cousins have indicated an interest in her marriage prospects. I have a mind to settle a dowry on her, Sister, for I know you are not in a position to do so.* Lucy looked up from the parchment and gazed out over her garden.

"Six hundred pounds is your dowry, Niece." She recalled Uncle Oliver's words from decades ago, and the freedom that had fluttered, birdlike, in her heart, as thoughts of independence first nested in her mind. "If you don't marry by twenty-five, it's yours to do with what you will."

Free to choose, she'd married at twenty-six and offered the dowry to Allen, who'd immediately returned the funds to her, along with a generous allowance. "You will spend this wisely and build up riches in heaven," he'd said. Perhaps she could find someone such as him for Luce. A man who would embrace her intellect and not be intimidated by her education. And love the gentle heart that lay beneath the prickly exterior.

She sighed and returned to John's letter. *It's time you thought about Luce's future. Allen is well on his way at court. James follows close behind, his schooling with the Villiers children assuring him the best connections. Babs will be grown soon, too. Luce must be settled. And perhaps, if she is steady, you will be too. Come to Lydiard, Lucy, and let us make amends.*

Marriage. Her girl. How swiftly this came upon them. And yet, John was right. If the Hungerfords were interested, then who was she to stand in the way of Luce's prospects? They were an old Wiltshire family, as venerated as the St.Johns. And although Luce may have nursed a hidden romantic longing for Edward when she was younger, their consanguinity prevented that match. But there were plenty of other cousins, further removed, who would suit. And, perhaps most importantly, she and her girls could settle back in Wiltshire—away from court and Westminster Hall, away from Puritans and Royalists, away from the memories of Francke and the terrible years of privation and sorrow.

How best to approach her opinionated daughter that marriage lay in her future? Lucy pondered, her thoughts perplexed. Allen. Allen and Edward would be her greatest allies. Luce would listen to them more than anyone.

She watched a tiny wren hopping around the tangled fruit bushes, pecking at the fallen ripe blackberries. Summer was turning to autumn, and nature was readying for the coming winter. Luce would turn eighteen in January. Time to prepare for her future, too.

14

The court was entertained with masks, stage plays, and sorts of ruder sports. Then began murder, incest, adultery, drunkenness, swearing, fornication, and all sort of ribaldry, to be no concealed but countenanced vices, because they held such conformity with the court example.

Luce Apsley
16th August 1637

Fairy-tale turrets adorned with colorful pennants capped the towers of Richmond Palace. A spritely breeze from the Thames teased the shimmering streamers, tossing them to and fro like exotic wings in flight. The castle was poised to levitate above the earth, so celestial did it appear, so ethereal in the golden August light.

Lucy calmed the fluttering in her stomach and marched forward, Luce and Babs on either side. Defying her better judgment, they attended this masque honoring the king and queen as they paused at Richmond on their journey to Whitehall. But Allen insisted, James pressured, Babs implored, and Luce was indifferent. For all four reasons, Lucy could not refuse.

Babs chattered in excitement, her words cascading. "First there is the antemasque. Then the masque, which will consist of disorder being tamed by order. And they finish with the revels, where we all join in."

"I know, sweeting. I have been to many a masque. They have changed little since I witnessed Ben Jonson and Inigo Jones collaborating at Whitehall." Lucy smiled at her daughter.

"You were there? You've attended the Banqueting House?" Babs asked reverently. "There were none nobler, and no better setting, either. You did not tell me this, Mother?"

Lucy's stomach tightened again. "It was a long time ago, my darling. Back when your father was honored by the king, and our favor was high."

"Perhaps he will remember you, Mother. You should arrange an introduction tonight."

"I think not, Babs."

"Leave court introductions to Allen, Babs," Luce interrupted. "Mother is only here to chaperone us."

Lucy was thankful again that she had taken her daughter into her confidence about her experience at court. There was no telling what Allen would have done with that story, for his ambitions were ignited as only a young man's could be. Luce would keep circumspect the old rumors and was not influenced by court ambitions.

"Oh, look. Look how beautiful." Babs's sigh was lost in the chatter of the other guests converging on the gatehouse, which was wreathed in hundreds of roses and draped with garlands of ivy and ferns. As they passed through into the courtyard and the sun dropped behind the high towers, a thousand torches blazed, and leaping shadows flickered on the walls. Gymnasts on invisible ropes danced down the sides of the sheer walls, their toes on the stone, bodies arching out over the crowd. Mr. Coleman's musicians played exuberantly, and Lucy and her daughters stopped, transfixed by the aerial gavotte.

"Ah, found you."

They turned at Allen's voice, and Lucy's nerves fluttered again at the sight of her son.

"Allen, your suit. Where did you acquire—"

"Brother, you almost look handsome—"

Allen bowed with as great a flourish as the pressing crowd would allow him. "William Villiers referred me to the tailor he shares with Prince Charles. I fancy he has worked wonders with Northumberland's relics."

Luce laughed. "Allen, you look completely the king's man. A Royalist, through and through."

"That I am, Sister. My future is with the king and his court, for I have never been as welcome as I have these last months here at Richmond."

Lucy was silent. William Villiers. Barbara's son.

"Come, follow me for the best view. James is holding space for us, and Lord knows he'll get distracted if a pretty maid crosses his path. Quickly, for the king and queen are about to appear."

Allen grasped his sisters' hands, leaving Lucy to follow them as he pushed through the crowd across the courtyard. She caught sight of James, and he waved enthusiastically, beckoning them to a spot across from the performance area and the royal balcony above. A persistent drumming quieted the audience, and from the large doors directly opposite, a herald appeared, a long scroll in his hands. The crowd grew silent, and in the cooling night air, his voice rang out.

"Tonight, we are gathered to honor his celestial majesty, the queen of the heavens, and the cherubim who have blessed their marriage." Silver stars were lowered from the windows around the courtyard, shimmering in the torchlight.

"We honor the prince of peace, and the mother of harmony." A moon and a sun joined the ornaments, and cloud banners that concealed the balcony were gradually pulled apart. Trumpets sounded and from the windows emerged the king and queen, their suits of gold emblazoned with diamonds and pearls, elaborate headdresses glittering.

Under the collective gasp of the crowd, Lucy felt Luce's lips close to her ear.

"He fancies himself divine, Mother. He declares himself as second only to God. What wisdom does that convey to the common folk?"

Lucy continued to stare at the spectacle, disturbed at the blatant relationship between God and king.

"It is not right, Mother. He is not divine. He is a man, like any other." Luce's whisper was horrified.

Lucy turned swiftly to her daughter.

"Hush. Do not say such things aloud," she shushed, causing Allen and James to turn to see what was being said. She frowned at Luce. "Guard your tongue well, Daughter. I share your thoughts, but know better than to express them here."

They continued to watch the spectacle unfold as the masque followed its predictable course. The balcony darkened; the king and his family disappeared. Great disorder resulted, actors playing the common man, peasants, farmers, merchants—all lost in a dark void, chaotic in their confusion to reach agreement between each other. The gibberish and discordant music reached a cacophony resembling the Tower of Babel.

Suddenly, an explosive thunderclap silenced all. Heralded by two men in green with great beards and brandishing clubs, spluttering fireworks accompanied a vehicle into the courtyard. Standing on its platform high above the crowd, the king and queen and two young princes, Charles and James, emerged from the smoke to pacify the mayhem. Consistent with the celestial theme, stars spangled from their clothes until the entire family appeared to be a divine apparition.

Lucy glanced at Allen's profile, illuminated by the flaring lights. Completely fascinated by the theatrics, his face was as happy as ever she had seen him. At his side, James appeared equally absorbed. Babs, in front of her, stood entranced by the music, and Luce . . . Luce glowered at the whole spectacle.

"It's the revels! Join hands for the revels!"

Pulled from Luce's side, Lucy joined the crowd of courtiers, where one and another exchanged hands and twirled in a wild dance. To the thrum of the tabors and wailing from the pipes, the dancing became faster and faster until the music suddenly stopped. Panting, out of breath, and laughing despite herself, Lucy looked up and found herself face-to-face with Barbara.

The crowd faded into the background, and as the music started up again, the dancers stepped around them. Lucy gazed steadily into the eyes of her sister, reluctant to speak, unable to move.

"You." In one word, Barbara cast Lucy back to all the previous confrontations, all the anger, hurt, and betrayal. "I might have guessed we would meet again after Oliver's funeral." Barbara's face was expressionless, but a twitch fluttered in her cheek.

"Barbara," Lucy acknowledged. "You look well."

"I am. And so do you appear to be."

Lucy sensed Barbara's appraisal of her gown, a remnant from the Tower days. It would still stand up to scrutiny. She remained silent. There was nothing to say.

"As do your sons, Lucy. How delightful to become reacquainted with Allen and James. Such charming little boys. Such delightful young men." Barbara fanned herself elegantly and looked around the courtyard, her eyes stopping. "And such good friends with my own."

Lucy followed her gaze and saw Allen and James with the Villiers boys, surrounding the young princes. There was no mistaking their standing now, for they were with Buckingham's children and the inner circle of court. Lucy returned to Barbara's smirk. How that expression persisted. She still looked like the cat that stole the cream.

"So fortunate, don't you think, that Allen was granted responsibility for you and your children, Lucy?"

Lucy started. "What heard you of that business, Barbara? And what concern of yours?"

"I made it my business, dear sister, when your son approached me for help—"

What was Barbara saying?

"—for if not for me, you would still be living with that Puritan, and your children would be destitute. Of course, the gossip that murmurs again around your name would be swept away, if you did return to him. There is talk already of your absent husband."

A darkness came over Lucy, her heart thundering in her ears. *Dear God, let me not swoon here and now.*

"However, I hear that you fit not well in that world either, Lucy. Perhaps you pay a little too much attention to your herbals and recipes for the liking of the local Puritans. Do not draw notice to yourself. Especially when you know not where your allies or enemies stand."

Theo. Barbara knew that Theo had intervened in the market.

"You may not know which land you belong in," Barbara continued as she fanned herself, "but your sons appear to have chosen. And chosen well."

Do not rise to her bait. Stay calm.

Lucy kept her voice level, inflecting irony and weariness into her tone. Two could play those court games, for Lord knew she'd trained well at Whitehall. "What more do you want, Barbara? What else could you possibly want of me?"

Barbara flipped her fan closed and tapped her chin thoughtfully. She looked around the courtyard again, her eyes pausing by the fountain, where young girls giggled at the antics of a jester.

"Ah. And there is my little niece, my namesake, Barbara. I was much honored when your husband chose to name her after me."

"Barbara, I swear, if you insert yourself in my family further—"

"No. I think that is all for now, Sister, for I have been compensated with loyalty." She paused as she saw Allen and William approach. "For now."

"Mother! Aunt Barbara." Allen had such a wide smile on his face, such a look of a guilelessness. He had intended no mischief in reaching out to the aunt who had the king's ear. The harm done was self-inflicted, her penance for keeping secrets. "I hoped you would speak."

Lucy managed a tight smile and felt a hand slip into hers, squeezing it reassuringly. She recognized Luce's touch.

"Mother, I think the time is upon us to leave. The hour grows late, and the company has become too rowdy for Babs. I think it is not appropriate for her to witness the behavior of the courtiers."

Lucy turned gratefully to Luce, who had gathered Babs to her side. "You are right. Allen, thank you for entertaining us this evening and for providing such a pleasant surprise." She looked again at Barbara. "Until next time, Sister."

She gathered her girls and, with an arm around each of them, walked away from the court. With every step, she could feel Barbara's eyes upon her. She refused to look back.

Their cozy parlor was lit only by the banked fire and a dozen candles casting an amber pool of light. In two chairs drawn close, Luce and her mother sat in their house gowns, hair loose.

"Babs is resting?" Her mother cradled her hands around the warm milk and honey left by Sarah in a pitcher by the fire.

"Fast asleep, already. The excitement tired her out." Luce poured her own cup and fell silent. A nightingale's song echoed through the dark garden, the fluid notes pouring into the quiet room.

A log cracked, stirring Luce.

"What did Aunt Barbara say, Mother?"

The shadows played over her mother's face, capturing the beauty there. In truth, she was lovelier than her sister, although life had etched worry on her brow. In this light, her mother appeared ageless. She continued to contemplate the fire.

"Mother?"

"Allen bought us a respite. And he did so with Barbara's assistance."

Listening to her mother's pained voice, Luce heard the betrayal behind the words.

"He was just trying to make good, Mother. And there is time to plan further. The warrants will last as long as we are being educated. James is receiving a gentleman's learning. Babs is still tabled at Mr. Coleman's for her music. And I continue to study Latin and Greek."

"But you grow into womanhood, Luce."

"What difference does that make?"

The nightingale ceased its caroling. Her mother glanced at the window. Darkness settled around them; even the nocturnal creatures quietened.

"Your Uncle John has invited us to Lydiard to discuss your dowry."

"My dowry?" repeated Luce. Her heart hammered. She had not expected this to happen so soon. Allen only just mentioned it in passing a few days earlier.

Nodding, her mother reached across and took Luce's hand.

"Sweetheart, I have no provision set aside for you. Leventhorpe refuses to help pursue any other pleadings now that we are estranged. If you are to make a good match, your dowry will be an advantage. As will the St.John name. John has pledged to support us in this."

"We talk of marriage? I am not yet of an age to marry."

"You will be, when you turn eighteen in January. And my responsibility is to provide you with the best opportunity I can."

Her mother worried often about the future. Allen's charge lasted only as long as they were still in education.

"Mother, I know how difficult this is for you. I have no intention of leaving you, of marrying." She paused, trying to read her mother's face. "But I will come with you to Lydiard, to make peace with Uncle John. His proposition is most generous. Even if he will not need to make good on it for a long time."

Her mother broke into a smile and kissed Luce's hands.

"Thank you, my darling. Thank you for not resisting me." Leaning back in her chair, she took another sip of her drink. "Babs should stay here. In fact, she can lodge with Mr. Coleman's school. She will be delighted to stay with her friend Susan. Sarah can accompany her, and Allen and James remain here. You and I will travel to Lydiard next week and hear what John has in mind."

Luce nodded. She would not oppose listening to Uncle John. But he could never persuade her to marry against her will.

15

She had gone into Wiltshire for the accomplishment of a treaty that had been made some progress in, about the marriage with a gentleman of that county.

Luce Apsley

28ᵗʰ September 1637

Lydiard. Her mother's beloved childhood home. The park unfurled around a glorious beech avenue leading, straight as an arrow, to a sprawling honey-colored stone mansion dozing in the late afternoon September sun.

The first tentative leaves of autumn whirled in front of Luce, descending in a bronze eddy. East of the avenue, a wide and shimmering lake appeared. A chevron of swans drifted amongst the bulrushes, while from the pale blue skies above the water Luce heard the shrieks of the hawks before she saw them. A boathouse beckoned from the far shore. Closer, a large cedar with an inviting wooden seat tucked under its protective branches dominated the parkland.

"My bench," Luce's mother mused. "John has maintained it, after all these years. I made some important decisions sitting there. Not least of which was to travel to your Aunt Eleanor's. Which is where I met your father."

Luce beamed in return. "Then I will always be grateful to that bench. For without it, I would not exist."

Hoof beats interrupted their conversation, a horseman cantering from the stable block toward them, cloak flying behind him. A covey of wood pigeons flew from the tree tops with a clatter, startling Luce's mare. The rider drew even and turned with a flourish, keeping the stallion on a tight rein so it pranced in place.

"Edward!"

"Cousin Luce. And Aunt Lucy. I've been waiting and waiting for you. I dare not set out to meet you, for fear you'd approach from the holloway, and I'd miss you." Edward's face shone with excitement, and his sparkling blue eyes mirrored the rippled surface of the lake behind him.

"Why are you here? We thought you were at Whitehall with the king?"

"Father ordered me to attend my favorite cousin and aunt instead. He thought you could use the company, Luce."

"Why? What is planned that I have need of a chaperone?"

Edward laughed.

"Not a chaperone, but an escort, sweeting. Father has arranged invitations to a round of visitations and events—even a Hungerford wedding for you to attend, to meet the local society. He thought you might enjoy your time more if I was on your arm."

Later, Lucy walked with John over to St. Mary's Church, a few steps from the old manor. The familiar crows croaked from the tower, and a chill wind whipped around the grave markers. An autumn aroma of a bonfire mingled with that of damp stone, creating the mournful scent of a waning year. Shivering slightly, Lucy pulled her woolen shawl closer and briskly hurried the last few steps into the church porch.

John pulled open the ancient door, and as they walked down the nave, Lucy studied the myriad of colorful wall paintings, evidence of the worshippers who had prayed in this church in centuries past. There was the story of St. Thomas Becket and St. Christopher, all familiar from her childhood. Drawing her attention away from the beautiful, simple drawings, Lucy gasped to see an enormous royal coat of arms and Tuscan screen spanning the entire width of the nave.

"Wonderful craftsmanship, don't you think?" John asked proudly.

"It's quite a statement." Lucy looked around her. The church had grown barely recognizable in the years of her absence, so crowded was the building now with monuments, and furbished with luminous stained glass in every arched window. Her Calvinist soul rebelled against the ornate trappings.

"We should be extremely proud of our shared heritage with the royal family," replied John. "I, for one, am a full supporter of the king and his resolutions."

"Even to prorogue Parliament and rule in its place?" Lucy questioned softly. "That is not the ancient law of England, John."

"Drastic times call for drastic measures, Lucy." John was brusque. "And when Parliament declined to support the king in his claims for ship money, they left him no alternative—"

"But to rule as a tyrant for years with no government guidance." She stared up at the decorative lion and unicorn, rearing on their hind legs, supporting the crown.

"It is his divine right, Lucy." John motioned to the St.John family pew. "Now, sit and listen, for I wish no more debates between us. I brought you here so we could speak in private." He sat beside her, and the cold air settled around them. The distant crows still cried, and a draft lifted the hairs on the back of Lucy's neck.

"I would have Luce marry a Hungerford, and there is one man I have in mind who will make a good husband."

Lucy's heart beat faster. This conversation was too soon, too practical.

"His land borders mine, and between us, we will be able to farm all the acreage from here to Swindon. He is pleasant and offers a good settlement in return for a fair dowry. And the St.John name, of course. It has taken some time to persuade him that the unfortunate episode with Francke is over, for he does not share the Puritanical creed that seems to fascinate you and your daughter."

"You have progressed far, John. I thought that the purpose of this visit was to discuss Luce's dowry, not arrange a marriage treatise." Lucy stared at a full-sized monument of John and his wives, lying as if in their marriage bed, children surrounding them. Great swags of marble, impassive angels, and ornate coats of arms decorated the immense canopy, crowned by the St.John falcon.

"Dear God, John, is that your tomb? And Anne and your children? And Margaret, your second wife not yet departed this life?" Lucy stepped up to the monument, unable to keep her hands from reaching out and touching her dear friend's cold visage. "Oh, Anne, you lie so cold, and yet you look as if you might rise and kiss me once again." She turned to her brother. "What cost was this, John? And why so opulent, so vulgar?"

John's face reddened. "Our cousin Queen Elizabeth herself set the fashion for family vaults, and in my church here, I may do as I wish."

"John, this is an attempt to ridicule divinity with an earthly pride." His exaggerated pretensions appalled her. "You are not royalty, nor will you ever be. The blood of a distant queen may run in our veins, but these aspirations to monarchy are well beyond any consanguinity with the royal family. I would have thought you'd have learned from my husband's troubles how fickle court is. I fear you go too far, Brother. In all things, you go too far."

She pushed past John, needing to clear her thoughts and think seriously about where this all was leading. Leaving the churchyard and John with his monuments, Lucy strode across the park to the sheltering cedar tree and her bench.

Allen's horse's hooves pounding, the gasping of the great bay as they thundered across Richmond Park, the shouts of his friends as they tried to keep up—this was pure joy. A wager rested on who could reach the gates of the palace first, and he could use a few more shillings in his purse. Allen glanced over his shoulder, and yes, the pack was falling behind—all, except that new fellow, whatever his name was, who had just joined them at Coleman's. Looking forward again, he urged Boreas over a fallen log, landing with surety in the mud on the other side. He pulled his horse's head quickly to the right, where a narrow path snaked. Let them find him now!

The path restrained him. Hoof beats. Damn it, he was being tailed. As the track opened into the final heath before the palace gates, Allen kicked Boreas into a full gallop and squinted behind him again. Against the crimson disc of the setting sun, the rider crouched low over his horse's head, gaining on him with every stride.

Together, they crossed through the gate, neck and neck, and maneuvered their mounts to a panting, gasping stop.

"You almost had me!" Allen shouted.

"One stride more and you would have lost!" called back the stranger.

"Allen Apsley. You are new here?"

"Yes. Just arrived. John Hutchinson, from Nottingham."

"Well, John Hutchinson, fair met, and welcome to the court. Let me buy you an ale before we return to Coleman's."

"My thanks, and I will accept, this time. Next time I will treat you, for the winner always buys."

Allen saluted the man. He was a fair horsemen and a wit. Just the kind of friend he enjoyed. He would know him more. Coleman had brought together a fine group of people his age. This promised to be an agreeable, festive winter.

The small consort finished the fantasia with a flourish. Applause broke out in Mr. Coleman's spacious music chamber. His evening concerts were a pleasant entertainment for the crowd before the palace's more debauched carousing.

Allen led the audience in an ovation, effusively calling out his praise, for he had recently embraced the composer's work in his own music studies. "Excellent. You do Mr. Byrd's work great justice, sirs. I particularly congratulate the viol player, for his part was well performed for all its complexity. Not an easy task, to play against the song."

"Thank you." John Hutchinson carefully put aside his instrument and bowed, his face flushed with praise. "I am afraid I am not as accomplished as you may think. I have the benefit of playing with excellent musicians." He gestured gracefully, including the other members of the consort.

The audience applauded, and under cover of the ovation, Babs leaned over and whispered to Allen.

"He's very handsome."

Allen looked at her, an eyebrow raised.

"And modest. And well dressed. And cultured," she continued cheerfully.

"And you are too young to be noticing such things." He smiled at his little sister. She was of an age where such things distracted her, and the more he could keep her a child, the happier he was. Babs was but fifteen. Luce was the one who needed to be thinking about the quality of a man, not her.

He stood and bowed graciously as John approached. John responded, his manners polished.

"You play well, John. You have an aptitude with the viol."

"A passable skill, Allen. I am glad to be tabled here at Mr. Coleman's to improve my God-given talent."

"You carried the harmony beautifully, Mr. Hutchinson." Babs was confident in her own knowledge.

Allen smiled. "My sister, Babs Apsley. She is the musician in our family."

Babs blushed. "Music is my joy, for you know I have no head for poetry nor languages, Allen. That is Luce's domain."

John bowed to Babs, causing her blush to deepen. "I am sure your playing is as charming as you are. For who are we to say which is favored more, words or music?"

Allen laughed. "Luce would say words every time, for she despises her lute and yearns only for her books for company."

"And who is Luce?" John inquired.

"My sister. She wrote the words to the song you just played," replied Babs.

"But not the music," added Allen. "Otherwise, the refrain would have sounded like someone treading on a cat's tail."

They all joined in laughter. Allen looked at appreciation at his new friend. He may have just arrived from the country, but his manners and wardrobe were most distinguished. John Hutchinson would fit well within the circle of friends at court, joining them in their days of hunting, dancing, and flirting with the maids.

Taking his arm, Allen drew John to one side.

"We have a picnic planned for tomorrow afternoon. Myself, William Villiers, and a few other friends. And, of course, the ladies of the court. Please join us. I fancy you would enjoy yourself, and they would enjoy you."

John hesitated. "I am not sure I am such good company in a crowd, Allen."

"Nonsense. You will enjoy the games—bowls, quoits, skittles—and the maids are a delightful distraction. I insist."

William Villiers suddenly burst into the chamber, chasing a small monkey dressed in a black suit with a white collar, dragging a silver chain. There were shrieks from the women and cheers from the men as he pursued the animal around the room, finally catching up with the creature in front of John.

"And I present Sir Misery Ape," William announced with a flourish. "Or should it be Goodman Lack-Love Monkey—"

"How now, Sir Desolation Puritan." Allen bowed deeply, flourishing his plumed hat at the little pet cowering on the floor. "Have you come to shut down our fun? Or may we tempt you out of your gloom and placate you with song and dance?"

He looked around the room, appreciative of the laughter and applause from his friends. His new friend John was frowning. Must be shy. He'd loosen up after a few days with the court crowd.

Crouching down and gently picking up the shivering creature in his arms, John carefully untied the points on the monkey's suit. Stroking his head, he eased the clothes from its back and caressed the little animal until it stopped trembling.

"Here is your quarry, sir," he said as he handed the monkey to William. "I think perhaps he has no place here at court, for in truth, he does not fit in this unnatural world."

There was a sudden hush, and Allen felt a twinge of discomfort.

A forced laugh broke the silence as William passed the animal to the girl standing by his side.

"Here, Mary, an orphan for you. Guard him well, for I fancy he has no friends here, except one."

The two men stared at each other until Allen stepped between them.

"No appetite for politics tonight, my friends." He motioned to the musicians. "Play a gavotte, good sirs, and let us dance, not debate."

16

Mr. Hutchinson was soon courted into their acquaintance and invited to their houses; where he was nobly treated, with all the attractive arts that young women and their parents use to procure them lovers.

Luce Apsley

19th October 1637

Babs sighed heavily. "And so, when he spied upon the mounting block the footprint of his deceased true love, the faithful swain could not leave it. Each day he lay by the print, kissing it and growing desperately melancholy, knowing that she had passed to that land from whence there is no return. There was no comforting him, and at length he languished away." She continued, her voice hushed with reverence, "Mr. Coleman's house has ever since had the reputation of being unlucky in love."

Allen glanced across the dinner table at John and winked.

"Seems to me that we're the opposite—lucky, not falling in love with a ghost," he teased.

"Especially one with such an earthly imprint," added John.

"Fie on you," cried Babs. "It is a true story. Fear for your own hearts that you not suffer the same fate."

"Never."

"Not I."

Allen laughed at his little sister's cross face and got up from the table. He placed a swift kiss on Babs's shining hair.

"Come, Babs, play something on the harpsichord for us. Leave those tales to the old wives that spin them."

Allowing herself to be mollified, Babs sat at the instrument while Allen filled his pipe, sitting in his customary place at the fire. John drew up a chair opposite him, where Luce would normally sit, for the window gave the best lingering light from which to read by. The evening was most agreeable, peaceful. John was good company, quiet when needed, but jovial too. Allen puffed meditatively on his pipe. He'd been burning the candle at both ends recently, and he needed to spend an evening at home, even if his mother and Luce were still absent.

He caught John asking him something, and turned his attention to his new friend, who was holding a book in his hands.

"Latin?" John repeated.

"Luce." Allen leaned over to look at it. "Yes. Looks like she's at her translations again. Don't see the fun in it, myself. Don't mind writing some poetry, but tedious work, translating."

John smiled. "It is demanding, but there is great satisfaction in working through the logic and seeing progress."

"Hmmm." Allen shifted in his chair. "So tell me, Hutchinson, where were you schooled?"

"In Nottingham and then at Cambridge. Does she spend much time reading?"

"Ah. An Oxford man myself. Who? Oh, Luce?" Allen pondered for a while. "Actually, I don't think she really does anything else. Except write. And create her medicinals with our mother."

Babs paused her playing. "She has gone with our mother to our Uncle John's house in Wiltshire. They are there to conclude a marriage treaty."

"Hold on, Babs." Allen knocked his pipe on the fireplace and took a sip of the Madeira he had poured for himself and John. The wine went down smoothly, a good vintage. "Uncle John's just talking about her dowry."

"I think she will return with a betrothal." Babs turned back to her instrument. "How I wish I were her, with a dowry and a husband and a wedding to plan."

Allen groaned and shook his head. "You are incorrigible. Luce will marry when she sees fit."

"When our mother and Uncle John see fit," replied Babs. "And I think they wish her wed within the month."

Laughing, Allen tamped more tobacco into his pipe and carefully lit it from a glowing taper he held to the fire. About to say something to John, he saw his head was buried in the Latin book, an intense expression about his face. Well, no disturbing him. He appeared about as interested in the conversation as a log on the hearth. Allen fell back into a reverie of his latest conquest, a sweet maiden fresh from Kent with a mouth as ripe as cherries. Life was good.

In truth, six weeks at Lydiard passed in a whirl of visits, parties, and dinners, to the point where Luce could no longer remember which name went with which face or what conversation had been repeated or was fresh.

And now, this grand finale: a Hungerford wedding at a neighboring mansion, where all her cousins, and her cousins of cousins, expected to meet their newly arrived London relative. Worse still, Uncle John was particularly insistent that she wear a gown that he ordered made the moment she arrived at Lydiard. She paced in the long gallery of the home, watched by her sympathetic cousin.

"Edward, I cannot breathe, and I feel like a prize heifer on display." The pale blue watered silk, stiff with semi-precious moonstones and decorated with scratchy starched lace, could have stood by itself, so rigid was the dress. "I am miserable."

"I know, Luce." Edward caught her hand and pressed it to his lips. "But you actually look quite lovely, and I would never have recognized the girl I rode to rescue from the Puritan's house."

"And I do not recognize myself, which is worse." She smiled gratefully at Edward, but tears brimmed in her eyes, threatening to spill over. "I don't know how much longer I can stand this, Coz."

Edward held her hand and drew her close to him. She relaxed for a moment in his embrace. The strangeness of the dress, the unfamiliarity of the Hungerford house, and the clutch of noisy relatives were overwhelming. She longed to be back at home, peacefully translating her Latin, quietly writing in her journal.

"Is it so very bad, sweetheart?" Edward asked curiously. "Most girls would love the attention and the chance to wear new clothes, to dance, be courted."

"I fear I am the odd one out, Edward. I despise the chatter; my head aches as if a thousand bees were buzzing in it. And the gossip and the tattling—I crave silence."

"I'll hide with you later. Do your duty at the wedding supper, and make my father and your mother happy with your conviviality. And then meet me in the library. It's the third room along the corridor behind the entry hall. No one else would even dream of setting foot there on a day like today."

Luce pulled back and smiled up at Edward.

"You are my savior, Edward. You know me as well as Allen does."

Her cousin grinned back at her. "I should do, Luce. You two may have different perspectives on life, but you share the same soul. And I love you both with all my heart."

He kissed her brow and gave her a little push. "Now, go and dazzle the company. Show these country cousins what a city girl with extraordinary learning and beautiful looks can do."

Luce took a deep breath and held Edward's words in her heart. She could do it. For his sake, and her mother's peace of mind.

The commotion in the banqueting hall almost forced Luce to turn tail and run, but as she paused in the doorway, Uncle John caught sight of her and beckoned her to his side at the head of the table. On his left was an empty seat. Her mother was placed on the other side. Apparently he was saving a place for her. As she slid into her chair, she nodded abruptly at the man sitting to her left, and bowed her head, murmuring a hasty prayer of courage. When she looked up again, the man was staring at her.

"Anthony Hungerford," he introduced himself. "I am of the Bourton Hungerfords. Your Uncle John is a cousin of my father. I recently purchased Hungerford land on the west of Swindon to add to my estates in Oxfordshire."

Luce nodded and smiled faintly. She looked past him to see if she recognized any other table members, and caught sight of Edward sitting at the very end. He seemed very far away, almost hidden by the loaded platters of roasted meats and cunning pastry arrangements that lay between them. He caught her eye and raised his glass to her, winking.

She reluctantly brought her attention back to her neighbor. "It is a pleasure to meet you, Mr. Hungerford."

"Sir Anthony," he corrected her. "We were fortunate to acquire much land and perquisites during the reign of King James. Our family fortunes rose with the tides of privilege and monopolies granted to your Uncle Giles Mompesson."

131

Luce's head was beginning to ache again. "My Uncle Giles suffered great humiliation at the hands of the Star Chamber and was exiled for many years. My Aunt Katherine died of heartbreak."

"And Giles has installed a suitably noble monument in her honor at Lydiard's church. He then returned to his estates. We remained friends." The man took a deep gulp of his wine, and Luce noticed his hand trembled slightly. "Good friends."

"Ah, Anthony. I see you are making the acquaintance of my niece." John leaned behind Luce and smote the man on his shoulder. "'Tis good to see you, my friend. And let us hope that we will see much more of you in the future." He laughed loudly and turned back to his food.

Luce was silent, for it was such an effort to make small talk. She saw Edward looking at her, gesturing with his head, encouraging her to converse with her neighbor. She sighed again.

"And your family, Sir Anthony? Do they travel with you to the wedding today?"

He cleared his throat and took another draft from his goblet, waving at the server to refill it. His face was flushed above an ornate, albeit old-fashioned ruff. Luce tried not to look at his puce-colored, veined nose.

"I am not married, Mistress Apsley. Your uncle kindly invited me, knowing that I was unaccompanied." He leaned forward, breathing wine fumes over her. "Perchance he felt the atmosphere of this event would bring me good fortune." Pushing something into her hands, he smiled broadly, revealing yellowed teeth. "Bride ribbons, for luck."

Not daring to look up, Luce froze in place, desperately wanting to be anywhere but at this table, at this time. If she was a heifer at market before, now she felt like the prize breeder.

For what seemed an aeon, she sat, answering with stiff politeness to Uncle John's comments about the bride and groom. Soon, however, both he and Sir Anthony gave up on creating conversation with her and, ignoring her discomfort, carried on an animated discussion about farming over her head. She folded and unfolded the ribbons in her hands, creasing them with her anxiety.

Finally, the signal came for the tables to be cleared and the dancing to begin. In the ensuing clatter, Luce excused herself, leaving Sir Anthony in mid-conversation.

She stood abruptly, the chair behind her falling with a crash. So much for subtlety. She saw her mother's face, questioning. All she could think of was Edward and the peace of the library. Gathering her skirts in her hands, she pushed through the crowd and slipped from the door into the quiet of the corridor. Breathing quickly, she followed the candlelight along the dark passageway, counting the doors until she found the third. Pushing it open, she walked into the wonderfully familiar and welcoming atmosphere of books.

"Oh, Luce." Edward was standing by the fireplace, its dying embers glowing gently in the dark room.

"Edward, I can stand this no longer." A great sob tore from Luce's throat and threatened to shred all the restraint she had been practicing that evening. "I can't talk to these people. I cannot listen to their speeches of the good of the king and the good old days of the court and the—"

"Luce, my child, what is wrong?" Her mother's voice from the threshold cut across her speech.

"Dear God, now what drama?" John pushed through into the room, walking directly to the fireplace and standing in front of Luce.

She stood her ground, as she had in those distant days at Westminster in front of the judges. Only this time, she was not defending her parents, it was herself. This was familiar territory. Edward's presence next to her was reassuring, and she plunged forward.

"I can do this no more. I am not intended for this life. I will not be put out to market like a breeding heifer. I refuse to be treated and traded for land and money. And I never, ever will marry such a man as Sir Anthony Hungerford. If I live and die an old maid, so be it. I am done with this lamentable episode in my life."

Her words fell like stones, and for a moment, no one responded.

"What mean you, Niece?" John's voice blustered into the room. "What impertinence is this that you bring to my plans? I would have you know there are not many young girls who have a dowry of eight hundred pounds and a name like St.John to take into a marriage."

"And there are plenty of other young girls who would readily accept their lot. But I am not one. I have no inclination to marry one with whom I have absolutely nothing in common."

John turned to his sister and shook his finger at her. "See! See what you and your husband's infatuation with learning and education for girls

133

have brought on your heads. You have a daughter now that considers herself above all else and thinks that she has a choice in these matters." He turned to Edward, who had been quietly observing. "And you? You do encourage your cousin?"

"She does." Lucy's voice was quiet.

"What?" John swung round. Luce held her breath as she watched her mother and her uncle face each other.

"She does. Have a choice." Her mother took a step forward and held out her hands, palms up. "John, you cannot force a young woman such as Luce to do your bidding. She is intelligent, educated, and knows her own mind. Yoke her into a marriage with someone such as Sir Anthony Hungerford, and you will destroy her spirit."

"It is not her place to decide. I am providing the dowry. This is my decision."

"Then keep your dowry," her mother replied. "For I would rather my daughter marry for poorer than suffer in riches."

The tension was unbearable, and just as Luce was about to step forward to plead forgiveness, Edward's cautioning hand restrained her.

"Father, I beg you, pardon them. Your sister and niece love you very much. They are extremely grateful for all you have done. But please understand they have lived a different life than you, than me." Edward carefully placed himself at John's side, and Luce's mother crossed to stand with her, putting her arm around her. "You have tried your best. Now let them go in peace."

"After all I have done, after all I have arranged! This is the way you repay me?" John stood still, his face contorted with anger.

"John, this is not against you. I just understand my daughter. And I know I cannot commit her to a life of misery. This is not the place for her."

Edward looked from Luce to her mother. "I think it best you leave, return to Richmond. Above all, you have expressed the truth, and by that, you have shown us all the courage that comes with the light of honesty. I shall arrange for you to be escorted home and make provision for your journey back. You will be home with Allen, James and Babs by the week's end."

Luce felt the tears slide down her cheeks now, the emotion of the last few hours released. "Edward, you put into words what I cannot express. I shall miss you so much. Please do not stay away from us for too long." She placed the bride ribbons, which she had been scrunching in her hands, into his. "Send these with the messenger to Babs. She will enjoy them. Tell them we are coming home."

Luce's mother took a step forward to her brother, but John turned his back on her, refusing to acknowledge her. "Go," he said without turning. "Go, and live the life you choose. I'll not renege on Luce's dowry. I am a man of my word. But do not ask for anything else from me again."

17

There scarcely passed any day but some accident or some discourse still kept awake Mr. Hutchinson's desire of seeing this gentlewoman, although the mention of her, for the most part, was enquiries whether she had yet accomplished the marriage that was in treaty.

Luce Apsley
15th November 1637

"Bride ribbons!" Babs's excited cry pierced the chatter and caused Allen to lift his eyes from the deliciously ample bosom of his dinner companion. "Bride ribbons!"

"What means this?" Allen demanded of the messenger, who stood by the table, mud-splattered and drooping with weariness. He twisted his hat in his gloved hands, clearly uncomfortable in the refined atmosphere of the Mr. Coleman's paneled dining room.

"I know not, sir," replied the man. "I was told to ride directly here by Mistress Apsley and present these ribbons to you. She and her mother return home. They will be here tomorrow evening, soon after sunset."

A clatter distracted Allen as John knocked over his goblet, resulting in a stream of wine flowing across the polished table. In the ensuing flap for cloths to prevent his suit being stained, Allen lost sight of the messenger.

"I say, Apsley, great work on arranging the treatise," bellowed William Villiers from his customary place at the head of the table. "Your sister was a difficult one to marry off, with that sharp tongue and reserved manner."

"She is not reserved," Babs replied hotly. "She is learned and kind and just shy in company."

Villiers snorted. "She is bookish and careless about her appearance. Nothing I would call companionable."

"And that is such a bad thing, that she is of such a humor that she is well acquainted with the traits you deplore?" John's voice silenced the dinner table.

Allen cleared his throat and gestured for more wine to fill John's empty goblet. His new friend placed his hand over it, shaking his head. Standing, he bowed to the dozen-or-so courtiers in the room.

"I will excuse myself, for I fear I am not good company right now. Something here does not agree with me."

"Must be the food is too rich for your stomach, Hutchinson," observed William. Mary Bayning gave a small laugh and leaned over to a companion, whispering behind her fan.

"Or the seasoning too poor for my digestion, Villiers. Good night, Allen, Babs." John's face was white as he hurried from the room.

Allen shrugged. Let him have his mood. John had been morose of late, pestering him about Luce. Within minutes, the chatter had resumed as Allen and his friends discussed the hunting party planned for the morrow, and Babs and Susan Coleman excitedly examined the crumpled bride ribbons.

Torchlights marking the palace boundary illuminated the gravel bridle path. As Luce rode the last mile through Richmond, she could not be more thankful for the freezing night which kept its citizens indoors. She just wanted to return home, to quietly enter her chamber, kiss Babs, and lie down upon her own bed. Craving solitude and only the company of her books, she counted each crunching step of her weary mare, bringing her closer to home and placing further distance from the events at Lydiard.

The trees outside her garden came into view, outlined black against the familiar starry sky, Orion standing guard over the rooftops. As she and her mother rode the last few yards along the edge of the heath, she caught sight of Babs and Allen standing by the gate, lanterns in hand.

"My darlings, we are home," she called, her heart lifting. "We are home."

As they drew up outside the house, Luce quickly dismounted, jumping down without care for the iced puddles on the ground before her. Throwing the reins to the groom, she pulled Babs and Allen into her arms, and they stood in a warm embrace, their breath mingling in the crisp winter air.

"You are cold through, Babs." Luce stroked her sister's cheeks, which were icy to the touch, and tucked her cloak closer around her neck. "How long have you waited?"

"Just a short time, Luce. I could not stand to be at Mr. Coleman's any longer. So, I persuaded Allen and John to escort me home so we could meet you the moment you arrived."

Luce hugged her. "You silly goose." She looked around. "John? Who is John?"

A tall figure stepped forward from the shelter of the hedge. His face was shadowed by a wide-brimmed plumed hat.

"John Hutchinson," announced Allen. "A good friend of ours. Met him at Coleman's. He thought the walk would do him good." He lifted his lantern higher, and the stranger stepped forward into the pool of light.

"A pleasure to make your acquaintance, Mistress Apsley." His voice was low, rich in tenor, soft in the quiet night. He bowed gracefully and stood back politely.

"Luce, you must tell me. The bride ribbons?"

Luce inclined her head to John Hutchinson and turned her attention to Babs.

"Come, you are freezing, sweetheart. Let us go inside, and I will tell you everything. Mr. Hutchinson, thank you for escorting my brother and sister home." She put her arms around Allen and Babs, and together they made their way to the front door.

"The pleasure is all mine." Luce turned at his words, and by the golden light of the lantern he held, she saw thick hair curling on the collar of his cloak and lively gray eyes reflecting the dancing flame. His bearing was formal, his countenance serious, contradicted by a generous mouth. She smiled faintly. She did not expect to find her attention detained by a courtier friend of Allen's.

Entering the house, she made to close the door. But not without realizing that he continued to stand at her gate until she saw him no more when the door clicked shut.

The following afternoon, Luce settled herself into her familiar upholstered chair by the hearth, her books spread upon a small walnut table by her side, her journal close to hand. The day was quiet, just her mother and Sarah for company. Babs could not miss her lessons, and Allen was at court. The peace allowed her time to arrange her thoughts, and she found great comfort in pushing the events of Lydiard to the back of her mind and focusing on her translation. She was lost in her world, and was startled when the parlor door abruptly opened and Babs entered.

"Luce, where were you?" Her sister ran to her side and planted a swift kiss on her brow. "I might have known. Back already with your book friends and forgetting all about me." She laughed, taking the sting from the words.

"Oh, Babs, I am so sorry. Forgive me. I lost my sense of time."

"Of course I forgive you." Babs whirled round. "Besides, John walked me home." She lifted her voice. "John, come into the parlor."

The tall man from the previous evening entered the room. Luce jumped up in dismay at the intrusion, knocking over the small table and scattering books, journal, and an ink bottle over the hearth. In one movement, John swiftly bent and righted the bottle before it spilled, replaced the table on its spindly legs, and then knelt on the floor, gathering the books while Luce stood in awkward silence.

"Virgil. And Lucretius." John stroked the spine of the intricately tooled volume, checking that no damage had been done. *"De Rerum Natura."* He stood with an easy grace and held the book to the light. A lock of light brown hair fell over his forehead, and he pushed it back impatiently. "Now that is an extraordinary work. *On the Nature of Things.*"

"Thank you," said Luce. She scowled to hide her disquiet. Pulling her old red woolen shawl more closely around her, she realized she was wearing her most comfortable and disheveled house gown.

"I found the Epicurean influence on Lucretius's work quite evident in the early verses," John continued.

Babs groaned theatrically.

"Do you think Lucretius embraced the philosophies entirely, or worked in isolation in his own interpretation?" he asked, lifting his eyes from the volume and looking directly at Luce. His face was thoughtful; a sweetness lingered in his visage.

"It is my opinion that Lucretius did not understand fully the work of Epicurus, for there are many times that he expresses—"

"Luce! Enough!" Babs almost shouted in her effort to gain her sister's attention. "Enough!"

Luce stopped abruptly and shook her head. Really, it was very interesting that this stranger from the court had expressed similar opinions on the Roman philosophers that she shared.

"My apologies, Mr.—"

"Hutchinson. John. Please call me John, as Allen and Babs have become cherished friends during my stay here." His smile was cheerful, and he did not appear to notice her untidy appearance, for his eyes stayed on her face.

"You board at Mr. Coleman's?" She stopped herself from smoothing her skirts. What mattered if cat hair lingered on the navy velvet?

"I do. I had originally planned to spend just a few weeks before traveling on to France, but I was made so welcome by your brother and sister that I have extended my visit."

"Allen and John have become good friends," said Babs. "They practice their fencing daily and compete on the tennis court to amuse William Villiers and his crowd."

It seemed much had transpired since she had left. "William Villiers? Aunt Barbara's son? Does Allen continue to spend time with him?"

"Allen and James both. They are rarely out of his company, or that of the young princes," replied Babs.

"I see. And do you subscribe to their circle, Mr. Hutchinson?"

"John." He shrugged. "I appreciate their skill in music and dance, for I enjoy both myself. And some are most erudite. But I am afraid I cannot always agree on their politics."

Interesting. Someone so cultured and fashionably dressed as John Hutchinson appeared no different than the fun-loving youth that decorated the galleries and chambers of the princes' court.

"In what manner, Mr. Hutchinson?"

"I hear much derision against all forms of religious worship, favoring only that preferred by the king, which is Catholic in its extreme. Those around the court stretch their superstition to idolatry to ask favor of the royal family, not through conscience." John's skin flushed slightly. "And it seems that they do not question the gradual erosion of men's rights that this king has embarked upon since he prorogued Parliament."

Drawing up a chair, John beckoned Luce to sit in her usual place. Obediently, she did so while he sat opposite her. "I have noticed that there has, in fact, been a faction at court that has embraced these philosophies to the point where they also consider the monarch divine. I fear that the Catholic influence of the queen has crept deep into England's . . ."

Luce barely noticed Babs's sigh as she left the room. Her eyes were on John Hutchinson as he spoke, his language articulate, brow furrowed in passion. He still held her beloved volume of Lucretius, his elegant hands absently caressing the worn leather binding.

John laid a primrose on the open page of Luce's journal, and she looked up, smiling at the token. "Come, Luce. Even I think you have spent too long at your books. 'Tis time to look outside, for spring has arrived, and you have not yet noticed it."

Luce glanced through the window. He was right. Winter was gone, the steel-gray sky banished by scurrying lamb-white clouds.

"Come, Luce," he repeated. "Time to take our discussions to the fresh air, and see if your arguments hold up in the bright light of day."

John's eyes sparkled above his burgundy wool cloak, the walk from Mr. Coleman's bringing a glow in his face. Luce glanced outside and saw an April morning bright with promise, blue sky beckoning above the lacy branches of the oaks on the common.

In the months since returning home from Lydiard, John's visits had grown to daily occurrences, and she found herself looking forward to each afternoon, when he would arrive with a new piece of knowledge or a fresh perspective on her reading. Her mother encouraged their discussions, oft times joining them, for her own education in Jersey of the Calvinist doctrine brought perspective in debating the king's influence on religious observance. Their conversations ranged wide, for John's depth of learning matched theirs. Luce found thoughts of him interrupting her day as she went about her tasks, stopping occasionally to gaze into nothingness as she recalled a particular point of animated discussion.

"Then I accept your challenge. I am sure my position will be even more clearly defined in the sunshine than here in my parlor."

Laughing, John handed Luce her cloak, which he had already removed from its peg in the hall. He was quite certain of his powers to persuade. And he was correct.

Stepping outside, Luce's spirits lifted. Spring had indeed arrived. Nestled in the roots of the oaks, carpets of primroses illuminated the dark earth, and the delicate yellow of the wildflowers reflected the April sunshine slipping between bare branches. It was too early for the oaks to bud, but there was a mist of green on the willows by the pond, and catkins dangled from the hazel trees that lined the bridle path. Luce joyfully took a deep breath, and the taste of spring lingered on her palette.

She caught John looking at her and smiled.

"You were right; it is a beautiful day to be outside. Thank you for awakening me to spring."

"It is my pleasure, Luce. This is the time of year when I most miss my home, for I would be outside all day, supervising the planting and stocking, along with the lambing."

"You farm the land yourself?" Luce was surprised. His fine hands were calloused on the palms, but she thought that was due to his swordplay, not laboring.

"We own more than two hundred acres by Nottingham," he replied. "Our family have held Owthorpe Manor for centuries. We consider ourselves custodians, not absentee land lords. The people of the village and the acreage surrounding have been the responsibility of the Hutchinsons for generations. I am proud to continue that role."

"And yet you came to London to study?"

John took his knife and deftly cut half a dozen willow branches, handing them to Lucy. She stroked the soft silver buds, the delicate stems.

"My father insisted that I further my education. I attended Cambridge, and I am enrolled in Lincoln's Inn to study the law this September. But I would prefer music and divinity."

"And will you stay in London, John?" This was the first she'd heard of his plans.

"For a while, I am sure. But eventually, I will return to Owthorpe, for my heart lies there, in my home, with my people."

He leaned over and drew a finger across the willow branch.

"So much promise hidden within a latent bud." She looked up, startled at his quiet words. His face was close to hers, his generous mouth smiling.

Luce lifted her face, and he hesitated for a moment before meeting her lips with his, gently at first, and then more firmly, kissing her until she felt such a pull in her heart that she responded. The willow branches crushed between them until she broke away, her breath stolen from her.

She said nothing, for her mind was whirling, until she looked up and met the eyes of her friend, her debate opponent, the man with whom she had spent hours discussing philosophy. Now, she saw a man of passion, of desire, a man who'd lit a spark in her that glowed like an ember within her heart, tilting this fresh spring day into the summer equinox of love.

"Did I offend you?" he asked gently. "For I have been desirous to do that since I first saw you, the night you returned from Lydiard."

"No. You did not offend me." She took a deep breath. "What mean you, John? You have just told me that you leave here soon for London with plans to return to the north. Are you trifling with me, passing the time as other gallants do at court?"

John grasped her hands earnestly, disregarding the branches dropping to the ground.

"Do not ever think me so shallow as to my intent, Luce. And never compare me with the insignificant wastrels that inhabit the halls of Richmond." He turned from her, and she admired his profile as he gazed at the towers of the palace which pierced the blue sky. "My future does not lay with the court or the palace. But I hope—with all my soul—that it may lie with you. Treat my heart carefully, Luce. For today, I place it in your hands, to do with what you will."

"What mean you by these words, John? What are you asking of me?"

"Luce, I am asking you to marry me." John took her hands and tenderly brought them to his lips. "Since the day I first heard your name, first picked up your books, first heard your poetry, I confess I have not thought of anyone else." He held her face between his palms. "Maybe it is true that Mr. Coleman's house is where devotion is engendered, for I have an ardent love for you which grows each day we are together. I have written to my father and explained to him my desire to make you my wife. He has consented."

"John, this is so sudden. And yet . . ." Luce paused, for the words in her heart would not leave her lips.

"And yet . . ." John prompted softly.

"You have courted me with honor and with affection. You have become my dearest friend through such discretion that I can hardly believe you would love me as a woman, too."

"Luce, from the moment I saw you, you generated such a powerful passion in my heart that I could think of no destiny other than to be bound to you."

"And yet, you said nothing?"

John kissed her hands again, lingering on the index finger that was perpetually ink-stained.

"My love, if I had declared my feelings for you when I talked of Lucretius and Virgil, you would have dismissed me completely as yet another courtier with vain flattery."

Luce looked at his bent head, his chestnut-brown hair reflecting the vitality of the sun, his broad shoulders muscular under his light cloak.

"And you desire me, John?" She had to ask, for a marriage without passion was no marriage.

"I desire you with all my heart, Luce. And without you, I am nothing. Will you have me? Will you?"

She looked at the man who pledged his heart and knew, from that moment, there would be no one else who could ever take his place, and her soul and his would always be as one. She was a mirror to his splendor, and yet without her to reflect him, he did not exist.

Luce smiled and thought fleetingly of Edward's words. This moment was hers because of her passionate belief in her true soul's desire. Without the courage of her convictions, she would be bereft of life.

"I will."

18

But there were two above all the rest, who led the van of the king's evil counsellors, and these were Laud, archbishop of Canterbury, a fellow of mean extraction and arrogant pride, and the Earl of Strafford.

Luce Apsley
April 4ᵗʰ 1638

Allen leaned back and crossed his booted legs, stretching out in the elegant upholstered chaise. He appreciated the opulent luxury of the sprawling Villiers apartments at Richmond Palace. Along with the generous company of the ladies of the court, of course, a clique led by Mary Bayning. The dismal poverty of his last years at the Tower seemed far away, and he found it very satisfying to be entrenched in the princes' court, now.

"Archbishop Laud was my own uncle's chaplain." William Villiers sipped thoughtfully from a gold goblet embossed with the Villiers crest: a lion rampart, ducally crowned. "His loyalty to the Duke of Buckingham and our family is steadfast. And when my uncle was assassinated, the king took great comfort in the company of Laud, when no other could soothe him. I believe him to be a devout and faithful man."

Allen held his own Venetian glass up to the fire, admiring the play of the flames on the ruby red wine. "Do you think Laud's latest edicts on the Scottish situation will hold?" he asked. "I heard tell that the Anglican prayer book was not welcomed with open arms at the Kirk of St. Giles." Allen paused and winked at one of Mary's friends, not remembering her name but enjoying her familiar curves. "'Twas said that a washerwoman threw a stool at the head of the bishop as he was attempting to read from the Anglican prayer book in place of the Scottish service. I do appreciate a spirited filly."

The group of young courtiers laughed. Mary crossed to William's side, leaning over the arm of his chair and kissing his lips. Her yellow silk gown draped in soft folds around her hips, her long curled hair falling forward over her pale bosom.

"You too, my love?" she asked. "What kind of woman do you appreciate?"

William pulled her onto his lap and kissed her in return, running his hand along her leg.

"A faithful one, who will wait for her love."

"Why so, sirrah?" Mary wriggled deeper into William's arms, and Allen watched as her dress shifted to reveal slim legs in white silk hose and crimson garters. "You have never kept me waiting afore."

"I have never ventured far from your side, Mary." William looked at Allen directly over her head, and he realized he was addressing him, although his conversation appeared to be directed to his bride. "But I have cause to ride north to the border, for the king has requested a show of extra security to be on hand."

Allen sat straighter. Although he had partaken in the fine malmsey always on hand in William's apartments, he was not so drunk that he could not appreciate the seriousness in William's voice.

"You ride with whom, Cousin?" Allen noticed that James was paying close heed. His brother was ever more fascinated with soldiering. William had the youth's full attention.

"I have been asked to form a small troop, no more than a hundred men. We are looking for volunteers who would consider an expedition on behalf of the king an honor. We assemble under Lord Goring."

Allen's anger rose. "That bastard. He declined the trouble of representing my father's estate and caused us much grief."

William shook his head. "His son. The old earl stays close to court's comfort. But I have formed a company of men under Lord Goring. He is an able soldier, notwithstanding his passions."

"Are you fighting the Scots, Lord Grandison?" Allen heard the excitement in James's voice. "Count on me, sir, for I would be out of this court life and with an army on the move as quickly as you ask me."

"Hold on, James," Allen cautioned. "You are still a minor and do not have your allowance in your pocket to make those decisions on your own."

"But I would if you granted the funds to me and came too, Allen." James paced the floor in front of the fireplace, and Allen smiled at his youthful enthusiasm.

"Are you ready for a soldier's life, James? Do you wish to leave the comfort of Court?"

"More than anything in this world, Brother."

Allen returned to William and saw that he was still studying him. "When do you leave?"

"Within the month." William laid his finger across Mary Bayning's ripe mouth to shush her small cry. "And we'll be back before Michaelmas. Will you join me?"

Allen hesitated. Life was good at the palace, comfortable. His position assisting the training of the young princes' hawks was enjoyable, and the office gave him a small income to meet his needs. The days stretched before him, tempting him with the promise of indolence and many lusty pursuits.

William gently moved Mary from his lap and stood.

"There is more to court life than just pleasure, Allen. Sometimes we are called upon to serve the king in more challenging ways than attending to his children or dancing in his masques. Your leisurely pursuits also carry the responsibility of king's guard. And I am invoking that duty now. Will you join me?"

Allen pushed aside the sting of William's words and stood, too.

"Of course I will. I was merely thinking of how best to tell my mother that her sons would be absent this summer when my sister is wed." He sighed. "And that our business is on the king's behalf to defend the Anglican Church against Calvinism. That won't be an easy conversation."

"Time that you made your own choices, and not those of your mother." William held his hand out, and Allen shook it. "I will see you at the armory tomorrow morning. You will need to get fitted for weapons and gear. At my expense."

"And me too?" James asked hopefully. The two men turned to him.

"Yes, and you too," said Allen. "It is your birthright to defend the crown against any who threaten it. Our father would expect no less of us. And although this may just be a handful of Scottish clergymen, it is the principle for which we fight."

"A prayer book?" James scoffed. "That is what we ride to defend?"

"It is a challenge to the unification of our three kingdoms. And that means one king, one state, and one religion."

Allen touched the falcon on his sword. *Be loyal always to your king, my son, for it is he we serve first and foremost, come what may.*

"Mr. Coleman's is no longer unlucky in love," Babs said confidently. "In fact, the new rumor is that anyone who lodges there may fall in love with the lady of his dreams. No matter how unapproachable she is—oops." She clapped her hands over her mouth, causing Lucy to smile at her daughter. Babs had hardly sewn one stitch since they had sat down, so entranced was she with chatting of her sister's forthcoming wedding.

"Luce had a very definite idea of who she might—or rather, might not—marry," she replied. "It is God's will that she had the courage to be true to her own heart and refuse her opportunity in Wiltshire, only to find love waiting for her."

"Literally," Babs giggled. "John was insistent that he accompany us to greet Luce on her return. He said that he had heard so much about her from me that he could no longer contain his excitement in meeting her."

"Who couldn't contain his excitement?" Allen strode into the parlor, bringing with him a spray of water as he removed his cloak and shook the rain from it.

"John. It is so romantic. He and Luce. Their courtship. The marriage plans—"

"Babs, please go and help Sarah with dinner," Lucy said firmly. "Allen and I have some matters to discuss."

Babs hurriedly stuffed her sewing into the basket and almost ran from the room. Lucy smiled. Her daughter was so vibrant. She hoped in her heart that she would find a match as suited as Luce's.

She turned to her son, amused at the resemblance to his father. So handsome, with his long curling hair and flashing dark gray eyes. A glittering diamond in his ear. And yet, something was different today. He was wearing new riding boots and a tooled leather doublet. He was carrying an extra dagger along with his sword.

"Allen?" Every mother's instinct rose in her mind. When had he grown so tall? And his beard now full, the same shape as his father's was. And his shoulders, broad, muscular. "Why did you want to see me alone?"

Through the plaster walls, Babs's sweet voice could be heard from the kitchen, singing a melody she had written to perform at Luce's wedding. Lucy's cat stretched on the bench by the window and rolled over contentedly as raindrops caught in the diamond-shaped panes. Such small, yet comforting moments.

"I am leaving. For the north. I ride with a troop. The king has asked it of us."

Allen was never one to mince words, but these bruised her like stones.

"The north? Where? Why?" Lucy could not quite fathom her son's intent. These were words spoken so often by her husband in years gone by. "For what cause? And why you? Why now?"

What had she missed by refusing to attend court, ignoring the gossip and rumors that scurried like the plague around the chambers and galleries?

"Just security. Nothing more. This will be a simple excursion to the border. We'll be back before Michaelmas."

"We?"

"James comes too—" He spoke over her small cry. "Mother, it is his duty, as is mine, to obey the king's command. We serve at his palace, we guard his children, and we are required to follow his orders."

"He's so young. And you. Neither of you have been trained in warfare, Allen. Times are peaceful since Buckingham died. There has been no need to bear arms or enter combat."

"This is not war, Mother. This is simply an excursion to show strength. It will make a man of James. If he is not permitted to come, he will run away anyway, so great is his desire to soldier."

Allen was correct. It was only a matter of time before this happened. Thank God they were called a simple expedition to the borders and not some foreign war which was taking her sons away.

"And so, you go together? When do you travel?" She was a soldier's wife, and now a soldier's mother. There was no changing this destiny that had crept upon her.

"Within the week. We serve under Goring, with the troop of Lord Grandison. William Villiers."

Oh, dear God, another anguished memory of his father, telling her a similar story of George Villiers, not ten years before.

"The king has given him a command of one hundred men. He selected me to accompany him," Allen continued.

"Again, Villiers." Lucy could not conceal the anger she held against the family that had caused so much devastation in her own.

"He is a good man, Mother. I know you have great issue with your sister. But put that to one side, for I serve under his color and represent the king by riding at his side."

"There is no talking you from this, Allen? You will miss Luce's wedding, and you were enjoying your advancement at the princes' court." Lucy paused. "And the money? What will happen to collecting on the warrants when you are gone?"

Allen pulled a paper from a drawstring pouch tucked inside his doublet.

"There is no changing my mind. And I have made provision for you while I am away." He handed her the document, a note with the king's signature and seal attached. "This is for five hundred pounds. William secured the warrant for me last night. You may use these funds for Luce's wedding and your household. This will ensure your independence. And there is more from whence this came."

Luce took the parchment and read it. The document made no mention of Francke. She could do with this money what she would. How strange was life. Allen's appointment to the king's army meant she did not need to appear in court again with Leventhorpe. No crawling back to him to return to Chancery. And although her name would always be Francke, her spirit was her own. Allen cared for her as his father had requested.

"You have thought of everything, Allen," she conceded. "You have truly grown into a man your father would be so proud of."

Allen stepped close and pulled her into his arms. She felt the smooth leather, cool against her cheek, the scent of the linseed oil bringing back a memory of her husband, the numerous times he embraced her before leaving her. She held her son tightly for a while, and when they finally drew apart, Lucy glimpsed tears in Allen's eyes. He smiled at her, and she saw again the boy behind the man.

"Go with my blessing, my darling. You are your father's son, and he looks down upon you at this moment with pride. Tell James to visit me before he leaves, so I may gave him my approval. Watch out for your younger brother, and return home safely, for while you are gone, I will not rest."

"We will be in good hands, Mother. This is an important undertaking. For the king—and for our family."

They both looked up as the parlor door opened, and Luce and John entered, laughing as they shook raindrops from their clothes. Luce's hood shimmered with damp, and a few drops glistened in her hair. Through the pain in her heart, Lucy found comfort in the balm of love.

"Allen! I have not seen you for a week." John greeted him with a grin. "You have been absent from Mr. Coleman's." He paused. "What is this? You are attired as if riding forth with a troop."

Luce looked swiftly to her mother and then to Allen. "What news do you bring, Allen? And why are you dressed so?"

Allen put his arm around Lucy.

"I was just telling our mother. James and I ride to provide security to the king at the Scottish borders."

"Security?" John asked, surprise in his voice. "Security for what, Allen?"

"Just a domestic matter. The Scots are not too keen on the fact that the king is requiring the Anglican prayer book to be read in Scottish kirks—"

"I should think not," Luce broke in. "They have their own church, their own covenant. It is not the king's place to impose on them his tyranny."

"'Tis not tyranny, Luce," replied Allen. "The king only wishes harmony throughout his three kingdoms. England and Scotland have the same monarch. They should have the same religion. Ireland as well."

Lucy stepped from Allen's arm, for she could see that Luce was mightily troubled. She did not want more arguments tainting her son's last night at home. She glanced at John, who caught her look.

"Now is perhaps not the time for debate, my sweet," he said gently. "Allen follows his conscience, and it is not our place to tell him otherwise. If we do, we are no better than tyrants ourselves. Although, I must admit, there are days when I tremble in fear from the fierce words that drop from your pen, so brilliant is your mind and fluent your language." He drew her to him and kissed her softly. "Save your words for those who deserve them, and exclude poor Allen from your wrath."

There was a moment of silence, and then Allen started laughing, as did Lucy. Grudgingly at first, Luce joined in.

"You are right, John," she replied. "There are opponents far more worthy of my time than Allen. I could decimate his logic in five parries. In fact, in about the time he would take to unsheathe his sword, I would have a treatise written that would floor him."

"Your pen is a mighty weapon, my love." John kissed her again. "Now, let us hear of your brother's adventure and raise a toast to our beloved kingdom. Long may our country be joined in peaceful worship of one God, in tolerance and openness."

Later, when the ghosts trespassed on her thoughts and raised her from her restless slumber, Lucy huddled by the casement window. The rain had ceased, and a watery moon now hung in the sky. Against the cloud-streaked firmament, the palace towers rose black, a few lights burning in distant chambers. Was one of those her sister's? Did Barbara also wake this night, dreaming of her own dead husband and her son riding for the king? Lucy withdrew into her thoughts as the memories crowded closer.

No matter this expedition represented adventure for these young men, unschooled in war, bolstered by the stories of heroic deeds and knightly conquests. Life was always the same. The youth went to war, fighting for old men's principles.

Lucy gazed through the window again as the first yellow streamers of dawn flowed across the lightening sky. To the west, the dark towers still loomed, all lamps now extinguished. Recalling the signs that had directed her past at Fonmon, Whitehall, and Lydiard, she nodded her head slowly. Light burgeoned in the east—in the direction of the city—while darkness clung to the west.

There was nothing left for her family here. With Allen and James serving the king, Luce's future lay distant from the palace, beside John. Babs would soon be of marriageable age, and she would be better served away from the temptations of court.

Time to leave Richmond and return to London.

19

Mr. Hutchinson employed his time in making an entrance upon the study of school divinity, wherein his father was the most eminent scholar of any gentleman in England, and had a most choice library.

Luce Apsley
13th May 1638

Bartlett's Court lay on the south side of Holborn's bustle. She'd traveled far from the lodging in St. Dunstan's, Lucy reflected, although that parish lay adjacent. As best she knew, Francke remained in Hatfield, entrenched in the Puritan community surrounding Ryes Manor. No more thoughts of that heartbreak, that dreadful decision. Banish those shadows from this happy time. Perhaps now, at last, she could enjoy a permanent home.

She opened the rear door onto a flourishing garden and paused on the step to enjoy the abundant plantings. Already, the May sunshine warmed the rosemary, its pungent scent greeting her with the familiarity of an old friend. Rosemary for remembrance. If she were to admit the truth, the garden appealed to her more than the house. In this secluded refuge, she'd settled peacefully, tending a healthy array of herbs and medicinal plants. Plague and ill humors may haunt the crowded streets of the city, but she was prepared with her curatives.

On first setting foot here, during her quest for a sanctuary for her girls and John, she knew this was a happy place. The previous inhabitants, a French Huguenot family, had created a garden equal to hers at the Tower. That, more so than the spacious and elegant chambers, convinced her to secure the lodging.

She also considered it great fortune that their home was close by St. Andrew's Church, which not only offered excellent sermons, but was also the church for Lincoln's Inn. John could make use of the pew the Inn rented there and enjoy the services with Luce upon their marriage. She smiled to herself. John was so eager for the wedding. Although he'd quickly arranged board with Edward at chambers within the Inn, he spent more time at their home than he ever did at his studies.

At Luce's call, she stepped out into the garden to look up at the house, admiring the crisscross brick work. As she thought—Luce stood at the window in the room that soon she would share with John. In just over a month, on their wedding day, he would leave his lodgings at Lincoln's Inn and move to Bartlett's.

"Come in soon," Luce called. "John's family arrives before long, and we have much still to do to make ready the betrothal dinner."

Lucy waved and gestured that she would be just a moment. She was not concerned about preparing for the final marriage discussions with John's father. A king's man from the provinces—a simple matter. There was time to pick the dandelion and cress leaves she'd discovered growing around the well and check the henhouse to see if the chickens had laid more since morning. Always, she found such joy in her garden.

"My son tells me you possess a formal education. And you are well schooled in the ancient philosophers, language, and logic." Sir Thomas Hutchinson beckoned Sarah to fill his wine, continuing to hold sway at the table and pinning Luce under his scrutiny. "I myself am a student of divinity and have spent many decades in meaningful contemplation of the word of God."

Relief. Here, at least, was a topic Luce could talk to her future father-in-law about.

"I respect your learning, sir. To commit your life to the study of the word of God is a vocation that must provide great solace to you."

"My father studies to the exclusion of all other things," remarked John. "When George and I return home to visit him, we spend more time sitting outside his door than within."

"But it does give us ample time to catch up ourselves, Brother," replied George, a younger replica of John, sitting next to him at the table. "For if it not for our father's divine studies, we would be as strangers, never speaking nor seeing each other." He dodged as John administered a playful punch to his arm, almost falling from his bench and subsiding under a glare from his father.

Luce smothered a smile while Babs giggled. Since John's father and brother had arrived at their home, she had eyes for no other than George. A lighthearted version of John, and as handsome as his older brother, George was as charming a young man as Babs had ever dreamed of.

"If you spent more time in the contemplation of the verses of the Bible, and in discussion with your religious tutors, you would have a better understanding of the workings of the court and enjoy more favor from His Majesty and Queen Henrietta." Sir Thomas turned to Luce again. "I hear that your brother is with the king?"

Luce put down her goblet and folded her hands in her lap. She recalled John's caution that his father was a loyal king's man who owed his current position to a knighthood bestowed by King Charles.

"Yes," Luce replied. "Allen accompanies our cousin, Lord Grandison, to the north. They ride under Lord Goring's command." *Say little more. And do not state your own opinion of Goring's exercise. This is not a man who is used to women expressing their thoughts freely.*

"Ah, a noble mission." Sir Thomas glared at John, his mouth settling into sour folds. "One I sincerely hoped my sons might have volunteered to join. For to carry out the king's orders is to carry out the will of God."

Luce composed herself as the silence around the table extended past five, past ten count. She felt a pain shoot through her temple and pressed her hand to her forehead. John's insights did not adequately prepare her for the barely-concealed disapproval she heard in his father's voice.

"My son follows in the steps of his father," Luce's mother said calmly, filling the hush with her cultured voice. "My husband served the present king and King James for many years, and Queen Elizabeth before him."

"Your husband, Lady Francke?" There was no missing the emphasis in Sir Thomas's question.

"Yes. Sir Allen Apsley. As both Victualler of the Navy and Lieutenant of the Tower of London, he served the king in Ireland and in the French Wars."

"Ah, yes. A difficult situation, I recall. He performed with honor, and yet the unpaid warrants . . ." The words hung in the air between them, and Luce wished that she could answer for her mother. Her head was beginning to pound, and she was running out of patience.

"My husband's service was never in doubt. Payment for his sacrifice has been slow to follow."

"He was a loyal subject of the king, no doubt, taking so much financial burden upon himself." Sir Thomas appeared to be leading the conversation in a specific direction. John's hand took Luce's under the cover of the table. "And your present husband, Lady Francke?" His eyes wandered around the room, as if expecting Leventhorpe Francke to pop out from the paneling. Really, he was verging on incivility. Luce opened her mouth to speak, but hesitated at John's warning squeeze.

"My husband, Sir Leventhorpe, is at his estates in Essex, Sir Thomas. He has a great deal of business interests there and is required to spend his time tending to them." Luce's mother gazed steadily back at Sir Thomas while Luce and Babs sat silent.

"And yet, you choose not to join him? Do you spend all your time apart? Or is it because I hear his manor at Hatfield is a hotbed of Puritanism?"

Luce could hold back no further. "My mother devotes herself to caring for us and ensuring my brothers were properly educated at the princes' court. If my stepfather decided that it was better for him to remain in Essex, which is not—"

"Father, let us remember that if not for Lady Francke providing an education for her sons at Richmond Palace, Luce and I would not have met." John spoke over Luce smoothly, and she realized that she had come close to offending his father. "And that is just too tragic to contemplate. We are here to celebrate our betrothal, not talk of the politics of the court."

Luce's mother took advantage of John's diversion. She placed a hand on Sir Thomas's arm and addressed her younger daughter.

"Babs, our guests have finished their meal. Would you care to play for us while John's father and I have a private discussion?" Luce looked up gratefully as her mother's gracious words broke the tension. "I am sure that George and Luce would be delighted to hear the music you and John have composed for the wedding feast."

The dinner party rose from the table, and Luce's mother inclined her head to John's father.

"Sir Thomas, let us conclude our business and permit the young people to enjoy their time together. I would be interested to hear more of your thoughts of the king. I remember when my husband and I were last guests in his privy chamber at Whitehall, his collection of art was most magnificent." Luce's mother effortlessly established her social standing and reminded John's father of her breeding and background. She slipped so easily between the worlds of the court and the Puritans. "In fact, King Charles and I were quite enchanted with his acquisition from Rubens of the portrait of. . ."

They withdrew to the other end of the parlor to sit by a large desk. The pain in Luce's temple moved to a dull throbbing behind her eyes, and her back ached. But the worst was over, and she knew that her mother would charm John's father and secure the terms of the marriage agreement.

Lucy closed the front door and leaned against it. Done. Sir Thomas returned to his lodgings at the The Greyhound, marriage contract in hand, dowry pledged. There was a moment when she feared that his suspicion of her Calvinism and the apparent lack of her husband in the negotiations would upset the entire arrangement. She thanked circumstance again that her brother's name and title carried weight, and that Luce's father's dismal financial legacy did not tarnish the valor of his deeds or undermine his loyalty to the crown. These times were complex, for loyalties were questioned, and she had no truck with choosing preferences. Of course, John's gifting of Luce's dowry concluded the contract in Lucy's favor.

Praise God Luce's abrupt change of heart at Lydiard had not jeopardized that gift.

Really, she experienced such an emotional relief from Leventhorpe's absence that she hardly considered the ramifications against her reputation, and she was so intent on establishing a home for Luce and Babs that she rarely ventured out to speak to neighbors. The excuse that business confined him to their Essex estates sufficed.

Pushing away from the door, Lucy checked that the fires were banked. She drifted through the quiet rooms, touching the furniture and hangings, becoming more familiar with the house. No taint of Francke marred this haven, and the ghost of her devoted husband wove through her heart and mind, bringing her peace. She had been so truly loved.

She wearily trod upstairs. The candle cast a pool of light in front of her as she climbed. She was more tired than she thought, for the effort of negotiating with Sir Thomas had been exhausting. Time for bed and rest, and on the morrow, she could start the wedding planning in earnest. A floorboard creaked as she mounted the top step.

"Mama?" Babs's voice came through the door from the chamber she shared with Luce.

"Shhh, sweeting, it's time to sleep." Lucy lifted the lamp and peeped inside the door. Babs was sitting up in bed, blinking like a little owl.

"Has he gone, Mother?"

"Yes, he and John and George have left for their lodgings. All is well." Lucy crossed and kissed Babs on her forehead.

"Mother, Luce is so hot, and I can't sleep."

Lucy lifted the lantern and leaned over to Luce's side of the bed. Her daughter lay on her back, hair tied back in a hood, a few damp tendrils of hair escaping. She appeared flushed, and beads of sweat glistened on her forehead. Putting her hand on Luce's brow, Lucy frowned, for her skin was burning. Luce murmured at her mother's touch but did not wake.

"How long has she been like this, Babs?"

"I don't know. We fell asleep quickly, for she complained of a headache and then took a sleeping draft."

"I see." Lucy laid her hand on Luce's brow again. "Babs, go and sleep in my chamber. I'll stay here with Luce."

Babs wriggled out of bed and tiptoed from the room. Lucy settled down next to Luce and blew out the candle. The day had been long. Surely just a fever, brought on by the excitement of the occasion. Maybe even the greensickness, for the prospect of marriage brought out the heat in any young girl's blood.

20

There is this only to be recorded, that never was there a passion more ardent and less idolatrous; he loved her better than his life, with inexpressible tenderness and kindness.

Luce Apsley
1ˢᵗ June 1638

Lucy jolted awake, her neck cricked from sitting propped up against the bolster. She immediately turned to Luce, who lay quietly, her face to the wall, and touched her forehead. Still hot. Carefully slipping from the bed, Lucy reached for the damp cloth by the pitcher on the chest. As she did so, Luce moaned and turned on her back, revealing her face to the rising sun.

Oh God, no.

In a step, Lucy was back to the bedside, washcloth dripping from her hands. Pinpricks of blood-red spots trailed across Luce's cheeks and forehead. Lucy untied the ribbons on Luce's nightgown. The rash coiled around her neck and collarbones. Smallpox.

Oh God.

Prayers vanished, and only a heart-wrenching plea to the Almighty remained. She smoothed Luce's hair from her brow and tucked the strand back under her hood. Her daughter's eyelids fluttered but remained closed. The pox tightened its grip and refused to let her wake with the morning sun. Pain spasms flickered across Luce's face; her fingers plucked anxiously at the light cover.

"Hush, my sweeting," Lucy whispered. "Be still, my darling. You must rest, and I'll bring you something to drink. Rest."

Luce's hands stilled, and she sank back into sleep. After watching her for a few moments, Lucy walked to the chamber door. Opening it slightly, she called through the gap.

"Sarah. Babs. Come here, please." Louder. "Sarah—I need you now, please."

Running footsteps along the corridor.

"Come no closer," she commanded.

"Lady Francke?" Sarah's voice was just on the other side of the door.

"Mother? What's wrong? What's wrong with Luce?"

"Babs, you have to be strong. I am going to need your help in the coming weeks." Lucy paused, preparing her words. "Luce has contracted smallpox—"

"Merciful Lord," Sarah breathed.

"Mother!" Babs cried.

"—and I cannot leave her chamber for fear of contaminating you both," she continued carefully. "Babs, I believe you will be fine, for the pox did not appear before you left. Only when the red spots rise do the humors release their spores and infection spreads."

Babs was softly crying.

"I want you to be strong," Lucy repeated. "We will nurse Luce through this. I have done so many times before in the Tower, under far worse conditions."

Sarah spoke soothingly. "There, Mistress Babs, your mother knows just what to do. And you and me, we'll help by doing everything she tells us, poppet."

"W-w-will she . . . die?" Babs gulped the words between her tears.

"No, she will not die. We will nurse her through the contagion." Oh God.

"But her f-f-face. She will be sorely disfigured." Babs broke down again.

"We will restore her to health and to her former beauty, Babs." Dear God, let these words hold true. "But now, I need you to help Sarah gather the curatives I need. Black salsify. Rosewater. Those I have clearly labeled in my medicinals. Please go to the apothecary and purchase jujube berries." She paused. "And Sarah—"

"Yes, my lady?"

"Sarah, seek out the alchemist in Blackfriars and obtain a scruple of calcined hartshorn."

"Madam?"

"He will know. Sir Walter Raleigh commended this to me. It must be calcined, heated, purified until just the white powder remains and the volatility has been removed. This will increase the efficacy of the compound."

A moan from Luce distracted her.

"Hurry. The sooner we can expose the pox and rid them of the pus, the more quickly Luce will recover and the least scarring will occur." She lightened her voice. "Send a message to John, and tell him not to fear. God has great things in store for Luce. We will pray to him to save her."

Lucy shut the door firmly to keep the contagion within the room. Days would pass before she could leave again. She had been in worse prisons, fighting ghastlier conditions. This was not Luce's time to die. Determined to cure her daughter, and to save the rest of the household from the ravages of the disease, Lucy prepared for war.

The pox spores settled into Luce's room and perched over her, gargoyles spitting venom upon her innocent forehead. This contagion would fight her hard for her daughter's life. She must marshal her every skill to vanquish it. Clean linens, floorboards swept bare, and a constant supply of small ale to keep Luce's thirst quenched were called for. And she had Babs and Sarah to worry about, too. If she could contain the management of the spores, she could stop the spread. She pictured them clinging to her skirts, a gaggle of wicked imps poised to disperse into her home and destroy everyone in their path.

Creating a plan where she isolated Luce and herself from the others, Lucy forbade Sarah to enter the room, demanding that she leave food and the bedpans outside. She covered the pans in a cloth for emptying, and each night while the house slept, she crept downstairs and disposed of the contents in the cesspit. As she stepped outside, she breathed the cool night air and considered it her ally. There were many doctors she had challenged in Blackfriars who were convinced that the worst humors hid in the gloaming and that patients should be protected from them with shutters and roaring fires. But Lucy had witnessed a difference at the Tower, where fresh air blew from the eastern salt marshes. If she could protect her patients from drafts, the clean night air often restored them by morning.

Sixteen sunsets Lucy counted. Fifteen moonrises. She kept the shutters open, knowing no evil humors of the night haunted fair Bartlett's. The sun arched from east to west, tracing the course of the Thames. And pursuing in its path, the waxing moon, growing stronger each day. Luce would follow the fortunes of the moon, for her horoscope inextricably harnessed her to the heavens. Lucy smiled as she remembered the dream that had come to her when she carrying Luce, where a star came down from the skies and rested in her hand. "We will have a child of extraordinary eminency," Allen had said when she'd told him of her dream. Luce would live and fulfill the prophecy.

"Mama?" Luce's voice. Barely a whisper, and yet heralding a broken fever and a return to the corporal world. "Mama, are you there?"

"I'm here, my sweeting."

"Mama, I'm scared. I cannot see."

Lucy swallowed her fear. "It is just the swelling, my darling. You have been ill. And now you are recovering. The inflammation was fierce. But it will gradually diminish." Please, God. Please no residual blindness, no lost vision.

"What illness?"

"A fever." No need to tell her yet of the dreadful pox, the marks that disfigured her child beyond recognition. "Here, sip some rosewater. Where do you hurt?" She poured a little cordial onto a spoon and carefully dripped the salve between Luce's cracked lips. The chamomile would quickly bring her the respite of sleep.

"My head, a little. My back." Luce lifted her hands to her face. Lucy carefully brought them down on the coverlet, and Luce weakly obeyed. They were bandaged to prevent Luce from scratching the pox scabs, to relieve her from permanently scarring her face.

"Sleep more, my darling, for it is the best cure for your illness."

"John?"

"Has not stirred from our home since you fell ill." *Terrified that he would lose you, out of his mind with worry.* His muffled weeping as he waited in vigil had seared into her mind. "I'll tell him you asked for him. In a few days, he can visit you." *And that will be the test, for if he sees beyond the terrible pox marks, he truly loves you.*

"Love you . . ." Luce's voice trailed as the posset did its work.

"I love you, my darling girl."

On the eighteenth day, Lucy stood at the open door of Luce's chamber.

"The danger has passed. She will live. The contagion has gone. You may see her, just for a few minutes," she said quietly to John and Babs, who had barely left their chairs outside the room the whole duration of Luce's illness. "And I warn you, the pox has left its mark. You must not frighten Luce with your reaction, for this will hinder her healing. No glass is in her room to reflect her image, and so, do not become a mirror to her fear."

"We will not, Mother." Babs had matured during this fearful time, growing more responsible as she served as the messenger between Lucy and Sarah.

"You saved her life, Lady Francke," John said, holding her hands between his. He had lost weight and become haggard, was not his usual meticulous self. "I could no more hurt Luce than take my own life. And I would that I could give my eyes for hers, to save her this terrible distress."

Lucy kissed his cheek. "Her eyes are healing, and her vision is returning. You will not need to sacrifice for her, John. Just love her, for she has a difficult journey ahead, and only those who look beyond the physical to the soul will be able to walk with her."

She stepped aside. John took Babs's hand. Together, they entered the chamber and paused by Luce's bed. She was lying against the pillows, her golden-brown hair bound in a thick plait, neat under a fresh white hood. Lucy saw afresh through their eyes the horrible disfigurement, the crusted pox scabs. John fell to his knees at her daughter's side and looked unflinchingly into Luce's face, ignoring the wretchedness of her deformity.

"My darling, my prayers have been answered by the Almighty God." He bowed his head and kissed her bandaged hands. "I am more yours today than the moment I first heard your name, the evening I first saw you. My life is bound forever in yours, through eternity. We will marry as soon as you are able to leave this chamber, for I cannot stand being apart from you for another day."

21

That day that the friends on both sides met to conclude the marriage, I fell sick of the small-pox, which was many ways a great trial. First, my life was almost in desperate hazard, and then the disease, for the present, made me the most deformed person that could be seen.

Luce Apsley
3ʳᵈ July 1638

As Luce sat on her bed and gazed at the finger-leafed chestnut trees through the window, the fat pigeon that roosted in the eaves struck up his cooing. His routine had awoken her every morning since her recovery. Today, the third of July, was as bright as any other summer morn she remembered in London. The early mist from the Thames released the honeysuckle's scent and muffled the sounds of the city stirring. And the faeries would be hiding in the garden at the Tower, where her mother's damask roses grew wild under the great stone walls, tended no more by her.

Tears welled from Luce's eyes, and her throat closed. So much loss.

She clasped her mother's lovingly sewn bride ribbons loosely between her fingers, turquoise silk glistening against the indigo of her velvet gown. Although her hair was loose, it did not cover the welts that coursed across her chest. She looked down at the fine French lace collar, carefully stitched by Sarah to hide the blemishes. How could he love her still, how could he love this hideousness? The tears spilled over to her cheeks, but she could not feel them, so thick still were the scabs. No glass was allowed near, but alone in the dark night, she touched her face and found it a stranger to her.

She could not do this to him.

"Luce!" Babs burst into the room. "Are you ready? The bridal procession is formed, and everyone is waiting downstairs. We leave for St. Andrews—" She stopped. "What's wrong? Why are you crying?"

"I cannot marry John. I am hideous, deformed. I cannot burden him with this face for the rest of his life." Luce tossed the bride ribbons to the floor and started tugging at her bodice. "Help me undress, Babs."

Babs shook her head. "You are wrong, Luce. You, of all people, know John loves you and is not troubled by your appearance."

"I will not burden him," repeated Luce. "Tell him I will not marry him. Go. Go now." She turned her back on Babs and refused to move. After a while, her sister left the room.

In the silence that followed emerged the little noises that delighted her: swallows rustling in the eaves as they flew from their nest, her mother's dog barking in the garden below. Simple, homely sounds. The day was continuing as every other day, and she would later work on her Virgil. Deep in that world, there were no critics of her face, no sideways looks of horror or sympathy.

A man's footstep creaked on the stairs. Luce's stomach tightened. *Be strong, for I must tell John.*

"Luce." Edward. Edward, who knew her better than any, save Allen. He would understand how she could not proceed with this marriage. How ironic that he had already saved her from one. Now, he was rescuing her from herself and the misery she inflicted on others.

She felt his weight on the bed, found herself pulled into his embrace. "My sweet cousin," he murmured. "What ails thee?"

Luce tried to speak and could not continue for the tears that choked her voice.

Edward held her tightly, wordlessly. Gradually, her sobs quietened.

"Babs found me and told me something I did not believe." He stroked her hair, soothing, as he would one of his horses. "If there is one thing I know about you, Luce, it is that you are the most courageous woman I know." Edward continued to hold her, his face resting on her head. "You rose above every teasing challenge from Allen and me. And most times you beat us . . . well, every time if our studies were concerned." His grin warmed his voice. "And now where has that courage gone, Coz?"

She shook her head. Courage she had aplenty. Courage was leaving a man on the day of her wedding.

"You, who stood in front of the Chancery judges and defended your mother against their wicked accusations? You, who stood up to Francke and all the deprivation you and your mother suffered at his hands? Where is that brave girl I love so much?"

Luce blinked to clear her eyes. This was not fair. Even he did not understand. Still, he would not let her go.

"And then, in Wiltshire, the woman who told her family that she would not marry into an arrangement that offered no love, the girl who became a woman in that moment, who showed such strength in refusing a secure future for the unknown?" Edward held her away from him and looked deep into her eyes. She saw no flinching, only the honest light of truth in his gaze. She stared back at him, daring him to look away from her hideousness.

"I am deformed, Edward. That woman no longer exists." She did not drop her gaze. Saying so made the words true.

"That woman is tempered to steel now, through the adversity that has been yours. That woman found love—deep and true love—through the honest truth of knowing herself." Still holding her gaze, Edward retrieved the bride ribbons from the floor and pressed them into her hands.

"John loves you. He loved you through the fear of losing you, through the joy of your recovery. He loves you better than his own life." Edward stood and pulled Luce to her feet. "John is the most honorable man, and holds you in such esteem, such love, such tenderness. Do not betray his love. And do not betray yourself."

Luce smoothed the bride ribbons, seeing the tiny primroses her mother had embroidered onto them. The flower John had given her on the day he declared his love. On the day he asked her to marry him.

"I'm frightened, Edward." There. The truth.

"We all have moments of fear, Luce." Edward's dear face was full of love. "But this moment, you have a choice about what life has dealt you. Do not choose bitterness, loneliness. Choose a better life, for on that road, wonders will occur that you have not even considered. And John waits downstairs to walk with you. Be the strong, courageous woman I know you to be. You will not be alone."

She took his hand. His touch was warm, familiar. She wanted to trust his words. "I have no worry. I can live a singular life. And I am no coward. Courage is refusing to marry the love of your life on the day of your wedding."

"And even more courageous is to face your fears and banish them in the light of truth." Edward held out his arm. "Choose the life that was predicted in your mother's dream, Luce. Give yourself a second chance to live again."

Those words, more than any, reached Luce's heart. Her mother had taken her second chance and married the man she loved. She'd lived with courage and defiance, a difficult life. But a full one. Perhaps Edward was right. A life in the shadows was a lie.

Luce separated the bride ribbons, running two between her fingers before solemnly tying them to his sleeve.

"Then I will face this fear. Vanquish it. And I will trust the love that you tell me conquers all."

Leaving behind her familiar chamber, which had borne witness to a fierce battle for her life, Luce walked downstairs to her wedding day. And when she saw John's upturned face at the bottom of the stair, a wide smile breaking upon his dear countenance, her heart's leap told her the choice was right.

Later, much later, when they returned after a quiet ceremony at St. Andrew's, where the priest was afraid to look at her face, she walked with John into their chamber. Her knees trembled, for surely this was the moment he would see the full horror of the monster he had married.

They stood in the room, the great tawny-curtained marriage bed between them, the candlelight throwing deep shadows into the corners. The warm July night embraced them, the curfew dusk quiet, the fading twilight gentle.

She looked at John as she slowly pulled at the laces in her bodice, urging his reaction as the indigo velvet parted to reveal a fine lawn undershirt. John untied her sleeves and eased the bodice from her shoulders, tenderly kissing her skin as he did so. She felt the brush of his lips against the scars and stared into a candle flame, braced for his disgust.

Lifting her to the bed and carefully laying her on the cool linen sheets, John removed his clothes, his fine swordsman's body lean and muscular in the golden light. Still, he looked into her eyes; still, he gazed with such love and tenderness and passion that she could not look away.

He plucked a full-headed rose from a bowl and pulled each dusky petal from the bloom, dropping them one by one upon Luce's nakedness. As the rose petals settled on her skin, desire surged through her, and the taste of his kisses, his sweet mouth, came tumbling back. John pulled another rose, and another. As he scattered the petals upon her and then lay by her side, she felt herself open as a flower greets the sunrise.

"I will not hurt you," John said softly. "You must tell me if you feel any pain."

She nodded, only wanting now to pull him to her, feast on his strength, to grow strong again from his love.

He raised himself on powerful arms and slowly entered her. The scent of crushed rose petals mingled with the fragrance of rosemary and thyme rising from his skin. As he gently lay on her, still bearing his weight on his elbows, the silky rose petals caressed her body. He leaned to kiss her, softly at first, and then more urgently. As his mouth possessed her, so too did his body, and she met him and joined him in the unity of their love.

From the casement window of her mother's parlor, Luce watched the cobbled square for John to return from Lincoln's Inn. Today was the first time he had attended in several weeks. Truly, he preferred studying divinity over law, and he attended his lectures with great reluctance. He emerged from the passageway, striding across the open space with the confident pace of a country man. Her heart twisted with love and joy. She would recognize that walk anywhere. The front door banged, and she turned from the window, eager to share her news.

"I have heard from Allen." Luce held a tattered parchment out to John as he entered the parlor. The letter was damp, the humidity of the August heat trapped within its fibers. "He does not expect to be home by Michaelmas."

John wiped his face and shrugged off his doublet, his linen undershirt clinging to his chest. He looked thoughtful. "Does he say why?"

"Only that the Scottish matter keeps him engaged." She placed the letter on the table and turned to her husband. "What have you heard in the city?"

Placing the books and perspective glass that he had just purchased for his father on the table, he took Allen's letter.

"There is a restlessness in the air. The queen's mother has arrived at Hatton House, here in Holborn. She keeps a room full of priests and hears

Mass three times a day. That is not going down well among the London guilds."

"But that has nothing to do with the Scottish?"

"They have formed a congregation to formally protest the prayer book." John scanned Allen's words. "The king has agreed to hear their request."

"Surely that is a good thing, John?" Luce stood at John's side, reading Allen's letter again with him. "Allen makes no mention of this. He just says that he is bound to stay until the matter is resolved."

"I do not like the sound of this, Luce. It is almost as though the king is playing for time."

"Is your father being summoned back to Westminster? Does Parliament meet to discuss this?"

"Not that he has said." John turned and held Luce by her arms. "Nor will the king encourage open debate. He has not held a Parliament in ten years. And yet . . ."

"Yet?"

"The news today is that the Parliament may be recalled." John's usually mild demeanor grew fierce. "No doubt the king only wishes to ask for more money. That is the only reason he would risk assembling the members after so long."

He turned to Luce and took her hands. "Edward leaves for the north tomorrow."

"What?" Did she hear right?

"Edward. He joins Allen at the border. The king has requisitioned more men." John reached out and caressed the frown from Luce's brow. "It is a strategy in the tournament of chess he engages in with the Scots."

"Is it safe?" These games men played.

"Completely. Edward is excited to go. He is as bored with studying as I am." John drew his finger gently across her forehead. "These scars are fading. Your mother is right. I think they will disappear over time."

Luce smiled back at him. "Don't seek to divert me, John. You tire of Lincoln's Inn?"

"The law is not for me, my love. If I am to spend my days entombed in the company of books, I would rather they be speaking of the glories of God than the crimes of men."

"What would you do?"

"My father's library contains more than a thousand books on the study of divinity. It will be mine one day. I think my time would best be spent acquiring the knowledge to understand these, rather than to pursue the law." John took her into his arms, and she felt the heat of him, the passion of his words.

"And how will we live, John?" The habit of the past years' frugality did not fade quickly.

"My father has a friend who owns a place in the Star Chamber. The seat next to him is occupied by a churlish man, a drunkard and an adulterer. He will be suspended, and I can purchase his place."

"The Star Chamber? I thought you did not care much for the king's private court?" This was a surprise.

"I can accommodate within my soul if I am pursuing a higher occupation in the study of the books. The requirements of my attendance will be minimal, and this is my way of serving the king, to keep my father content."

"And so, live for your desire, my husband." Luce drew her finger down John's throat and rested, for a moment, on the cleft where a pulse beat steadily. "As I do for mine." She kissed her fingertip and touched his mouth and, as she did so, caught the sudden hot passion in his eyes. She drew his hand to her waist. "We are alone, for once. Leave the talk of our future, and let us take the present that is offered."

22.

There was a wicked queen, daughter of a mother that came out of the bloody house of Guise. Those who were chiefly active and instrumental in the justice executed on this wicked queen, were the reformers of religion in Scotland.

Luce Hutchinson
17th November 1638

Allen peered across the dark hills of the Middle Shires. Lightning flared over the humps and tossed deeper shadows into crevices carved by ancient waterfalls. Another November night storm rolled through the Scottish border country, and he pulled up the collar of his leather coat as fat raindrops spattered on the ruined stone wall in front of him.

Damnation, he could have been settling by the fire at the Angel Inn, ten miles away in Berwick, where he'd left James grumpily polishing bridles. Instead, William had sent him on another patrol, a futile trek along the Roman wall.

The king demanded constant watches to demonstrate to the Scots the strength of the English army. And yet, what of the might of Scottish army, hidden in these hills? Thank the good Lord that Edward joined him, for in truth, this was a bleak and unwelcoming land, mysterious in its shifting weather and shadowy landscape. In his gut, he knew he was being watched. But in these treacherous lands, a single man or an entire army could be concealed, and no one would know the difference.

"We did not fulfill our promise to your mother and return home by Michaelmas," remarked Edward, standing hunched against the weather. "Do you think we may by Twelfth Night?"

"I hope to God so," replied Allen. "Although, the king is building a presence here, rather than reducing it. You say you encountered many others on the road north, all riding toward the border, not away from it?"

"I did. And all in great spirits to serve the king and carry out his command, whatever that might be. Although I admit when we stayed in

Newark, we did not receive a welcome reception from the locals." Edward pulled the brim of his hat farther over his eyes as the rain intensified and shifted out of a puddle that was rapidly filling up against the broken rampart. Tethered to the tumbledown byre a few yards away, their horses whickered as a clap of thunder echoed around the hills.

"The men of Newark are most disgruntled with the king and his rule," Allen said. "I felt the same suspicion from them six months ago. Apparently, feelings are not diminishing. The city is a lodestone for Parliament's cause, I fear."

"Come, let's shelter before we are soaked through. This weather is good for neither God nor man, and no beast is even stirring tonight." Edward strode to the byre and quieted his horse, which was restlessly shaking its head at the approaching storm.

Allen followed, glad to leave his lookout position. This country was deceitful in its swift-moving storms and sudden downpours, and there was as much vexation in reading the skies as understanding the dour inhabitants. At least they were uniformly taciturn in their dislike of the southerners, while the blasted weather was completely unpredictable in its moods.

As the men stood under the thin branches of a stunted fir, they were both quiet for a moment, eyes peering into the darkness of the Scottish hills. After a while, Allen spoke over the drumming of the rain.

"So, Luce is recovered?"

"I have told you this. Do not fret. She is well and happy. John takes good care of her."

"And her complexion?"

"As I said. Marred, but the scars will fade in time. When she first emerged for her wedding, even the priest was afraid to look at her, but John cared not one whit for her appearance."

Truly, Edward bore Luce great affection.

"He is a good man, Allen, and loves her dearly."

Allen kicked a loose stone. It rolled down the hill, clattering when striking a rock. "He had better. If he should hurt her heart by a careless word or thoughtless remark—"

"He will not," Edward assured. "You have a fine brother in John. He is loyal and loving and a welcome addition to our family."

Allen grunted. He still remembered the late-night debates at Richmond with William Villiers. John Hutchinson was a man who would not withhold his opinion, no matter if the truth offended. But then, Luce was just as forthright.

"If Luce's appearance is as compromised as you tell it, John will say so."

"And if you think Luce is afraid of honesty, then you underestimate your sister," replied Edward. He stroked the neck of his horse and looked up at the sky. "I think the storm is passing. Let's make for Berwick and see if we can at least get back by daybreak."

A cold east wind whipped across Allen's cheek, and a patter of raindrops fell on his head from the spindly tree. As he peered to the heavens, a watery moon appeared between the racing clouds, offering a glimmer of light by which to see the path back to the Angel Inn.

"The weather has shifted again," he said. "I am sick of this unpredictable clime. I'm ready to return home, Edward. But I know not when."

"The king does not recall us, yet. Let's return to the garrison and make the best of our lodging. A warm fire and good company await us."

"It awaits us in London, too. I'm going to tell Villiers that I am done with this pretense. There is nothing to keep me here. The entire exercise has been futile. The Scots stay on their side of the border, and we sit here."

"Serving the king will further your cause at court. Before I left, it was quite obvious that the king is counting who is loyal to him and who have disappeared to their estates. Serving with our cousin Grandison on this mission is advantageous. The Villiers name carries value with the king."

"Is that why you joined us?" Allen gathered his reins and mounted his horse. He circled the animal around and pointed its head east.

"I have no legacy. All goes to my oldest brother. You know my father sticks to the inheritance protocols. I must earn my money, and volunteering for the king's army is as good a way as any." Edward rode across to Allen's side, and they carefully picked their way through the rubble of the ruined wall. The land was so desolate that not even the peasants ventured to steal the stones for their own use.

"But you are Uncle John's favorite. Surely he has made provision for you?"

"No." Edward kicked his horse into a canter as soon as the track appeared clear in front of them. "No provision. It is all up to me."

The mummers for Twelfth Night made a fortune at the Angel Inn that year, for the bored soldiers spent their coin on calling for more entertainment, both from the players and the town whores. This was not Whitehall nor the King's Men players, but it passed the time. With no certainty of a return to London, Allen was as free with his money as any of his friends. While he was persuading a doxy follower of the company to give him a private performance of a particular nature, he received a summons.

"Keep her warm for me," he yelled to his comrades. The innkeeper's son led him away from the warmth of the taproom to the cold staircase that wound its way through the middle of the inn. "But don't spoil her too much!"

He laughed at the groans as she modestly tucked her shift back in her bodice and sat at a trestle with her back to his friends. She at least ignored them and was prepared to wait for him. That was a good sign.

The boy led Allen along a narrow corridor with uneven floorboards and a rank smell of mice from the attic just above them. He stopped, banged three times on a door, and flung it open. Eager to return to the taproom, Allen hastily walked inside.

"Apsley. I have an assignment for you." William Villiers did not look up from his papers as Allen entered the cramped parlor. "You are to return to Whitehall with a message for the king."

Thoughts of the doxy fled. Ah, a mission that did not require endless riding back and forth along a ruined wall gazing out over blank hills. Finally, a break in the tedium.

In two strides, Allen crossed the meagerly furnished chamber. "Of course, William. It would be an honor." Villiers sanded his signature and then sealed and stamped the parchment with his signet ring. Allen poured himself a goblet of wine. "I can leave tomorrow morning."

Villiers held up his hand. "Leave now. The news is critical. I have put as much as I dare trust in writing. The rest I will leave for you to tell His Majesty in person." He crossed the room and thrust open the door. No

174

one stood outside. He closed it again and leaned against the stout frame. "The Scottish bishops have rebuffed Laud and the king's request of them. They will not tolerate the English prayer book in a Scottish kirk." Villiers dropped his voice even lower, making it difficult to hear him over the crackling fire. "The Covenanters are amassing an army, Coz. They intend to make a fight of this. And all we have is a few volunteers who have been riding the border as if it were a yule hunting party."

Allen's cousin pulled a second parchment and scribbled a quick note, also folding it and sealing it. Barbara Villiers's name was scrawled across it.

"And why not send your usual messenger, Cousin?"

William looked up. "The king demands secrecy. He plays both sides, and does not want to reveal anything to his enemies in London. My mother is the queen's favorite lady-in-waiting. She can get you an audience."

Allen's stomach tightened. This was not the news he was expecting. So much for heading to London for the comforts of home.

"I did not know your mother was at Whitehall."

"Ever since the Earl of Suffolk's ill health forced his retirement from court, her time has been in demand by the queen." William pulled a fistful of coins from a chest on the table.

"Theophilus Howard? Your mother's lover?"

"And your mother's too," William shot back.

Allen started. "Old gossip. Her name was cleared."

William counted coins into a purse. "Not according to my mother. But those were their battles, not ours, Cousin."

An olive branch. Best take it.

"And your request of the king?" Allen ventured, although he knew the answer.

"Men. Horses. Armaments." Villiers handed Allen the messages and a purse of coin. "And quickly. Go to my mother first. She will get you access to the king. Take Edward with you, and ride like the wind. I will keep watch over James. This is no longer an exercise, Allen. This is war."

The Great North Road pointed spear-like from Berwick to London, plunging into the heart of England, crossing moor and vale, following the tracks of the ancient Romans. A tutor in the Tower had once captured his imagination with tales of disciplined centurions marching the length of England. Allen had spent the last six months patrolling their blasted border wall—at least now they could help him achieve his mission by giving him a straight road south.

After filling their packs with meat, cheese, and bread, and knocking back a cup of the landlord's smuggled brandy for warmth, Allen and Edward mounted the inn's fastest horses. They galloped through the deserted streets of Berwick, a snowfall muffling the hoof beats. The track was easily navigated, for the snow had lain thick all day, and no thaw threatened ice. Distant starlight revealed the path ahead, and suddenly, a rush of exhilaration ran through Allen. He turned to see Edward riding by his side, bent over his horse's neck, and at that moment could not imagine a better place to be in all of England.

He let out a whoop as they left the sleeping town behind them. Guided by the frigid North Sea glinting under the dome of the night sky, they galloped south toward Newcastle and the string of towns leading to London.

23

Now, although religion were the main ground of those bloody quarrels, yet there were, in all these countries, many disputes of civil right, which for the most part bore the face of the wars.

Luce Hutchinson
11ᵗʰ January 1639

Hicks Hall lay at the end of the Great North Road, hard by Smithfield Market. Allen and Edward arrived and were assailed by the sights and sounds of a London robustly enjoying its day. To combat the freezing weather, smoky braziers burned in front of churches, offering warmth to parishioners. Merchants called from the shelter of their shop doorways, housewives and their servants chattered with friends and scolded apprentices, and the cries of mutilated and diseased beggars punctuated every street corner.

After the silence of the borders and the blur of his week's ride, the clatter and crash of humanity swept over Allen. Lord, it was impossible to think in this riotous city.

Dismounting at the milestone marker and turning in their horses, the men parted ways at St. John Street.

"Edward, go to Holborn and let my mother know that we return to London." Allen was eager to complete his mission. "Have her prepare beds for us, and tell her that I have a duty at court and will be at her home as soon as I am able."

"Are you sure you don't want me to come with you?" asked Edward. "You could have a long wait."

"I'm not using the conventional way to seek an audience." Allen slung his leather saddlebag over his shoulder and gazed over toward the spire of St. Paul's Cathedral, confirming the direction of the river. "I'm heading to Whitehall now. I'll be in Holborn tonight."

Allen navigated through the crowded streets into Blackfriars and strode down the gentle slope to the water steps. This was familiar land, for his mother had brought him here many times on her expeditions to the alchemists and herbalists of this ancient ward, and belonging welcomed him. London would always flow through his veins, and the cobbles beneath his feet felt more familiar than any other path he had trodden.

Reaching the Thames and relieved the tide was running in his favor, Allen hailed a wherry. Perched on the hard bench, which painfully reminded him of his long week in the saddle, he joined the throng of traffic heading upriver toward the towers of Whitehall. Pray to God that the king was in his winter palace and not elsewhere. With any luck, the inclement cold kept him within its protective walls. And hopefully, the queen stayed with him. If Henrietta Maria was in residence, then his Aunt Barbara served her. He could gain access to the king and deliver his cousin's message.

As he strode through the outer reception rooms of the palace, Allen realized his great leather coat and mud-splashed riding boots were awkwardly out of place in the refined atmosphere. Cursing, he swung into a velvet-draped alcove and rubbed fiercely at his boots and coat with the back of a hanging, removing the worse of the travel stains. He removed his hat, smoothed his bedraggled hair, and replaced it firmly on his head. Court niceties must be sacrificed for the speedy delivery of William's private message.

Access to the king was through Barbara Villiers. At the doors to the queen's rooms, he presented the guard with the note from William, directing him to immediately deliver the message to the queen's lady-in-waiting. As he waited, he grabbed some sweetmeats from the sideboard. He was starving. And thirsty. He helped himself to a cup of wine. And another.

Finally, the door opened, and his aunt appeared, holding his note. He kissed her cheeks in greeting and knelt to receive her blessing.

"Allen. My son writes you have urgent business with the king." Barbara moved swiftly to the point of his visit. She made no mention of his sudden and unkempt appearance. This was a woman who was used to thinking quickly.

"I apologize for my unexpected visit. I have not stopped to change my clothes." Allen stood up and removed his hat. "William asked that I travel hastily and in secret. He felt that if I came to you first, you would gain me access to the king. My visit is unofficial and must stay that way."

"I understand." His aunt drew him to one side of the antechamber, away from the curious looks of the courtiers that stood gossiping in small groups. "Go out to the Privy Garden and meet me at the doorway in the far southeast corner, behind the privet hedge that borders the path. I cannot admit you through this chamber; it will draw too much attention." She held out her hand dismissively for him to kiss and turned quickly away.

Ivy clambered so thickly around the narrow door that, at first, Allen did not see a way in. Then, when it opened a crack and he glimpsed Barbara's yellow silk skirts, he sprang forward into a dim hallway and slammed the door shut behind him. He entered a corner of the Stone Gallery, and with Barbara's dress providing a beacon ahead, he followed her through the crowds of promenaders. She did not look back as she quickly slipped into an alcove. As he hastily caught up, he bumped into her while she pulled aside a hanging and slid a key into a small door.

"A way to the maids of honor's rooms." Barbara turned the well-oiled lock and took a lantern from a high shelf just within the passage. "From there, we will enter Her Majesty's apartments. The king waits for us. No one will know you have visited."

"Why the secrecy, Aunt? William did not share with me the reason." Allen ducked his head as they made their way down the dim passage. A few lanterns glowed in small bricked niches, but there were puddles of darkness between each lamp. The air was stale, cold.

"The king is secretive with his plans. He does not encourage idle gossip about the Scottish cause."

"And I would raise suspicion?"

Barbara paused, lifting the lamp higher. In the candlelight, her eyes glowed luminously, and her high cheekbones cast hollows in her face, emphasizing her full mouth. She appeared fey, otherworldly. How much she resembled his mother. And yet, life's journey wrote a different story on her face.

"Anyone raises suspicion in the atmosphere of the court today, Allen. Rumors that the Scots are not accepting the king's will are flying from the lips of the gossips." She turned and opened a door onto a narrow staircase. "And they know my son serves the king on the border. Any news from Lord Grandison is worthy of speculation."

Allen grabbed the thick, twisted rope that served as a rail and carefully climbed the stairs, which were not cut to accommodate a man's foot in a great riding boot. As Barbara opened another door at the top, he blinked with the sudden rush of light. They stepped into a chamber draped with tapestries and a hundred candles burning to keep the mid-winter gloom at bay. A stuffy warmth and strong aroma of musk and attar of roses assailed him, the contrast from the cold corridor causing him to break a sweat. Really, these women went from one extreme to another. Frigid secret passages and stifling rooms.

He sighed and pulled his hat off again, running his fingers through his hair before putting it firmly back in place. This was getting wearisome.

"Come. William indicated your message must be delivered with all haste." Barbara beckoned him forward, and together they walked from the private maids of honor's rooms to the queen's chamber. A single guard stood outside, his eyes staring straight ahead. If he thought anything unusual of Allen's presence, he did not acknowledge it.

The king and queen sat, as if any normal couple, on a finely carved chaise by the ornate marble fireplace. The king, half-turned to Allen, was a slight figure, smaller than Allen remembered from the Richmond masque. His suit of red silk glowed in the roaring firelight, and his abundant hair tumbled over his shoulders. Next to him, the queen sat stiffly, her wide cream skirts glistening with pearls. She appeared doll-like, so tiny was she, her little feet barely touching the floor.

Several ladies were sitting by the graciously curved bay window, sewing by the last of the winter light that filtered through the diamond panes. A musician softly plucked at the strings of a lute, and several small dogs ran over to sniff Allen as he stood awkwardly by the door. One, a brown-and-white spaniel, yapped loudly and pissed on his boot.

"Richelieu! You are most impolite!" The king clapped his hands and waved at a page, who ran to Allen's side with a large cloth. The queen giggled. Allen suspected that the rapidity of mopping up and the underlying odor in the chamber signified this was not an unusual occurrence. He also noted the dog was named after King Charles's enemy during the siege of Saint-Martin-de-Ré.

Barbara took Allen by the arm and led him forward. He removed his hat and bowed deeply to the royal couple, remaining bent over as the king spoke.

"Allen Apsley." His voice was soft and musical. "The son of one of the noblest men I have ever known."

Allen stiffened, his heart leaping in his chest. *Steady, my son, steady. The king is an old friend. Remember you not the tales of the battle of Ré?*

"Stand up. And approach so I may see you better," the king commanded.

Walking closer to the king, Allen stopped a respectful five feet away from him. He bent his head, holding his hat awkwardly in both hands.

"Come closer. I do not want to shout. I hear you have traveled far with news from my nephew Villiers." King Charles looked Allen up and down, his searching gaze remaining for a moment on his face. He had a singularly mournful visage, his large brown eyes drooping at the corners. The lace at his neck was the finest Allen had ever seen.

"Your Majesty," Allen responded. "I have indeed come from the borders of Scotland." The fact that the king referred to his cousin William as a nephew did not escape him. All the Villiers children were as family to the Stuarts.

"My God, you have a look of your father about you." King Charles's voice was emotional. "He was a noble knight, young man, and a brave one. If not for him, we would have had suffered even more in the French War. Your father's careful planning saved many a life."

If not for his money, you would not have had your ships victualed and your men fed. The unpaid warrants still stung.

"Thank you, Your Majesty." Allen drew William's letter from his breast. "I have a message here from Lord Grandison. He commanded me to deliver this with haste, for your eyes only."

He bowed and handed it to the king, who remained sitting on the chaise. The queen stood and turned to Barbara.

"Let us leave the men to their talk of soldiers."

She walked to the window where the maids sat and picked up a book lying open on a bench. "Read to me, Barbara. I would hear more of Mr. Jonson, for his conversion to the true faith is a matter I greatly admire."

The king watched with affection as his wife and Barbara Villiers sat together, their heads close as they leaned over the pages.

"A good woman, your aunt," he remarked. "Trustworthy. Her son resembles her, and his dear uncle Buckingham." He opened the parchment and read it quickly before tossing the document into the cavernous fireplace, his luminous eyes fixed on the dancing flames.

Allen, not dismissed, stood uncomfortably. The exhaustion of the journey was creeping up on him, and the effort of courtly subterfuge, the fug of the room, and the plinking of the wretched lute were beginning to wear his patience. He shifted from one foot to another, causing the spaniel to yap again. Oh Lord. Not another piss.

His attention caught, the king turned his gaze back to Allen.

"So tell me, Mr. Apsley, your opinion." He gestured to the letter, curling and blackening in the fireplace. "William says the Scots are amassing on the borders. That he hears rumors of armies being raised. That there is great dissention in the Scottish parliament. That a mighty covenant is being formed."

"I know nothing of the parliament, sire. But there are signs of increased activity along the borders."

"And you think the Scots will invade England?"

"Yes, Your Majesty. They know we are few, spread thin. If I were their commanders, I would strike first."

The king frowned slightly and took a sip from a crystal goblet that was at his side. "Your father gave me much good intelligence when George Villiers and I planned the siege of Ré." He ran his finger around the rim of the glass, staring at the life-sized portrait of himself and Henrietta Maria that hung over the fireplace. Allen followed his gaze. In the painting, she handed her husband a laurel wreath.

"My father was a courtier from the days of Queen Elizabeth," replied Allen. "He was battle-worn, and a loyal subject to your father and to yourself, Your Majesty."

"That he was, Allen. That he was." The king turned, his eyes full of tears. "Those days, when your father and the Duke of Buckingham and I planned our expedition, those were like the stories of the days of old. We fought with God on our side to relieve a besieged people."

"Yes, Your Majesty." Allen was nonplussed. His father had spoken little of these times, the expedition itself being such a disaster, with so many men dying and the battle lost.

"As is the case in Scotland now." The king continued his musings. "These people are held captive by the ignorance of their Covenanters. They seek relief; I am sure of it."

Allen said nothing. There was no place for his opinion. The king was reaching a conclusion on his own.

A woman's voice broke into the quietness from across the room. The tone was deep and strong, and Allen turned, startled at who would interrupt the king.

"The bishops. They are warriors of God. You must support them." Queen Henrietta Maria was staring directly at her husband, her brown eyes glowing with a brilliant fervor. "The people need you to show them *la vraie foi*—the true faith."

"Maria, this is a delicate matter."

"It was not so delicate for your Scottish *grand-mère*, Queen Mary, *chéri*. She lived and died with God in her heart."

With a firm nod of her head that set the diamonds in her cap sparkling, the queen closed the conversation and resumed her reading with Barbara. Her outline against the window resembled that of an avenging angel in a cathedral window, rays of the setting sun radiating from behind her. Allen shuddered, as if a goose walked over his grave.

The king returned to his contemplation of the fireplace. "Just as Richelieu did at the Isle de Ré, the Scots are preparing for a siege. A siege to withhold against the true word of God." King Charles scooped up the spaniel and held the struggling dog in his arms before tossing it down again. The creature yelped and ran under the chaise. "Then, Allen, we shall do likewise. Ride back to William. Tell him that I shall come north. And bring with me God's army."

24

Yet about the year 1639, the thunder was heard afar off rattling in the troubled air, and even the most obscured woods were penetrated with some flashes, the forerunners of the dreadful storm which the next year was more apparent.

Luce Hutchinson
23rd January 1639

This, indeed, was happiness. Lucy surveyed her family gathered around the dining table. Luce and Allen side by side, inseparable as always. Sweet Babs, eyes large with wonder as her brother and Edward told of their adventures with the king's army. And now John at the table, his place next to Luce a welcome addition.

To have her children home together was a great blessing. Only James was absent, but Allen assured her that his heart was with his regiment, and in God's truth, she'd witnessed over and over the lure of the military to the men in her family. His was a well-trod path to manhood.

The moment Allen strode into the chamber was beyond price. Chilled, with coal smoke clinging to his traveling clothes, his presence filled the room. Grabbing a lantern from the mantel to illuminate Luce's face, Allen softly stroked his sister's cheek as tears ran down his own.

"It is a miracle," he whispered hoarsely. "The scars are not hideous, Luce. Even by this light, they do not shock me."

Luce smiled back at him and lifted her head proudly. "'Tis God's work, and the love and tender care of our family."

"I feared the worst deformity in you when Edward brought the news." Allen's voice broke. To be sure, her son wore his emotions on his sleeve and cared not for who saw them.

"Mother nursed me to health with her remedies of hartshorn and powder of myrrh. And Babs and John never left my door. It will be a long journey to restore my countenance, but one day, I will be as I was before."

John put his arm around his wife. "You are more than you ever were before, my love, for you fought a lethal battle with courage and endurance and survived with a badge of honor."

As Lucy swallowed tears at her son-in-law's touching words, Allen clasped John to him and hugged Babs. The room resounded with laughter and chatter. Sarah arrived with heaped dishes of capons and guinea fowl, salted herring, and a flagon of wine. Lucy looked around the festive table, committing to memory the precious sight of her family's happy faces.

"Marriage suits you, Sister," Allen set his knife down and pushed his empty plate away, the stripped bones of several birds evidence of a meal well enjoyed. Both he and Edward ate ravenously, and Lucy guessed their week on the Great North Road provided little in the way of sustenance. "You have a contentment about you I have not seen before."

Luce clasped John's hand and nodded. "Thanks be to God, the reason sits before you. Without John, I am not sure I would have survived the difficulties of the last year." A shadow crossed her face, and John lifted her hand to his mouth and kissed it softly. Such a simple, loving gesture.

"I am sorry to hear of your loss," Allen replied gently. "Mother wrote and told me of the twin babies that miscarried."

"It was not meant to be. They came too soon after my illness, and God took them for his own." Luce kissed John's hand in return. "But we are young and healthy, now. God will grant us future blessings, we are sure."

"To future blessings." Allen raised his goblet in a toast. "And to the king."

They echoed his words, for to drink to the king's health was a family tradition at every meal.

"To the king," repeated Edward, who sat on Allen's right. "And to our mission."

Edward's words jarred, for Lucy had yet to hear the reason of their return to London. These were the times she appreciated the closeness between her son and his cousin. Thank God for Edward, whose sensible head would always temper Allen's impetuous disposition.

Edward also pushed away his dish. Raising his glass to Luce and John, he turned to his cousin. "So, Allen, tell us of your experience at court today. How far did you get with the message from Lord Grandison?"

"Why, to the king's presence, of course," replied Allen. "It was simple enough once I reached William's mother."

A silence fell around the table, and Lucy gripped the edge of the table. How long before this talk of Whitehall and the court would not affect her? She suspected the mention of Barbara would always beget trouble. She met Luce's gaze and knew her daughter recollected the story of their old rivalry.

"And where was your audience with the king?" Lucy asked, forcing herself to sound natural. The royal court was her son's domain, his chosen world. She must allow him the freedom to talk, even if she despised it.

"In the queen's chambers. Aunt Barbara arranged it. She serves the queen now that the Earl of Suffolk has retired. They say he is exiled from court in his mansion on the Strand." Allen paused, changing the subject. "The king spoke of Father."

Lucy nodded slowly. So, it came to this. And a mention of Theo. The past was haunting her again. "They were close once."

"Why did you not tell us?" Allen and Luce spoke together, as they did so often.

"Your father wished all that behind him. His way was not the way of the corrupt court. Although he counseled the king and Buckingham, he did not embrace their morals. Besides, your father despised the Earl of Suffolk and would not tolerate his company." Lucy took a sip of her own wine, its warmth flushing her cheeks. "When Buckingham led the disastrous voyage to free the Huguenots in France, and failed with such loss of life, your father refused to speak of the horrors he witnessed."

"And yet, the king praised him and called him noble," Allen countered.

Lucy recalled a long-ago meeting in Whitehall between her husband, Buckingham, and the king. "He would. The king was inexperienced, unseasoned. Your father gave an indecisive young man with little courage the confidence to command an army." She paused, her thoughts in the past. "It was a tragedy that Buckingham did not have the experience nor the character to lead. Men such as your father paid a high price."

"And so perhaps the king wishes to make up for bygone mistakes," Allen mused. He poured another goblet of wine, slopping it as he misjudged the brim of the cup. Lucy motioned to Luce to move the flagon out of Allen's reach, and she did so without him noticing.

"What mean you, Allen?" John's question was quiet but direct.

Allen shrugged. "The king fights for his religious beliefs as did the French citizens of La Rochelle. Except, this time, he is eager for a victory that quashes the insurrection of the Covenanters and convinces them to accept the English prayer book. Maybe that is his way to avenge the deaths of the past. Including our father's." He drained the wine and slammed the cup on the table, making Luce jump.

"Insurrection?" repeated John. "A strong term for the actions of an independent authority that merely wishes to maintain its ancient laws and method of prayer."

"And an authority which questions the king's right to repossess lands that were once held by the Catholic Church," added Luce. "It seems appropriate the king's bishops are unwelcome in Scotland, for the country has enjoyed its own freedom of worship for many years. The Covenanters merely want to maintain the purity of the kirk."

"What?" cried Allen. "Purity? What say you, purity? Are these damnable Puritan opinions in our midst?" His words slurred.

"Allen, I think it is time for you to rest," Lucy interceded quickly. "It has been a long day, and you must be weary." She nodded at Edward, who stood and attempted to take Allen's arm.

"Leave me be, Cousin. I need no support from you." Allen pushed away from the table and lurched to the door. "'Struth, I ask again, what is this legacy from Leventhorpe Francke? I thought myself rid of his radical influence when I cast him out. I have entered a hotbed of Puritans in mine own home—"

"Allen, no," Luce soothed. "You misunderstand us. We are simply stating our belief in the Scottish right for free worship of their religion."

"And I am simply stating that I will carry out my orders from my sovereign, the king, to enforce his divine right to administer the church and land throughout England. And Scotland." Allen's shout drowned Luce's quiet voice. John stood now, his arm protectively around Luce, and the very air hummed with the emotion that suddenly boiled over.

Lucy fought the alarm surging through her. She slowly stood.

"What orders, Allen? What has the king commanded?"

Allen turned to her. "Why, to be a loyal citizen, Mother, and to follow in the footsteps of my noble father." He looked around the room at his family and swept an off-balanced bow. "We are preparing for war. I join William Villiers and the king himself in raising an army against the Scots."

Lucy's hand flew to cover her mouth, and she could only stare at Allen, his words echoing in her mind. Again? Again, a man she loved took up arms for this king? And James? He was but seventeen. Did he follow his brother to war? This could not be true.

John broke the shocked silence.

"It is war, Allen?" His voice was calm.

Allen turned to his brother-in-law and responded to the quiet words.

"If that is what it takes, then yes. I have seen for myself the king's resolve. He is not one who will be swayed from his purpose. And his purpose is to carry out the divine word of God and unite his kingdoms in a common prayer book and one religion, one administration." Allen rubbed his forehead tiredly. "I'm sorry. The day has been long. I must rest. We can talk more in the morning before I leave."

"You leave again, already?" Lucy picked the one phrase she could respond to.

"Tomorrow. The king requires me to return to William with his response." Allen looked at Luce and John. "I have no argument with you, Sister. I am just doing my duty to my king."

He left the room. Silence remained.

Edward kissed Luce and Lucy. "It is Allen. He speaks with his heart before his head. You know he will think differently when he awakes. I will ride back with him. I bid you good night."

Lucy sat again at the table, the scraps of the dinner a cruel testament to their happiness just a short time earlier. Always, this king seemed to destroy whatever joy she seized. He had robbed her of her husband. Now, his cause stole her sons. She looked up at Luce and John, tears blurring her sight. They stared back at her, clearly shocked at the abyss that had suddenly emerged within their family.

They were all so young, so innocent.

Allen rose early the next morning. Walking into the scullery in search of ale and bread, he found Sarah carving great slices of ham. His head pounded, and he gratefully accepted a chunk of bread and washed it down with a mug of cool ale.

"Your mother said to be sure to pack food for you and Master Edward," she said. "As if I'd let you go off to them heathen parts on an empty stomach."

Allen hugged her. "Sarah, you have always looked after us, as long as I remember."

"Aye, and I'll be here until they carry me out, so you come back from your adventures safe, otherwise you'll have me to answer to."

"I will. I promise. And you look out for my mother and Luce, please."

"You's got Mr. Hutchinson looking after them, now." Sarah nodded to the garden. "And he's up early hisself. He's a restless one as well."

Following her gesture, Allen blinked a few times, clearing his eyesight. John stood in the early morning sunshine, wrapped up in a greatcoat and brimmed hat. He was staring up at the chestnut trees, whose bare branches laced against the white morning sky. There was time before Allen left. Pulling on a cloak from the peg and lifting the latch, he walked outside into the frosty air.

His boots crunched on the gravel as he approached John. He stopped a few paces short, his breath clouding before him. The cold air cleared his thoughts. "I must talk with you, John."

John brought his gaze from the sky to Allen and smiled. "Do you feel better this morning, Brother?"

"I did not feel bad last night." Allen's words rushed to defend, as they did so often. "John, I have no personal grief with you. Lord knows you respect the right of our king as much as anyone. But I am sworn to serve the king, and that I will, just as my father did before me."

"Just as my father served, and as I serve too," replied John. He took a step toward Allen and held out his hand. "You caused no insult to me, Allen. Your time here is too brief for us to argue. And Luce needs no protection from me in your debates. She held her own long before I appeared."

Allen laughed and grasped John's hand in return. "That she has. You have married a fierce intellect there, and one well trained from a young age. I swear, when we were at our lessons, she would run rings around our tutors, putting James and me to shame many a time."

John smiled. "And that's why I love her. I would not quench that spirit for any family squabble." His face grew serious. "Walk with me a while. I

189

would hear more of your view on the king's troubles. Last night, you said war. How could this escalate?"

They walked to a narrow door cut in the wall at the end of the garden and let themselves out into the passage beyond. London was just stirring, the first cattle and carts being driven up the Holborn Hill to Smithfield Market. Choosing to stroll west toward Lincoln's Inn Fields, John and Allen fell into step through the awakening streets, each absorbed in their thoughts. On Chancery Lane, Allen stopped a pie man and bought hot pasties, handing one to John as he bit into the fragrant pastry, carefully preparing his words. John must understand his position.

"The king is insistent that the Scots accept his religious administration." Allen wiped crumbs from his mouth. "And Archbishop Laud is not going to retreat from his God-given role to enforce the king's rule. I was charged by my cousin Grandison to be a trusted messenger to the king. My news is fresh from the borderlands."

"But surely there is a way the king will accept the views of the Scots. It's the land of his birth, the land of his forebears. Does he not have a compassion for their independent ways?"

Allen paused, struggling to put into words the observations he had made during the last months.

"We know the king believes—above everything—in his divine right to rule. And that he represents the true religion, the best for his people. Archbishop Laud fans that flame until it burns blue in the heart of our monarch. That conviction is what dictates his actions, and in many ways, what compels men to follow him." Allen sighed. "Look, I know you and Luce question his devices, and would say that Parliament has a right in the governance of our country. My father served the king before me. My cousin Villiers is committed to the king's cause. I would serve him with the same dedication. The centuries of tradition our country is founded on rest on these simple dictates."

They approached the gate to Lincoln's Inn Fields. John pulled it open, and nodding to the watchman, they entered the quiet space.

"I always come here when I need to think," John said softly.

Allen looked at him. "Me too."

John smiled. "We are not so different, are we?"

"I think we are more alike than oft times we care to admit."

The two men walked the paths for a while in silence.

"So how long will you be gone, Allen?" In the quiet stillness of the ancient refuge, there was such peace, while beyond the green hedges, the sounds of a London fully awake chanted a distant hymn. Allen did not realize how much he'd missed the city until he found himself in these moments.

"Till the business is done. I hear next the king will ask his lords to muster their men—"

"He'll summon the nobles to bear arms?" John was shocked. "That hasn't been done by a monarch for centuries."

Allen kicked a stray pebble on the path. "The trained bands of militia are already on patrol around Berwick. The king does not have funds to raise a formal army and is reluctant to recall Parliament, for you know the tribulation that will bring. He's ruled without government for the past eleven years and continues to assume he can do so."

"This has gone much further than I feared. What else, Allen? What else do you know?"

Looking around him and confirming they were still alone, Allen lowered his voice. He repeated the words that William Villiers had revealed to him before he left Berwick. "Arundel will oversee mustering soldiers."

"Arundel? Arundel? He has no experience. What games is this king playing, moving troops around our country as if knights on a chessboard?" John snapped his mouth shut, emotions chasing across his normally calm features.

"It's a show of force, John. The king has no intention of going to war against his own people. He won't ask more of the cities or counties. He's relying on his nobles to support his cause. It's just a matter of assembling the companies at the border and presenting an argument that will convince the Scots into accepting the king's request."

"And if they don't?"

"They will. They have no alternative. They do not want war any more than we do." Allen looked up as the sun rose over the chapel in Lincoln's Inn Square. The bell struck nine, and its toll was echoed by the churches of St. Dunstan's and St. Clement's. "It is getting late. I must leave. Will you return to the house with me?"

"I will say my good-byes here, Allen." John's face was thoughtful. "I have business to attend to at the Star Chamber. I may as well continue."

191

"The Star Chamber? That is not a place I would think to find you, John."

He shrugged. "Needs is as needs must. I seek a position, for neither my father nor his estate provide an income, at present. Everything goes to his new wife and family, for he does not countenance George and me, nor our politics. The estate in Nottingham will be mine one day, but in the meantime, I must augment my income."

"I have a favor to ask of you while I am gone." Allen was reluctant to put this into words, but he could not leave without a commitment.

"Certainly. What is it?"

Allen looked out across the Fields. His eye was drawn to the lodging he had lived in with Edward when he was studying to plead before the judges at Westminster. How distant that time already seemed, how naïve his plan.

"The king is chronically short of funds. He has little access to money." He turned to John. "He is not going to make civil matters his priority when he has an army to feed."

"What means that for your mother?"

"She may have to go back to Francke to plead their suits again before Chancery." Allen fought down the old anger. "I would ask you to do all you can to prevent that, with your training here at Lincoln's Inn. And if you need to take her under your protection while I am gone, until I can bring this back to the king's attention, please do so."

"Without hesitation, Brother. She is as mine own mother. Rest assured that I will care for her and Babs."

Allen nodded. A raven hopped on the ground in front of him, its raucous caw immediately conjuring a memory of Tower Green. He shook the image from his head. He must be on his way.

"There is one final word." On the one hand, he was betraying his king's mission, the secrets that William entrusted him. On the other, this was his family's well-being at stake.

John looked at him intently. "What, Allen?"

"This may not end as quickly as we think. Or as cleanly." Allen paused, searching for the nuances. "If Parliament is summoned, the king will expect much of them."

"As Parliament will of him," John replied. "He cannot expect a sitting to be smooth after ruling for so many years without consulting them."

"Just be aware that the situation could be explosive. And if so, then please remove from London and take our family safely to your estates. The conflict between the city and Whitehall may be a violent one."

Allen could see the confusion on his brother-in-law's face. He had already said too much. Time to leave well alone.

"Good-bye, then." Allen briefly hugged John. "We have traveled far and fast since we first met at Richmond, my friend."

John did not question more. "So has the country, Allen." He clapped him on the shoulder. "Godspeed, Brother. Keep yourself safe as you carry out our king's mission, and may this come to a quick resolution. My prayers are with you. And keep that unpredictable temper of yours—"

"I know, I know, under check." Allen laughed. "And you keep Luce well, John."

"Always. We share a common soul; our life is as one." John smiled.

There was his friend, the man who fell in love with the character of his sister before he even saw her. Allen nodded. "We are joined as family, now. Let us not be divided over England's squabbles."

25.

The gentleman who had professed so much love to my mother, in her absence had been, by most vile practices and treacheries, drawn out of his senses, and into the marriage of a person, whom, when he recovered his reason, he hated.

Luce Hutchinson

14ᵗʰ April 1639

Lucy slipped from the house, leaving Luce and Babs to their tasks. Just going to Blackfriars, she told them. Simply visiting the apothecary, replenishing her supplies. Her heart beat fast at the lie. And at the end of Fetter Lane, instead of turning left and crossing by Shakespeare's house into Blackfriars, she turned right toward the Strand and Suffolk House.

She did not need to reread the message commanding her to Theo's side, for the words repeated themselves with each step. *Come, Titania. Come, for I am not long for this world, and I would see you one more time. My conscience demands it. Do not deny a dying man absolution.*

Delivered that morning, the messenger wordlessly handing her the missive and departing.

Suffolk House was a great monolith of a building facing onto the Strand, close on Charing Cross, back to the river. Two quarter-hour chimes rang from St. Martin's Church, and still she stood across the busy thoroughfare, staring up at the building. Thirty-six huge windows. A gatehouse four stories high, topped by a fierce black lion. Turreted towers on each corner. And a deathly stillness over the mansion, for in the time she paused, no one came or left.

Which window concealed Theo? And what was his message for her? She could still leave. She could leave the past, as she had before. *Do not deny a dying man absolution.*

She owed him nothing. But to herself, perhaps she owed something.

The servant who answered the gatehouse door was untidy, his livery stained. He showed little interest as she announced herself. And as he led her into the central courtyard, the building quadrupled in size; each face presented to her another thirty, sixty, ninety windows. Entrances every few

194

yards indicated private apartments, and it was to the very end, to the southwest corner, that she was led. The servant flung open the door and gestured for Lucy to enter into darkness. A stale smell of unaired rooms and a sharper odor of something more unpleasant greeted her.

"He's upstairs."

A silence settled in, and her footsteps echoed loud on the wooden floors. She glimpsed the ground-floor receiving rooms but could make out little in the gloom, for the shutters were closed, and there appeared to be no furniture. Upstairs, the only open doorway diffused light from the south, and she walked in, heart racing.

Theo reclined on a daybed facing the window, a tapestry draped over him. That, and a small side table and chair were the only pieces of furniture in the large chamber. A few poor paintings were hung on the walls. The fireplace was empty, and the remains of a meal along with a large flagon of wine stood on the table.

Theo stirred. "What do you want, Dickon? And I sent for more wine. Where is it?"

Lucy walked forward slowly. He did not turn, and so she had the advantage of gazing upon his profile before he saw her. His skin was a sickly yellow, and his auburn hair was now gray and thin. The hand that rested on the counterpane trembled.

"Theo. Theo, it is I."

"My God, Lucy. Titania. You came." His old voice for a moment, a rich timbre that she'd once loved. "I did not think you would."

"I could not ignore your plea." Lucy crossed to the window, and he struggled to sit upright before falling back on the grubby pillows. "What has happened to you, Theo? This jaundice, these terrible conditions . . ." Her words failed as she looked around the derelict chamber.

His smile was a grimace, for the flesh had fallen from his bones. "I am ill, Lucy. My physicians say my time is come."

"Did you contract a malady abroad?" Her experienced eye told her otherwise.

He shrugged. "Of the temperament, perhaps. I have not been careful with my health, nor my finances. Now both appear to have ruined me."

"But your children?" Lucy hesitated. "And Barbara?"

His smile disappeared. "I am of no use to any of them. They do not care what happens to me. My debts far exceed my income, and nothing remains of my estate. And I am retired from court, for I cannot maintain that life."

Lucy took his hand and noticed the liver marks scattered across the skin.

Theo looked up at her. "You would not have deserted me, would you, Lucy?"

She could not answer. There was no benefit to reliving the past. And destiny was already written at birth. Their path was never meant to be.

"What did you want to tell me, Theo?" If she could help him prepare to his afterlife by relieving his conscience, she would do so, for the sake of all that he had once been to her.

He pulled her hand to his mouth and, with dry lips, brushed it with a kiss. All she felt was pity.

"I would say that I repent of all the pain I have caused you, Lucy. I repent of the deceit, the lies, and the damage I brought about." He moved under the carpet and grimaced. "I thought I could run your world as I ran mine. I thought your desires would usurp your integrity. But, in the end, I ruined your reputation; I married another and made your sister my mistress."

Yes. You did. And if not for her husband's generosity and faith in her, Lucy would be an outcast, exiled from court, with no family or children. True, her life had not been easy, but the thought of a shadow court life with Theo over the joys of her marriage and her children could not be contemplated. That, more than anything, filled her heart with generosity.

"I absolve you of the hurt you caused. And there is no taint remaining. My son serves with his cousin, Barbara's boy. And although we do not speak, there is no hatred left in my heart for her." She took her hand from his and smoothed his brow. The flesh was clammy, cold. He closed his eyes.

"One more thing I have to say, Lucy."

He tired. His eyes wandered to the flagon and she guessed he was craving a drink of wine. This was a symptom of the corporal disease, an unending thirst for alcohol.

"I must go soon, Theo. What else do you wish to tell me?"

He licked his lips. "That time I saw you in Bishop's Stortford. With the Puritans. And I warned them away."

"Yes, I remember it well."

"Those times are a hundredfold worse upon us. I still have my spies about court. And the queen's priest attends me each week." He crossed himself in the old way. His other hand clasped a crucifix against his breast. "There will not be a peaceful resolution to this conflict between king and country, Lucy. And London is in the heart of the argument."

She nodded, not wanting to break his train of thought. He was weakening and becoming more distracted with each word.

"Leave, Lucy. Leave this city, if you can, and take your children. Go back to Lydiard, or find a safe harbor in the country, far from Whitehall and Westminster and the king and Parliament." His breathing was hard now. His bloodshot eyes flickered to the door as the servant entered with a flagon of wine. "Barbara chooses to stay. Her son and the court mean everything to her. If you need help, go through him. A conflict comes, and danger stalks the citizens of this city. Leave. Leave London. And do not return."

As she bent to kiss his forehead, she caught the whisper of his final words. "And leave me. Leave me."

Luce's mother insisted they leave, insisted danger to Luce's unborn child lurked in the very air of Bartlett's. She was unrelenting that John find them a home away from London, and quickly. Luce had not witnessed such determination since the Westminster hearings. And all because her mother was warned that plague stalked the city. She remembered the day her mother returned from the apothecary at Blackfriars, distracted and disturbed, telling them she had heard of men dying on the steps of St. Anne's Church, seeking shelter but instead gaining entry to the kingdom of heaven.

By May, Luce found herself reclining on the mattress of the tawny bed in the back of a canopied cart, surrounded by hampers and baskets, linens and coverlets. With every rattle, every bump, she was reminded that the child she carried inside her was more precious than the material comforts of home. Still, she could not but help feel so guilty that she was responsible for her family's flight.

Worse, she was committing Babs to an unknown life in the country, far from her friends and her familiar surroundings. She hoped to God that the house John rented was not like Newington Barrow—dilapidated, forgotten, with a cheap rent and no amenities.

Gazing south toward a bank of dark clouds that settled behind the spire of St. Andrew's, she swallowed to dislodge the lump in her throat. Silently, she bade good-bye to the church where she married, in the parish where she first dwelled with John.

"It is no more than a three hours' ride," John reassured as he rode up alongside her, his bay stallion controlled under his firm rein. Such beautiful hands, such a caring man. Luce could not have wished for a more attentive husband. The moment her mother expressed concern about Luce's health and that of his child, he was off. For three days, he relentlessly rode the villages and towns that lined the Great North Road, stopping at inns and churches, asking if any knew of a home to rent. And in his determined way, on the fourth day, he found the Blue House on Enfield Chase, close by Barnet.

"It is sturdy and gracious, and sits high on a knoll," he'd told them when he'd returned, lease in hand. "There is no damp from the woods nor mold from the river. The house has been well maintained, and there is a garden."

"But where is this place?" Babs had asked petulantly. Her mother had looked at her sharply.

"It is not far—less than half a day's ride, Babs. If you pine to be here with your friends, I can escort you to stay for a few days. And this is not for long, just until the plague subsides and the air is clean again."

Luce sighed and eased her back. A pot had escaped from a basket and the handle was digging into her side. This was by no means the most elegant way to travel, but her mother forbade her from riding. She longed to be free and ride with the rest of her family and not be stowed in with the household effects like an old woman.

She gazed steadily from the back of the cart as the road stretched behind them. The spires of London faded into the western horizon. A dark shape appeared on the road, moving quickly toward them. Troops again. This was more than happenstance. She watched as yet another throng of horsemen caught up with them, slowed to a walk, and passed by in a jingle of harnesses. There must have been five or six such groups that had traveled the Great North Road in the past two hours—men in armor and great battle coats, riding huge war horses caparisoned and tacked with rich cloths and shining leather. No one journeyed south. All rode north. Luce wondered if the soldiers were joining her brothers and Edward. She sent a prayer along with the travelers as they cantered on ahead.

Gradually, the houses appeared farther apart, and within the hour, they were in a woodland, the city forgotten. The loamy green fragrance of new growth filled Luce's senses. Birdsong washed over her, echoing through the ancient trees, and John broke into a merry melody. Babs joined him, her sweet voice harmonizing with his. Luce dozed, her hand on her belly. If they were all together, they would create a home wherever they landed.

She started, John's shout echoing back from the head of their little procession.

"We're here! Welcome to the Blue House, my darlings!"

He was so proud. And rightly so. Before them stood a comfortable, newly-built manor house, square on a rise, with an iron gate and neat wall around. A pale blue lime wash caught the late westerly sun rays, turning the home a delicate mauve, reflecting the lavenders that tumbled over the stone paving. To the south, an apple orchard frothed white with a mass of blossoms. A blackbird warbled his evensong, and a thrush responded in harmony.

"It's beautiful, John." Relief flooded her. "A perfect place for our son to be born." Luce turned to her sister. "Babs, it will be like Richmond. We can picnic on the heath, and look—I see a church tower just across the chase. There must be a town there, where we will find friends, I am sure."

Her mother nodded approvingly. "It is well situated. The air is fresh, and the soil is fertile. Luce will carry her child to term safely here." She turned to John. "You have done well to find this for us, my son. Thank you."

John dismounted and helped Luce climb down from the cart. She was stiff from the journey and a little light-headed as she stood up. He caught her as she swayed and tenderly wrapped his arm around her. Together, they walked to the front door.

The decision to move to the Blue House was a good one, and as she watched her daughter thrive in the fresh country air, Lucy knew she had been right to insist they were safer outside of the city. Theo's message weighed heavily on her mind, and the pregnancy was a perfect excuse to move without worrying Luce. Now, as her daughter's time approached, Lucy's thoughts drifted to the future. Life was simple here, quiet. She sensed John was feeling a similar calmness.

She stood by the fire, rubbing her hands together to dispel the October chill. John was seated in Luce's chair, a holdover from Richmond, clutching her pillow to his chest.

"The Blue House has been a haven you have secured for us," Lucy said.

"I promised Allen I would take care of you." John sat up straight and adopted a dignified tone. "You and your daughters are well provided for."

"And for that, I thank you, John. I am grateful we are in your trusted hands until Allen has established his place at court." She paused. The night grew dark around them. There was silence upstairs, no sound from Babs nor Luce. An air of expectancy lingered, and she sent a prayer to heaven for the safety of her daughter in her impending ordeal.

Setting a taper to the fire, she lit several lamps around the room. A warm glow encircled them. Her place was to keep John calm, for it would not be long before Luce's labor started.

"Have you thought of the future, John?" she inquired. "Your studies at Lincoln's Inn are over. And you are not yet sworn to the Star Chamber."

John nodded seriously. He waved his hand at the bookshelves surrounding them. The owner of the house had left a stack of books along with the furniture.

"Here is but a small sampling of a library," he replied. "My father has nigh on two thousand books at our home in Nottingham, all devoted to divinity and the study of the word of God. He promised to me one day." She watched as his face lit up with excitement. He was certainly her daughter's husband, and each day, she saw why Luce had fallen in love with him.

"And you would study divinity? And live your life away from court? A life spent under the tenets of the Puritan philosophy appeals to you more than sitting in the Star Chamber and passing judgment on men?"

John nodded again. His cheeks were flushed, and he blinked a few times before continuing, as if gathering courage. "I have hired a tutor, one of the best in the south, to teach me divinity and philosophy. If I am to inherit one of the finest libraries in the kingdom, I must know how to understand its contents."

Lucy nodded. She knew what was coming, and spared him the difficulty of breaking the news to her. "And you would move back to Nottingham and devote your life to the study of God's word? Has your father made provision for an income? I had not heard."

John nodded, a grateful smile breaking out across his handsome features. "You know that the Manor of Owthorpe is mine, as his oldest son. The estate is more than two hundred acres and generates a fine income. The hall's tenants are leaving, and the time approaches when my father will wish me to return."

This was where life was leading. Perhaps this opportunity to start afresh was a destiny determined by Theo, his parting gift. "Do you intend to travel to the north soon, John? The land is quite wild there, I hear."

John laughed. "Nottingham is a very pleasant town, Mother. A thriving city with fine houses and culture. I would not take Luce to a barren outpost. Most importantly, our home is far from court and the sycophants and falseness that prevail in that world."

Lucy nodded. "You make a good provision for my daughter. My heart is content that you care for her so. Babs and I will return to Bartlett's, when the pestilence has left.

He looked at her with surprise. "But you both will come with us, won't you?" He leaned forward and grasped her hands. "Your home is with us. We are a family now."

Tears filled Lucy's eyes. Such a good man. She ducked her head, unable to speak.

John continued, "I am no soldier, such as Allen. It will be a quiet life. I prefer to grapple with the words of the ancient philosophers than the clubs of the Scots."

Lucy laughed with him. "And yet, you are a skilled swordsman. I've heard Allen say you would fell any man at court should he taunt you for your bookish ways."

John placed his goblet down by the fireplace and pushed back his long hair from his forehead. His voice grew serious, sober. "I may be learned, but that does not make me a dullard, nor reluctant to defend my beliefs or my family. Besides, my father grows old, and I must be prepared to not only inherit his library, but to run his estate and be responsible for the people who live there."

There appeared a new maturity in John's voice.

"Your father remains in Nottingham. And yet he represented the county in Parliament at Westminster. Does he ever come back to London?"

"Not for any length of time since the last Parliament assembled. And yet . . ."

"Yet what?"

"And yet, he wrote me this past week to state the king may have to recall Parliament. And if that happens, he will take up residency in London again."

"Do you think Allen's mission on behalf of the king to muster the nobles may not be successful? That the king must resort to calling Parliament to fund his Scottish wars?"

"There are many grievances that must be settled first before the Parliament will grant the king any money. The members are angry. Those discussions will be fierce—" John broke off as Babs burst into the parlor.

"Luce's pains are starting, Mother. She calls for you."

John's eyes widened, and he clutched the arm of Luce's chair.

"Ride for the midwife, John, and return with her quickly." Lucy pushed her sleeves up from her arms and quickly kissed his cheek. "Tonight, your son will be born."

26

The king had upon his heart the dealings both of England and Scotland and harboured a secret desire of revenge upon the godly in both nations, yet had not courage enough to assert his resentment like a prince, but employed a wicked cunning he was master of, and called kingcraft.

Luce Hutchinson
4th August 1639

Allen shifted his position on the city wall at Newcastle, the dark town at his back, the woods beyond the clearing concealing God knew what enemy. The Scots were on the move. Twenty thousand of them pouring over the border, according to their briefing that morning. Now, at midnight on August 28, Lord Conway convened a council of war in this city, and his colonel, Sir Jacob Ashley, was readying them to defend Newcastle to the death.

This instant was the pinnacle of Allen's life. The swordplay with the yeomen at the Tower. His father's lectures on keeping a cool head and hand. The interminable training last summer in the Berwick shithole. And six months drilling with William in the tiltyards of Whitehall. All led to this moment.

He turned his head and grinned at Edward, crouching next to him behind the parapet by the West Gate. His cousin nodded. Reunited that week when assigned to Ashley's brigade, they fell immediately into their old ways, as if never separated.

Squinting over the battlements to troops positioned in St. John's Yard, Allen looked for James. The shadows were too deep on this moonless night. He was well taken care of under Goring's command. A relief, really, that someone else was responsible for disciplining his younger brother. James was becoming a firebrand, his youthfulness always spoiling for a fight.

All afternoon, a deep booming of artillery fire from the battlefront reminded them of how close the Scots were. Come nightfall, the cannon quietened, but cessation did not bring the relief Allen wished for. The silence was ominous. He'd heard tell of these moments, veteran troops describing the minutes before battle when a calm descended. Men's thoughts turned inward or flew to their families. Talk revolved around home. Or jokes were shared to avoid the specter of fear.

"So, Luce is happy?" Edward whispered, his voice distinct across the few feet between them. The time must have been close to two in the morning by now. Still no sign of messengers or troops outside the walls. Still the council met.

Allen dragged his thoughts back to Edward's question, remembering the letter the messenger had brought that afternoon.

"Yes, Luce is very happy. Her twin boys are healthy. And John dotes on her."

Edward nodded. "He is a good match for her."

"He is." Allen peered out at the forest. In the dark, the woods crept closer to the walls, menacing. "Not what I would have wanted for her, him also being so serious, God-fearing. But he is reliable and loyal. Perhaps, after the childhood we lived, that decided her. And she loves him very much."

"Anyone who reads a book for pleasure is serious in your view." Edward cast an eye over the woods and suddenly tilted his head, alerted by a movement. "Did you see that?"

"What?" Allen peered through the darkness.

"There." Edward transferred his weight and pulled the musket up to his shoulder. "A line of horsemen, breaking from the forest."

Allen heard others along the wall shift and the clatter of metal on stone as muskets were raised and steadied on the ramparts. A dozen or so soldiers galloped toward the city walls, their dark cloaks streaming behind them. Moments later, the great oak gates were winched open, followed by the creak of the iron doors and hooves striking cobblestones.

"Which way to Colonel Ashley?" a voice shouted, urgent in its lack of caution.

Shouts responded, and the horses cantered toward the King's Hall. Allen and Edward glanced at each other and then looked again to the west. Something was about to happen. Allen braced himself and uttered a quick prayer for Luce and his mother. His father's voice echoed in his mind. *Steady, my son, steady.* He watched and waited.

Within minutes, news spread with the swiftness of embers riding the wind. Whispers scurried back and forth across the ramparts, swirling like fog wraiths around his head. He knew not what to believe, each staccato statement bringing a new lurch to his belly.

"The Scots have broken through."

"They invade England. War is upon us."

"There's been a great battle fought at Newburn."

"We leave. We do not stay to defend Newcastle."

The last news hit him as a hammer. Retreat? *Retreat?* His own shock was reflected in Edward's face.

"Muster! Muster!" The shout echoed around the town walls. At the command, Allen and Edward sprang to their feet, staggering slightly as they stood for the first time in hours. Following their comrades, they raced to the King's House, where the council met.

"We leave now," shouted Colonel Ashley, standing on the steps, lit by the orange glare of blazing torches. His booming voice commanded silence among the troops. "The Scots approach. They avoid Berwick and head for Newcastle. Twenty thousand of them. They crushed our men at Newburn and are now no more than five miles away."

"If we leave, they will overrun the city," Allen muttered to Edward.

"If we stay, we will all be slaughtered," Edward responded.

"We withdraw to Durham immediately. Their advance guards ride hard. The artillery is not far behind." Sir Jacob mounted his horse and signaled for his troop to form. "Foot soldiers, gather your packs and assemble here to depart in a quarter of an hour. Cannon, horse, you join us too. Lord Goring and his troops ride ahead of us. Our only hope is to retreat and meet the king and his army, who advance to York. We must march fast. We leave, and leave now."

Allen grabbed Edward's arm. "James has already left. We must follow him, straightaway."

Together, they sprinted across the square, dodging through the chaotic crowd of townspeople who had turned out of their beds at the commotion. When news spread of the retreat, a great wailing and sobbing broke from their throats as they begged the troops not to abandon them to the marauding Scots army. Allen's heart wrenched at a woman with two young boys pleading with a soldier to take them along, trying to save her sons from the inevitable slaughter.

Allen paused for a moment, unsure.

Edward pushed him forward. "We have to leave."

"But—"

"We cannot help all of them, Allen. We must obey the command. The king needs us."

Grabbing their packs from the billet, Allen and Edward fell into formation with the rest of Ashley's brigade. James was ahead somewhere, already safely out of the path of the advancing Scots. The city gates swung open again, and three thousand men marched across the bridge over the River Tyne, leaving Newcastle defenseless to face the Scottish army.

By the time they crossed the moors, Allen had been able to piece together the events of the week and understand the hopelessness of their situation. This was reinforced even more by the company of the battle-wounded from Newburn, bundled into a line of drays that trundled alongside his dispirited troop. These men groaned and cried aloud as the carts lurched along the rough tracks, with wounds such as he had never imagined.

He had witnessed army men begging on the streets of London, missing a leg or an eye, a knot tied in breeches or a puckered scar signifying the extent of the wound. These marks were commonplace. For God's sake, even his father, fighting at Ré with the Duke of Buckingham, had returned home with a consumption that killed him, sparing his family the trauma of absent limb or mutilated face.

But these men were war personified, in all its horror. The great gouge of a sword thrust, evidenced by a blood-soaked bandage stuck to a man's heaving chest. An arm's stump, hewed above the elbow. A shattered thigh, white bone splinters circling a black bullet hole. And in the heat of the day, when the carrion crows circled overhead and the stink of shit and blood mingled with the sweat of the living, Allen choked on the vomit that rose in his throat.

Then came the death carts. Men heaped three, four deep, arms dangling, heads lolling, eyes staring to the sky. Every so often the drivers paused, and a lifeless soldier was hauled from the wounded to the dead, hurriedly slung on top of the pile so as not to slow down the march.

His throat stung with acid from his empty stomach. A fresh wind sprang up from the west, and he turned his face to suck in the air, gulping great breaths to calm his nerves.

Those boys, those two young lads standing in front of their mother in the Newcastle square. Were they alive? Or was their fair-haired innocence already ravaged by a Scottish blade?

It was sixty miles from Durham to York. Sixty miles of unrelenting marching, right foot, left foot, right foot, left. A convoy of defeated men and dying heroes. God's blood, there was no glory in retreat. Where now were the rewards, the titles, and patronage from Lord Goring? What use were these family connections if they ignored relatives in these times of need? Even Cousin William had been one of the first to leave. He rode ahead of them, James caught up somewhere with the dragoons.

Edward nudged him. Ahead, across a final vale, the towers of York Minster skewered the pale dawn sky, the pinnacles sword-thrusts into the body of heaven. And from where they stood, all the way to the city walls were fields of tents and men as far as they could see. This was a force indeed. And English, not Scots. For the first time in days, Allen's heart lifted.

"Names!" A soldier with a clerk seated next to him barked a command as they entered a field crushed full of militia. On the makeshift table, a sheaf of parchment ruffled in the breeze, weighted by a stone. The muster lists were formidable.

"Allen Apsley."

"Edward St.John."

They spoke simultaneously and were pushed through into the meadow, the next men and the next recorded into the muster. Finding a patch of grass close by a stream that flowed at the boundary, they threw down their packs and dropped to the ground.

The march was over. Newcastle and Durham had been handed to the Scots. But with the force assembled here, they could advance again. Now, to find James, unite with the king and exact retribution upon the Scots.

After a month camping in the field outside of York, the mood of the men soured. Allen and James watched as yet another group walked brazenly from the pasture, their belongings slung over their shoulders. No longer concealing their desertion, these men were heading back to their homes for the winter. And who could blame them?

"Jesu, is there war or not?" Allen exploded as he stuffed a turpentine-soaked rag into the barrel of his matchlock musket and rubbed the weapon vigorously. Target practice. If he had to clean the gun once again before firing it for real at a Scottish arse, he would turn it on himself.

"Still no word, Brother?" James looked up from his perch on a stool, where he'd been kicking his heels in rhythm to the strains of the fife and drums. Drilling was now demanding hours each day, and his platoon was resting briefly before being summoned back for another round of maneuvers. "You should consider joining me in the dragoons. We are being primed for action. Not like your foot patrols."

Allen scowled at his younger brother. James had grown this last year, both physically and in cockiness.

"You're not going to like what I heard, then," Edward announced. He'd walked up just as Allen spat on the engraved silver inset in the handle and polished furiously with his sleeve.

"Now what?" Allen slammed the gun down. He wiped the sweat from his forehead. This northern sun was brighter, hotter than the gentle orb that warmed London's misty skies. Even in October it made the middens stink.

"The king is reconciled to a negotiation." Edward picked up the musket and held up the barrel, squinting down it. "You missed a bit." He handed the gun back to Allen, who snatched it from him.

"A negotiation? What the hell does that mean?" What kind of decision was a negotiation when the king amassed twenty thousand men within striking distance of the border and loyal Highlanders commanded ships along the coast from Berwick to Aberdeen?

"I just came from William's briefing," replied Edward. "We are to prepare to welcome the Scottish representatives and escort them to safe passage. The king negotiates a settlement."

"This cannot be," cried Allen. "We are no longer a band of untrained recruits. We have a fighting unit, ready to enforce the king's word. To negotiate now would be to lose any leverage we have."

Edward shrugged. "Our small platoons have discipline and training. But most of the men—those who are left—are inexperienced, reluctant.

The king realizes that he cannot deploy an army of complete amateurs. We'd all get slaughtered."

"We can train them. Look at what Lord Goring's commanders have put in place for discipline now." Allen was frustrated beyond means. All this time wasted, this effort for naught.

"Allen, most of the men from the country don't even have weapons. And those who do, walk with bows and arrows. The king uses this show of manpower as a tactic to extract a settlement from the Scots. And besides, he's already offered them."

"What?"

"The agreement terms. The king proclaimed that if Scotland settles and order is restored within the kingdom, he will not pursue force. And he will insist the English Parliament pay for his war."

"You've learned a lot in the last few hours." Allen squinted up at his cousin. Edward had proven a head for tactical thinking, and William was inviting him to many of his briefings.

Edward nodded. "William and the Earl of Holland ride across the border to issue the pardon to the Covenanters. And the army leaders come here to treat with the king."

"Under what terms?" Allen asked with disgust. So much for mustering a fight to unite the kingdoms.

"No more rebellions, accepting the king's will, disbanding the Covenanters—"

"Hush!" James jumped from the wall and lifted his hand. "Hush. What is that sound?"

Edward and Allen turned. Through the still afternoon drifted the wailing of bagpipes and the regular thump of marching feet. Louder and closer, the pipes now filling the air with a sound like no other Allen had heard before. Over the brow of the hill appeared first a dozen and a dozen more, and then a full band of Scottish fighters, pipes playing, drums beating, and their kilts swaying to the pace. The wail of the bagpipes resonated deep within his chest, and as the rebels marched by them toward the town, he let out a breath he was hardly aware he had been holding.

Edward moved first.

"Looks as though the negotiations are starting." He looked at James. "Want to come with me and see what we can do to prepare? There'll be more where those came from. I could use the help."

James's face lit up, and he fell into step with Edward. Together, they strode across the field and turned toward York. Allen was left alone, the musket lying useless by his side. War was averted. Parliament would surely see the king's side of the situation and release funds to pay reparation to the Scots. He would think about riding back to London. William was bound to be back at court soon too, and there was always a place with the princes.

Life went on. Perhaps he'd stay with Luce and John for a while on his way back. The Blue House sounded pleasant, and it would be good to enjoy some of Sarah's cooking again.

And the future? Allen shrugged and picked up his musket. He could put that weapon away in favor of his dress sword.

27

The parliament, beset with so many difficulties, were forced for their own vindication to present the king with a petition and a remonstrance of the state of the kingdom, wherein they spared him as much as truth would bear, and complained only of his ill counsellors and ministers.

Luce Hutchinson
17th March 1641

Leaving the twins at the Blue House with her mother was like severing a limb. But both Luce and John agreed that the city was no place for their precious boys, and when John's father had insisted that they come to visit him while he was in London for the opening of Parliament, they'd invited Babs to join them. George had accompanied his father from Nottingham, and Luce knew it would mean so much to her sister to see John's lighthearted brother again.

And here they were, riding through the narrow streets of Holborn, St Andrew's spire a welcome sight above the jumble of roofs. Something was different, though—a sense of watchfulness, unease—as they approached Sir Thomas's house. On the street corners, groups of soldiers in the king's livery stood idle and watched as the citizens went about their business. And by St. Dunstan's Church, a crowd of black-clothed Puritans huddled in the yard. As Luce rode past, she glimpsed a man in the stocks, pamphlets stuffed in his mouth. Horrified, she caught John's eye and gestured at the scene. John frowned and shook his head, kicking his horse forward. Within minutes, they arrived at Sir Thomas's home.

The ride shook Luce, for never had she witnessed London as on edge as the city was that day. Safely inside the house, she, John, and Babs joined Sir Thomas in the dining room. The unease in the city was making itself felt in Parliament, too. According to John's father, the list of grievances presented to the king was far beyond anything that he or his fellow members ever anticipated. And to hear his disgust at the dinner table that evening, Luce wondered if this was the biggest insult to the king in living memory. She listened as John tried to reason with his father.

"These members of Parliament are concerned that the king is ill-advised."

"And so they threaten to impeach Archbishop Laud? The king's own chaplain? The queen's confidante?" Sir Thomas Hutchinson was purple with rage. He was in a foul humor, and Luce widened her eyes at Babs across the table. The house in Holborn was large, well proportioned, and comfortably furnished, as befitted a respected member of Parliament. It was just a pity that the conversation was not as hospitable. She was not sure she could stand to hear more of her father-in-law's declarations. Only the prospect of seeing Allen at Whitehall the next day kept her from leaving again, pleading the excuse that her boys needed her.

"The king opened Parliament with his acknowledgement that there were grievances that he would hear from his members," John pointed out, his tone mild.

"And then the whole damned lot of them stood up with their list of woes! Lord Digby from the West. Edward Hide from the North. Culpeper speaking for Kent. And then Hide again on ship money."

"They have been silenced for more than eleven years, Father. The king has refused to listen to his people."

Sir Thomas ignored him and continued speaking. Luce could feel John's frustration from across the table. "And then this religious business. The declaration that our own English ministers have been oppressed by Laud and the bishops—"

"True," murmured John.

"And to challenge the intent of Archbishop Laud to bring peace across the three kingdoms—"

"It is not his place, nor any of the bishops, to rule on policy once they wear the bishop's hat. It is a miter, not a crown."

This was the John Luce knew of old from the debates at Richmond, when her cousin Villiers challenged his views.

"Enough!" roared Sir Thomas. "Do I have a heretic for a son?"

John bowed his head. When he raised it, tears glistened in his eyes. She and Babs dared not say a word.

"Father, salvation lies in the doctrine of our church. At the king's request, these bishops and Archbishop Laud would have us swear an oath designed to blow up our Protestant religion. The Parliament and the king should govern together for the betterment of our citizens. Not in exclusivity. That is all. That is all these men are saying."

No one moved as John and his father stared at each other. George cleared his throat.

"Let us remember we have our new family here with us, and not dredge up old arguments."

Sir Thomas nodded abruptly. "These are not matters for women's ears."

"Do not trouble yourself that you have offended us," Luce rushed to confirm George's point. "Debate about the rights of worship is always lively in our home."

"So that is where my son learns his radical ideas? Your household, madam, seems a viper's nest of twisted thought." Sir Thomas pushed his chair away from the table. "Not even mentioning that your cousins, Oliver St.John and Oliver Cromwell, lead this group of miscreants. I think it best you excuse yourselves, for I do not wish to hear extreme Puritanical tenets under my roof."

He left the room, and shortly after, the door slammed. John dropped his head into his hands and rubbed his face wearily.

"We see less eye to eye than ever," he sighed. "My father represents Nottingham, but I do not think he speaks for the men of the county. He puts the king's interests before those of the citizens."

"Should we leave, John? I do not want to offend your father more." Luce felt ill with anxiety, somehow feeling responsible for the rift within her family.

"No. He will calm down. Besides, he leaves early for Westminster, and tomorrow you see Allen. You do not want to miss him. Too much time has passed. After that, you and Babs return home to the peace of the Blue House."

"You do not come with us?"

"I want to hear more of the proceedings, Luce. Our future is bound up in these debates, and I would hear firsthand the grievances, not my father's interpretation of what he wants to hear." Shadows from the fire flickered over John's face. "These are my friends and neighbors he is representing. I fear he is aloof from their needs. When I return to

Nottingham, I want to be sure I understand what the country is asking of the king."

Through the silence, the watch called the nine o'clock curfew. Luce sighed. It was upsetting to think that she may have offended her father-in-law. And yet she had no regrets that she had spoken her mind.

George threw a log on the fire and poured more wine for each of them. "No point in worrying about Father, now. What's done is done," he said. "John, I have no more stomach for politics tomorrow. You can listen at Westminster. Babs, would you like to show me the menageries at the Tower? Perhaps you have a favorite Barbary lion from your time there who will recognize you?"

George's invitation brought a smile to Babs's face. Luce relaxed her shoulders. Babs should enjoy a day of fun. And after John escorted her to Whitehall, she could have Allen to herself.

John commanded their carriage to leave Luce at the great hall within the palace walls, where Allen was waiting for her. With a hurried promise to meet later at Westminster, her husband rode to attend Parliament's session.

"Walk with me, Luce." Allen settled her fur-lined cloak more tightly around her shoulders and took her hand, examining her French leather gloves. "Ah. Weren't these Mother's?"

Luce nodded. "Yes. She thought they would be appropriate for London. I was quite happy with my black calfskin, but—"

"She has her own definitive ideas of how to dress in Whitehall." Allen laughed while Luce pulled a face and smoothed her dark brown skirts. She never had been one for adornment; in fact, Babs accused her of great negligence in her habit. Blinking in the bright winter sunlight, she hugged Allen. It was so good to hear his laugh, see his sparkling eyes. He had matured, his jaw stronger, his look harder. And his clothes were those of a Royalist courtier, rich layers of burgundy and navy velvet embroidered with the Villiers silver thread.

Too long they were separated.

And, deep in her heart, she feared for his safety. John's accounting of the Scottish war, although carefully worded to calm her, only sent a tremble of fear through her, reminding her of the times her father had traveled to war.

"It's a beautiful morning, Allen. Where shall we walk?"

"Through the Privy Garden and toward the river. You said you wanted to talk in private." Allen paused. "And there is nowhere in this palace that does not have hidden ears."

She nodded. "There are things we should discuss."

"Let us walk through the hall and the Long Gallery. Come, you may see for yourself the artwork the king has collected. His passion was ignited by the Duke of Buckingham, you know. In fact, our parents attended many an evening here with the court."

Memories rushed back from their childhood at the Tower: so many happy times when her father was home, so many anxious moments when he was gone.

"Show me," she replied. "I know Mother would be curious to hear how it all looks now, despite her feigned indifference."

"Does she ever speak of the times she was at Whitehall?" Allen asked. "When Father died and she married Francke, she buried those memories completely."

Luce shook her head as Allen pushed open the tall black oak door to the great hall. She opened her mouth to respond and shut it again as they entered the extraordinary chamber. Above her head, the soaring roof vanished into darkness, statues and carvings looming ghostly in high niches. Colorful tapestries of biblical scenes hung on every wall, and the black-and-white tiled floor magnified their footfall with every step.

"This is remarkable," whispered Luce. "Look at these hangings. The gold and silver thread alone is worth a fortune."

"The king is a great collector. Come, there is more."

Walking through the hall and letting themselves out of a small door behind the dais, Allen led Luce through a maze of chambers crammed with ornaments and curiosities, clocks and globes, crystal and chandeliers. Musical instruments and leather-bound books filled niches and cabinets. Rich silk curtains hung at every window; exquisitely detailed carpets were draped over tables, while yet more tapestries of classical scenes graced the walls. In some rooms, languid courtiers looked up as she passed and paid scant attention to her. In others, a greeting was called out to Allen, which he politely returned.

Luce was speechless. The never-ending rooms, the scale of the halls, the sheer number of possessions were overpowering.

Her thoughts returned unexpectedly to the black-clad Puritans in the churchyard at St. Dunstan's, their preacher in the stocks, his words stuffed in his mouth. Did the king know what was being done in his name? How could he know what the common people wanted if he cocooned himself in this chrysalis of a palace?

Allen steered her through the antechamber, the air redolent with the mingled scents of cloves and oranges from the numerous pomanders.

"We'll walk through the Long Gallery," he said. "It is a good place to see and be seen."

"And you play these games, Allen? Do you enjoy these trappings and what they signify?"

"What do they signify, Sister?" Allen asked carelessly, bowing his head to a highly powdered and painted woman who approached them. With a flick of her fan, she acknowledged Allen, but ignored Luce. "They are but the regalia of a royal palace."

"But the wealth, the money this must have all cost—"

"It is the king's privilege." Allen guided Luce through the crowded chamber, and she saw that they were emerging into a long gallery. "Now, Luce, what do you think of this?"

She could not say more. The gallery, which stretched beyond her vision, was filled with paintings of classical allegories, religious parables, portraits, hunting scenes, and more tapestries. The ceiling was carved stone, picked out in gold. The wainscot featured thousands of engravings, exquisitely detailed figures, and fantastic creatures. But the portraits overwhelmed her. Hung three, four, five high, stretching from floor to ceiling, from door to door, the expressions of religious fervor completely revolted her. Did this king deify himself to the point that his divine right to rule permeated his entire existence?

In silence, they walked the Long Gallery. Reaching the very end, Allen threw open a small door and led her into the garden.

"This is the life you choose, Allen?" Luce held his eyes with hers. "This reliance on material things, this blasphemous, blatant depiction of wealth—"

"Luce, it is art; this is the inheritance of the nation."

"An inheritance hidden from the people and acquired by taxes extracted from the shires of England." She stormed ahead of Allen. This was not what she imagined their reunion would be. Where was their closeness of childhood? Why had they grown so far apart in principles? Suddenly, she had an idea.

"Come with me." She turned back, demanding his attention. She gave him no choice, for now she walked swiftly, her cloak occasionally catching a hedge and sending a sudden snowfall to the ground. She knew he was following; he always did.

By leaving the palace through the Holbein Gate, the spires of Westminster Abbey gleamed just a short distance ahead. Allen caught up with her and strode next to her. Within minutes, they were at the massive doors of Westminster Hall. She softly stroked the pale stone surrounding, unadorned, smoothed by countless common people who had, for centuries, crossed freely this threshold.

Luce turned. Allen's expression was impassive.

"In here, Allen, Babs and I defended our parents against the corruption of the Duke of Buckingham. In this court, you vowed to uphold our father's name and his reputation and restore honor to our family." Luce dropped her voice, and Allen bowed his head to listen, refusing to meet her eyes. "And in this chamber, a Parliament meets for the first time in more than a decade, representing the people of this nation."

"The king has ruled wisely without them—"

"The king has brought our land to the brink of war, taxed his people far beyond their means, and imposed a papist prayer book through the illegal actions of his bishops."

Luce gestured through the doors of the hall, where a hundred, two hundred men were milling, talking at such a pitch that their voices reached through the ancient doors to the outside porch.

"Parliament is back, Allen. It is back. And it is not going away." She clasped his arm, forcing him to raise his eyes and look at her. "The king can no longer hide in his palace or summon an army or furnish his privy chambers with art bought with his subject's taxes."

"You are speaking treason, Luce."

"I am speaking truth, Allen."

He turned from her and gazed into the great hall. She followed his look and saw that the angels were still flying from the ceiling, the white harts still standing guard over the people.

"We have traveled far in the last few years, Allen. But always together, always with the purpose of keeping our family safe and together."

"And we still do, Luce. We still do." His voice cracked a little. Her brother was close to tears.

"Allen, I know not what lies ahead. But times are changing. We must vow never to change, too." A few flakes of snow drifted from the now-leaden sky. Luce shivered, and not only from the cold. "John and I have been talking. We are removing to Nottingham—to Owthorpe, John's home."

"You are leaving?"

"Yes. The Star Chamber will be dissolved within three months. There is no position here in London. We both know that the king lives on credit and that the warrants will not be paid." Luce brushed a snowflake from Allen's dark hair. She loved her brother so much. "We cannot afford to stay. But John has the manor at Owthorpe, and there is plenty for him to do there."

"Mother? And Babs?"

"They come with us," Luce replied. "We have room and can care for them. You have done well these past few years with the income you were able to collect—" they stepped apart for a moment as a half-dozen men burst through the door, voices raised in heated debate, "but times are different, now. You have chosen to stay at court. James serves in Ireland with Edward. Nottingham will be peaceful, quiet. And, in time, I think George may make a proposal to Babs. We will have a family home again, one that cannot be taken away from us."

"Then I send you with my blessings, for the choice is yours and John's." Allen looked up at the sky. The clouds were lower, the snow falling more heavily. "You should leave for Holborn before the weather closes in. Let us go into the hall and find your husband. He's assured to be at his favorite bookseller."

Luce took his arm. "You will do well at court, Allen. You already have. But promise me you won't forget where you came from and the battles you and I have fought together, side by side."

"I promise, Luce." Allen swept her into a fierce hug. "I vow we will always come first."

"I promise too, Allen. Always our love for each other and our family first."

28

Yet the very next day the king came to the House of Commons, attended with his extraordinary guard, of about four hundred gentlemen and soldiers, armed with swords and pistols, and there demanded five of their members, whom not finding there (for a great lady at court had before informed one of them of his coming, and the house ordered them to retire), he returned, leaving the house under a high sense of this breach of their privilege.

Luce Hutchinson
9ᵗʰ January 1642

John dropped the letter from his father and slumped back in the chair, his face white with shock. "The king could not intervene to save his own key advisor. Parliament demanded that the Earl of Strafford be executed. Death has been done."

Luce was equally startled at the news. She put down the jug of apple blossoms she was arranging in the parlor of the Blue House and crossed to John's side to read the missive for herself. "Parliament wanted to blame someone other than the king for our woes in Scotland and the Irish wars. But I am astounded. No clemency from the king? No pardon at the scaffold?"

"No. Parliament bound the king's hands so tightly with their grievances, he had no choice but to sacrifice his favorite. It was not enough that he did not resist Archbishop Laud's trial and execution. The Parliament is removing all those they perceive as a wicked influence."

Luce rested her hand on her stomach. She was with child again, and this time she was strong, healthy. The country air agreed with her. Serenity ruled her days, and the far-off thunder of the storms in Whitehall would not disturb her family's tranquility.

She shrugged. "Now the king will temper his rule with Parliament's guidance. Archbishop Laud is dead. Strafford is dead. Parliament has removed the wicked advisors that guided him ill, and the king must listen to the advice of the men who represent his subjects."

John caught Luce's hand and slowly kissed her palm. She felt a delicious flutter in her heart. She loved this man with such a passion, such devotion.

"You are a most fair and logical wife, my darling." He ran his lips over her wrist, his beard tickling the delicate skin under which pulsed her life blood. "It is a pity that Parliament and the king have not your wise counsel."

As her desire warmed her, the babe kicked, and she laughed.

"They have no need of our counsel, John. We can save our wisdom for the governing of Owthorpe and the betterment of your land."

Pulling her to his lap, John laid his head on Luce's breast and stroked her stomach.

"Are you certain you are ready to leave London and all that you are familiar with, my darling?" His voice was muffled, but still there echoed anxiety in his words.

She smoothed his hair and kissed the luxuriant curls. He was so very handsome, with such a fetching countenance.

"I am ready as soon as our baby is born, John." Her own household, a home to manage, an organized country estate where her boys could thrive. "My mother talks to me daily of her life at Lydiard and how happy she was there when Uncle John brought their family back together. And now that Babs and my mother come with us, our family will be complete." She showered kisses all over his head and gasped when he pulled her head down and kissed her deeply and passionately on her mouth.

"I will keep you happy, my darling wife. Our home will ring with the laughter of our children, and the land will be rich and fruitful. I have so many ideas to bring wealth and certainty to our people, and you will be a wonderful lady of the manor."

The letter drifted from John's lap to the floor and was forgotten as they kissed.

In Lucy's view, the manor of Owthorpe did not compare to Lydiard's graceful aspect and golden warmth. In fact, it was positively cold and bleak. The roof of her daughter's new home emerged through the trees, tucked behind a sprawling farmhouse. She peered from the carriage window, pushing aside the stiff leather blind that gave scant protection from the driving rain that pursued them on their journey.

The land was moderate, she conceded, flat and rising toward a crest to the north. Ridges in the fields indicated the land's arable history, where the villagers had farmed their strips for centuries. A spatter of rain flew into her face, and she shook her head. This bleak land offered little protection from the west wind, and the standing water made mud of the track that wound its way from the main road. She could not tell where the estate boundary existed, for fields lapped at the feet of the house. Across the way, to the south, a small church stood by itself at the end of a footpath from the village.

Still, this was home, and one that could not be taken from them. And although the very mention of this provincial northern outpost, four days' ride from London, struck trepidation in the hearts of their friends, she was secure in her decision to accompany her daughter to her new life. She glanced across the dim carriage at Luce and smiled to see her daughter slept, her month-old babe clasped firmly in her arms. Three boys now, and John as proud a father as she had ever seen. Lucy shook from her memory the bleakness of Ryes Manor and her loveless marriage to Francke. There was nothing similar in these circumstances, and yet the paucity of the land and the cheerlessness of the surrounding country encouraged those awful memories to return.

As the carriage slowed, John rode up. Bending over the saddle, he peered into the window.

"Welcome home, Mother," he called, rain dripping down from his nose, his hair flattened under the brim of his hat. Lucy laughed. Not even the downpour could dampen his spirits.

The carriage lurched on its final turn, and the iron wheels rumbled on a wooden bridge as they crossed over the remains of a moat, half-filled with water. This was ancient land indeed, a reminder of an era past where none knew from whence their enemy would come. The jolt shook Luce awake, and the babe, Jack, who set to wailing in hunger.

Lucy drew a patient breath. At least the twins traveled with Sarah and Babs in the second carriage.

"Come, sweeting, come to Grandmother." She lifted the baby from Luce's lap and held him up to the window, carefully supporting his wobbling head. "Welcome home. Welcome."

"We are here?" Luce stretched and rubbed at a damp spot where Jack had dribbled on her, shrugging when the spit didn't disappear. "At John's home?"

"At your home, darling," Lucy corrected. "Yes, we are here. And a beautiful, spacious house it appears."

In the middle of nowhere.

William's firstborn, christened Barbara in honor of her granddame at Westminster on November 27, looked much as any other babe, Allen thought. This one, however, was the center of attention. Lord knew the Villiers turned any occasion into a party.

He slung back his goblet of wine and held it out for a refill from a passing page. 'Twas another occasion to get drunk, for if he wasn't going to expire on a battlefield, he was certainly going to die of boredom. And now, the highlight of his social calendar was attending a baby's christening. God's teeth, he was restless. Perhaps he should join Edward and James in Ireland after all, and get some soldiering under his belt with Goring.

"She's beautiful," his Aunt Barbara simpered, leaning over the baby. "She has your eyes, William."

No doubt his aunt was flattered that her grandchild was named after her. Good Lord. The creature was just a few days old. She didn't even open her eyes. They were scrunched tight while she screamed.

"She has a spirit to her," pronounced Prince Charles. No Villiers function would occur without the attendance of the royal princes. Allen was grateful for that connection, at least. The prince peered into the baby's face, his own swarthy skin dark by comparison to her pink-and-white complexion. "I think she might be quite challenging to manage, William."

Villiers smiled. "Do not concern yourself, Your Majesty. You'll be out of the schoolroom before she joins it. And besides, with her place at court, she will quickly learn etiquette."

Prince Charles held his finger out, and the baby grasped it tightly. He stepped back and laughed. "She has quite a hold on me!"

"Barbara Villiers," admonished Allen. "Barbara Villiers, let go of the prince." He reached over and uncurled her tiny fingers.

He stopped as his cousin's hand clasped his. For a moment, they were all locked in a children's game—the baby's tiny fingers, the prince's olive-skinned young fist, and the two soldiers' calloused palms.

"Allen. A word." William approached.

Nodding his head in deference to Prince Charles, Allen allowed himself to be drawn aside to the tall windows overlooking the tiltyard. The Villiers lodgings at Whitehall naturally came with the best views and freshest air. At least he was out of the coal bunker and boarded now on the outermost row of rooms guarding the privy chamber.

"What is it? You look anxious."

"I need to ask you to commit to something. But I cannot tell you what it is."

"That sounds very mysterious."

William nodded. "It is cautionary; that is all." He looked around the chamber, and his eyes stopped on Prince Charles. "I have a pledge to the king. He asked to me to find others who will join me. Will you?'

"Will I what?" What guessing game was William playing?

"Pledge secrecy and be available to me if I call on you in the king's name." William's voice was low, and Allen had to lean forward to catch his meaning.

"I am always available to defend the king, William."

"This is not necessarily a defense, Allen. But that is all I can tell you."

"Nothing else?" Allen followed William's glance and watched the young Prince Charles walk away from William's daughter and strike up a conversation with quite the prettiest maid in the room. He may just be eleven years of age, but he knew the powerful effect of his charm.

"The king is ignoring the remonstrance that Parliament agreed on last week. He thinks that if he does not pay attention, the demands will go away. Only eleven votes gave it majority, but still passed the declaration." William took Allen by the elbow and pulled him even farther from the christening party. The cold November light shone hard on his face. There was more concern in his cousin's face than he had ever seen before any battle preparation.

"Does the king dare to challenge the will of the House of Commons?" Allen asked. He recalled the heated debates with John and Luce, their insistence that the king would have to listen to Parliament's grievances and answer them satisfactorily.

"Not yet. But the Irish war and unruly Parliament disturb many families. They hearken back to the days of Queen Elizabeth and long to return to her wise rule." William's tone commanded Allen's obedience. "You remember the loyalty of our fathers to their king. Do not leave Whitehall. I may call on you at any time."

Allen bowed his head and tried to contain the sudden rush of excitement that filled his belly. Perhaps there was more to staying in Whitehall than he originally thought.

The summons came early on the morning of the fourth of January and took him by surprise. The messenger, dressed in Villiers colors, stood at the door waiting for a reply as Allen read through the scribbled words. Pushing his hair from his eyes, he threw the note on the table.

"Tell Lord Grandison I shall be at the tiltyard at noon." The page bowed quickly and scampered off.

Allen splashed water on his face and pulled on his linen shirt. The girl in his bed stretched and sat up, her plump breasts spilling over the cover. Would he have time for . . . no, the note commanded him. He picked her gown up from the floor and dropped it on the bed, giving her a deep kiss as he did so. "Sweeting, I have business to attend to. You need to be on your way."

Allen pulled shut the door of his rooms and clattered down the narrow steps, buttoning his thick winter jacket. His wardrobe had improved along with his lodgings, for at least his stay in Whitehall put him back in the center of power. Working for the Villiers family meant there were always pickings; their cash was abundant, and they were generous with loyal relatives.

He strode past the old great hall, pushing aside the uncomfortable memory of his last visit there with Luce, and walked through the Palace Gate, crossing the wide yard by the Banqueting House. Directly opposite was the barracks for the Foot Guard, and that was where William had summoned him. He stopped dead still. There must have been three or four hundred armed guards assembling in the parade ground. What the hell was happening?

Half a dozen drummers struck a beat, and their insistent sound formed the men into columns of marching men, twenty abreast. Searching for his cousin, Allen caught sight of William at the rear of the guards. As he fell into step beside him, the thrill of the muster gripped his belly.

"Where are you heading? What is going on, William?" Allen noticed they were picking up more men as they marched through the palace grounds and almost tripped when the king's coach and his mounted attendants pulled out of the yard.

"The king rides to Parliament," William shouted, his voice drowned by the incessant drumming and marching.

"To do what?"

"To arrest those members he accuses of treason for challenging his right to rule!"

The advance to Westminster took no more than ten minutes, but with every step, more joined, until the crowd behind swelled to a thousand or more. The curious, the loyal, the king's subjects, all dropped into line behind the royal carriage as it drove toward Parliament. When the spires of the abbey and the turrets of the hall came into view, Allen harkened his sister's words, spoken so recently. He called her speech treason. She called it truth.

The king, a slight man in a blood-red coat, descended from the carriage. Behind him, black trees traced stark against the pale stone of the abbey. The crowd, dark in its winter wool, poured into the open space, restrained by the guards. Clouds raced in from the north, the air brittle with cold. Accompanied only by his personal guards, King Charles marched through the arched wooden door and into the ancient hall. Allen glanced at William and beyond to the foot soldiers. The whole crowd held its breath, such a blanket of silence descended. Never had a reigning monarch entered the House of Commons. And never had a king accused his own Parliament of treason.

"Stand ready," murmured William. "The army knows what to do. Follow their lead when I give the signal. We cannot allow rioting."

No more than a half hour passed, and a shifting and whispering blew across the gathered citizens. The king reappeared, still surrounded by his guards. His head held arrogantly high, he walked slowly from the hall back to his carriage. As the footman opened the door, he paused and surveyed the crowd, who fell silent again. He looked at them for what seemed an eternity and then nodded once and climbed inside.

Allen followed William across to a huddle of courtiers who were standing in front of Westminster Hall, recognizing one of them as Sir Edward Hyde, his mother's relative. A close confidante of the king.

"What news, Cousin?" he asked.

Hyde turned to him. "Ah, Apsley. Good to see you here. The birds have flown. The traitors received warning the king was coming and fled to take refuge in the city. The king demanded to know their whereabouts, but the Speaker of the House refused, saying he only answered to Parliament."

William looked across at the army of foot soldiers marching back to the Palace of Whitehall.

"I fear the worst now, for the city will not release them to the king. They declare loyalty to Parliament first."

Allen stared at them. "And so the king is at war with his own Parliament?"

Hyde nodded. "A war of principle. And God save us all from where that leads next."

29

The king meanwhile in the north, summoned divers of the nobility and gentry to attend him, and made speeches to them to desire a guard for his person, pretending danger from the parliament.

Luce Hutchinson
April 17th 1642

Within the month, the king fled to Hampton Court Palace, Allen accompanying him. There was no purpose in staying at a deserted Whitehall without the court. Besides, the king's move was an important strategy in facing down Parliament and its rude actions. Allen had no intention of being left behind and associated with the London rebels.

Even more reason he should stay close by the court was to convince people of his loyalty to the king, and not to his mother's distant cousin, the solicitor general. He was embarrassed enough that Oliver St.John had crossed the king and convinced Parliament to execute the Earl of Strafford; the last thing Allen needed was to be associated with his Parliamentarian relative, who advocated turning control of the armed forces over to an independent lord-general.

"Parliament, and our cousin, the solicitor general, overstep their boundaries. The king has always commanded the military and the navy, thus protecting the welfare of his people." William Villiers paced back and forth in his private rooms, just a few doors away from the king's apartments and equally sumptuously furnished. The floor creaked with the pounding of William's footsteps in his riding boots, and the very air in the room hummed with his vigor.

Allen mentally congratulated himself again on his choice to follow his cousin at court, and nodded. "And yet, Parliament seeks to usurp this power and take control of the military and the armaments stored in each county. We must distance ourselves from this treasonable suggestion."

As he spoke, Allen looked to Edward for confirmation. "You've just arrived from Lydiard. What news from the west?"

Edward had not changed from his military garb—no armor, but still with his black leather greatcoat and sword. Allen sought reassurance, for William was as nervous as a cat these past few days.

Edward drew off his worn gauntlets and tossed them on a red velvet bench; they landed next to a fine linen embroidered kerchief forgotten by some careless lady. It was an unsettling combination—one so rough, the other delicate.

"My father says that the counties are fearful the king leads us into a deeper war with Ireland. An organized Irish campaign will create a hundred years of chaos and bloodshed for our people." Edward walked over to the diamond-paned windows. "Although my father understands the king's position, he feels for the common people. The moderates in Parliament seek to prevent the king from further wars, for the good of their constituents."

Allen fought down the shock of Edward's words. It was one thing for James to be serving in Goring's army on patrol in Ireland. It was a completely different world if he was embroiled in a full-scale war.

Joining Edward in the enclave, Allen followed his gaze to the small clusters of courtiers in thick furs and extravagant velvets strolling the gravel paths in the formal gardens. A flight of stone steps led down to a sloping emerald lawn, which dissolved into the Thames amidst a fringe of rushes. The king's barge was moored at the bank, azure-and-gold pennants fluttering. A haze on the willows predicted an early spring. No scene could be further removed from a battlefield.

"It is not Ireland we have to fear," said William quietly as he stood next to them. The cousins watched the king approach his courtiers, causing a silent ripple of bows and curtsies. "If Parliament pushes our cousin St. John's Military Bill through as an ordinance, they do not require the king's signature to authorize each county to secure its own magazine and ammunition—"

"Effectively putting Parliament in control of all armaments," finished Edward.

William nodded. "Each county's lord lieutenant will be responsible for its own force, and then Parliament rules the military, not the king."

The men turned at the door opening, and Mary Villiers entered, accompanied by a nursemaid carrying the baby. The infant was dressed in an elaborately embroidered gown that swept down to the floorboards, yards of gossamer glinting with gold and silver thread.

"William, enough of these gloomy faces," Mary cried. "See, your daughter has learned today to laugh, and she brings mirth to all around her. Come, join with me in playing with her, my love."

The nursemaid held out the little girl to her father as he swiftly crossed the chamber and caressed her cheek with his finger, adoration chasing anxiety from his face. Allen held Edward back.

"Have you heard of the queen's movements?" he asked his cousin in a low tone.

Edward shook his head. "No. I have not even slept one night here at Hampton Court."

Allen glanced over at Mary. "The queen has left for the Continent, along with Prince Rupert. She rode with a small party, for swiftness, leaving her court and attendees here. She is petitioning her family and allies for support, for money to finance the king's cause. Rumor whisper she took crown jewels with her to pledge security."

"What cause?" Edward asked. "What would the funding go toward?"

"If the Militia Ordinance passes, the king will call out a commission of array—" Allen began to explain.

"Dear God, Allen, that hasn't been done in two centuries!"

"No matter," Allen said. "He will not let Parliament be the sole controller of the military in his own kingdom. He will raise his own commission, call on all the lords of the land to muster private armies. 'Tis said he spends day and night writing lists containing the names of the lords he counts on to be loyal to him. He will distribute his foreign funds to these men to muster ten times more in return."

"He compels his subjects to choose, to declare an allegiance to their king or Parliament?" Edward turned and contemplated the figures in the garden.

Allen sighed. How curiously the gravel paths and square flowerbeds checkered the land. The courtiers resembled chess pieces as they followed the king in his slow promenade.

"He has not said as much," Allen replied. "But I think, in his mind, there is no choice. These commissioners will be the foundation for the king's party across the country. Some have already declared. Their name is formalized—Royalists."

"But he will divide each county in half. How can he command men to choose?"

Allen shook his head. "I know not, Edward. But we will watch closely where these loyalties fall, for we do not want to be enemies of the king. Our future rests on his patronage."

Absent the queen, the court became a palace of men. The halls filled with the sounds of rough voices raised in discussion and swift footsteps pacing from the privy chamber to the lord's apartments and back again. More than five hundred armed nobles gathered, each committed to serve the king.

Allen attached himself to varied groups, hearing the arguments presented, the opinions put forth. Mostly, he listened, fearing to bring attention to himself by misspeaking in the company of these seasoned soldiers and courtiers. John and Luce's warning echoed in his mind as the words flew around him. What was the basis for the king to raise a personal army? And yet, how could Parliament subvert the wishes of their divinely appointed sovereign? It was against the natural order of the world to question the king's authority to rule.

If it wasn't for Edward's steadfast presence, he may have joined in with the bored young men who drank themselves into a stupor each night, boasting of their exploits, toasting the king's strategy. Instead, as the weeks dragged on and the tension heightened, Edward was the one to whom he turned for reassurance. Thus, when the news finally came that the king commanded them to Newmarket, the cousins resolved to ride together.

Allen's uneasiness did not lift as they kicked their heels in the countryside of Cambridgeshire, for although the king and his close courtiers stayed within the royal palace, those on the periphery were forced to fend for themselves. The small towns and villages surrounding Newmarket were not welcoming to this horde of Royalists that took over the taverns and drank the kegs dry. And, in Newmarket, emerged another nickname for these king's men—Cavaliers. 'Twas fitting that this mispronunciation of the Spanish for "horseman" would evolve at the king's racecourse.

The loose friendships of the courtiers were forming into closer alliances, bonded by the hostility of the country, where Puritans dominated the landscape. There were no open arguments, no obvious challenges. And yet, as Allen recalled the stark atmosphere of Sir Leventhorpe Francke's manor and environs, the landscape was dauntingly familiar.

"I've written to my sister." Allen looked up from the cramped desk in the tavern's attic he shared with Edward. The roof was pitched so steep that nowhere could they stand at full height, and there was room only for a flimsy iron bedstead with a sagging straw mattress. Their coats hung on pegs; boots, gloves, and swords were piled in a corner. A circular hole with a broken shutter high in the wall belied the original storage purpose of this space that had cost them most of their wages.

"Did you write to Luce of the confusion here at court? Perchance John will know more from his father. Or maybe your mother will have heard about the solicitor general from her cousins." Edward was seated on the rickety bed, sharpening his blade. With every swipe of the iron, a squeak of the bedstead accompanied the rasping.

"I tell her we travel with the king." Allen blew on the tattered parchment, for no sand was available to dry his words. "We hear he goes next to York. And that perhaps we can call on her before he returns to Whitehall, when this whole business is resolved."

"That would be a great relief." Edward put his sword down and stretched his arms high to relieve the muscles. His fingertips touched the ceiling, and he laughed. "Frankly, any time with Luce and your mother would be delightful after this rank accommodation. I long for clean linens and a decent meal."

"So much for the glorious life of a courtier. I wonder how much better William has it."

"Infinitely so, Coz. He sleeps in a comfortable bed under a ducal coronet, with the king in the next chamber." Edward stood up, careful to keep his back hunched. "We are but poor relations. But we *are* relations. Let us not forget, and ensure our loyalty to William is known by the king. We must be included on those lists if we are to progress with our plans to earn our fortunes at court."

Market day, and Nottingham's narrow streets were crammed with all manner of stores, and as Luce browsed from one to another, pleased with the quality of the merchandise on sale, the bells from St. Mary's Church rang noon. Time to meet John at the town hall, for his business must be concluded by now, and he would be eager to return home to Owthorpe.

She walked through to Weekday Cross Market, where stood a fine gabled building, fair enough to be located on London's Fleet Street. Even with the usual throng of stallholders and customers, the square was busier than usual, and approaching the town hall, she recognized the mayor's wife in the middle of a crowd of people.

"Mrs. Hutchinson, your husband is inside with Lord Newark," the woman called, her cheeks red with agitation. "There is a great argument about the munitions, for the king intends to borrow our powder, and Mr. Hutchinson refuses to let him."

The crowd grew by the moment, and at her words, cries arose.

"They can take my blood before he should have one measure of our powder!"

"Throw my Lord Newark from the window, for he shall not take what is ours, no matter what paper says he may."

Luce squeezed through the crush and ran up the steps into the main chamber of the hall. Behind her, heavy footsteps signified more of the countrymen followed. At the sound, John emerged from an upper chamber, Lord Newark and the sheriff at his side. Her husband held his hand up for calm, and the crowd fell quiet.

"My friends, Lord Newark asks on behalf of the king that he may take our powder. The king says that he is assured that we will do so cheerfully, and serve his wishes."

"We will not part with it, nor leave our families undefended," shouted a man next to Luce. "Would you ask us to deliver our swords too, that our wives and children are at the mercy of the armed men that pass through here daily? Over my dead body, sir!"

The muttering grew loud, and the demeanor of the crowd changed. The mayor's wife wriggled her way to the front and stood by Luce.

"Do not leave us naked and defenseless," she shouted. "The king has no authority over our ammunition. We've paid for it; we own it."

The crowd shouted its agreement and pressed forward, taking Luce along.

John held his hand up for quiet again. His face was calm, his bearing purposeful. He commanded the room with his dignity and fine manners.

"Lord Newark, you have your answer. We will not part with our powder, and I will not have blood spilt in the defending of such. You will have to cut me down first."

Lord Newark arched his high brows and pursed his small mouth. It was evident to Luce that he was most displeased with Nottingham's response to his request.

"Perhaps, Mr. Hutchinson, the king may borrow your powder. I pledge on my honor that it will be returned."

Luce prayed for John to remain staunch. *Remember the warrants,* she said silently. *Remember how useless this king's word is.* She caught his eye, and he returned her look, his face grave.

"I am afraid not, my lord. For the ammunition is the county's property—all men have an interest, and all say it remains with us."

Lord Newark turned bright red and, taking the sheriff by the arm, ran downstairs and pushed his way through the crowd. Pausing at the door, he shook his fist at John.

"Hutchinson, your part in this has been noted. I am sorry to see failure in this town, for the king was assured of this county's affection toward him. I will personally acquaint His Majesty with your insolence and insubordination."

The room fell quiet.

"I thank you, Lord Newark," John called. "For if the king must receive information about me, I am fortunate it is from such an honorable person as yourself. In the name of God, let my reputation stand."

Lord Newark slammed the door behind him, and as John approached Luce, the crowd applauded, cheering his courage. He stood before her, his eyes alight with the emotions of the moment.

"What brought you to this moment, my love?" whispered Luce. "What brought you to speak for all the men of Nottingham?" Around them, the story was already being told and retold. Soon, word would spread across the city and out into the county. John Hutchinson represented all of them. John Hutchinson defied the king. John Hutchinson saved their lives.

"I just wanted to prevent mischief this day, Luce," he replied. "It was wrong, what Lord Newark was doing. He would have forced his way in and stolen the ammunition. And, if I had not intervened, blood would have been shed."

Luce looked around at the men of Nottingham, now joking about the incident, rejoicing their munitions were safe, their families protected. They were her neighbors, people that she knew now as friends. Pride swelled in her breast.

"You did well to stand up to Lord Newark and the deception he tried to pull on our fair town. Blood may still be shed, my love. But not this day. And not on your hands."

"Unrest often precipitates matters of the heart." Lucy held out her arms to Babs. "And so you are to marry George. I . . ." She held her girl tightly, the unbidden tears preventing her from finishing her sentence. Her youngest, betrothed. Her duty was done. She thanked God in her heart and her husband in heaven that she had safely reached this moment.

"Are you sad, Mother?" Babs pulled away, her sweet face a picture of concern. "Do you not approve of George? I thought you welcomed him into your heart." She looked around the church, the ancient building now empty of the morning worshippers. "Owthorpe is our home now, and John and George are our family."

"These are tears of happiness, my darling," Lucy rushed to assure Babs. "I want only the best for you. You are my precious daughter, and George's temperament and yours are so well matched I cannot imagine a more pure alliance." She hugged Babs again, and swallowed the greater anxiety that hid beneath the immediate happiness. "I am happy, and joyful, and give you my blessing, my darling. Your father would have loved George's spirit, his love of life, for his character mirrors your own."

Babs gathered up their prayer books, and took her mother by her hand. Together they walked to the front of Owthorpe's church, its simple stonework and colored glass creating a cool contrast from the brilliant June morning.

"Do you agree with John? Do you think war is coming, Mother?" Babs touched the petals of a damask rose in a bowl on a table, its scent drifting through the small church. "George wishes to be married as quickly as possible, for he fears that armies may form and he will be sent away."

Why did this king always bring a cloud of sorrow to her family? Babs should be excited, preparing for her marriage, not fearful that her husband would be snatched from her side.

"I think that the king and Parliament will confront each other and there must be a civil discourse," replied Lucy. "I cannot believe that the king would intentionally jeopardize the welfare of his own people to prove his right to rule over them."

Babs was silent, listening.

Enough. Enough of this fear for the future.

"But right now, we have a wedding to plan," continued Lucy. "George wishes to marry here, at Owthorpe, or in Nottingham?"

"Here, Mother. In this church, among the people of the village who have known him since he was a child." Babs pulled a flower from the vase and tucked the bloom behind her ear. "And I shall be his country bride, with flowers in my hair, and we shall open the hall and invite the village to dine. . ."

". . . and we shall drink to the happiness of the bride and bridegroom with our own ciders and ale . . ."

". . . and we shall dance to the old country tunes . . ." Babs giggled. "Well, perhaps not Luce."

Lucy joined her in her mirth. "Your sister will dance at your wedding, Babs. If John doesn't insist, George will."

30

The parliament sent the king word, that if he would not disband his forces, and rely upon the laws and affections of his people for his security, as all good princes before him had done, they held themselves responsible for securing the parliament and preserving the kingdom's peace. Whereupon they voted, 'That it seems that the king, seduced by wicked counsel, intends a war against the parliament.'

Luce Hutchinson
August 21ˢᵗ 1642

Allen stood at York Minster's Great West Door, admiring the tracery work and carvings of Adam and Eve. This was surely a noble monument, far more impressive than the bleak Puritan chapels that were springing up around the country. Speaking of which, his brother-in-law's message had come as a surprise. What business did John have in York? And why did he send a letter through William, asking to meet here today?

He peered through the crowds of armed soldiers who swaggered and tramped the narrow streets of the city, bands of swordsmen on foot and mounted Cavaliers, progressively turning the town into a garrison. When did so many arrive? Each day, the king's presence attracted more and more followers, until the townspeople hid behind their barred doors and the countrymen stayed away from the city.

Allen looked to the sky, small clouds drifting in the summer breeze, the great minster tower appearing to fall toward him from the movement of the clouds behind. He jumped at a touch on his shoulder and reached immediately for his sword.

"Steady, my brother."

So good to hear John's familiar, calm voice.

"You startled me."

John smiled and clasped him in a hug. "It seems the entire city is on alert."

Allen nodded. "These are not tranquil times."

"York is full. There is no room for more, and yet on my journey here from Nottingham, the road was crowded with Cavaliers riding to the king's side." John shifted his stance, and his sword hilt glinted in the afternoon sun.

"And you? Why ride you to York, John?" Allen eyed his brother-in-law. "What business have you with the king?"

"Walk with me in quiet, Allen." John looked around to the archbishop's palace across the green. "Over there, we can talk in private without others hearing us."

They fell into step, silenced by the confusion around the minster. Bands of Cavaliers reeled in and out of inns, shouting slogans and cheers for the king, while the clatter of horseshoes striking the cobblestones drowned any reasonable hope of conversation. Beating drums, fifes, and singing filled the air. There was not a woman or child in sight; York was armed and on edge.

In the peace of the archbishop's gardens, the silence washed over Allen, and he became almost light-headed, such was the contrast. This evoked the time he and John had walked Lincoln's Inn Fields, where they'd first discussed the troubles. Surely only a short while ago. And yet, how clearer their stance now. John led him to a corner where two stone walls met and a willow tree by a quiet pool offered a canopy of shade. Positioning them so they could see anyone approach, John took a flask from his belt and offered it to Allen, who drank deeply of the cool ale. Taking a draft himself, John put his hand on Allen's arm.

"What know you of the king's state of mind?" he asked, his question abrupt.

"His mind?" Allen paused. A swan glided into view on the pond, its reflection mirrored on the smooth water. "He is resolute. He has suffered greatly this past year with the loss of Strafford and Laud." The swan continued its effortless drift, leaving barely a ripple. "He was humiliated by Parliament. That does not sit well."

"And the petitions?" asked John. "Have you seen him entertain petitions from the counties?"

"Daily." Allen shrugged. "He receives them, but does not read them. They are full of the same complaints. They want to keep their munitions. They want representation in Parliament. Why do you ask?"

John's face tightened. For the first time since leaving Whitehall, Allen felt deep unease strike his heart.

"I bring such a petition from Nottingham."

"You? You lead a petition to challenge the king's order?"

John nodded. "Today, I presented to the king a petition signed by 4,540 hands of knights, esquires, gentlemen, freeholders, the mayor, aldermen, and other inhabitants of the town."

"So many . . ."

"They protest the command to turn over the town's munitions to the king. To relinquish the powder, the carbines, the armaments. I refused to do so."

John refusing the king's request? Speaking on behalf of the citizens? What rebelliousness was this in his brother-in-law?

"Their duty is to accede to the king's desires," Allen replied. "Surely you see that, John."

He nodded slowly. "I understand, Allen. Truly, I do. This troubles my heart and soul to the very depths of my being."

"And yet?"

"And yet, I cannot let my neighbors be undefended, their lives in danger because they have no protection, no stores of powder, no defense of their town and trade." The willow branches dappled shadow across John's face, making his expression hard to read. "Lord Newark came to Nottingham this past week. He demanded our powder and tried to remove our ammunition," he continued. "In the king's name, he wanted to confiscate all our defenses against the dangers of these times and leave our wives, our children at the mercy of any and all armed men that pass through our town."

The minster bell tolled the hour. Twelve strokes reverberated through the quiet gardens, and when they stopped, the silence was deeper than before.

Allen took a deep breath. "Why you, Brother? Why are you the one appointed to represent Nottingham to petition the king?"

John smiled and stepped forward into the sun. "I resisted Lord Newark and sent him on his way empty-handed. I told him I would defend our town's ammunition, and if there was blood to be drawn in these times, I was willing to be the first to fall."

"The king will be informed of your name and actions, John." Allen eyed his brother-in-law and remembered the times they had practiced their swordplay at Richmond. How easy to forget John's skills, what with his bookish airs and quiet manner. "Are you prepared to defend yourself further?"

John nodded. "Our family has represented the people of Nottingham in Parliament for generations. The citizens trust the Hutchinson family to do what is best for them and preserve their safety. I return now to tell them I have represented them to the king, that he has received our petition."

"And your father is a Royalist? He just spoke his public regard for the king."

"Yes."

"And you are for Parliament?"

The swan, suddenly disquieted, flapped its wings and rose from the lake with a clatter, breaking the glass surface into a thousand ripples.

"I am for the people. And if that means Parliament, then yes, I am for Parliament."

Christ's nails. And did that mean his sister and mother stood with John? The beating wings of the startled bird merged with a distant drumming.

"Then God help us if he does not attend to the petitions, John, for you stand in opposition to our king and country."

John's mouth tightened. "What causes you to believe the king is the country, Allen?" His brother-in-law turned a somber face to follow the flight of the swan across the bright sky. "God help us," he echoed. "God help us all."

York to Nottingham was but a three-day ride, yet with the king's companions, guards, and three thousand undisciplined supporters, the journey took five. The king called upon his Cavaliers to answer John's petition, and they did so by descending on the town that dared to challenge the king's authority.

Allen and Edward rode in the middle of the convoy to Nottingham, coated in the powdery earth kicked up by the thousand horses that rode ahead. The fields of ripe wheat shimmered through the dust motes, an early August harvest heralded by the golden grain. There were no towns large enough to accommodate such a cavalcade of men and horses, so when the king stopped for the night, they were forced to camp in fields, fend for themselves, find fodder for their mounts. Each morning, they straggled together again, forming the train that moved inexorably south, fused by a common goal to support the king in his crusade.

A Cavalier army was slowly evolving, and as the men rode together, order began to emerge from the chaos, and discipline found its way back into the hearts of men. They rode in wordless silence, with only the jangle of harnesses and the clopping of hoofs to herald their progress. But as they rode, Allen and Edward met the eyes of the farmers in the fields, the laborers in the villages, and saw doubt in their faces. No longer was this a royal progress. This was a military march.

On the fifth day, they were just ten miles from Nottingham. They sought out William, who rode close to the king's guard.

"We travel through to Owthorpe," Allen told his cousin. "My sister's home is just an hour's ride south of Nottingham. We will stay with Luce and John until we know what the king does next."

William nodded slowly. "Stay alert, and be aware of any movement of men or munitions," he replied. "The king lodges at Thurland House. Be in the town tomorrow afore noon, for he commands us all to attend him."

Allen and Edward embraced their cousin. There was a gravity about him that brooked no questions. In silence, they mounted their weary horses and pointed their heads south, skirting the town of Nottingham and riding through to Owthorpe Hall.

Lucy sat in the parlor, somnolent in the summer weather, the ticking of the clock loud as the pendulum marched relentlessly through the still afternoon. Each tick brought Allen closer to home; each tock punctuated the reason. She stilled her hands in her lap and looked across at her girls. Luce pressed close to John, sharing a bench, reading stacks of broadsheets that he had brought back from York and Nottingham. Babs played cribbage with George, their heads bowed over the table, hands linked.

She longed for the sounds of her son arriving. She dreaded the provocation that brought him. John's recounting of his conversation at

York was enough to convince Lucy that Allen was pledged to the king's cause. His confirmation that Allen, Edward, and her brother were all listed on the commission affirmed their loyalty. And, the latest honor from the king's court—that he was now Sir Allen Apsley, knighted because of patronage from William Villiers.

The crunch of horse hooves on the gravel outside the manor broke into her musings. Through the open windows came Allen's voice, and Edward's, as they ordered the grooms to care for their mounts. The clock's heartbeat deferred to the clatter of arrival.

Luce and Babs jumped up, raced to the door, and ran outside. John and George stayed with Lucy, standing on either side of her. With tears swelling her throat, she stood to receive her child, her son, her beloved Allen. And when he walked in, all dusty from the road, his eyes bright with excitement, his sword at his side, she knew he was lost to the king's cause.

She held out her arms, and he bent to kiss her cheek and embrace her. She could not let go until she had swallowed her tears and pulled her emotions under control.

"Where's James?" she asked, her heart leaping in her throat. "Does he not ride with you?"

Edward took her hand, his expression kind. "He remained in Ireland, Aunt, with Lord Goring's troop. He is in good health. His passion to remain with his military brothers surpasses any desire to return to England."

A mother's lot, to give up her sons in times of trouble. She pulled herself together. Allen and Edward were here at this moment. James must follow his own destiny under the protection of her prayers.

"Well," she said. "Welcome to Owthorpe. May this always be a place of refuge for you."

The men became boys again: hungry, dirty, full of tales of their adventures. Lucy arranged baths and asked Sarah to brush off their coats and wash their shirts. Attired in borrowed shirts and breeches from John and George, they ate voraciously and drank toasts until the flasks were drained.

"To my new brother," Allen raised his goblet to George. "Welcome to our family, for this is wondrous news to return to."

"Thank you, Allen," George grinned and lifted his own tankard. "I cannot take full credit for this. I must admit my personality is such that anything my older brother accomplishes, I feel compelled to match."

Allen laughed. "We are fortunate, then, that we had a sister to spare." He turned to Babs. "I recall when you first caught sight of John at Richmond, you thought him most pleasing to the eye. God's will is provident that he had a brother to spare, too."

Laughter rippled around the table. Truly, these children were as well-matched as any she could think of. Now, if James could just return home, her family would be complete.

"The king is here, then?" Lucy asked. "He brings his cause to our doorstep and calls upon the men of Nottingham?"

Allen nodded, his mouth full. "William stays with him at Thurland House, with the Earl of Clare and other Royalists. We are commanded to be at his side tomorrow by noon."

"For what reason?" John leaned forward, eager to hear more.

"He intends to make a speech, as I understand," Edward replied. "Will you come with us?"

"We all will." Lucy was firm. "This is an event I want to witness."

"Is Nottingham safe?" asked Babs.

"John and George are respected by all in the town," said Luce. "Do you not think we will be treated with the utmost courtesy?"

"The citizens of Nottingham are our friends," George added. "We have nothing to fear of our own people."

"This is true." Allen pushed his chair back and reached for his wine. "Ah, how many nights did we dream of sitting here, Edward?"

"Too many, Coz. It is certainly a respite from the army camps to spend time with you, Aunt."

"You could stay here." Luce's voice carried across the table. "You could stay. There's room here. John can provide a home for you until the king's matters are sorted."

What did she guess? Lucy thought. What unsettled her daughter to make that spontaneous offer?

"Our place is with the king," replied Allen. "We have trained for a time such as this, Luce. You cannot deny our duty."

"Where lies your loyalty, Allen?" demanded Luce. "Your family deserves the truth."

He shrugged, his broad shoulders strong under the fine linen shirt, the beautifully cut doublet. Court was good to her son.

"Why, Luce," he replied, "As God is my witness, I am loyal to His Majesty and faithful to the Parliament. My heart lies with the men of this country and their wish for peace."

"By forming armed bands of Cavaliers?" cried Luce, her voice rising. "My heart is loyal and faithful too—loyal to the Parliament who represent the rights of men, faithful to the tradition of monarchy. Consider your own world order, not mine."

Allen stood too, his soldier's physique suddenly charging the atmosphere. His color rose. "The king is as a father to the people of this nation. He knows what is best for them."

"Is that why he commandeers our ammunition, leaves our towns defenseless, our women and children vulnerable to any band of armed men?"

"Keep to your writing and notebooks, and leave the business of government to men."

Lucy prayed for the storm to subside. Thus always ranged their arguments, until one caught the other's eye, and a shared smile would appear, contagious and healing. Please God this night was no different.

"Tomorrow, we ride to Nottingham to attend King Charles," she said. "He speaks to unite our country, to stand down the armies. Tonight, let not differences divide us."

"Let us put politics aside." This time, George spoke up. George, whose lighthearted character could be counted upon to relieve any tension. "Edward, Allen, would you like to stroll a little before nightfall? The country here is most conducive to walking, and we can show you the land and its boundaries."

Allen and Edward looked at each other. Edward nodded at his cousin and smiled at Luce.

"We would enjoy that very much," he replied. "I think a little cool air would be just what is needed."

Luce opened her mouth to speak and then shut it again as John held out his arm to her.

"Shall we?" he asked gently. "Let us show Allen where our hearts lie, in this home of ours."

Lucy's family left, their voices harmonious again, even a few bars of a plaintive harvest song sung by Babs. She moved to the window and pressed her forehead against the wavy glass. They walked across the moat bridge toward the verdant fields beyond, a glorious golden sunset suffusing high clouds with hues of pink and red. For one more night, she could believe that the world was a safe place for her children.

And so, to Nottingham, and the castle mount. Lucy's stomach churned. Were all the memorable events in her life to be set against the backdrop of castles and palaces? It seemed so, for it was at Whitehall that Theo betrayed her, at Castle Fonmon where Allen proposed to her, and the Tower where he'd died in her arms.

Now, today, her daughters stood with her at the foot of the mount, while somewhere in this crowd of courtiers and Cavaliers, her son waited on the king. The citizens of Nottingham thronged in the streets around the castle, and as she took the hands of Luce and Babs, they walked together up Friars Lane. The closer they came to the castle yard, the denser the crowd, and she despaired of finding Allen or John.

"John said to meet him by the top of the hill." Luce peered through the mass of people. "That is the most likely place for the king to appear. We are almost there."

A light breeze from the River Trent stole through the crowds, bringing a coolness to the thundery August evening. The air was heavy with a brewing storm, and Lucy was grateful for the brief freshness.

"There's John," called Luce. "Come, this way."

As they squeezed through the crowd, a drumming began that was picked up by various soldiers stationed at every street corner. The insistent beating caused the crowd to still and quieten. Lucy and her girls arrived next to John, and they stood close together, the pounding reverberating in their ears.

"Look," John murmured so that Lucy had to strain to hear him. "It is Prince Rupert. And Prince Maurice, the king's cousins. And the Duke of Richmond, dead Buckingham's son-in-law."

Across the crowd, not more than a hundred yards away, stood a cluster of noblemen, their gorgeous lace-and-silk clothes singling them out from the courtiers around them. The Duke of Richmond's golden hair gleamed in the setting sun. She searched anxiously for Allen, but could not find him nor Edward in the mass of people.

"More nobles arrive—and Prince Charles," John said. "And he is attended by Edward Villiers, William's brother—"

"And Allen? Do you see Allen?"

The drumming increased in fervor and now beat a tattoo that changed tempo to an insistent roll.

"Yes," John said, his height helping him see over the heads of those in front. "Here, tread forward and up on these steps. You will be able to see Allen and Edward."

Lucy took John's hand and climbed up the stone stairs; Luce and Babs followed. They held each other tightly to keep their balance. Across the small square, Allen and Edward stood to solemn attention, shoulder to shoulder with other Cavaliers.

More drumming to the left of them, and all fell silent as a convoy of riders parted the crowd.

"The king comes," said John.

"It's William." Luce was the first to recognize her cousin. "William rides with the king's party."

The king and a small group of nobles clattered past them in full armor. From her perch on the steps, Lucy was level with the party. Seeing William was as if looking at Barbara's face, for he carried her unmistakable elegance and fine features. He stared ahead; she did not know if he saw her in the crowd. A dozen men carrying the king's standard on their shoulders walked gravely behind the horsemen.

"Surely not," breathed John. "Surely he is not going to raise the royal standard. That is a challenge against Parliament that few could misread."

Lucy wavered on the step and almost lost her footing. "He must just be hoisting it to declare his residency at the castle."

They watched, standing silent with the crowd, as the king rode across the drawbridge and through to the castle grounds. Moments later, against the darkening storm-clouded sky, the great standard was unfurled from the highest tower. The pennant hung limp for a moment and then snapped to life as a gust of wind flew from the valley below.

"What emblem is this?" Lucy was shocked. Never in all her years at the Tower or Whitehall had she witnessed such a thing. The ensign was brilliant blood-red bearing a white cross of St. George, embellished with a crown and a pointing hand. Flapping on the storm gust, the wind revealed words emblazoned across the length of the flag. The courtiers surrounding the king threw their hats into the air and whooped aloud. The crowd became sullen.

"God save King Charles! Hang up the Roundheads!"

Lucy blanched at the direct challenge to the Parliamentarians. The nickname from the streets of London had become a rallying cry from the king's men.

"*Give unto Caesar his due*," read John. "Dear Almighty God. The message is clear. The king has declared war on his own Parliament."

"War on his own people, you mean," responded Lucy. In the deepening night, torches flaring, other standards were raised, battle flags of the nobles who surrounded the king. The forces were rallying, the old feudal custom awakening men's ancient loyalties. Flickers of lightning illuminated the distant horizon, a fiery backdrop.

"We should go." John turned abruptly and held his hand out to Lucy. "We should return to the safety of Owthorpe."

"Allen," she cried. "Allen stays here. I must see him before we leave."

The shifting crowd closed in around her, and for a moment, Lucy glimpsed her son's face in the dying rays of the blood-red sun. His eyes caught hers, and a silent message of love leapt between them. He nodded slowly and then resumed his fixed stare ahead, guarding the king and the banners of war.

She looked from Allen's face to that of Luce, standing next to her, eyes brimming with tears. The chasm of conflict yawned between her children, and she could no longer bridge it with words and kisses.

A crash of thunder echoed from the castle walls, and in the last of the fierce sunset, a gust of wind tugged at the royal standard and blew it free from the tower. For a moment, the banner hung in the air before furling and tumbling to the dirt of the inner bailey of the castle. As one person, the townspeople gasped their shock at this terrible omen.

Her son-in-law put his arms around her and Luce while George sheltered Babs from the pressing crowd.

"Come," said John. "Come. We must hasten home. War is upon us. War is upon us."

31

My dear, do not be concerned for I am presently detained in Northampton, with My Lord Essex's army, to whom I have successfully delivered plate and horses diverted from the king's troop.

Your ever loving husband, John
17th September, 1642

Luce handed John's creased and tattered letter to George and sat down painfully next to Babs on the bench before the fireplace. This was a girl child she carried high and wide, and who caused Luce an agony in her back such as she had not experienced before. And still three months before the birth. God willing, John could return by then, else she may have to travel back to her mother in Owthorpe on her own.

"'Tis a pity that John was called to Northampton," Babs said, wistful. "George and I hoped he could enjoy visiting with our friends here in Leicester. Perhaps by Martinmas, this conflict will be resolved."

George read the scribbled words and laughed.

"Not likely by the tone of his letter. John seeks to remain neutral. But I would say stealing the king's horses speaks louder than words, and that he is as loyal to Parliament as the rest of us. His letter may have taken a while to reach us, but his words fly from the page."

Luce rushed to defend her husband. "John wishes only for peaceful discourse to resolve these differences. He pins his hopes on the petitions from Parliament to defend the citizens." Her husband wrestled with his conscience, wanting only a peaceful outcome.

"Even with our differences, Father supplied us with money for armor and weapons when we asked him." George winked at Babs. "Guns encourage discourse. And very respectable Roundheads we are, to encourage conversations with the Royalists."

Babs shook her head. "Do not call yourself such, Husband. Neither you nor John will ever cut your hair in that disgusting fashion, nor give away your velvets and lace."

George laughed. "True, my beauty, true. We may pack them in trunks until we are recalled to court, but we will not dress in Puritan drab."

Luce smiled to see her sister and George so happy with each other. Fate dictated they be brought together—she had fallen in love with John; 'twas no great surprise that her lighter-hearted sister had pledged herself to his high-spirited brother.

Turning back to the letter, she wondered again how soon John would arrive. Armies were on the move across all of England, and for certain the troop of Prince Rupert's garrisoned next to them in Leicester did no harm to the ordinary citizens of the town. Hopefully, they would leave soon, and John could ride freely and take her home.

A blast of trumpets echoed from the street outside.

George strode to the window. "Another troop comes into town. More Cavaliers to join Prince Rupert." He leaned against the frame, watching intently.

"Are we safe?" asked Luce, her voice low. "They know John resisted the king's command to hand over munitions. Will they take retribution on us?"

Laughing, George turned to his sister-in-law and wife. "I think we are quite safe. If I'm not mistaken, the troop is wearing Goring's colors. And your brother is leading it."

Allen laid his hat on the table and took Luce and Babs into his arms. What a joyful twist of fate he should be garrisoned next to their friend's house, even if only for one night. His only sadness was that his mother was not with them.

"I am sorry I could not call upon you as soon as I arrived," he said. "Prince Rupert insisted we attend his briefing, which ran deep into the night."

"But you came now," Luce replied. "How long can you stay?"

"I'm afraid I leave again this afternoon." Allen looked over his sisters' heads and frowned at George. "We continue our patrols. I ride south, toward Oxford, where the king has his court." He saw George catch the deeper meaning of his words. The offensive had begun. "Where's John?"

"He traveled to Northampton—"

"Sister, tell me he had nothing to do with the king's supplies being diverted to the Earl of Essex."

Luce fell silent.

"Luce, they are searching for him. A Captain Welch is appointed to find him. He approached me last night to see if I knew anything from you." This time, Allen did not conceal his concern from any of them. "If he asks again, you must protect John. Say he is in Owthorpe or Nottingham or somewhere. Do not say he was in Northampton."

George clasped Allen's hand. "We hear your words, Brother, and thank you for your warning."

Allen put his other hand over George's and pressed it tight. "Keep them safe, George. And hasten back to Owthorpe the moment Rupert's troops have left. You'll be secure there."

A banging on the door startled Luce to her feet as she rested in the parlor the next morning. With the entire household out watching Prince Rupert's departure, only she and George were at home. Glancing up the stairs to the chamber he shared with Babs, she saw no movement, and so opened the door.

"Mrs. Hutchinson?" The soldier stood close to the door, his stance intimidating.

"Yes."

"Captain Welch. I am here to speak to you of your husband. Unless he is here, of course." The man smirked, his dark eyes narrowed, peering into the hallway behind her. He took another step forward. "Do you mind if I come in?"

Luce opened the door wider, as if she had nothing to hide.

"By all means, Captain Welch. My brother, Sir Allen Apsley, mentioned you might be calling. You are most welcome in our home."

"How interesting. Did he also tell you that we intercepted your husband's letter before sending it on to you? He is in Northampton, stealing supplies and diverting them to the king's enemy, the Earl of Essex."

Luce forced herself to remain calm. Behind her, upstairs, she heard the creak of a floorboard. George was listening.

"I think not, Captain Welch."

"You deny the letter? I read it for myself."

"I deny my husband is in Northampton." She gave a quick prayer that George was following. "Let me call him down, now. John? John!"

Captain Welch's expression changed to one of disbelief as George clattered down the stairs, shrugging on his jacket.

"Yes, my love?" he replied as he kissed Luce on the cheek. "And who is this?"

"Captain Welch. He thinks you are in Northampton." Luce stared at the man, daring him to deny her. The silence between them lengthened.

"And I appear to be in Leicester," responded George. "May I see you out, Captain?"

Later, when all returned from the excitement of seeing Prince Rupert's troop ride out and were settled in the parlor, Luce fell to telling her friends of her adventure. As the parlor resounded to much laughter and merriment, the maid interrupted them.

"Beg pardon, madam, but there is a Captain Welch to see you, with another gentleman."

The room fell silent. Luce put her finger to her lips and winked. "Now, let us continue the jest," she said. "You must not call George by his name. And, Babs, for once I am commanding the attention of a man who is in love with you. That is a rarity."

Captain Welch strode in, accompanied by another Royalist soldier.

"Captain John Hutchinson?"

George stepped forward. "Why, man, have you yet to believe your own eyes that I am here? You have brought a witness to prove to yourself that I am not riding around Northampton, stealing the king's horses?"

Babs giggled, and her laughter appeared to irritate Captain Welch. The mood of the room shifted.

Luce stepped next to George. "John, best that we offer Captain Welch our hospitality and let him state his business." She did not want George's natural high spirits to carry this joke too far.

"Our business, madam, is to arrest your husband." Captain Welch and his companion drew pistols from their waistbands and stepped forward to

George. "John Hutchinson, I am authorized by Prince Rupert to imprison you for the crime of treason. I have a company of dragoons outside to bring you into custody."

In the silence that followed, Babs's cry of denial pierced the air. "This is not John, it's not John! This is his brother, George, my husband, I swear."

"She's right—you must listen," Luce wept. "This is not John Hutchinson. We were deluding you."

"Tell that story to Prince Rupert," snapped the Royalist. Shoving past her, Captain Welch and his companion grabbed George and marched him from the parlor. Her last glimpse was of his face, white with fear.

Allen reined his horse at the brow of Edge Hill to keep the stallion from sliding down the steep escarpment. With sides heaving, Boreas snorted at the abrupt tug on his mouth and stamped in place. Ill-tempered brute, but as fast and strong as the wind he was named for. Next to him, Edward held his own horse in check, steam rising from the mount's sweating sides in the cold October air.

In silence, they gazed northwest across the broad plain spread below, heathland stretching as far as the eye could see, ending in a distant range of hills. Only, Allen didn't look to the horizon. He was fixed on the Parliamentarian army assembling below, a mass of horses and foot soldiers creating a formidable wall close to the foot of the escarpment. To the rear, closest to the village of Kineton, cannons anchored in the marshy ground.

"'Tis Dutch formation," Allen stated. "Cavalry on either flank, infantry in the center."

"I'd say about two thousand men." Edward shaded his eyes. "And more coming by the moment. Word is out that our armies engage. Look." He pointed to the east, where a stream of men and horses advanced to the heath.

"We are evenly matched." Allen looked back toward their own Royalist fighters. "Perhaps more in our favor. William commands a large troop of horse, and we have more dragoons on our flanks."

Edward turned his horse away from the edge. "We must ride down with care. The terrain is steep and rugged."

"And we will have the advantage of power and speed." Allen turned his horse. "Time to gather our troop. Are you ready to lead your men into battle, Captain St.John?"

"As ready as you, Captain Apsley."

Allen laughed at the sheer euphoria that coursed through his body. Here he was, commanding a troop of horse, under the leadership of his cousin William and Prince Rupert. They held the winning position; the king was here, as were his sons. A glorious day for the cause. A glorious afternoon to strike at the heart of the Parliamentarians. Petitions, his arse. There would be petitions all night, once they'd won this skirmish. The waiting and training since Nottingham was worth every moment. Victory would be theirs today.

He and Edward rode through Prince Rupert's battalions, arranged in the complex Swedish diamond formation, to their own position in the second line under Lord Byron. God, what good fortune was theirs to serve under such an experienced warrior, who had proven himself over and over on battlefields throughout Europe.

A drum started up from the heathland below, pulling Allen's thoughts to the immediacy of this skirmish. The throbbing rhythm was drowned by a louder drumming from the Royalist platoons surrounding him on the escarpment. He tightened his grip and felt Boreas quiver beneath him.

"The king! The king!" The monarch and his sons, mounted on great warhorses, emerged from a camp pitched toward the back of the escarpment on the Edge Hill side. Beside them, Prince Rupert, a white dog at his horse's side, stood outlined against the bright sky.

A barrage of artillery fire crackled from the Parliamentarian ranks; invisible bullets whistled through the air above Allen's head. Answering fire volleyed from the Royalist soldiers. The acrid stench of gunpowder choked his throat, staining the cold, clear October air. White smoke drifted across their hill and quickly cleared, while down below, the enemy was barely visible, so thick hung the smoke in the valley.

Giving his red Royalist sash a final tug in place, he lifted his gauntleted hand. To his right, Edward did the same. The eyes of his men were fixed on his raised arm.

With a great shout, Prince Rupert gave the order to attack. Allen signaled his troop to maintain their tight formation, and descending the escarpment, they reached a controlled canter. All moved forward together, presenting a block of horses and armored men that appeared invincible to men on the ground. Closer and closer they rode toward the opposing army. Cannon fire roared from ahead and behind, and yet Boreas never flinched. The menace of their calm and controlled appearance panicked the enemy into firing out of range.

A blast on the trumpets and thundering drums incited the horses to leap forward, and within a second, Allen galloped Boreas across the heathland, Edge Hill at his back. Such was his speed, there could be no stopping, no turning back—only forward into the battle.

Ahead, Prince Rupert's troop disappeared into the smoke, and as another volley of shots rang out, a horse in front screamed and fell heavily on its side, pinning the rider underneath. Allen galloped past, catching only the wild rolling eye of the creature, the bloody open mouth of the trapped rider. Boreas did not balk, and as they crashed into the remains of the front line of the Parliamentarian army, Allen drew his sword and slashed at anything in his way, man or beast.

Screaming and crying raged around him, the marshy land churning and pellets of mud flying into his face. His sword slashed into soft, vulnerable armpits and rang off breast plates. A gurgling shriek told the truth of his aim. And when a broadsword whipped in front of his visor and he instinctively slashed upward with his own blade, a disembodied arm flew in front of him, the weapon still clenched in its fingers. A stink of blood and shit and filth filled his nostrils, and he urged Boreas forward, knowing that to slow for one moment would endanger the safety of the men behind him.

Allen glanced to his right, wanting to see Edward—and there he was, crouched over his pommel, armor shining in a sudden ray of sun that penetrated the smoke. His cousin rode as one with his mount, his sword covered in gore. Next, over his shoulder, Allen saw his troop intact, a tight compact of men holding the formation, just as he had drilled them.

The smoke cleared. Perhaps a hundred yards away, Prince Rupert's troop of horse continued its gallop, unstoppable in the weight and speed of a thundering advance. And now, as they spread out, he could see beyond to the scattering of Parliamentarian forces. They'd broken through enemy lines.

He tightened his reins, preparing to signal an about, but hesitated. Rupert's troop continued to gallop across the flat plain with no sign of slowing. To Allen's left, the constant clash of swords and clamor of drum signals indicated fierce fighting underway. Why did Rupert not circle back and attack the Parliamentarians from the rear?

Lifting his arm and dropping to a canter, Allen looked back over his shoulder. No foot soldiers were left between his unit and the king. In less than an hour, they had effectively routed the entire left flank of the Parliamentarian army.

Edward cut diagonally across his unit and rode up to Allen. "We should rally and return to attack the rear," he shouted.

"I agree," Allen yelled back. "But Prince Rupert pursues the retreating forces. We must follow his lead."

"Is this wise?" Edward pointed to the west with his sword. "They are in fierce conflict. William is there somewhere. That is just where his troop advanced."

"I don't know; no signal tells us. We have no choice. We ride with Rupert!" Allen kicked Boreas back into a gallop and gave the signal for his troop to follow. They streamed across the wide-open battlefield, pursuing the retreating Parliamentarian cavalry.

Only when they were clear of the carnage of dying men and horses did Allen start to tremble, and he sheathed his sword to better grip his reins.

Rakes. Staves. An ancient longbow and sheaf of arrows untouched. The gorge rose again in Allen's throat as he walked Boreas back through the carnage of the heath, retracing the steps of their advance. These men were not soldiers. This enemy was not armed for this kind of conflict.

Boreas stepped over a mangled body and kicked a head that lay to the side, eyes and mouth fixed hellishly wide. Jesu. Most of these men wore tawny sashes, Parliamentarians all. But to the west, heaped where they fell, lay foot soldiers draped in red. Royalists. The center of the field was where the fighting had been fiercest. And now, in the darkening October night, the cries and groans of men rivaled the very witches and ghouls that haunted this most evil of months.

After the wild gallop away from the skirmish in pursuit of the fleeing Parliamentarians, Allen had thought the battle won, a clear victory for his side. But not this. Not this morass of severed limbs and horse parts, the earth soaked in vomit and urine, and pools forming where the fluids could no longer be absorbed into the soil. Allen breathed through his nose, his sash now bound around his face—for to open his mouth was to taste the very blood of his fellow Englishmen, running in streams on this desolate heath.

Small skirmishes still broke out, and suddenly a weak cheer echoed as a man in William's colors recaptured the royal banner from a fleeing Parliamentarian. Quiet and exhausted and fought out, with the fading light making it impossible to distinguish between red and orange sash, Allen and the Royalist horse wearily cantered back to Edge Hill to join the king.

Small fires were burning outside the tents, and after seeing that Boreas was watered—for there was no hay for feed in this hasty camp—Allen unstrapped his breastplate and flung himself down on the ground next to Edward. He drank long and deep of a flagon of beer, but could not yet face food. The roasting flesh hanging from a spit over the fire appeared delivered straight from the battlefield.

Edward passed him another flagon.

"William is safe. You should try to eat something."

Allen shook his head. He rolled over and settled his breastplate as a bolster, looking up at the clear sky. Orion laughed down at him, invincible in his field of black.

Did I serve you proud today, Father? Did you watch over me as you said you always would? Is this war, then—this filth, this fear, this feeling of utter emptiness when the battle is done?

Steady, my son, steady.

Allen sat up abruptly, Edward's eyes upon him. He gulped his beer and smiled at his cousin while seizing a hunk of roast flesh from the spit.

"Best keep our strength up, Coz. And not waste this ale the quartermaster has provided."

Around him, the terrible groans of the wounded echoed through the camp. The empty heavens looked down upon him, and he wished for the comfort of his mother's dream of the star coming into her hand and promising fame to her child. He wished that he, not Luce, be the lucky one of eminence. For if distinction was to be gained through war, he doubted himself worthy.

32.

The Lord Viscount Grandison, my cousin-german, was then in the king's army, to whom I immediately dispatched a messenger, to entreat him to oblige me by the procurement of my brother's liberty, who, upon my imprudence, had been brought into that trouble. My lord sent me word, that, for the present, he could not obtain it.

Luce Hutchinson
November 17th 1642

George's captors had removed him to Derby, where the prison overflowed with Parliament's men accused of defying the king. Luce had brought Babs back to the safety of their own home in Owthorpe. But her parlor was as much a prison as the Tower, for Luce's guilt held her captive. The familiar room brought cold comfort. In the fire's flames appeared faces contorted with pain. In the crackling of the logs, came the creak of the ropes. She remembered the hideous machinery that lay deep in the Tower.

She could not contact John in hiding. Allen was unreachable.

"William Villiers, Lord Grandison. He rides with Prince Rupert." said her mother after the third day. "You must write to him. For the sake of our family, and his loyalty to Allen and James, plead for your sister's husband."

And so, she returned to the old family connection.

Luce knew what it had cost her mother to plead to the Villiers for help. But there had been no other to turn to. Cousin William could intervene, for the sake of kinship in these uncertain times. She wrote to him to plead for the life of her brother-in-law.

Luce examined her hands. Her fingers, as always, were ink-stained. Her journal lay on the table close to her side. She might not have a sword to defend her family, but her pen was powerful. And the letter she'd sent to William had been impassioned, imploring, begging him to release innocent George. He had no love of combat. They made no difference to

257

the war; they chose no side. Independents, they fought for neither king nor Parliament.

She lay back on the divan as Babs sat on the floor beside her. Luce's newborn, a weak girl, mewed in her cradle. An early birth, brought on by the fear of George's capture, John's absence. Luce turned her face to the wall. Dear God, let this innocent babe live. Surely all this was her fault. She must make good on her terrible mistake.

She stroked her sister's soft hair. These months of fear had taken a toll on Babs; a new maturity settled on her features, and her character had grown solemn.

"Read me again William's letter. Read me what he says," Luce murmured.

Babs pulled the letter from the small table by their side.

"He is doing his best to free George, who refuses to swear an oath that he will not take up arms for Parliament. He says it is not safe for John to return. The king commanded Rupert to order a troop of forty to hunt down John." Babs's voice broke, but she cleared her throat and continued, "Our cousin writes in haste, for he rides to Oxford to join the king. The Earl of Essex has mustered an equal force of Parliamentarian soldiers, who stand between the king and London." Babs looked up, fear in her eyes. "He makes no mention of Allen, nor Edward or James."

Luce bit back a sob as took her sister in her arms.

"They will all be safe, Luce. They have to be safe," Babs soothed. She rocked Luce as if she were a child herself, and they clung together as the darkness fell around them.

Lucy held her granddaughter tightly in her arms as she walked the length of the solar. The infant was sickly, and Lucy feared she would not survive. All around her hung the news of death.

With the passing months since the child's birth came news of the war, the real war, the war where men hacked and butchered and slaughtered each other, corpses angrily eviscerated like pigs at the Smithfield meat market. Lucy prayed night and morning for the safety of Allen, James, Edward, John, George, William, her brother's children, Eleanor's son—all the laughing boys she loved so well. Prayer was her constant companion, a litany that ceaselessly chanted in her heart and mind, wherever she was, whatever she was doing.

Dear God, let them be safe. Dear God, keep them from harm. Dear God, never let them face each other on a battlefield.

She stood by the tall windows and gazed over the summer countryside. Lucy loved this room, of all the chambers in Owthorpe House. The wall paintings, of hunting scenes and minstrels, beautiful ladies and mythical unicorns, comforted her. And the south-facing windows caught the July twilight long after the rest of the manor was in darkness. Out of the window, a shadow against the golden wheat fields caught her eye. Lucy froze, the baby giving a small wail at her sudden stop. A troop of horse approached, twenty men, at least. She could not tell whose colors they wore. But they were headed directly for the Manor.

At the hammering on the door, Luce caught up a fire iron and ran across the darkened hall. The windows were all shuttered, and the only light came from lanterns by the cold fireplace. Her heart thumping, she gestured to Babs to hurry to the kitchen, where the few servants they had with them were supping.

"We are closed for the night. We cannot open the doors," she shouted through the thick oak. Dear God, let them not ram the door, or force the shutters. Babs crept back, with a sorry group of men. Old Tom the gardener, seventy if he was a day, his grandson, and the simpleton kept for the kitchen chores.

"Ride on to Nottingham, travelers," she cried. "We have nothing to offer you here."

"Luce! Open the door. Let us in!"

Dear God. John's voice.

Tearing at the bolts, bruising her fingers, Luce flung open the door. John and George strode in, followed by a dozen or more Roundhead soldiers.

"My darling, my darling," she sobbed. "And George, you are safe."

Babs gave a cry and flung herself into her husband's arms, while John gathered Luce into a fierce embrace. Her mother ran into the hall, the fear on her face turning to joy as she understood what had happened.

"We are safe," John said. "And ravenous. We have ridden through from Leicester tonight—"

"And we still have further to go," added George.

"Food, for Colonel Hutchinson," commanded Luce to the gathered servants. "And these men. Quickly. Bring whatever meats we have, ale, cheese. And lay the food all on the table here."

She turned to George.

"We thought you lost, Brother. We heard you were on your way to the Tower."

George nodded, running his hand through his hair. He looked exhausted, and yet elated to be home. "'Twas close. If not for Lord Grandison, I would be there now."

"My love, my darling," cried Babs. "But you are safe, and unharmed?"

George nodded. "That I am. And released from custody."

"But not from the war," interrupted John. "We are not safe here at Owthorpe any longer. Prince Rupert has sent a troop of forty from Newark to look for us. William's release of George was not to his liking."

"But why?" asked Luce. "We have no side in the war. We are independent."

George looked at John. "The battle at Edge Hill—"

"Allen and Edward?"

John replied. "Safe, both of them. And James has just been recalled from Ireland."

Luce closed her eyes. "We heard there was a battle. And that there were casualties. But news has been unreliable here. Were many men were harmed?"

"Worse. Far worse." John's voice shook. "Thousands were killed. And for naught. There was no conclusion, no clear winner or loser. Those who said the war will be over by Christmas now say conflict just begins."

"Englishman slaughtered Englishman. And all because this tyrannical king— this mere man—believes his way is the only true way." George stood shoulder to shoulder with John, and Luce saw a new intent on their faces. "We will not let him continue this bloodshed. We join our brothers in the Parliamentarian cause and fight for the freedom of all Englishmen."

"And that means you fight against Allen and James, and Edward," Luce whispered. Her mother and Babs drew close. The hall was quiet, even the soldiers standing silent.

"We fight against the king," replied John. "War has broken out over all of England. We pray that we will never meet on a battlefield."

"But now, we must get you to safety," continued George. "Rupert's Cavaliers will not be so respectful this time. Tonight, under darkness, we ride on to Nottingham, all of us. The castle holds for Parliament. The fortress offers the protection that Owthorpe cannot."

John kissed Luce's forehead. "You must pack all you can, my darling, and be ready to leave as soon as these men have rested and eaten."

Luce nodded. This was not the time to question or debate. A deep calm descended upon her, and she knew what she needed to do. She turned to the group of soldiers, standing at a respectful distance.

"Eat," she gestured to the table, now full of food. "Eat, and rest. We will be ready to leave when you are done."

Taking Babs and her mother by the hand, she led them away from the exhausted men. Let them have their peace, and eat undisturbed.

"Listen to me," she said. "We do not know where our beloved men fight, nor their future. We do not know any of our destinies. But we have been in terrible situations before, and we have trusted in God's plan for us." Luce softly blotted a tear rolling down her mother's cheek. "And along with God's plan, we have our own courage, and will to survive. All of us. Allen, James, Edward—they must not have the distraction of fearing for our safety from their own forces. We move into the castle, and we wait out this war."

Her mother nodded. "God holds our fate. But we can affect our destiny." She turned to Babs. "Come, let's pack the needs for the children and prepare them for the journey. It is but an hour to Nottingham Castle. We must leave immediately."

Lucy stood with her daughter in the great hall of Nottingham Castle, surrounded by chests and boxes. No Queen's House at the Tower was this. Nottingham Castle was a garrison, and the highest point for miles around. Built on the mount over a warren of secret caverns carved from the sandstone, this was a brutal stronghold that five hundred years of hostilities had not leveled. This bleak fortress was not going to change its character for Lucy and her family.

"Take our clothes to the chamber allotted to us," Lucy ordered the two soldiers who helped unload their trunks from the cart. "Be careful with that case of medicinals. I will take it to the stillroom." She turned to Luce. "I fear we will need these curatives more than anything else here."

Luce nodded, her eyes wide. As soon as they arrived from Owthorpe, John and George were called out to lead a skirmish against a troop of Royalists that were attacking a bridge over the Trent. Once they rode past the crumbling gates, the drawbridge was raised. No one was leaving or arriving until they returned. There would be no sleep for them tonight.

"Sarah and Babs are settling the children into their room next to ours," Luce replied. "We had best prepare for the return of John's troop. I fear there may be injuries among them."

"It is our lot to nurse our loved ones wounded in war." Lucy gave her daughter a quick hug. "You'll be all right, Luce?"

"It feels so familiar, as if we are back in the Tower's stillrooms, taking care of Father." Luce smiled. "I am fine. I feel strong, and I cannot bear to sit with the children and wait to hear. Let's check your supplies and see what is to hand here."

They walked across the cavernous hall, their footsteps echoing on the stone floor. Through the clerestory windows, in the early dawn light, Lucy glimpsed a flag flying from the old tower built over Mortimer's Hole. She shivered at the thought of Queen Isabella's paramour, a tortured man whose legacy named the caverns below. The rest of the towers surrounding the yard were ruined, in great disrepair, for no money was spent to maintain this fortress in times of peace.

She shook her head. How had this come about? Did they envision only a year ago that brothers and friends, fathers and sons would be facing each other on a battlefield and that England would be tearing itself in two? Since the royal standard had been raised and the king rode away, Nottingham held the castle not for the Royalists, but for Parliament.

Her thoughts rested on Allen and James, never far from her mind. How proudly Allen had stood by the king. How excited was James to fight at his cousin's side. Where were they now, and when would they return to her?

The door to the hall flung open, and John strode in, pulling off his gauntlets.

"You are safe," exclaimed Luce. "And George?"

"Out of harm's way and drinking a round with his men," replied John. "No Royalist will get between George and his ale."

"What did you see, John?" Lucy asked quietly. "Who threatens us outside the town walls?"

John pushed back his hair, still worn long and curling on his shoulder. He saw no need to cut it to declare his loyalty to Parliament. He paused, as if preparing his words.

"They ride to surround us. Rupert's troop. Lord Byron and his army are lined up at all the northern bridges, and as we beat them back from one, they disappeared into the forest, only to gather at another crossing. By tomorrow or the next day, they will attack again." He reached out and held Luce against him while taking Lucy's hand. "We were fortunate to leave Owthorpe and take shelter here. We must prepare for a siege. We can defend the town and the castle until help arrives. I have sent to Leicester and Derby to lend me men."

"I thought you said we would be safer here," cried Luce. "And now you speak of sieges and defending ourselves against the enemy."

"We *are* safer here," replied John. "Owthorpe now lies in the midst of enemy ground. I know not what looting or destruction may be taking place. But we would not have survived the onslaught of the king's army that has encircled our town."

"How many men are here, John? And surgeons, doctors?" Lucy's mind flew to the practical.

John paused. "We have but fourscore men. George and I are the only officers. And no surgeon."

In the quiet following John's statement, Lucy's thoughts went immediately to her grandchildren, tucked away in the high chamber. She would rather die than let any harm come to them.

"Then we shall prepare to defend ourselves and hold out until help arrives," she resolved. "This castle has seen many a battle fought outside its walls, and has never been breached. The defenses will not be penetrated this time, either."

Luce picked up the case of medicinals and turned to John. "Show me where the stillroom is, my love, for we have work to do. This war will not be bloodless, and if my mother and I can apply our learnings to help save men's lives, that we will."

Gunfire. Lucy woke with a start. Gunfire shattering the dawn in reveille, shots ricocheting off the stone walls. She grabbed her robe and jumped from the bed she shared with Luce, who was already at the slit window.

"It is as John predicted. The enemy is within the city walls," Luce gripped the stone, her knuckles white. "They have taken St. Nicholas Church, and fire cannon at the castle gates."

"Where is John?" Lucy looked to the door that led to the children's antechamber. "The children?"

"They are safe. He sent a soldier to guard the door. Sarah is keeping them calm."

Another volley of shots brought Lucy's attention outside to the castle yard, and she gasped at an old man lying in a pool of blood, the bullets flying around him and sending up puffs of dirt.

"They need to bring him to us," she said. "We must help him."

"He has been there since first light," replied Luce. "The bullets fly too thick for him to be retrieved. He stopped writhing a while ago. I cannot believe there is life left in him."

"Come, Luce. Dress quickly, and let us go to the stillroom, at least." Lucy pulled on her gown and tied an apron firmly around her. "I cannot watch from here."

The great hall of the castle was deserted except for two soldiers who stood at the door, guns in their hands. They pressed up against the stone walls and peered through the narrow slits to the yard outside.

"What see you?" asked Lucy. "And where is Lieutenant Colonel Hutchinson?"

"Beg pardon, ma'am, we are not at liberty to say."

"He is my husband," Luce said angrily. "You can tell me where he is."

The soldier shook his head. "The enemy came into town disguised as women, in the night," he replied solemnly, his country accent strong. "We are to take no risk in what we reveal. You could be the enemy."

Lucy and Luce looked at the soldier and then at each other. Holding their hands over their mouths, they laughed until they were choking at the thought of them being Royalist fighters. The soldier stared ahead, impassive.

"Enough, they will think we are mad women," gasped Luce. "What can we be thinking?"

"In the midst of fear, laughter lies close to tears. Hysteria is a humor that is unpredictable." Lucy tucked her hair under her hood. "I've seen this before, in the Tower. When a man faces death, sometimes he calls to God. Other times, he gibbers like an idiot or laughs like a maniac."

"John will return soon," said Luce. She took a deep breath and became serious. "Let us prepare a room. There are wounded soldiers out there, and we need to care for them."

There was little to do except watch the battle from behind the walls, for their casualties were light. None rode outside the castle walls, and although George's men fired back at the enemy, the stronghold was designed for defense, and little harm came to those inside.

On the fifth morning—just as Lucy thought she could no longer stand the incessant gunfire, the shouting, the cannon pummeling the castle walls—she stood in her chamber and watched John run across the yard from the tower over Mortimer's Hole. Five soldiers followed him. The group kept close to the tumbledown buildings that ringed the yard, now even more derelict from the enemy onslaught.

She ran down the narrow circular stairs, her hand grazing the wall as she steadied herself.

"Where do you come from, John?" she asked as he entered the hall. "And who are those men?"

"I've been in the town. Through the tunnels. They link with the cellar of the Lion's Den by Market Square. We are secretly meeting with our allies there to overthrow the enemy." His weary face told of his exploits.

"And you see no danger in this? What would happen if you are discovered, John?"

"Of course there is danger. But if we don't get help, we will be overwhelmed."

"And the men? I did not recognize them."

"Soldiers from within the city who have been hiding in the tunnels. We bring more in each day. Fourscore men more have mustered here at the castle since Lord Byron began the siege."

"And next?"

John looked around the deserted hall.

"Where is Babs?"

"Upstairs, with Luce and the children." A stone weighed in Lucy's heart. "Why?"

"George rode out early, before dawn, with all our men. A small party stays to keep up the cannon fire to distract the enemy. We are ridding the city of the Royalists." John took his sword from the sheath, his eyes red with exhaustion. "Derby's men ride to our relief. We have one hour to ensure these strategies coincide. Prepare yourself, Lady Mother, for there will be many wounded and dying brought to your door."

Lucy nodded. "We shall care for them all. And, John . . ."

He looked at her wearily. "Yes?"

"Bring us all men, you hear? These are fellow creatures, not enemies."

And, somewhere, perhaps a woman would be doing the same for Allen.

John nodded. "I will. There are some that won't agree, but I will deal with them." The great door of the castle slammed behind him.

Most of the wounds were gunshots, most dangerous of all. Her mind focused on the dozen men she treated, Lucy worked tirelessly, Luce at her side, as they cleaned the wounds with their balsams and dressed them with plasters and poultices. Although her nursing at the Tower was more in diseases and distempers, Lucy knew how to keep a man drugged to prevent the pain and how to break a fever brought on by duress. Extracting the lead bullets out of the wounds was critical, for leaving them in caused a man to lose feeling in his limbs, and even brought on blindness.

Pride filled her heart as she worked with her daughter. Under their care, not one man died, friend or enemy. And while she and Luce worked in the stillroom, nursing their fellow creatures with no regard for their religion or loyalty, John and George crept through the cellars of the city and ambushed the enemy, opening bridges and streets again to let the Derby Roundheads in. War ebbed from the castle walls, and men emerged from the tunnels and caverns to rejoin their families.

For now, Nottingham held for Parliament.

33

The king was the most obstinate person in his self-will that ever was, and so bent upon being an absolute, uncontrollable sovereign, that he was resolved either to be such a king or none.

Luce Hutchinson
October 17th 1643

Oxford unfurled for Allen as a legacy to his youth. As he rode Boreas through the fortified city, the streets around Trinity College hinted a faint familiarity, dreamlike in quality. He recognized the alleys and walkways. The inn on the corner was still named the Sunne. Fair orchards stretched behind the college, a pleasant walk where he and Edward had escorted many a maid to view the blossoms.

And yet, the environs were as remote as the moon. Was this what war did? Numb senses until only vision was left?

He cleared his mind. No room for fancy in this day. Court waited, the new court in Oxford established by the king now London was lost to the Roundheads. Bastards. That they should refuse God's appointed ruler entry to the capital of English power was the most presumptuous challenge yet.

How congenial to rejoin William and the Villiers family. James might be returning too, if the stories from the road were true. Now, if Edward showed up from his mission, the old drinking club would be reunited. These last few months on patrol were appalling. No comfortable beds, no decent food. And, most of all, a complete lack of female company.

Praise God these excursions ended now. Following his knighthood, a commission waited for him with the king's signature—appointed as lieutenant governor at Exeter, thanks to William's intervention. Take him off these blasted patrols and at least into decent lodging.

Oxford looked the same. Didn't recognize anyone he knew yet, but the town was bursting with Cavaliers, all armed and ready to ride forth again. Christ's nails, was there no break? Newbury was a disaster, thousands of lives lost in this last bloody battle. Not his, though. He'd done his part and more. God, he could use a drink, a bed, and a whore. Not necessarily in that order.

The spire of Christ Church soared against the brilliant October sky as he rode up South Street, and as he approached the king's court, the guards and crowds noticeably thickened.

Leaving Boreas in the care of a groomsman—thank God, finally some decent feed for the poor beast— Allen pushed his way through the mass of men standing idle within Christ Church's cloisters and spilling into the hall and grand staircase. The vaulted entry to the great hall was packed. Apparently here the king held his council meetings, judging by the number of scribes and secretaries milling around. He assumed the king was lodged within the college, and as the guards barred his way to the sunlit yard, he showed his pass with the king's seal. William must be somewhere around. He could collect his commission, celebrate their reunion, and head out of this madness.

"Where is the king?"

"In the deanery, sir." One of the guards gestured to the long terrace of buildings that lay through the arched doorway.

They stood aside and parted their pikes with a clang, and he slipped through into a large quadrangle. Honey-colored stone residences surrounded gardens bearing the last of the summer blooms, and birdsong filled the soft air. How distant from the clash of battle was this space. A sense of tranquility descended upon him, for here was the king's rightful privacy, his protection from the masses that thronged the outer buildings.

The gravel crunching beneath his boots echoed from the stone faces of the quadrangle; he slowed. Approaching him was a funeral procession— a small party, no more than a dozen, black-clothed and somber, the widow deeply veiled, as were the other women surrounding her. A normal sight these days, all too common. Allen paused, removed his hat, and stood deferential in a doorway as they drew closer. And then he realized that the king and queen were in the heart of the party, their small figures somehow vulnerable in their mourning black. Must have been someone important, for them to participate. Damn, meant kicking his heels around for another wait while this insipid ceremony was conducted.

As they drew level, the woman next to the widow turned her head and stumbled. He instinctively reached out his hand to catch her, and at that moment, his eyes met those of his Aunt Barbara. The procession faded into the background as her veil fluttered in the slight breeze, black lace marring the blue sky.

"No. No. No . . ." Allen took a step back, and all sound around him ceased.

Beside his aunt, he recognized Mary Bayning Villiers. He could only raise a hand; words would not come forth from his closed throat.

Allen found himself following as they processed solemnly within the cloister and entered the great doors of Christ Church chapel. Later, he could not recall walking from the courtyard to the church. A choir lifted its voice to heaven, the chorale piercingly sweet, echoing the melodies from the quadrangle. Lying on a bier in front of the great altar was a coffin. The funeral hatchment of Grandison was draped over it. How envious he had been of William that night at Battersey when the clergyman had read aloud Oliver's will. And now, what did the title bequeath him? Death held no regard for rank. Clenching his teeth, Allen glared at the ornately carved ceiling, the jewel-toned windows, the saints in their niches, searching for God but finding only the void.

Dry-eyed, he stared ahead at the coffin, the black-clothed figures surrounding it. Dear God, they even brought the baby, little Barbara, to the funeral. He would make sure she knew what a hero her father had been. Tell her of the man, the strength of his character. He'd promised William, and he must make good on his word. There, that was something he could do.

So. Their first casualty of war. Denial stole the balm of tears. He couldn't go up there to the altar. They'd understand. He wasn't dressed befittingly. He wasn't prepared for a funeral. He'd come to enjoy William's company, not lay him under a granite slab.

No words, really. Not even memories, for to open that volume would expose his heart. Damn, he needed a drink. And whatever other hospitality in Oxford a soldier could get lost within.

A touch on his arm made him lift his head. One of the mourners stood before him.

"William died two days ago of wounds sustained nobly defending the city of Bristol." The woman was deeply veiled, and he could not make out her face. "You'll come back to the deanery; there is food and wine. You are Allen, aren't you?"

He nodded.

"Come, come with me." She held out her arm. "My brother talked often of you. He loved you very much."

Allen hesitated. The woman's voice was clear and soft and comforting. "I am your cousin Anne, Lady Dalkeith," she said. "Come. Come be with your family."

Inside the gracious reception rooms of the deanery, Anne drew Allen away from the other mourners, to the window facing the cathedral garden. He squinted at the verdant lawns rolling from the terraced beds, so bright were they in the golden autumn sun. The chestnut trees promised a fine crop of conkers. Funny, the little things that drifted into his mind. When had that childhood world vanished?

A stone wall ran the length of the garden, and within was cut a small archway, indicated by a green wooden door.

"The king ordered the entrance made," Anne said, following his gaze, "to privately visit the queen, who stays at Merton College across the way. There is a path direct to her lodging."

"He makes himself at home here, then."

Anne nodded. She glanced over to the king and queen, standing next to Barbara across the spacious chamber, sipping blood-red wine from crystal glasses. "Oxford is the center of his power, now. And here, they are safe and can live undisturbed by the outside world."

Allen turned from the window. The land was all too green, lush, peaceful. The room was too hushed, the murmur of condolences stifling. He longed to be outdoors, away from this rarified air.

"And you, Cousin Anne? Do you live safely, undisturbed? And does your husband, the earl, fight somewhere on the king's behalf?"

Anne put a hand on his arm. "We all fight on the king's behalf, Allen, in our own way." She pushed back the black veil, and William's piercing blue eyes reproved him in the afternoon light. "My husband raises money for the king from his Scottish estates. And I serve the royal household by waiting on the queen. She depends on me to bring stability to her life and children, to support her as she lobbies on the king's behalf with our foreign friends. Not all fighting is on the battlefield."

Allen shrugged. To each his own.

270

"I must pay my respects to your mother," he said. "I have to get to Exeter. To take on the responsibility of the king's defense."

Anne removed her hand. "Then who am I to stand in your way?" She smiled calmly, and he once again glimpsed William in her features. "Let me go to her with you."

Together, they crossed the room and stood dutifully a short distance from Barbara. The king turned at their approach, and Allen bowed deeply before standing to attention before him. Since he'd last seen him at Whitehall, age had crept upon the king; gray coiled in his beard, and dark shadows rimmed his large brown eyes.

"Your Majesty," Anne began. "My cousin, Sir Allen Apsley. He has just ridden into Oxford and did not know of William's death."

The king inclined his head at Allen. "I remember you from Whitehall. And your father was a heroic man. You served with William?"

"At Edge Hill, Your Majesty."

"Ah, that was a great victory," replied the king. "We fought well that day. William's strategy was instrumental in winning on that field."

Allen said nothing. That was not the version that was out in the common narrative. Most thought the battle evenly tied—no winner, no loser. In his mind's eye, he saw the heaped dead, tawny and red sashes blood-soaked and indistinguishable from each other.

His aunt took a step forward, and from the corner of his eye, he saw Anne put a hand on her arm.

"My William is dead."

"Aunt Barbara, my deepest condolences. He fought and died defending the king, for his beliefs." Allen bowed to her.

"And you live." The words fell into the room as if a stone dropped into a well. Allen jerked his head up. "Tell me that your mother does not rejoice in my pain."

"Mother, you must rest," Anne's quiet voice interrupted. "Your grief taints your words. William is with God and at peace. He died proudly in the service of the king. Allen loved him dearly."

Allen's aunt pushed back her heavy veil, revealing a face wretched with grief. No cosmetics, no powder to disguise the ravage of sorrow. He barely recognized the woman whose charm had captivated the court at Whitehall.

"Remember this visage, and tell your mother."

Allen was wordless. That even in this deep grief his aunt should still think of the old rivalry proved those wounds cut deeper than any received on a battlefield. He bowed deeply again, not even wanting to kiss her hand. Best to leave.

The king raised his eyebrow, beckoning Allen to join him. He suddenly felt exhausted. Really, he just wanted to saddle up Boreas and ride west.

The king cleared his throat and inhaled through his nose. To Allen, it seemed he was searching for words. And then he remembered his father speaking of the king's stutter, the tricks he employed to control his impediment.

"Sir Allen. I recall now that William recommended you for the Exeter garrison. He believed you well-suited to commanding our defenses there." The king moved his mouth again, swallowing several times before continuing. "I trust you desire to live to his expectations of you."

Allen nodded. "Your Majesty, I will defend Exeter with my life and keep its citizens safe for you."

"Just as your sister defends Nottingham for the Roundheads?" Barbara's voice cut across their dialogue.

The king blinked. "What mean you, Lady Villiers?"

Barbara laughed, a brittle sound that crackled through the hushed room. At his side, Anne stiffened. The queen placed a hand on Barbara's arm.

"Why, his sister, the colonel's wife, of course," rejoined Barbara. "Mrs. John Hutchinson. Luce Apsley."

The king's face turned white. "Colonel John Hutchinson of Nottingham?" His tone was controlled, but nuanced. "The enemy who caused us to declare our intention in that city?"

Steady, my son.

"My sister Luce is married to John Hutchinson, Your Majesty."

His aunt's voice broke the silence again. "An interesting dilemma, Nephew. Are you loyal to your king, or loyal to your family?"

All eyes were on him. What game was she playing, making him declare his allegiance in such a way?

Steady.

The king's doleful eyes looked only at him. Allen gathered his thoughts, pausing to gain control of the conversation, not rush to his own defense.

"Aunt, my condolences again to you on your loss. William was like a brother to me. And in this present time, we all wish that there were no choices to be made, no loyalties to declare except those to our king and our country." He took a deep breath; so far so good. Now, how would Edward end it? The king was still staring at him. More was needed. He slowly knelt before the king and raised his face to speak from his heart. "Your Majesty, I would ask for your blessing, in the name of my father, who fought and died for you, and my cousin, whom we honor today. My sister agreed to marry John Hutchinson long before loyalties were doubted. Let us pray that my service in Exeter helps bring this conflict to a hasty end, that all men are loyal to England, and that William's legacy is peace, not war."

Anne, at the king's side, nodded. He fell quiet and bowed his head again. The moments ticked on. Even Barbara dared not interrupt this silence.

That throat clearing again, and the pause before the words.

"You speak assuredly, Sir Allen. You will serve me well in Exeter, where men's loyalties waver and change like the wind. William knew what he was doing when he recommended you." The king touched Allen's shoulder softly. "Travel on your way. Defend the west for me. And know that if the king calls on you in the future, as the father of your country, his is the voice you should listen to first. Be sure your love is not divided."

34

Sir, since I writ this letter I am certainly informed that there are above a hundred Cavaliers lying dead in Thornleigh and Sansom woods, and Nottingham coppice, the weather being so sharp that their wounds bled to death, and some of them starved with cold, and we have since found many of them dead in the town that were wounded, and hid themselves in houses, and there bled to death.

John Hutchinson
17th January 1644

The road to Exeter lay a direct ride from Oxford, now the west held strong in Royalist hands. Perhaps that land gain embodied William's legacy. His leadership at Edge Hill, the victory at Bristol—his cousin Lord Grandison's efforts turned the tide of war. And, possibly, his sacrifice may well end it.

Allen couldn't put thoughts into words to offer comfort to his aunt; the sooner he left Oxford, the less he'd be required to speak to anyone. And surely she understood, within the torment of her grief. She knew a soldier could honor the fallen in silence.

Checking again that his commission rested safe within his leather jacket, Allen traveled two hours on the Great Western Way when he realized how close he rode to Lydiard. He could call on his uncle. Perhaps even by fortune, he might know of Edward's whereabouts. They had separated after Edge Hill, and he wasn't in Oxford. No sign of James either. Edward's troop served somewhere on the eastern front, toward Cambridgeshire.

So flowed the war. No news for months, and then hearsay was served up—cold with age and untrustworthy.

Skirting Swindon, Allen turned Boreas north, and within a few minutes, happened on the ancient holloway to Lydiard. Autumn had arrived early this year, and the tunneled track already caught a drift of golden leaves.

Ahead, the tower of St. Mary's Church beckoned through the trees, and he kicked Boreas into a canter as he passed the graveyard and turned into the manor house. Here lay the Lydiard he remembered from the summers he and Luce had traveled to the country, where his parents had thought them safe from the pestilence encircling the Tower.

There stood the tree he and Luce used to climb, his mother's weathered bench beneath, overlooking the lake. He rode to the stables and reined in abruptly. At least twenty horses stood tethered, a Royalist troop, by the look of their trappings. His uncle appeared not as neutral as he claimed.

Throwing Boreas's reins to a groom, Allen strode to the manor house doors and flung them open. A flood of voices engulfed him. He walked into a hall crowded with men, the reek of sweat, ale, and tobacco pervasive.

For a moment, he stood, searching for his uncle, not recognizing anyone. And then, a golden head across the smoky room.

"Edward! Edward!" Allen pushed his way through the soldiers, not caring who he elbowed and shoved to reach his cousin. "Edward, it's me!"

Edward spun on his heel, and a great smile broke out across his face. "Sweet Jesu, Allen," he cried. "Where the hell have you been?"

Allen clasped his cousin to him, and his heart gave a great leap. He did not know how much he had feared for Edward until he held him alive in his arms.

"On patrol in the midlands," Allen replied. "And then in Oxford, picking up a commission to Exeter. Whose troop is this?"

"Mine. I rode straight through from Newark. We rest here before heading to relieve patrols in Bristol." Edward pulled Allen through the crush of soldiers and found them a quiet spot by the fire. He grabbed a tankard from the board and placed it Allen's hand. "God, it is good to see you. I was concerned you were caught up in the disaster at Newbury." Taking a deep draft from his own ale, his face grew serious. "You heard about William?"

"I just left. How did you get the news so quickly?" Allen asked. He'd departed almost immediately after the funeral and knew of no messenger leaving before him.

"Quickly? William died six months past, Allen."

Oh, Christ. The old familiar numbness crept into Allen's heart. "Not your brother?"

Edward nodded. "At Cirencester. He transferred from the King's Life Guard to serve with Prince Rupert. He was killed under fire—wait, why did you say quickly?"

Allen swallowed the rest of his ale. "William Villiers. He died two days ago in Oxford. From wounds he incurred at Bristol."

Edward fell silent. So, he too knew the emptiness. Allen's uncle crossed the room toward him. He'd aged. His beard was trimmed neatly, his hair carefully combed to his collar. But, under his eyes, great hollows were impressed like bruises.

"Allen."

"Uncle John." Allen knew not what to do with his arms. He gripped his mug. "It pains me to hear of William's death."

John nodded, his expression grave, and put his arm lightly across Edward's shoulders.

"Thank you, Allen. These are difficult times. And losing a son to war is an indescribable pain."

"Father, Allen brought more news from Oxford." Edward leaned into his father slightly, and Allen envied their closeness, always apparent when they were together.

"Yes?"

Edward lifted his hand to touch his father's. "Our cousin, William Villiers. He died two days ago from wounds. He stormed Bristol but fell in battle, nobly."

"He was laid to rest in Christ Church; the king attended," Allen added and then stopped. His uncle did not need to hear of another burial.

"And your aunt? How fares my sister Barbara?" John's mournful eyes probed Allen's for the truth.

"Not well." Allen did not know what else to say. How could he explain the lamentation he'd witnessed, the hostility?

After a moment, John stirred himself. "You stay with us tonight, Allen?"

"Yes, please, sir. I have to be in Exeter by week's end. I raise a regiment to support the campaign in the West Country."

"Then avail yourself of our home, Allen. Perhaps even your old room is ready for you." John smiled. "Family must stay close in these times. I am glad for my boys to be together."

He turned and walked away, his back stooped. Grief did that. It extracted the light of life and replaced radiance with a dark abyss.

"His troop is well disciplined." Allen raised his voice to be heard above the wind. The weather had turned overnight, and winter's bleak white light replaced autumn's golden promise.

"The men love him," replied Uncle John. He'd walked across the windswept park to join Allen at the railings as they watched Edward put his troop through their paces. "They'd do anything for him. And he them."

"We all would." Allen fell silent as he watched Edward in his three-quarters armor lead four rows of four men, his charger prancing as he held it on a tight rein. Ahead of him, his trumpeter blew a blast on his horn, and as one, the troop moved into the slow canter maneuver Allen remembered from Edge Hill. Now, the men executed the movement with a precision and accuracy that confirmed frequent deployment.

Another gust of cold wind, and the men's great cloaks flapped, revealing the swords and carbines at their sides. Guns were inserted into the open holsters strapped on their cobs' necks. They trained as they fought—fully armed.

Allen shivered and drew his cloak closer. The change in weather unsettled him. Over the railing, the sails of Lydiard's windmill creaked as they caught the air and turned.

"Winter is not far away," John remarked. "I pray this war be resolved within the year." Still staring at Edward, as if he could not watch him enough, he continued, "What hear you of your mother? Does she still stay with the Roundhead Hutchinson? Or does she return to Puritan Francke?"

Allen paused before answering. He did not need to argue with John. The incident with Barbara was conflict enough. "John looks after her and Luce and Babs very well. He keeps them safe in Nottingham Castle."

"He is a Roundhead and fights against us, Allen."

"He fights for his convictions, Uncle. Just as we do." Allen tried to explain his brother-in-law's intentions. "John believes the king badly advised. He just wants him to listen to the people."

"The king alone, by God's great goodness, can preserve our religion and protect the laws of the land and liberty of its subjects." John drew his gaze from Edward, who turned his troop and now led them at full gallop across the parkland. He rode as one with his mount, strong and graceful. "John Hutchinson and your mother think otherwise. They choose to usurp the natural order that has maintained peace in this land for centuries."

The ground trembled as the troop thundered by. Allen watched Edward disappear over a crest in the land. The old emptiness returned. "I should be leaving, Uncle. I have a long journey ahead." He put his hand on his uncle's arm, and the older man looked up at him, his eyes watering. "Take good care of yourself, and tell Edward I'll expect to see him at Exeter soon. I'll be sure to give him a warm welcome."

John nodded brusquely and turned to look for his son to appear over the brow of the hill. Allen walked away, hearing the trumpet blast that portended Edward's return.

Exeter wasn't as derelict as he'd imagined, considering how long the city had lain in enemy hands, how devastating the fight. Allen's thoughts returned to Luce, under siege herself in Nottingham. She was safe inside the castle walls, surrounded by the town. Riding into the Exeter, he also saw the privation of a blockade, the ruined buildings blasted by cannon shot, the shattered church spire, streets blocked with rubble and masonry.

Still, far away in the Midlands, protected within the castle, high on the mount, Luce and John were safe from the front lines of battle. Those clashes still rang in his mind at night, chasing sleep, keeping him cold company in the long predawn hours.

No, Exeter was quite tolerable, and after several weeks of working hard with the castle force to restore organization to the town after the flight of the Parliamentarians, Allen could see out the war in the west. He'd raised a regiment of good Devon men, solid fighters all of them. Just needed a lieutenant to act as his second in command under him, then he'd be set to supply reinforcements to the king whenever called upon.

Leaning back in his chair, he pulled another piece of meat from the platter before him. The table within his private chamber groaned with food and wine, and a fire burned brightly on this cold December night. The laundry maid he'd found changing his bed linens this morning showed promise. She'd blushed prettily when he'd suggested he might have need of her services later this evening, and he wouldn't be surprised if he heard her knocking soon.

He raised his wineglass in a silent toast to William Villiers. There was a certain irony that he'd achieved his ambition—just as his father had governed the Tower, now he governed Exeter Castle. And both of them did so with the patronage of their Villiers relatives.

A banging on the door interrupted his thoughts. 'Struth, that wench wielded a strong arm. Allen didn't feel like moving away from the fire, so he raised his voice to be heard through the thick oak. "Come in. Sit with me, and we'll share some wine." Loosening his doublet, he undid the knot on his points.

"Well, that's an invitation I've waited an age to hear." The door crashed open, and a burst of laughter rang out in the chamber.

"What the—James?" Allen leapt to his feet and clutched his unlaced britches, which threatened to drop around his ankles.

James threw his hat down on the table and swiftly pulled his brother into an embrace. Cold, smoky night air still clung to him, and beneath the leather cloak, Allen could feel the muscle and bulk of his brother's body. Eye to eye they stood, and Allen glimpsed his father reflected in his brother's broad shoulders. He was no longer a boy.

"I heard you were making yourself comfortable in the West Country," James said, tugging playfully at his brother's laces. "So I thought I'd join you. See for myself how the Villiers patronage suited you."

"Where the hell have you been?" demanded Allen. "And why is this the first I've heard from you in over a year?"

James shrugged off his cloak and reached for the flagon of wine. "Here and there, Brother," he replied. "Wherever the pay is the best and the fighting the fiercest."

"You no longer serve with Goring's troops?"

James downed the wine and refilled his glass. The firelight played tricks on the angle of his jaw, casting shadows that made him look thirty or more, mature, seasoned. "No." he drained his wine again. "Too many old men, too much marching, not enough fighting. I raised some money. Equipped a ship that's moored at Torquay, and I'm running supplies up and down the south coast. Christ, I'm hungry."

"Help yourself." Allen gestured to the table. "I take it you're staying?"

James cracked a chicken leg from the carcass and stuffed it in his mouth.

"If you'll have me." He grabbed the other leg and pulled the tender meat from it. His long fair hair fell into his face, and he shook it back impatiently. "I heard you raised a regiment."

"You've heard a lot." Allen assessed his younger brother. War had seasoned him. But the fire still burned in his eyes. "Yes, I have. All but a lieutenant—"

"Good. I'll start tomorrow." James looked up from the table and grinned, confident in his ability to charm, as always. Allen shook his head, laughing. His brother hadn't changed a bit.

Deep snow blanketed the inner bailey at Nottingham, and although the January dawn was still hours away, Luce left the warmth of her bed early, her worries chasing away sleep. John had warned her of an enemy buildup east and west of the town. Although he'd sent men out to reinforce the earthworks, he fretted the defenses would not hold.

After commanding her mother and Babs to keep watch over the children as they huddled in the cold chamber, furs heaped around them, she prepared the hall to receive the injured. By the smoking rush lights that dripped puddles of orange light and threw great shadows on the ceiling, she folded woolen blankets and ripped rags for bandages. Their supplies were precious. She hoarded the wax candles for when her mother required light to stitch flesh in the dark winter afternoons.

Eighteen months had passed since that August day when the king had raised his flag and declared war. And only recently had she heard again from Allen. A trusted messenger traveled cross-country with a letter stating that he and James were safe in Exeter, living comfortably within the secure boundary of the fort. Edward he'd last seen at Lydiard, and very well he'd looked, too. Her brother wished them all a good new year, and was comforted to know that John provided her and his mother with the same protection he was enjoying within Exeter's sturdy walls. Perhaps this war would conclude with them both in their respective castles, and they could celebrate together the next Christmas.

As she methodically laid out the instruments to extract bullets, the balsams to pour into the gaping wounds, the plasters to hold men's limbs together, Allen's words ran through her mind. He was not telling her the whole truth, either. There was only so much their mother could bear. When they'd received the news in December that both Aunt Barbara's and Uncle John's firstborns had been slaughtered, Luce had known both she and Allen were complicit in protecting their mother from the details. She was relieved Edward stayed at Lydiard, for his father must have been grieving sorely.

The boom of cannon shook her out of her thoughts, and she jumped up. Her husband's prediction was correct. The enemy breached the town again, and once more the castle stood as the last stronghold. She peered from the slit by the door, which afforded her a view across the snow-covered yard. In the gray light of dawn, black figures fell back from the gates to the outbuildings, the flash of fire from the muskets flickering before the shot sounded. There was no riding forth at this moment. The cavalry would fight as foot soldiers—all to defend the castle, to keep Nottingham for Parliament.

John's tall figure ran past the window, joining the men by the gate. Much of the cannon fire issued from St. Peter's Church, which must mean the enemy occupied the streets and houses at the very edge of the castle walls. The snow swirled in countless flakes, and now, a band of men on horseback sallied forth, followed by the foot soldiers. Her heart thundered hard in her chest. John's men attacked, attempting to drive the enemy back from the walls.

All she could do was wait—wait, for the injured and dying to be brought to her.

It was past three of the clock and almost dark again when John walked into the great hall, George at his side, along with a handful of officers, weary and filthy. They threw themselves down on the fur rugs by the fire, easing off their boots. Luce ran to him, needing to touch his face, his chest, to see for herself that he was safe.

"John. You are not injured?"

"No. But we have several who are. They are being carried here, now."

"And any others—"

"No dead this time." He turned to her, his eyes hollow, sorrow in every crease on his face. "We chased the enemy from the town. We pushed them from the city gates. And then, we pursued them through the woods as they retreated." John took a deep, shuddering sigh. "We hunted them for over two miles in the snow by the trail of their blood, by the dead left as markers along the way."

Luce stared into the fire, but still the image of the white snow stained red beneath black trees burned in her mind.

"We counted a hundred Cavaliers lying dead in Thornleigh Woods. They bled to death, the weather being so cold that none stayed to treat them. They are local men, Luce, who know these lands as well as I do." His voice choked, and he swallowed. "We brought prisoners back—those we could move who were left behind to die."

"I will tend them." She maintained calm, for his sake. She must be practical, not let her emotions break through. "Do not put them in the chapel or the dungeon. Bring them to the infirmary. I care not who criticizes me for saving the enemy on this day."

"Yes." John stroked her face with trembling fingers. "Save all you can, my love. We cannot last much longer, Luce. Six hundred men fled from us today, flinging their weapons that they may run that much faster. And yet I believe these numbers will further be swollen with reinforcements. When their commanders learn how small a troop we are, they will return."

"John, you must write to Parliament. Oliver Cromwell's star ascends. You must use my mother's influence, remind him his cousin is married to ours. Tell them of your actions. Plead for assistance, for without relief, we will not sustain."

John nodded. "Help me write when you have finished treatment. I have no words left in me, and your pen is more eloquent than mine."

He turned back to the hearth and George, spreading his hands out to the fire. The men sat quietly, lost in their own thoughts, not talking, barely moving. The great doors opened, and a flurry of snow drifted into the hall, preceding the first of the wounded on stretchers. Cavalier or Roundhead, it did not matter.

They were God's children, and they needed her help.

35

The queen was by the parliament voted traitor for many actions, as pawning the crown-jewels in Holland, encouraging the rebellion in Ireland, heading a papistical army in England.

Luce Hutchinson
9th May 1644

"Queen Maria travels to Exeter, now the way is clear." Allen tossed the curled and creased parchment onto the battered table that served as his desk. He grinned at James. "Looks like she'll be here by the first of May. We'll have to make provision for a royal entourage."

"Why?" James asked. "And what are we supposed to do? This is a garrison, not a palace."

Allen shrugged. "Provide security. Ensure she is well protected. I can only think she journeys to France again. I'm sure she'll just be passing through."

"She can't stay here." James stood and stretched, looking around the cramped guardroom. "We have no privy chamber, no solar or gallery for her ladies." He minced a step or two, lifting imaginary skirts. "Besides, the ladies we employ here are hardly fit company for a queen."

Allen chuckled and picked up the message again.

"Bedford House. She'll reside there. They are informing us so we can provide additional protection." And a chance to impress the queen with his hospitality and knowledge of royal protocol.

"Good. She can stay there. Don't expect me to entertain her. That's your specialty, Brother."

"It's my responsibility."

"And mine is to our men. Essex's Roundheads are on the move again. I'm going to take the troop to Barnstaple, see what kind of manpower we have in North Devon."

"You're excused." Allen walked to the narrow window and looked east across the gentle countryside, where cloud shadows chased sunshine across the rolling green hills. Somewhere out there, the queen and her

283

followers approached, the royal court wherein lay his future. "Perhaps the tide of war is truly turning. I think this bodes well for the summer. I promised Luce I would see her and mother ere Christmas. Maybe peace is on the horizon."

Allen paced the hall at Bedford House, his footsteps creaking on the warped floorboards. Dear God, this place was positively ancient. Not exactly Richmond or Whitehall. Jesu, would those spaniels travel too? And his aunt? He did not relish seeing her again after her last outburst.

He paused to once again straighten the moth-eaten embroidered carpet covering the ancient oak table. If the queen enjoyed her stay, it would be helpful to his next position. After all, if the war was concluding, the king would need plenty of good men to advise him when he returned the court to Whitehall.

A soldier shoved open the door and saluted Allen. "They are at the gatehouse, sir."

"Thank you." Allen strode to the steps as two carriages and a dozen armed outriders drove across the green. Interesting. The queen traveled swiftly, no train of followers to slow her down.

The second carriage drew up before Allen, and he swept a deep bow. A pair of crimson French leather riding boots descended the step.

"Your Majesty," he said. "I bid you welcome to Exeter."

"Inside, and quickly, Sir Allen," replied a brisk voice. "We do not stand on ceremony today."

Allen straightened and took a pace back. Those eyes, particularly beautiful, luminous, haunting.

"Madam . . . Lady Dalkeith . . . Anne . . ."

His cousin looked beyond him and surveyed the façade of the house, pulling a face. "My mother stays with the court in Oxford. The king thought it best that I escort the queen. My mother is still not well."

She lifted her hand, and he brushed it with a kiss.

"And now, we must bring the queen inside. I hope you have arranged a comfortable chamber for her." Her face expressed doubt.

Anne turned and opened the carriage door wider. The queen slowly emerged, clinging to Anne's hands, tentatively putting a foot on the step.

284

She was as Allen remembered her from Oxford, yet frailer, smaller. And dressed in a loose gown with a fur around her, even on this beautiful spring day. As she alighted, the coat fell open. Queen Henrietta was heavily pregnant.

Allen's eyes met Anne's. She nodded slightly. This was not the visit he'd expected. Once again, the Villiers were impacting his life.

"We were to stay in Bath, but the Earl of Essex leads the Parliamentarian advance toward the west. We are safer here in Exeter until after the child is born." Anne was much like her mother. Not one to mince words. "I shall need a woman to help," she said over her shoulder as she assisted the queen through the open door. "A local girl, one who is well connected and versed in child rearing. And fresh milk, honey, soft white bread. Good wines. And is there no fire? We must have fires lit; the queen feels the cold most desperately."

Jesu, did this woman not know there was a war raging around them? And that Exeter's merchants were still for Parliament? Where the hell was he going to obtain white bread and fine wine?

Allen set up a temporary office in Bedford House in an effort to meet the queen's demands. It was the morning of the third day of her stay, and it felt like a month already. Managing a troop of dragoons on a march across the Pennine Hills was easier than organizing a temporary royal household. The stream of locals that arrived by the hour, hoping for employment, irritated him beyond belief. Country yokels, all of them, with no idea of how to behave around aristocracy. He despaired. Why the hell hadn't he gone on patrol to Barnstaple and left James in charge?

"Next," he called wearily. Lady Dalkeith was threatening to write to the royal chamberlain if he did not find suitable staff by the end of this day. He did not need King Charles questioning his ability to look after his precious wife and unborn child.

"I heard you were needing help." The slight Devon accent softened the words, tinged the woman's educated voice with just a slight burr.

"Yes." Allen did not look up and continued reading his morning dispatches. "What experience do you have with babies?" Really, this was painful. The king had sent his own personal physician to monitor the birth.

The queen's sister-in-law had dispatched a French nurse from Austria who had taken up residence in the birthing chamber and sent demands to the kitchen all day.

And now, he'd spent half the blasted morning dealing with foolish maids when he had a garrison to run. What was his cousin Anne up to with the queen, that she couldn't interview these women herself?

"I have younger sisters that I tended from birth, my mother dying when I was but ten."

"Mmm." The king was still in Oxford, this morning's report told him. Why had he sent his wife on this long journey to the west when she was so great with child? Did he fear for her safety that much?

"I'm Frances Petre. My father, John, was knight of Bowhay Manor. He sat on the city council until his death last year. He was a most loyal king's man and would have considered it a great honor for his daughter to serve the queen."

That would explain the accent. At least not another country farm lass. He pulled another missive from the pile. "And why do you think I should hire you to assist in the queen's household?" Ah, a brief word from Edward. He was recalled to Oxford with his troop. Must be something strategic going on. He scratched a note to his cousin on the back of the parchment to send back with the court messenger that afternoon.

"Sir Allen, you are in need of someone who knows the area well. Who can perhaps persuade the merchants to supply the demands of the queen as she approaches her time."

She wasn't giving up easily. So far, she was passing the test.

"And you can?" Still not looking up, he reached for the sand and his seal.

The soft voice carried a hint of mirth. "I've known them all my life. And their families, their histories. There's enough that still cling to the old religion. I think I could find enough grounds for persuasion, should they prove reluctant to part with their goods."

He glanced up at that and met sparkling hazel eyes, twinkling in amusement above rosy cheeks and a full mouth.

"You resort to blackmail, madam?"

"Are you engaging me for the position, Sir Allen?"

He dropped his gaze back to his papers, but for some reason he was distracted from reading the words. This woman knew how to negotiate.

"If you can bring me champagne and manchet, yes."

"And fresh honey and cream from our Devon cows." She paused. "I think perhaps you are in need of some informed help, Sir Allen. This is not a garrison you are commanding, but the residence of the Queen of England and the king's unborn child. There are standards to maintain."

"You go too far, Mistress Petre." How dare she insinuate that he was not paying attention to the queen's needs?

"And you do not go far enough, Sir Allen. I shall return shortly with the provisions the queen desires and the arrangements in place to supply more."

Her skirts rustled as she curtsied, and he only lifted his eyes when the tapping of her shoes on the floorboards told him she was leaving. Her skirts swayed from her hips; her glossy brown curls lifted from her shoulders as if imbued with their own energy. She did not look back at him as she left the chamber.

Frances Petre. He found himself writing her name on the parchment instead of Edward's. He scratched the words out until it was illegible.

True to her word, Mistress Petre not only returned with the best quality white bread in the West Country, she also brought soft Devon wool blankets, jars of honey, fresh butter, and a dozen bottles of champagne. Provisions flowed to Bedford House, and each morning as Allen called upon his cousin, he had to push his way past half a dozen merchants and plump farmers' wives, laden with fresh trout or the first sweet June strawberries.

Anne Villiers lifted her eyebrows at Allen.

"Your girl is ingenious. Rich findings. We have not seen supplies such as these in Oxford for a year."

"She's not my girl." Allen stood by the fireplace in the stuffy chamber. Even kindling in June, Mistress Petre secured to supply the queen's chamber. Although he'd taken to visiting Anne daily at Bedford House, he still wasn't accustomed to the queen's demands. Frances Petre knew better, it appeared. He often saw her if he waited in the chamber long enough. And now the babe was born—a sickly, mewling girl—the queen's demands were even greater. "But she does know her way around the local merchants."

"Mistress Petre appears to have also improved the caliber of the servants attending us," she continued. "I think perhaps she has hired maids based on attributes other than their physical ones."

Allen grunted. He'd noticed that the quality of service had improved greatly with the disappearance of the more buxom serving girls.

Anne continued her musings. "The queen is much taken with Frances. She would not look out of place at Richmond or Whitehall. But I suspect she is of more value to you here."

"I have no need for a housekeeper."

"She is more than a housekeeper, Allen. And her family in Essex, the Baronets Petre, are well loved by the queen for their catholic loyalty. She is most delighted that you chose Frances to care for her."

"You meddle, madam, in something that is none of your business." Damn, the room was hot. "Frances Petre's family connections are no concern of mine."

"I'm a Villiers. Connections are my business. Her grandfather served with yours under Burleigh at the court of Queen Elizabeth. You are of the same cut." Anne smiled sweetly at Allen, and he could not help but laugh. She possessed the same easy charm as William, along with her mother's allure.

Frances entered the chamber, her arms full of dainty little garments.

"More gifts for the baby," she announced. "This time, Honiton lace, the finest in all of England." She held her arms out to Allen. "Feel the quality, Sir Allen, the softness. See the tiny stitching. And look, roses, butterflies, ferns, all woven into the collars. You must agree, these garments would turn any child into a royal baby. Even a soldier's."

Allen scowled at Frances and backed away from her. He always felt she was teasing him, and yet, he could never catch her out. Every time she spoke to him, there was a merriment in her voice that reminded him of Babs.

"I came to let you know that I ride out with the troop tomorrow," he said. "'Tis a simple mission, one that should not take more than a week. I join my brother to keep the roads clear for Prince Maurice. He is moving his army through to Cornwall."

"We'll be here when you return," responded Frances. "The queen recovers her strength daily, and the baby grows stronger, too. The Devon air is beneficial for them. It enhances the temperament and brings sweetness to the disposition. You will profit from partaking the fresh air on your expedition."

Allen scowled. There she went again. "I shall see you shortly."

"And we look forward to your joyful homecoming."

Frances curtsied, a small bob that deferred to his rank, but not deep enough to be subservient. Anne laughed and took the clothes from her.

"Leave him be, Frances. You confuse him sorely."

Allen bowed stiffly and turned to leave.

"God go with you, Sir Allen," called Frances. "You will find us here in excellent spirits. May we welcome you back in the same humor."

How he returned, he did not remember. And when he reached the safety of the garrison? No more than ten days after leaving Frances, maybe twelve. James may have counted the days. They were meaningless. The queen still stayed in Exeter, Anne with her; that much, he saw when he returned.

How foolish to think this tide of war turned. Instead, a river ran red with men's blood. Its banks were strewn with severed limbs and dead horses and useless armor and broken pikes.

Cropredy Bridge. Another unknown English place name that would now be seared into men's memories. The insignificant crossing on the map where James met up with him and they led their troops to escort Prince Maurice. And where the Roundheads had been waiting.

This had not been the plains of Edgehill, nor the siege of Basing. No exhilarated gallop across wide open fields, Prince Rupert leading the charge, his magical dog Boye at his side.

Nor a strategic blockade, waiting for the castle to surrender.

Cropredy Bridge. A narrow deathtrap of stone, an overturned cart blocking escape. And two armies of Englishmen that hacked and slashed for every inch gained, every yard lost.

How proud flew the flag—gyronny to honor the queen, black and white with a red cross for George and England and the day the king raised his standard in Nottingham.

289

How red bled the flag, soaked in men's blood, hurriedly washed in river water, damp across his saddle.

Yes, he came home, and so did James.

But what was home, but the place where his nightmares roosted?

She stood by the fire still burning in the queen's parlor. Anne was absent, the queen preoccupied with the child in her chamber. No maids lingered, no serving woman to distract, no anonymous wench to wipe the tormenting images from his mind.

Instead, Frances remained, her flower-scented hair so clean and shining, her eyes soft, her mouth trembling.

He tried to say something normal—the weather, perhaps, a polite query of the health of the baby.

No words came forth.

She moved to him, grasped his head, and pulled his face to hers. Breath sweet as honey, skin soft as silk, mouth as full as the ripest strawberry. Sweet Jesu, did this woman anticipate every need, know the emptiness within him that he refused to admit?

He lost himself in her kiss. And when he finally broke away, he saw an emotion in her eyes that he had seen in no other woman's. Compassion. She wordlessly led him to the chair pulled up by the fireplace, placed a flagon of wine at the arm, and left him with his thoughts.

As he stared into the empty grate, he became conscious of her sitting on a stool by his side, quiet, still. And her presence soothed him.

"I need your protection." A few days later, Anne confronted him while he sat by the dead fireplace in his guardroom. Only the queen enjoyed the comfort of a blaze now. Wood was in short supply, and the wet July night chilled his bones. Even Frances could not produce miracles as the Roundheads advanced, cutting off supplies. Lady Dalkeith had arrived at the garrison accompanied by a single guard. No frail-hearted courtier was she.

He stirred himself from his thoughts. "Of course. As long as the queen and you stay here, I pledge myself to your safety."

"That's just it." She sat on the bench opposite him, the skirts of her serviceable riding gown falling around her. She crossed her boots at her ankles and leaned forward. The ghost of William commanded him from her eyes. "The queen leaves for France. She fears she will become a hostage if the Earl of Essex breaks through the lines. He will not guarantee her safe passage—in fact, he threatens to imprison her in London."

"You go too? And Frances?" Her words demanded his attention.

"No. That is why I have come to ask this of you." Anne reached for his hand. "Cousin, the queen does not think her baby will live. And she would rather leave the child with me than take her on a voyage that will be certain death."

"She abandons her child?"

"Her Majesty's love for the king is greater than any love for her children. She would not endanger his life by risking her own captivity by the enemy. A sickly child will slow her progress. She returns to France to raise more money, more arms. She knows the child is safe with me, and she trusts Frances with her well-being. I can negotiate to transport her daughter safely back to our kin in the east. Cromwell will be more interested in the queen's flight than the child and me."

Allen nodded. "Of course you have my protection. And Frances, and the princess. We are well defended here in Exeter, and when you secure safe passage, take a troop with you." He stood. "Does the queen make for Falmouth?"

"Yes. She plans to leave in the morning. Once her mind is made up, she has no patience to delay."

"Then I'll send James with her. She'll travel swiftly with him."

Would she have stayed if she'd known the king rode with Prince Maurice to be with her? Allen did not know.

Queen Henrietta Maria was stubborn, courageous. He'd witnessed firsthand her steel will and determination. Most noblewomen remained in their chamber for weeks after delivering a child. Despite her terrible weakness from the birth, she was up and dressing in her leather doublet within a fortnight, reincarnating her self-stated title of "Generalissima."

When she bade her child good-bye, no tears fell from her eyes. She looked only forward, to the help she could raise for her husband, Anne said. She had no use for sentiment. Besides, she still did not believe the child would live, so why grow attached?

At least, that was how Anne and Allen explained Queen Henrietta Maria's absence to the king when he arrived in Exeter. No ceremony for him, he rode as a soldier, swiftly, with a small escort. His great brown eyes shone with tears when he realized how narrowly he had missed his wife. He truly adored her, realized Allen.

At the new font in the cathedral, paid for by the merchants that Frances encouraged to celebrate Exeter's princess, the small party stood with the king. Anne Villiers held the tiny baby girl, with Frances and Allen next to her. The bishop stood by the king, murmuring a prayer. The rest of the cathedral was empty, occupied only by the saints on their pedestals.

"Her name, Your Majesty?"

The king looked at his daughter, the youngest princess.

"Henrietta," he replied. "In honor of the bravest woman I know."

And then the fleeting moment of peace was over.

Outside the sanctuary of the cathedral, Prince Maurice's arrival had turned Exeter into a massive armed camp. Allen estimated the army had swelled to fifteen thousand men. The king would not stay, for together, the royal cousins marched west to Cornwall. The Earl of Essex would be cut off, his army driven like sheep into a pen.

Allen had received his orders to ride east to the ragged battle line, hold up the Roundheads while the king's Cavaliers formed an impenetrable wall. The east of England may be in Parliament's control, but the men of the west would stand for the king.

Allen placed his hat back on his head. Time to go. Frances, the baby in her arms, stood in a shaft of crimson sunlight that pierced the stained-glass window above the font. He nodded good-bye. Anne had already negotiated their passage to the eastern counties. She'd be gone by the time he and his troop returned.

36

*My husband and his brother scorned ever to yield the castle on any terms, to
a papistical army led by an atheistical general. George told Lord Newcastle,
'If my lord would have that poor castle he must wade to it in blood'*

Luce Hutchinson
17th September 1644

This death march, a trail of fleeing wounded Roundheads from Lostwithiel
to Poole, could not surely be real. Not this, on top of all the battle
slaughter? Cornishmen robbing and killing the defeated Parliamentarians,
asserting they were reclaiming their own plundered property. Slaughtered
for a saddlebag, a trumpet? The defeated troops carried no weapons, for
all were confiscated as spoils of war.

Riding out from Exeter to join the Cavaliers, Allen took control at the
king's command. Even Charles could not condone the massacre of his
own people and settled surrender terms on Essex's ruined army, ensuring
a truce until Poole. So, they marched, and Allen rode.

March.

That in itself was an irony. These men could barely stumble. And if
they didn't walk, they deserted. Men pushed through the high Devon
hedges and straggled across steep-ridged sheep pastures. Let them go. Let
them struggle and hobble and whimper like hunted foxes. He was not
going to stop a man crawling home to die. Day after day, the lines thinned
through death and attrition.

He saw no hope of returning to Exeter now. They rode on to relieve
Basing, Banbury, Donnington . . . the string of castles that held for the
king, now besieged by the Roundheads. Fighting ebbed and flowed
throughout the countryside, county borders swept under a wave of blood
and vengeance. Was there a corner of England left not saturated with
displaced families, widows, maimed veterans? What, in all this confusion,
could be called a win or loss?

Did Luce still defend Nottingham Castle? Did his mother and sisters
peer from the slit windows of the tower keep, faces pinched with

exhaustion, stomachs empty with starvation? Allen felt sick. And he'd thought them safe within their fortresses. They were deathtraps.

He kicked Boreas on. A mile from Poole, the advance riders told him. Time to leave this stinking line of decaying, dying Roundheads and rejoin his troop. God save King Charles, Prince Maurice, Prince Rupert, and the Cavaliers. Time to finish off the enemy. Secure the west. On to Newbury.

The fog from the rivers flanking the camps first silvered the October dawn. Allen stood and stretched, brushing the heavy dew from his cloak, rubbing his face to banish the sleep from his eyes. Arriving by dark, he had not seen the extent of the armies. But now, as the sun rose, the troops spread out before him, clustered around the king's standard. Westerly, Prince Maurice's flags hung limp in the dampness.

He turned to an officer next to him. "Who else is on the field? I see Prince Maurice. Is Prince Rupert here?"

The man shook his head. "Not after Marston Moor. He is not in the king's favor."

Allen nodded. Word in the taverns was that the king blamed his nephew for the disastrous loss and refused to allow him to fight at this side. The king's territory shrank daily. Cromwell pushed deeper and deeper west.

"Goring's troops, then?" Was there a chance he might find Edward?

"Yes. They are camped to the north, the other side of the Cheveley Road." He pointed past Allen. "Looking for someone?"

"Yes. My cousin. I lost contact with him earlier this year."

The officer shrugged. "We've all lost contact with someone." He looked around. "I just want to be done with this. I'm leaving if this battle don't go well for us."

Allen nodded. "I'm going to see if he's there. Thank you." He was not going to entertain desertion. Not yet.

Damp river air flowed into his lungs, and as he followed the lane north, a singular lightheartedness fell over him, and he whistled softly. He couldn't think why until he realized that Frances Petre's face filled his thoughts, her soft lips smiling, enticing, distracting. Picking up his pace, he stopped whistling and swung into a measured march, falling into step with other troops.

The camp was laid out with similar precision to the king's, and Allen walked toward the central tent, where Goring's flag flew. He sensed the river just across the lush field, where several troops were warming their horses. He glanced at them, glanced away, and then stopped. That charger looked familiar, the Cavalier's set of his shoulders . . . and the troop, easily the best on the field.

"Edward!" Allen started shouting before he was even within range, running now across the rutted field, dodging other horses. "Edward!"

The rider held up his arm and halted his troop. Allen pounded onwards, his feet twisting in rabbit burrows, drops of moisture kicked up in his face.

"Edward. Sweet Jesu. Found you." He was breathless, no other words.

"Oh God, Allen." Edward jumped from his horse and flung off his helmet. "Jesus."

Allen burst out laughing, and Edward joined him as they hugged and banged each other on the back. Edward was just the same. Laughter in his eyes, his hair still long, though tied back this morning. And a new scar across his cheek. Made him look quite rakish.

"I see you have a new badge." Allen gestured at the wound.

Edward drew off his gauntlet and touched his face. "Marston Moor."

"You were there?"

His cousin nodded. "It was a mess."

"I heard." Allen looked back at Edward's troop. "Don't let me hold you up."

Edward smiled. "Thanks. We practice a little harder today." He looked to the west. "Cromwell lies just across there."

Allen whistled. "Cromwell. His Ironsides are a good fighting unit."

"They are. But we are better." Edward pulled his gauntlet back on. "Where are you positioned?"

"Dragoons. Right flank of the king's troop. We'll follow you in on foot."

"Good. Just don't wait too long. We intend to flatten Cromwell. You'll want to finish them off."

Allen laughed. "See you at dinner."

Edward mounted his horse. "Keep a spot for me at the table." He put his helmet on and raised his arm again. He and his horse cantered toward the river, their formation as tight and controlled as it had been the day Allen had watched them at Lydiard.

Did the lingering musket smoke that hung in the air make visibility impossible? Or perhaps the clash of the drums, the bugles blasting directions, the shouts of men, the screams of horses threw Cromwell's Ironsides into confusion? Would he ever get that noise from his head— the screams of animals and men mingled in agony? Whatever hung over Newbury that day, it served his troop to their advantage.

Allen walked steadily, his musket held in front. Boreas he'd left tethered in camp. This was a foot campaign.

Ten paces, fire, reload.

Ten paces, fire, reload.

God knew where Edward's troop was, but they'd cleared a swath with their charge.

Ten paces, fire, reload.

The screams lessened; the smoke drifted as the light faded. Five paces, fire—here was an Ironside holdout. Reload. Fire. Screams.

Marshy ground, river must be close. Ah. Yes. There. Roundheads dead, cut down as they'd crossed, stepping stones of bodies, diverting the current. Black water flowing.

Edward's troop should be returning.

Hoofbeats.

Cromwell's cavalry?

Old Ironsides was running a campaign at Newbury such as Allen had never seen before. The horsemen indistinguishable from each other. The hundred banners depicting God and his miracles. The shouts to heaven and fervent prayers as they forged forward. This was not the mounted confusion where he'd followed Prince Rupert, his white dog pacing through the gloriously caparisoned Cavalier horses. There was a force at work here he'd never before encountered.

Ten paces. Prepare to fire.

Goring's cavalry. Lower muskets.

And Edward was . . . Edward was . . .

Edward was leaning over his horse's neck, helmet off, golden hair spilling, light in the gloaming.

Christ on the Cross, enough pacing. He ran, marsh sucking his boots, clutching at his feet.

"Edward."

The horse stood still.

"Is it dinner time?" Strong voice, thank God.

"Jesu." Laughing. "You jest, Coz."

Where was the injury? Where had he taken the hit? Not his chest, not his head, his leg did not bleed. Damn this hellish darkness. God's Wounds, was this it, by his rib?

A groan.

Allen's fingers found the spot the bullet had entered, glancing off Edward's breast plate, penetrating his side.

"I can bind this for you." Already removing his sash.

"Get me to the field hospital, and they will find room for me."

Allen paused. "I should take you to Lydiard."

"You don't need to do that. The surgeons with the king are skilled in battle wounds. The hospital is in the castle."

The field emptied. The troops disappeared into the night, bequeathing the land to the dead and dying. Putrid with the foul smells of death, the miasma from the river trapped the ill air and turned it into stinking drops that clung to his cloak.

I'm leaving if this battle don't go well for us.

This was not desertion. This was going home.

After backtracking through the king's encampment, Allen gathered Boreas and led Edward and his horse. The land surged with confusion—fires blazing, soldiers shouting for each other, seeking news of dead and wounded. The walking injured leaned on men's shoulders, staggering to the field hospital within Donnington Castle.

Allen stood at the edge of the earthworks surrounding the tower, trying to make sense of the scene in front of him. Christ's nails, the defenses stood taller than him, with great trenches betwixt, where a man could fall and never stand again. Campfires burned around the perimeter, all the way up to the castle walls, throwing great shadows against the stone.

The night was a gateway to hell—the cries of the dying, the smoke wreathing across the land, the stench of blood and death filling his mouth and nose. He climbed with Edward and the horses as far as he could up the castle track, joining the grotesque procession. As they moved closer, the path congested, and the maimed and wounded—heaped high in their carts—screamed louder. Dear God, this was the road to Hades, and he refused to condemn Edward to the care of some demon butcher.

And no finding James in this mess of thousands. He couldn't afford to spend time looking.

Newbury to Lydiard. A half-day soldier's ride, no more, with time to stop at a tavern for an ale or two. On a black October night, where the stars were veiled and the high-hedged lanes dark, with one man injured, the journey would take twice as long.

Blood seeped from Edward's side, darkening the red sash, albeit slowly. He could not sit upright; he drooped over his horse's neck. The journey to Lydiard would consume most of the night. And dare anyone challenge them.

Pushing against the flow of soldiers, Allen turned Boreas's head west. As they left the river for higher ground, the air cleared a little and freshened. The stars shone through breaking clouds with enough strength to get a sense of direction. As best he remembered, Lydiard lay northwest of Newbury. If he could find his way to Swindon, he could deliver Edward safely home.

He found himself talking, of their time at Oxford, their boyhood at Lydiard. "Remember the Sunne Inn?" he asked Edward. "Remember the tree in the park we always climbed? Remember how Luce always finished our lessons first and then laughed as we struggled to keep up with her?"

How much Edward heard, he did not know. But he stayed on his mount, his horsemanship instinctively keeping him stable. West-northwest, along the carter's tracks that crisscrossed the hilly downs, they walked their horses. Damn, the night grew frigid. If they could just go a little faster, it would warm them. He tried a trot, but the pace made Edward groan and sway.

Too dangerous.

Occasionally, men joined them—Roundheads or Royalists, he knew not. No orange or red sash showed in the dark to distinguish. The night was a great equalizer. He had no fight left in him, nor did his companions.

Boreas led, his white mane reflecting the stars, his ears pricked. How often he had gazed across his head. But never had he imagined leading Edward, injured, home to Lydiard.

The stars wheeled in the great dome of the sky above his head; the track emptied, and soon, just Allen and Edward were left.

God, who somewhere looks down upon Mother and Luce, protect us and keep us. Show me the way to Lydiard. Luce, give me a sign that you are praying for me. Father, guide my steps, for the love of God.

A shooting star twinkled in the distance, faintly, so that he barely saw it. But the celestial sign appeared, and God gave him comfort. For, there on the horizon, outlined black against the starlight, he saw the spires and towers of Swindon's churches.

Almost home.

"Sir Allen Apsley and Sir Edward St.John, urgently to see Sir John St.John." Allen stopped at the guards to Lydiard's gates.

"Your papers, sir?" They were armed with carbines and swords. John posted a strict guard.

"Run, you fool. Run to Sir John and tell him his son is injured."

They gaped at him.

"Run. Now." He pushed past the guards and walked the exhausted horses to the front door of the house. As he dismounted, the door was flung open, and John, in his nightshirt and robe, ran down the steps.

"Allen? What . . . Edward? Edward?"

"It is a flesh wound, no more than that, Uncle," replied Allen. "But he needs rest and sustenance. We have traveled from Newbury this night."

"Who did this? What force took down my son?"

"Cromwell's Ironsides." Allen rubbed his eyes wearily. "They fight differently than we have ever seen before. They attack with God on their shoulders."

Edward stirred, attempting to reach his carbine in the holster.

"He is delirious." Allen gently moved his cousin's hand away from the gun. "He needs rest."

Tenderly, John helped Allen remove Edward's feet from the stirrups. Two soldiers rushed up to join them, and together, they lifted Edward from the saddle. He groaned as they did so, and John whispered to his son.

"Hush, my love, my boy. You are home. Hush."

"Home?" Edward's voice was weaker than Allen had heard before. "Allen brought you to me."

"Allen? And Luce? Is she here? Am I safe?"

John smoothed his son's matted hair from his brow as they carried him up the steps to Lydiard.

"Yes. You are safe."

Oliver Cromwell leaned back from Nottingham's high table and belched loudly. Luce exchanged a swift glance with her mother and turned her eyes to her lap. Really, this man was just an elevated Cambridgeshire farmer, and his manners left much to be desired. If John had not insisted that they entertain the newly promoted lieutenant general, she would not have given him the time of day. But she must be cautious. His jovial bluster concealed a deeper vein of a darker character, and he discomfited her with his probing eyes.

"So, as I understand it, madam," Cromwell took a slurp from his goblet and raised it in a toast to Lucy, "your cousin, Sir Oliver St.John, married my cousin, Elizabeth Cromwell."

Luce's mother nodded. "Yes, Lieutenant General Cromwell. Our family in Bedfordshire are close friends with your cousins."

"And in these times, best that family knows who to trust and who is a traitor within the relations." In the firelight, his heavy jaw caught the shadows, his eyes blank and unreadable. There it was again—a flash of insight that lurked beneath an innocuous statement.

A silence fell upon the table. Luce dared not look at her mother nor John. She knew they all thought of Allen.

With a sudden roar of laughter, Cromwell thumped the table. "Naught so strange as kin, I say." His sudden change of mood was unnerving.

"And are your family all in Bedfordshire, Lieutenant General Cromwell?" Lucy asked. Luce let out her breath. Her mother would steer the conversation out of dangerous territory.

"We have kin in Essex too," he replied. "Not far from your brother, I believe. The Barringtons of Barrington Hall, near Hatfield Broad Oak." Cromwell leaned forward abruptly and stared hard at Lucy. "Come to think of it, Dame Francke, is not your husband—"

John's sleeve caught his goblet, tipping it over, and a stream of red wine bled across the board toward Cromwell. Ned, who was serving the table that evening, jumped with a linen and blotted it, then refilled John's cup.

Nodding his thanks, John turned back to Cromwell. "My apologies, sir. But no harm done. Now, tell me of your recent visit to Parliament. I would hear more about the new-modeled army and your role as commander."

Again, a sensitive topic averted.

John continued. "I hear the army is being reduced and concentrated into a fighting force that aims to bring the war to an end within the year."

Luce longed to hear more. Pray to God this meant that an end was coming. Pray God that Allen, James, Edward, and others could return home.

"Parliament is reducing the army to twenty-one thousand dedicated fighters," replied Cromwell. "These men are appointed not by their position in society, but by their aptitude to bear arms. All men are equal under God, Colonel Hutchinson, and in my army, we stand together without social rank. We fight to obtain a righteous peace in this kingdom, and we will win with God on our side."

Luce looked at her mother and then back at her husband, who nodded his agreement. This man did, indeed, share their belief. And he led an army prepared to die for their cause.

"Such fervor, and such new thinking," responded Lucy. "And to establish equality for all men. It might just be the flame that burns the brightest in England's fire."

Cromwell nodded enthusiastically. When he smiled, he was charismatic, charming. Luce could understand why men followed him.

"The Cavaliers still follow the old ways, their leaders selected through their rank in society, not their fighting ability." His eyes now reflected the firelight, zealous, mesmerizing. "And so, they crumble and fight to save only their own skins, with little loyalty to their units. They dress all in their finest, with no thought to uniformity or common cause. The Cavaliers hang on to the beliefs of the old injustices, where no man can get ahead without the dishonesty of perquisite and benefactor. And, after the battle at Cropredy Bridge, we knew we had to change the way we approach this war and end it rapidly for the good of the people—not draw conflict out to despoil and corrupt our country further."

"In this new way of thinking, General Cromwell, do you foresee a Parliament that will represent the people's needs, will hear their wishes and act upon them?" Luce glanced at John. This was the foundation of their belief, the cause which they stood for above all others.

"I do. And we will need good honest men to attend Westminster on their behalf." Cromwell leaned over to John, his eyes bright with zeal. "I heard the seat for Nottingham is vacant, from your father's death, John. My condolences to you."

John shifted in his chair. "We were estranged. He did not see eye to eye with us, nor embrace the freedoms we are espousing."

"And yet, the people elected John their governor," continued Luce. If her husband were too humble to speak of his triumphs, she would speak for him. "And he refused a significant bribe from the Royalists to betray them. John represents the true heart and beliefs of the citizens of Nottingham."

Cromwell nodded. "I thought as much. I heard your father's sympathies lay more with his Royalist Byron relatives than with you." He reached out and grasped John's hand. "There's a place for you in the new Parliament, John. When the fighting is over, the rebuilding will begin. We need men of integrity such as yourself, men who the people trust, who will make the difficult decisions and stand by them. All good Englishmen deserve their grievances redressed, and men like you, honest, simple, of the people, will be the future of our nation."

In the pause that followed his declaration, Luce reflected on the plain righteousness and integrity of his words. Cromwell's way—the way of the people—promised hope for the future.

If they could all survive the present slaughter.

37

My husband understood well, and as well performed when he undertook it, the military art in all parts of it; he naturally loved the employment, as it suited with his active temper more than any, conceiving a mutual delight in leading those men that loved his conduct; and when he commanded soldiers, never was man more loved and reverenced by all that were under him.

Luce Hutchinson
27th January 1645

Luce placed her quill back into the inkpot and flexed her fingers. She spent hours each day at her notebooks, recording the war and the deeds of those who fought so hard for freedom from tyranny. In the future, her children would understand for themselves the reasons their parents had challenged the king's assumptive divine right to rule.

She glanced at John, sitting across from her at the worn table, a slight frown on his face as he read through a pile of documents. Luce loved this morning ritual—he going through his dispatches, she recording the news of the previous day.

John caught her looking at him and raised an eyebrow, passing her a parchment.

"Cromwell suggests I travel to London to discuss his campaign here in Nottinghamshire. He despairs that Newark continues to hold for the king, when all around us men are loyal to the Parliamentarian cause."

"He values your mind, John. He knows you are a strategist."

"I believe Cromwell gathers intelligence to challenge the Earl of Manchester's leadership of the army," replied John. "The earl let Newark remain in Royalist hands, and his ineptitude at Newbury this past fortnight handed a victory to the king. Cromwell does not believe Manchester capable of leading the army. He has invested too much in this war to see his vision squandered by another."

Luce nodded. "Cromwell is ambitious. We witnessed that when he dined with us last."

"And yet he prides himself on having the common touch." John paused. "Remember what he told us he wrote to Manchester: *If you choose godly, honest men to be captains of horse, honest men will follow them. I would rather have a plain russet-coated captain who knows what he fights for and loves what he knows than that which you call a gentleman and is nothing.*"

"He speaks for many men with those words." Luce ignored the pain in her heart. Allen was a gentleman. Edward too, born and bred. What were these false ranks that elevated one man above another and caused such labels to be applied that could never be removed? Were they all not God's children?

"Are the roads safe?" she asked. "Is there passage through to London?"

"Yes." John pulled another dispatch from the pile. "The king's armies are in Devon and Cornwall; some encamp in Wales. After Newbury, they retreated west. Apart from Newark, little remains of them in the entire east of the country."

Somewhere in the west. Allen, James, Edward. The gentlemen of the king. Her family.

"So you will leave for London?"

"The armies are resting for the winter. No one is on the move. And it is time I checked on my father's house in Holborn. It has stood empty since his death." John looked at her, and in the angled morning sun, Luce caught the exhaustion behind his eyes. The responsibilities aged him, in this role that he'd never asked for. She must be his backbone, for he was a cautious man, slow to make a decision. If Cromwell wanted his counsel, then she must see that he gave it.

"I will pray for your safety, my darling, and your wisdom in guiding your discussions with the Parliament and army. You will need all your skills to satisfy both, for their objectives are not always aligned."

"As I pray for yours. George will remain here; the winter bodes quiet." John stood up and folded her into his arms. His familiarity nurtured her. "I feel in my heart the tide is changing, my love. And, with the ebbing of the king's hostility, will come the flowing of a wave of optimism and hope across our country. Cromwell brings new leadership to our cause. He is a careful thinker and believes in sharing power between army and Parliament and king. There is room for all men to live together peaceably in our beloved nation."

"You did the right thing, Allen," John said as Allen prepared to leave, holding his shoulders in both hands and gazing up into his eyes. "That was no desertion. 'Twas a choice any man would have made at battle's end."

"I could not leave him with the field surgeons." Allen gazed across the peaceful park, the ground rolling away from the stable block toward the lake, a dusting of snow sparkling on the grass. This was a place of gentle recovery, where Edward could regain his strength. "The conditions were appalling, with so many wounded and dying, and not nearly enough to tend to them. And my troop—those who survived—left for the west."

"You are right. He is better here at home. Where I can guarantee his safety." John's eyes watered, and a lump formed in Allen's throat. He swallowed, the coating of ice returning to his heart. He took a step back. Time to saddle Boreas and move on.

"I share your sorrow at my cousin Jack's death, Uncle." Allen put away the memory of that long ago night at Battersey, the cousins who had laughed and drank together. Three dead, one wounded. Why was he still standing?

"Two sons this war has taken, Allen. Two of my boys, felled on an English battlefield, far from home, dying alone. Barbara's son, killed at Bristol. I thank God Edward is safe here with me. But I agonize for my youngest, Walter. He yearns to ride out, and I cannot countenance to lose another—" John turned away, a sob wrenched from him, his frail shoulders trembling.

Allen reached out to him, but John did not notice.

"Edward is safe here with you, Uncle. And the fighting ceases. Perchance this winter we will find a way to negotiate a truce that holds, for neither side wants this slaughter to continue."

John nodded, his face still averted.

"I should leave." Allen touched his uncle's arm. The strength was not there anymore. When had he become the taller of the two, the decisive one?

John turned and composed himself. "Yes. You return to Exeter?"

"No. There is a greater need in the north of the county. I've been appointed governor of Barnstaple. Goring took a surrender from the

Roundheads a month ago. James is there, with a small force in place, but I must raise more to increase my troop. Barnstaple is not friendly to the king's cause, and I will need a firm hand and armaments to enforce rule."

"God's speed, then." John hugged him and kissed his cheek. "And thank you, Allen."

Old Ironsides. Cromwell's nickname stuck with his troop of horse, too, Allen reflected. He'd never seen a formation on the field like that before. The battle could have been lost or won on a whim of fate. Edward's cavalry had gone head to head with Cromwell's force, beating them back under the shadow of Donnington Castle. They were good, but Edward was better in that marshy terrain. Why had he been wounded in that skirmish, of all those he'd encountered?

As Allen left Lydiard and rode west toward Devon, he wondered at the happenstance of the bullet finding its target through Edward's armor. When they'd stripped him and examined the wound in his side, there had been such a little amount of blood, and such a small hole.

No matter. Satisfied that his cousin was resting comfortably in his boyhood room at Lydiard, his fever abating and John's capable surgeon promising a full recovery, Allen could ride out with a clear conscience.

Allen shook the specter of his uncle's sorrow from his mind and pulled his hat brim down deeper against the February cold. If he rode at cavalry pace, he could reach Frome by nightfall. He rode alone, no one to hold him back. And no one waiting for him, either. He pushed the image of Frances from his mind. Why would she enter his thoughts at this time?

Barnstaple was a complete and utter disaster. No question about it. The Roundheads had done nothing to preserve the garrison during their occupation, and the entire miserable town was lacking in any kind of defensive work. The walls crumbled to the touch; the gates could have been breached by a flock of sheep; the castle stood in ruins.

God only knew why it had taken so long for the Royalists to reclaim the town this past summer—probably due more to the stouthearted Parliamentarian citizens than any brick or mortar defense.

Allen frowned as he looked down from the garrison, perched high above the town. The River Taw gleamed in the distance, and a copse of masts indicated the location of the quay, the hub of the town's commerce. And there lay his biggest problem.

Barnstaple was fiercely independent, naturally loyal to Parliament. Despite its wealth, trading, and rich merchants, this blasted town was not about to embrace the king's cause, nor anyone who represented it. There was more trade going in and out of this town than Bristol, now, and its residents should take the same kind of civic pride in building and maintaining the defenses. Instead, they decorated their houses with fancy plasterwork ceilings to celebrate the Spanish Company trade and drank toasts to their wealth in ornamental goblets. Time to make these smug merchants contribute to the king's cause.

He was charged with hastening the rebuilding work over the winter while the armies stood down. And with the five hundred men from surrounding towns he'd raised into service, Barnstaple was finally able to boast a reasonable defense. The area was prosperous. Devon wool fetched a pretty price even in peacetime, and the demand was far greater during war. The taxes and fees from the local farmers funded his building efforts nicely. The days may be short, but he was able to pay well for the work.

For a moment, his mind flashed back to the Tower, of all places, and his father. Why now? Allen sighed. No matter. It must have been an echo from the days of victualing armies and a memory of the endless lists of supplies. He could use some of those armaments now, with rumors that Cromwell would be on the march as soon as the weather lifted. Never mind. He'd fortify this miserable garrison until not even a rat could get inside. Barnstaple was now the king's town. And so it would remain.

Striding down Bear Street to the East Gate, Allen scowled at the group of laborers that appeared to be doing very little but smacking their picks on the rubble. The wall had not grown one span since he had put them to the task that morning. He could almost believe they were doing so intentionally. Stalking over to them, he raised his voice.

"You there. Get to work." The men swung their picks half-heartedly, and one man intentionally turned his back on Allen and spat.

Allen beckoned one of his troopers over from the adjacent post.

"Throw him in the gaol," he commanded, pointing at the laborer. "Now."

The other men bent their heads and swung their picks harder. The culprit grinned and hawked again, this time the spittle landing on the trooper's boots.

Allen slashed him across the shoulder with his riding whip and stomped over to the dirt mound. A similar lack of progress was apparent. Jesu, the fact that he had to rely on the blasted citizens of this blasted Roundhead town was not good for his temper. He would need to set a greater example of Royalist control. He'd string up the mayor and burgesses if he had to. This garrison was not going to see Roundhead rule again, so Barnstaple had better get used to working under the king's governance.

Ha. A good rule for the country to live by, really.

He walked back over to the men by the wall.

"No Sunday rest, this week or next," he ordered. "They can conference with their ministers and receive instructions on saving their souls after my wall is built."

Ha. Ironsides, eh? By the time he'd rebuilt Barnstaple, they'd be calling Sir Allen Apsley "Ironarse." Edward would like that one. He'd share that joke with him when next he saw him.

Luce looked up from her notebooks as her mother arranged the tiny bundle of snowdrops into a green bottle and placed it on the table next to her. Without noticing, the March afternoon had faded away, leaving just the fire to light her writing. The sweet fragrance from the white blooms drifted across the table, the warmth from the chamber releasing their delicate aroma.

"Thank you," she said. "You always do find the first of the flowers."

Her mother brushed one of the buds with the tip of her finger. "This time last year, we could not even contemplate looking for snowdrops. We were solely concerned with saving men's lives and fending off starvation."

Luce nodded. "There is a strange quietness around us. Only Newark holds out for the king. John writes there are no Royalist armies for fifty miles, except for that last garrison."

"Babs took the children into town today, to the market. We would not have imagined that even six months ago." Her mother looked at the muddle of papers on Luce's desk. "You have heard from John?"

"Yes. He meets with Cromwell and others in Westminster daily. Even our cousin, Oliver St.John, talks to him of what lies ahead and asks him to commit to the new government."

"Oliver. It is a privilege for John to be taken into the Solicitor-General's confidence." Lucy stood still for a moment. "I wish that this honor could have been Allen's, too."

Luce checked the ink was dry in her notebook. She paused, for not often did her mother speak aloud of her son.

"Allen chose his way long ago, Mother. It is not a decision we condone."

"And yet, he and John were so close when we were all at Richmond. They had so much in common."

Luce snapped her notebook shut. "Do not speak of those times, for we lived under the tyranny of a corrupt monarch who encroached on our freedoms and ignored the will of the people."

"Can you not be neutral, Luce?" The break in her mother's voice caught Luce unawares.

"You are losing heart, Mother, in our cause?"

"England has lost more than any of us, Luce. Our sons are the heart of this country, and each day, more die for this cause. If we could find our way to peace and acceptance, then my sons will come home, and you will be reunited with your brothers."

This was not the time to waver.

"I would remind you of the lesson John read to us before he left," replied Luce. "*And he shall judge among the nations, and shall rebuke many people: and they shall beat their swords into plowshares, and their spears into pruning hooks. Nation shall not lift up sword against nation, neither shall they learn war anymore.*"

Her mother remained quiet, her face in shadow.

"My husband is gaining a reputation for level-headed counsel," Luce continued. "He is called upon to give his wisdom to the leaders of our cause, to be the judge of what is right for our country. He is asked to represent Nottingham in Parliament when government is restored."

A silence, and then her mother replied, following Luce's lead.

"As Cromwell forecasted, in his father's old Parliamentary seat? Yes, I can see the citizens electing him. He has their confidence." She started tidying the piles of parchments on the table. "Really, Luce, you keep things in such a muddle. Now that messages are getting through to us, you must be more organized. Look, here's a letter that's not even opened."

"I forget, when I'm writing." Luce took the letter. "This could only have come a day or so ago."

"That is my brother's seal."

The sharpness in her mother's voice caused Luce to fumble with the document and drop it. Her mother picked it up and quickly cracked the wax. Unfolding the yellowed vellum, she read the contents, holding the letter to the firelight in order to read it. A small frown appeared on her face.

"What is it?" No doubt, some new drama with her mother's sister, Barbara, or some other such complaint from her uncle.

"News of Edward. He was wounded back in October at Newbury. He does not recover as quickly as John would think. He asks me for any remedies that will restore him."

As her mother handed the letter to Luce, she pushed back the hair from her forehead, and the firelight caught the shadows in her cheeks. The past year had left its mark on all of them. Luce read the lines quickly and looked at her mother. "He says this was just a flesh wound. Would that take five months to heal?"

Her mother shook her head. "No. Especially in someone as young and healthy as Edward."

"What shall you do?"

"Gather my best recipes and medicinals and send those to my brother without delay." She was preoccupied as she pulled out a fresh sheet of parchment and reached for Luce's quill.

Luce stopped her. So similar were their hands—the capable, healing fingers, the square, calloused palms. No court lady's, but infinitely more valuable.

"I have a better idea. We will take them to Lydiard ourselves."

"You cannot mean that." A spark leapt in her mother's eyes, and Luce felt a responding excitement.

"I do." Luce gripped both of her mother's hands and spoke hurriedly. "John tells me the roads have been clear for months. No army is within forty miles of Lydiard. Babs loves to care for the children. George can send an escort with us. We'll be back before John returns from Westminster."

Her mother's face lit up. "Do you think we can?"

"I know we can. Edward needs our help. And I am not about to trust his care to anyone else."

"Lydiard is a Royalist house. John may not approve of you traveling there."

"*Neither shall they learn war anymore.* It's Edward," replied Luce. "That is reason enough. Nation against nation. Family against family. He will understand." She smiled. "We are still one, under the skin. If it were not for Edward, John and I would not be married, remember?"

38

All the time my mother dwelt in the Tower, if any were sick my mother made them broths and restoratives with her own hands, visited and took care of them, and provided them all necessaries; if any were afflicted she comforted them, so that they felt not the inconvenience of a prison who were in that place.

Luce Hutchinson
8ᵗʰ April 1645

Her bench was now gray and weathered under the cedar's spreading branches.

Subtle signs signaled different times. As they approached Lydiard House, Lucy noticed the fields by the windmill were churned over, a sign that troops of horses had trod the earth. Lydiard's face looked out over a bowling green, now a parade ground occupied by a group of village boys. No more than ten years old, they marched to the command of one standing on a mounting block and shouting orders.

"Are you glad to be home?" Luce called, the March wind catching her words.

"Glad? Home?" Lucy thought for a moment. "Lydiard will always be in my heart. But I am not sure this is home. The sights are familiar, but as if from a dream, not a life I have led."

Trotting the last hundred yards to the stable block, they quickly dismounted and made arrangements with the head groom for the care of George's escort of troop. The suspicions of the loyal servant were allayed when he recognized Lucy.

"Let us find my brother," said Lucy. "Come."

Picking up her bag of medicinals, Lucy took her daughter's arm as they crossed the gravel and entered the great oak door leading into the house.

Dear God, was this John? This old man who approached, his beard grizzled, shoulders stooped? How long had it been? Ten years, maybe, no more. Time had been treacherous to her brother. And grief had robbed him of his vitality.

"John." She put down the case and held her arms out to him.

"Lucy? Is that you?" Even his voice conveyed the frailty of sorrow.

"We could have sent back a messenger with Edward's curative." She hugged him, so fragile, thin under his padded jacket. He stood still, his arms at his sides. "Luce thought we might be the best medicine. And so, here we are."

John shook his head. "You came, even though this is a Royalist house?"

Luce spoke first. "This is our family home above all, Uncle John. And Edward needed us. Will you not welcome us?"

"Your husband agreed, Niece?"

"He does not know. He travels to Westminster to meet with Parliament. But he would say there is room for beliefs and loyalty to live harmoniously within kinship."

"It was Cromwell's bullet that smote Edward." John began to tremble.

Lucy stepped forward. "John, we are family. We have traveled far. Can we not see Edward, bring him a restorative to help him recover? You did write to me for assistance. Would you be so proud as to turn us away?"

Lucy watched as her brother struggled with what to say. Please God, do not let his foolish pride get in the way this time. Could he not accept this simple gesture of love?

"This way." He said no more, but turned and led them through the hall to a well-stocked library and on to a smaller chamber.

Lucy looked at her daughter and saw her own relief reflected in Luce's face.

In the corner of the room, facing tall windows overlooking the park, an ornately carved sleeping chair rested. The high back was angled so that Lucy could not see the occupant, but a hand lay on the armrest. With Luce at her side, she quietly approached the chair. Edward reclined in the upholstered seat, propped by cushions and covered in a warm coverlet. He slept, his eyelashes dark on his pale cheeks, his breathing soft. His beard was neatly trimmed, and his freshly-washed hair flowed loose on his shoulders.

Luce exhaled. "He is not in bed," she whispered. "He must be feeling better."

Lucy nodded. "Let us sit here, in the window seat, and wait for him to awake." John pulled up a stool by the side of Edward's chair.

Edward's eyelids fluttered open, and he blinked. They were the same beautiful blue Lucy remembered, and in the late-afternoon light streaming in from the parkland, they shone in his pale face with a luminosity that pierced her heart.

He stared at Lucy and Luce, and there was a pause while she let him adjust to the surprise of seeing them there.

"Edward," Luce said softly. "Edward, we came to you."

His eyes continued to stare at them, and through them, to the park beyond.

"Who is there?" he asked. "Why do you torment me with Luce's voice?"

The shock in Lucy's heart was echoed in John's words as he took his son's thin hand between his own and caressed it.

"Edward, Luce is really here. She and your aunt arrived today. They bring restoratives to make you well again." John carefully placed Edward's hand back on the arm of the chair and looked at Lucy. "You see, Sister, my son is blind."

Edward broke the silence.

"Luce? Aunt Lucy? Is it really you?" His voice trembled as he struggled to sit upright.

"Shhh, Edward. Yes, we are here." Lucy placed her hand on his brow, and he lay back against the cushions. Luce stifled a sob.

"I am happy," he murmured. "I wanted to see you so much, Luce. Now that your mother is here, I already feel my strength returning."

Lucy made a small movement with her hand, gesturing Luce forward to Edward's side. She mimicked a smile. Luce nodded.

"Edward, we bring my mother's best curatives and our company to restore you," she said lightly. Lucy could see the effort it cost her. "Now, recovery is in your hands; take your medicine and obey everything I tell you."

Edward smiled. "You haven't changed, Coz." He turned his head in her direction, and Lucy's heart sank to see how thin his face was, the hollows beneath his eyes. Under the blanket, his body barely disturbed the cloth, so slender was he. Nodding at Luce to stay with Edward, she drew John to the other side of the room.

"How long, John? How long has Edward been in this condition?"

John shook his head, his face crumpling. "When Allen brought him here, he was in pain and delirious. But soon after my surgeon removed the bullet, his fever broke, and he recovered his strength. He walked in the park, talked about returning to his troop."

Lucy gripped John's arm. "Where was the bullet? And did you see it?"

"In his side." John indicated his waist, just below his ribs. "Somehow his armor had not been buckled tightly. The bullet notched the breastplate as it entered his body." He looked at her with puzzlement. "No, the surgeon removed the shot and disposed of it with the sash that Allen wrapped him in."

Dear God. The worst place. If the bullet had shattered bone or lodged in a thigh, it would have been extracted, whole, held up for all to see. In Edward's side, there was no hope of the surgeon finding it without damaging those essential organs, unless he was especially skilled. Better he pretend to remove the shot and bind the wound quickly, announcing success, collecting his fee.

She glanced back at Edward and Luce, who were talking softly. Knowing that her words would forever change their lives, she told John all she knew.

"John, there is a malaise that creeps over a man from lodged bullets that has no cure. And recently, armies have been mixing copper with the lead to amplify these dire effects. You must be prepared for worse to come. Fatigue, appetite loss, blindness . . . all are symptoms of this insidious poison." She took John's hands, tears streaming down her face. "Edward is dying, John. And there is nothing I can do."

Luce sat by the window next to Edward's chair. They had adjusted the back to its lowest position so that he reclined, the sunshine still warming his face. This seemed to reduce the pain, relieve the pressure on his side. She watched him sleep, dreams chasing across his face, the tension ebbing and flowing as he lived in his twilight world. Soon, he would stir and ask for another draft of medicine to ease him back to sleep.

Would Allen arrive today? She looked again to the park through the windows, longing to see her brother galloping across the fields. Her mother had advised her it was time to write, time to summon him to Edward's side. Afore Easter, she'd said. *Afore Easter, Allen needs to come.* April had arrived last week, and Easter Sunday was on the sixteenth. She'd written to the garrison in Exeter, praying her letter find its way to him, that someone would know where he was. He must come soon.

She dozed a little in the quiet of the morning, catching up on lost sleep. The nights were the worst for Edward, when the house was silent and no daylight through the glass thawed his chill. In the day, he turned his face to the sun like a flower, seeking its warmth. At night, the moon rose across the park and spilled its cold beams across the lawns, and the shadows playing across Edward's countenance drained the life from him. Then, she sat sentinel, keeping silent company, daring the night to steal him away.

A sound. Did Edward stir? She opened her eyes, and there stood Allen, horror on his mud-spattered face.

She lifted her finger to her lips. "Hush. He rests," she whispered.

"How could this be?" Disbelief in his voice.

Luce moved to her brother. She held him tight in her embrace, held him as if she would never let him go.

"Come, walk with me. He will sleep a while longer."

Allen allowed himself to be drawn from Edward's side. Taking her shawl, Luce clasped his hand in hers, and together they walked through the quiet house to the park of their childhood. As she told Allen of the hidden bullet, the poison, the advent of Easter, he started to shake.

"Allen, you must prepare yourself." Luce looked back to the house. Her mother stood at Edward's window, watching them. She turned to her brother. "He has accepted this, and waits now only to join his brothers in heaven."

A great cry came from Allen, such as she had never heard before. She knew the sound of physical pain, the groans of dying men, the screams of soldiers injured in battle. But not this guttural, visceral shout against loss.

Her eyes returned to Lydiard. Her mother turned from the window. Clouds scudded across the sky, an April shower pattering around them, releasing the scent of hidden things growing under earth's dark cover.

"It will be Easter's promise to us, Allen." She held her weeping brother in her arms. "'I am the resurrection and the life: he that believeth in me, though he were dead, yet shall he live.'"

"Would that I were dead." Allen's words were muffled. He raised his head, anguish tormenting his face. "It is my fault that Edward will die."

Luce reeled back and clutched his arm. "You cannot mean that. You saved him by bringing him to Lydiard."

"And delivered him into the hands of an inept surgeon—"

"You weren't to realize—"

"The surgeons on the battlefield know more—" He broke down sobbing again. Luce could not imagine a more mournful sound.

"Allen, listen to me." She shook him and made him look at her. "You do not know this. You do not know if they would have had any more success. You do not know if he would have lost so much blood that he could have died on the field at Newbury. You did what you knew in your heart to be right." She turned him to look back at Lydiard, the old stone house resting in the verdant parkland, the church tower peeking over the tile roof. "You brought him home. Would we all could have that gift when we die."

If there was a day to choose to die upon, thought Lucy, there was one no more apt than Maundy Thursday for Edward. The feast of the Last Supper, the account Jesus gave of his washing the apostle's feet.

A new commandment I give unto you, that ye love one another; as I have loved you, that ye also love one another.

She arose early on God's Friday and cut willow branches to symbolize the palms of Jerusalem and Jesus's last journey. Early roses she gathered, and sharp-scented lavender. Of all these she made garlands, working alone in the church, distracted to keep her fingers occupied while her mind wandered free with her memories. Her eldest children, John's favorite son, the three of them inseparable. Tears brimmed from her eyes and dropped to join the dew on the young blooms as she wove and tied the April flowers. And when she was done, she hung the garlands from the alter rails, the pews, even John's stone tomb that had caused her argument with him at her last visit.

Thanks be to God Lydiard stayed a Royalist house, for the church and its family monuments, its ancient wall paintings, were protected from the Puritan destruction. This was the comfort of home, the belonging, the continuity of ancestors. She looped the last garland around the carved wood of the enclosed family pew and bowed her head to the monument of her grandparents, crowned with the remembrance of an older brother, drowned when she was a child. The Puritans would have destroyed these family memorials, condemning them for idolatry. And so continued the conflict, even in her own heart.

A click of the door and the footsteps of her family. Allen and Luce walked on either side of John, joining her in the pew. Walter, Edward's younger brother, followed closely behind. They gazed upon Edward's coffin, strategically positioned in the aisle beneath the royal coat of arms. She was glad she had placed the simple nosegay of primroses on the lid. She could not deny that Edward had died fighting for the king. But she could immortalize him with a memory that endeared him to her most. The primrose, the flower she'd stitched on Luce's bride ribbons, a marriage saved because of Edward's intervention.

Next to her, John's arm pressed close. Perhaps he took comfort in her presence. When the prayers were done and the last hymn sung, the servants and mourners left the church. Walter and John remained, staring stonily ahead.

They sat in silence for a while, and then John's tears flowed.

"My boy, my boy," he repeated. "My golden boy."

Lucy turned to him, and as she did so, the bright light of the northern window shone in her face. Next to the window, an empty wall.

"John," she whispered. "John, listen to me."

He lifted his head, his eyes red-rimmed, his face slack.

"Look." She nodded toward the window, over Edward's coffin, past the royal coat of arms. His eyes followed hers. "There. A place for Edward, a place for you to remember him." She took his hand. "You can set a monument to him there, John, one that will always stand true and strong and brave. One that time cannot change, cannot age."

"In his armor," added Allen from John's other side. "Dressed in his armor, as I last saw him. Ready to do battle for all he believed true."

John inclined his head. "And with his troop, Allen. As when we watched him train. His troop, here at Lydiard."

Allen nodded. "There was no man better than Edward in horsemanship or bravery, Uncle. That day at Newbury, he routed Cromwell."

The conflict again. But, in God's abode, there were no sides, no cause, no choice to make. Never had Lucy been more proud of her son.

"He was my best friend, Uncle," Allen continued. "His wisdom will be his legacy to me."

"And me too, Allen." John reached across and took Luce's hand. "He loved you dearly, Luce. Always know that."

Luce nodded. "I know. I always knew." She covered John's hand with her own, completing the family circle within the pew. "He returned me to life, Uncle. For when I was scared, he comforted me. His love guided me to happiness. And so will his memories, for the rest of my days."

Lucy wept then, for the loss, for her brother's grief, for the agony dwelling in her children from the actions of men who tore this country apart. She took Allen's and Luce's hands and joined them in her own. She glanced at Walter's stern profile, his mouth set as he stared at his brother's casket.

Enough. Surely now, enough.

Allen could not promise Lucy when he would next see her. His departure was another loss, another journey into the unknown.

"The war still rages in the west," he said as they stood together at the stables. "This moment, this sorrow, has suspended time for us. But outside these walls, men still kill each other, and battles continue."

"Allen, there must be an end." Luce was holding his horse's reins, as if she could prevent him from leaving. "John believes he will be seated in Parliament before the end of the year. He thinks it is just a few months before the king realizes he must compromise."

Allen shook his head. "Your husband is deluded. There will be no compromise." He stared back at the church tower, the tracery of crosses etched across the blue sky. "Edward's death must be avenged. I will not rest until I have fought every last battle."

Luce dropped her hand as if scalded. Lucy watched her children wrenched apart again, their shared grief torn by the political currents that still governed their lives. She dipped her hand in her pocket and drew out the keepsake she had been waiting to give them.

Dividing the ribbons, she handed one to each.

Luce looked at the crumpled, stained satin, the tiny stitched primroses faded but still discernible.

"My bride ribbons," she whispered. "Where—?"

"Edward carried them in a tiny leather pouch against his breast," Lucy replied. "I found them the first day, when I checked his wound."

"A talisman," Luce said softly. "I gave them to him on the day of my wedding, when he showed me the meaning of bravery."

"And now he sends them back to you. To you both." Lucy was dry-eyed as she turned to her son. She had said good-bye too many times before. She must be the mother he needed at that moment.

"Take it, Allen, and remember all they stand for. 'Love one another as I have loved you.'"

Allen touched the ribbon to his lips and tucked it inside his shirt. Turning Boreas's head away from Lydiard, he kicked the beast to a gallop.

Lucy and her daughter watched as he disappeared across the park.

39

*The wolf came into the fold in sheep's clothing, and wrought more slaughter
that way among the lambs than he could have done in his own skin.*

Luce Hutchinson

17th June 1645

God knew why he rode north to Leicester, instead of returning to
Barnstaple. Why he hunted for war.

In a fog of grief after leaving Lydiard, Allen rode into the bloody siege
of fair Leicester, Parliament's holdout. The screams of its trapped citizens
muffled the sigh of Edward's last breath in his mind. The blood flowing
through the streets replaced the image of Luce's tears. But how much more
hideous seared the scenes of war, than the memories of Edward's funeral?

There was no God, for no God would allow men to behave the way
they did in fair Leicester.

The abyss pursued him. Waited for him. Lurked in the empty eyes of
the soldiers who drank at every tavern. Not that he spoke to them. He had
no words left. No sleep. Just oblivion. If he just continued riding, drinking,
riding, drinking, then he'd keep away the devil's phantoms. When he rode,
the images couldn't crowd his mind. When he drank, unconsciousness
shielded him.

Was Nottingham next for the siege breakers? The town lay but a half
day's ride from Leicester.

Now he was ordered to his garrison, back to Goring, who held the
west. Others from his troop followed the king north, Newark in their
sights.

Dear God, was Nottingham next?

So flowed the war. No rhyme nor reason. And his training? His
discipline? Those months on the borders, in Whitehall? All chaff in the
wind in this helter-skelter skirmish of a campaign. Where went the king?
And Rupert, whose reckless bravery commanded men's hearts? Cromwell
would exact retribution for Leicester. General Fairfax, too. They'd
established a front at Naseby, Allen heard. Cromwell. Fairfax. And their

newly modeled army. Those two combined forces against the king and Rupert. Would to God he could be there. But his orders were clear. Goring commanded him to Devon.

He turned for the south and Barnstaple.

His soul flew to Nottingham.

After galloping across Wiltshire and Somerset, a three-day ride which passed in a blur of alehouses, Allen reached the gorse-golden hills of Exmoor. He slowed to rest Boreas as he smelled the brine of the ocean, and soon, the sparkling Channel came into sight, lying like the Virgin's robe across the horizon. Across the water gleamed the shoreline of Wales. His parents had fallen in love on that distant coast. His father's proposal, he'd heard tell, was one tendered with these hills of Devon in their sight.

Well, a pretty story. But where had it led them? Heartache and pain.

The garrison in Barnstaple waited for him. No doubt his troop slackened, and the building work slowed. There would be much to do. All along the route from Leicester, whispers in the Royalist alehouses told of the power of the New Model Army. What name was this for a fighting unit? More of Cromwell's propaganda?

Still, he could not underestimate the man. He rode into battle with God on his shoulder. If one believed God chose sides in this slaughterhouse. And his men, disciplined to hold fire and shoot as one. After all, it was a bullet from his troop that had killed—

No. Think elsewhere.

A west wind lifted the damp hair from his neck, and Boreas whickered, breaking his thoughts. He reined behind a farmer and his son pulling a sledge piled high with wool along the track. Allen's urgency diminished, and suddenly he wanted to walk these moors as if they were his own land, be this farmer with his strong young son and a sweet wife waiting for him in his own home. He shook his head. The worst kind of thoughts for a soldier.

He kicked Boreas on and cantered past the man, not looking back.

From the brow of the hill, Barnstaple lay before him, a compact town with church spires impaling the setting sun, and the River Taw a glistening ribbon wrapped around the distant quay. The fort lay between him and the defensive walls, but from here, it looked no different from when he'd left. Jesu. Did nothing get done if he was not there to do it himself? A few more miles, then, rest. And James better be ready with some good reasons if things had slacked off. The men in Bristol had hinted that Prince Charles, now head of the Western Army, marched toward Dunster and Barnstaple. If Allen was going to entertain him, the garrison must be functioning perfectly.

God, remember how demanding Queen Henrietta's household had been? His cousin Anne Villiers? The nursemaids, the supplies, the constant stream of requests. Thank the Lord he'd found Frances . . .

Damned sun low in his face, making his eyes water.

The next morning, James worked alongside him, shoveling the dirt to mound up the earthworks beneath the walls.

"I wrote to Hyde to grant me a commission for rigging my ship as a man-of-war," James said, his voice muffled as he leaned over a ditch. No man was spared the labor now, for Barnstaple's defenses were still sorely under-built. "As God's my witness, I will intercept those poxy rebel sailors and blow their arses out of the water."

Allen rested on his shovel and wiped the sweat from his forehead. The June sun was beating down hard, and he hadn't stopped working since sunrise.

"Your frigate in Torquay?" he asked. "You would bring it around to Barnstaple harbor?"

"If Hyde would approve my commission, I could be shipping coal on her, blasting the enemy out of the waters, opening up the shipping routes again." James dug more furiously, sending up a shower of dirt over Allen.

"All that, eh? You singlehandedly could turn the war."

"Damn it, Brother, don't be so bloody arrogant." James's face was bright red, and Allen could see he was close to losing his temper again. "It might not have come to your attention, but I am aware that these defenses are disastrous and the Roundheads still march west. If they take Bristol and set up a blockade, we are lost."

"I don't need you putting yourself in more danger than you already are, James."

"And I don't need you acting as nursemaid."

Allen returned to his shoveling. "This morning's dispatches tell me the prince travels to Dunster, not twenty miles east of here." Really, James was getting out of hand with his schemes. His temper was unpredictable, and there was little reasoning with him. "Go and ask him for your commission. And good luck with him listening to you. Prince Charles has greater things to worry about."

"I will." James flung down his shovel and stalked off, leaving Allen alone with his thoughts. And that was not what he wanted.

The plague in Bristol drove Prince Charles through to Dunster and on to Barnstaple, traveling with his court in carriages and on high-stepping horses. Accompanied by three troops of horse from Lord Hopton's garrison, they rode into the town on Midsummer's Day. Afterward, Allen blew up the arch of the bridge over the River Taw to complete the defenses. Now, just one way in and out. Easier to guard a single road.

Allen scrubbed his hands to remove the dirt from his fingernails and smoothed the calluses from his palms. He tied his best hair ribbon and pulled his last remaining lawn shirt from the trunk. The moths had arrived first, but there was little he could do. William would have been horrified.

He stood at the gate to the garrison as the prince and his entourage traversed the narrow lane, the carriages slowing as they were pulled up the gradient. The war was down to this moment, then. Just him and the prince. No William, no other Villiers courtiers. His father's voice echoed in his thoughts, his words reminding him of his loyalty to his king and the royal family. And he also remembered his father lying desperately ill in his chamber, his vitality gone, his health broken from supporting the king and Villiers. What were those loyalties that attracted and repelled like a lodestone for heartache?

"Sir Allen." The prince dismounted and stood eye to eye with him. He'd matured. An unsightly countenance, with those heavy features weighing down his face, but curiously charming. For a boy of fifteen, he was taller than most men about him. "It has been too long since we have seen each other."

"Your Highness." Allen bowed. "My apologies for the barren accommodation."

The prince laughed. "Allen, compared to some lodgings I have occupied, your town is Richmond on Twelfth Night."

Allen smiled at the reference. What a different world that masque recalled. Then he had first seen the court in splendor, witnessed the power of his Villiers cousins.

"You and your company . . . we will find lodging for everyone." Allen calculated there were at least ten ladies of the court that followed the prince. Allen would command Widow Beaple to rent him her rooms. God knew her mansion was rich enough, her late husband having lined his pockets with privileges exacted from when he had thrice been mayor. "It may not be a palace, but I can assure you of a comfortable bed."

"And perhaps a wench to warm it for me." The prince laughed. "My friends consider this a great adventure. Not much is needed to amuse them." He drew Allen to one side. "Now tell me, tell me of my baby sister and your cousin, the splendid Lady Dalkeith. For I hear it was your hospitality in Exeter that secured my mother, and which by certainty saved the life of my newborn sister."

Allen nodded. Seeing that the carriages and horses were organized, he beckoned for a flagon of wine and took the prince to the guardroom of the garrison. Sitting on a hard bench with cups of wine in their hands, Allen told him of his mother and her struggles in childbirth, her sadness at leaving England, and her fortitude to save her family.

The prince's eyes filled with tears as he heard the story, and he hugged Allen at the end of the telling. A singular loneliness hung over Prince Charles, reminding Allen again of how young he was and how much he had seen. His wrists, surprisingly delicate and bony, stuck out from the brocaded sleeves of his jacket. The prince had no doubt grown much this past year, and yet no tailor served his needs to make a new suit of clothes for him. That, more than anything, struck Allen as the most poignant feature of the young royal.

"Sir Allen, you have truly done my family a great favor. I think, without your assistance, my mother and my sister could well have died in Exeter."

Allen shook his head. "I did little but provide shelter, Your Highness," he replied. "My cousin Anne Villiers is the one to thank."

"Villiers, always Villiers," mused Prince Charles. An expression of sadness crossed his swarthy face. "I miss William."

Oh God. Not more talk of the dead.

"I do too, Your Highness." Allen beckoned for more wine. He stood and led the prince to the mess hall, where his troops were seated. A roar of conversation washed over them, breaking the intimacy they had just shared. "Now, although our entertainment is sparse, perhaps I can introduce you to some of the pleasures of Devonshire."

The prince looked up, a gleam in his eyes.

"I have arranged for a charming group of young ladies who are only too excited to dance for Your Highness," Allen continued. "Perhaps you would care to—"

"Bring them hither," interrupted the prince. "We should certainly enjoy this entertainment."

Allen smiled. This was the kind of royal pleasure he remembered enjoying. Wine. Music. And the lovely Devonshire maidens to distract the prince. Oddly, of late, he found little favor in them.

Opening his eyes, Allen found himself lying on the hard stone floor by an ash-filled fireplace. A dog lay licking its balls six inches from his face. Christ's nails, the sun was bright. A shadow fell over him, and he blinked several times. His head was about to split open. He felt around for his sword, for he thought he'd removed the weapon before the night had blackened. Before the phantoms had roosted on his chest, squeezing the breath from him.

"Is this what you're looking for?" A woman's shoe kicked his sword toward him. He grabbed it and sat up, rubbing his head.

"Water," he croaked. "Get me some water, woman."

He drew his hand across his eyes and then yelled in shock as the contents of a jug of water were dumped on his head. "What the—"

"Best cure for a sore head," said Frances. "That, and a good breakfast. When did you last eat?"

Allen peered through his dripping hair. "You? Why are you here? What brings you to Barnstaple?"

"Oh. At least you remember where you are." Frances sat down on the bench and contemplated him. "And don't you look fine."

Allen stood and buckled his sword, tucking his soaked shirt back into his breeches. "What do you want?" He refused to face her.

"I came to deliver a portrait of the princess to the prince," she replied. "And tell him how his baby sister fares. Lady Dalkeith sent me with an escort when she heard the prince lodged here—a troop of Barnstaple men who were returning home."

"Oh, she did?" Allen turned and walked toward the door. "The prince is in his chamber, I'm sure. He may not be stirring for a while. You can sit there and wait."

"Thank you. I will."

Allen snorted and left the room. He did not need to do more. She knew her way around a garrison. He tripped over a sleeping dog on his way out. What the hell was Anne Villiers thinking, sending Frances Petre across the county on a fool's errand with some blasted painting? Did she not know how dangerous the land was, or contemplate how he would return her, with every man needed to protect the prince and keep Barnstaple for the king?

"You dared to leave and travel to Lydiard?" John's face was flushed with fury.

This was not the welcome return of her husband Luce had expected. She looked up from her seat at the table, her quill poised above her notebook.

"It was for Edward's sake," she replied. "The roads were safe. You told me so yourself."

"We are at war." John strode to the table and picked up piles of documents. His dispatches had piled up while he'd been gone, and his first priority was to go through them. "There are still battles being fought. The carnage at Leicester was the worst yet of this abominable war. The slaughter, the absolute disregard the king's men had for their own people was beyond belief. I cannot countenance any who had a hand in that massacre. And even here in Nottingham, you know that George lost men defending the bridges into town from plunderers."

"Of course I do. My mother and I were here. We nursed those who were injured."

"The Royalist army is like a rat in a sinking ship, Luce. They feel the water rising, the tide turning. They will become more vicious, more unpredictable, as our forces move to crush them."

Luce's own temper rose. "We put our family before the cause, John. Allen, too."

"So did you enjoy your taste of Royalist hospitality at Lydiard?" His voice was peevish.

"I am here. Unharmed." Luce flung down her pen, disregarding the ink splotches across the page. "Edward has died. Is that not enough grief for me, without you pouring more on me with your petty accusations?"

John raised his voice to a level Luce had never heard before. "I have been fighting my own battles, Luce. Against those within our cause who seek to bring me down through jealousy and envy. Do you rush to my side to defend me?"

Luce jumped to her feet and swept her notebooks to the floor. She was trembling, so unfair was John's tone.

"Every one of these is filled with accounts of your endeavors, John. I record everything you tell me. I fight to save your reputation as much as I fought to save Edward's life."

He stared down at his dispatches, ignoring her.

"My words will preserve your deeds more than your actions ever will be recorded." She walked around the table to him and bent close to his ear. "Do not think that your heroics will go unnoticed, Husband. Every petty little slight, every insult, and yes, every brave deed—where you have ridden out unknowing if you will return—is recorded here."

She straightened. "One day . . . one day, our children will read these and know who you were. Be grateful for that. For Edward has no children, no record of his character and bravery, no one but Allen and me to remember his legacy."

"Perhaps his father will raise a monument to him too, in that papist church of his."

Luce slammed both hands on the table. John finally looked up at her.

"You take your Puritan principles too far, Husband. When this war is over, and our families are reunited, you had best remember who remains true and loyal to each other. For while you may scorn that I rode to a

Royalist's side to try to save his life, do not forget that, before he died, your own father disowned you for your beliefs."

John turned white, shock in his eyes.

"Yes, John. There have been times when I have had to choose between my family and you, and I will always love, honor, and obey you, as my husband. But do not think this means I disown my family, who choose to follow the principles they defend just as strongly as you do."

She sat then, the fire expended, her words still flowing.

"That day in Whitehall, when you left me with Allen. The day we separated, our beliefs tearing us asunder—" John reached for her hand, and she grasped his. "—Allen and I promised each other, John, that we would never let this war divide us." She was dry-eyed, emotion spent. "And we never will. Meeting again at Edward's funeral was no different than every other time we have been together. He will always be my brother, and I will always be loyal to him."

John sat, his head bowed. Minutes passed, and Luce let them. She had nothing else to say. Eventually, John looked at her again.

"I have not had to make the choice you did, Luce," he said softly. "If war came between George and me, I would rather die than let it separate us." He blinked back tears. "Forgive me for my weakness. I spoke from fear of losing you, not from animosity to Allen and Edward."

Luce gently brushed the tear from his cheek.

"Remember how we first met, my love? Allen and you were like brothers, so close you became. Do not forget those bonds that transcend war's violence. Do not allow hatred and politics to kill love and brotherhood."

John nodded. He brushed the dispatches to one side and leaned to the floor to pick up one of Luce's spilled notebooks.

"Read to me, my love," he said, handing the leather-covered book to her. "Read to me your account of the war and our lives."

40

If we must leave the light, why do we stay
By slow degrees more painfully to die

Luce Hutchinson
31st July 1645

"The Earl of Bath invites you to dine at Tawstock Court, Your Highness." Allen handed the message to Prince Charles as he sat with him in the garrison's mess hall. He enjoyed that the room had become an impromptu chamber for the prince, who preferred to spend his days with Allen and his troops while his court frittered time away in Widow Beaple's spacious house. "Lord Bourchier's hospitality warms with the advent of summer."

"Or with the advent of opportunity," replied Prince Charles. "Ever since he was publicly humiliated with his failed commission on behalf of my father, he has tried to ingratiate himself back into our graces."

"Lord Bourchier? Has he finally seen the folly of his arrogance?" Frances curtsied to the prince as she approached. She was holding a bundle wrapped in a red cloth. "He rode into Exeter with his band of Cavaliers as if he were the king himself. My father had much to do to reassure the locals that he was not at war with them. The men of Exeter and of Barnstaple do not take kindly to him."

Allen looked at her package suspiciously. After three nights at the garrison, he was still trying to arrange for a troop to escort her back to Exeter. But with the prince's arrival, no one could be spared.

"What business do you have with us, Mistress Petre?"

"The prince's business," answered Charles. He held his hands out to accept the gift from Frances. "Did you really find one?"

Frances smiled sweetly at Allen, then turned to the prince. "She is just six weeks. A little young to leave her mother." She and the prince bent their heads over the towel as he gently drew it back and revealed the brown-and-white freckled head of a dozing spaniel pup.

"How on earth did you find her?" the prince asked wistfully.

Allen shook his head. Nothing surprised him about her anymore.

"Frances can secure most anything you ask for, Your Highness," he answered. "She is a magpie, finding all manner of precious things and bringing them back to her nest." He touched the little puppy's ears. So soft. Frances's fingers brushed up against his, and he pulled his hand back quickly. "If it were not for her endeavors, your mother and newborn sister would have suffered greatly during their time in Exeter."

The prince took the puppy into his arms and held it close to his face. The creature licked him enthusiastically, making him laugh.

"Then we must express our thanks. And if a pleasant night of dining and dancing at Tawstock Court would go a little way to conveying our appreciation, Mistress Petre, you shall join us." Charles hugged the squirming puppy. "For once, let us forget this war around us. I shall send my musicians, my cook, and we shall feast as if we were at Richmond again."

Allen bowed. As he straightened, he looked at Frances, bright-eyed with flushed cheeks. Who could resist her excitement? For one night, he could leave James in charge of the garrison while he entertained the prince.

Allen had not visited Tawstock Court before, and when he approached the gate pillars, he shared the prince's amusement at the stone dog statues that bayed to the sky. Each decorated with red Royalist ribbons around its neck, they were a simple yet effective reminder to the local population of Lord Bourchier's loyalties.

The lane narrowed. Allen and a handful of troops took the lead as the prince and his court, his musicians—and somewhere in there, Frances—crowded aside him. Another troop brought up the rear, and as the party clattered through the three-story stone gate with its arched entry and arrow slit windows, Allen recalled the Byward Gate at the Tower. This felt the same, the sudden change from light to dark, the deep, hollow stone arch, and the guards standing shoulder to shoulder to salute the prince. Evidently Lord Bourchier was taking no risks with securing Charles's safety during his visit.

Within the fortified mansion, Lord Bourchier had indeed created an atmosphere reminiscent of court. Tall vases of fragrant summer flowers were placed on every surface, and the rich furnishings and tapestries glowed in the late-afternoon sun streaming through the mullioned windows. The house was old, and yet every comfort was planned, for the uneven stone floors were covered with expensive carpets, and long velvet curtains hung at each window.

The abruptness of this wealth and opulence assailed Allen, and he suddenly felt nauseous. Stepping back into the shadow of the doorway, he let the prince and the court flow around him, chattering like sparrows. His heart thumped within his ears, and the room blurred around him. Beyond the windows, brightness dazzled. Only the rolling green lawns were visible—fields, really, surrounded by woods where soldiers could hide and shoot their muskets without being seen. Was that a movement by the tallest oak?

A hand touched his arm, and he jumped and then looked down into Frances's calm eyes. He could barely take in the richness of her turquoise gown, the pale ivory of her bare shoulders, before she guided him to a quiet corner.

"Breathe, Sir Allen. Close your eyes and breathe. This feeling shall pass. I am here with you," she soothed.

He struggled, trying to pull his arm away from her, but she held him firmly.

"I have seen this in men before," she murmured. "It is a reaction that comes when too much assails the senses. And it is especially common in those who have returned from battle."

He fought the rising fear that threatened to choke him. What in God's name was the matter with him?

"I'm here, Sir Allen. I will not leave your side."

Her voice was the only clear thing in this moment, for he feared his heart would burst from its cage and that he would fall on the ground as if possessed.

"Hold your breath. Hold for a count of fifteen. Then breathe again." Frances continued to hold him. Such beautiful skin—soft, white, flawless. No blood, no gaping wounds.

"The prince and his court are enjoying themselves," she said. He grasped onto her words as a drowning man clutches a timber. "There are many delicacies being served. I see artichokes and raspberries, fresh cherries and strawberries. Such a change after army fare. Now hold your breath again."

His palms grew slick with sweat, but his heart was slowing, and the thunder in his head was distant, now. He still did not trust himself to speak.

"No one has noticed us," Frances continued. "We may stay here for a while. Let us turn and look out of the window. How beautiful are the gardens. Breathe deeply. You are past the worst, Sir Allen."

A strand of her chestnut hair curled around her delicate ear, and in profile, her lips were as full and ripe as the strawberries on the table. She was whole. Pure. Untouchable. And yet, she stood next to him, saved him from his humiliation.

"I thank you," he rasped, then cleared his throat. "I must have contracted a fever."

She nodded. "There are many explanations for an attack of that nature on the mind and body." Lifting her hand, she gently laid her fingers on his brow. "You will be fine, now. Come, let us join the prince's party. This may be the last time for a long while that we attend a court feast."

Across the chamber, Charles looked up and waved at Allen and Frances, a broad smile on his face. Allen offered Frances his arm, and together, they walked to the prince's side. He embraced them both.

"My noble soldier and his beautiful lady," said Charles. "Now, tell us again of your experience at Newbury, Allen. I would hear once more your description of the New Model Army's tactics."

Frances pressed closer to his side, and he shut his eyes for a moment before he relived the battle of Newbury.

Returning to garrison life, Allen put the attack on his senses behind him. The sudden sickness at Tawstock must have been caused by the heat and something he ate, and he was grateful that Frances had ensured he did not disgrace himself. Still she lingered in Barnstaple, lodging now with the prince's court at Widow Beaple's house. It seemed she'd made friends with the women who traveled in the prince's company, for he had rarely seen her at the fort in the week since Tawstock Court.

Each morning, he and Charles strode through the town to inspect the fortifications. The prince's gaze was always drawn easterly, his questions of Allen consistent. Were there sufficient troops to defend the vulnerable face of Barnstaple's hastily erected earthworks? What else was needed to strengthen the town walls? How much this prince already knew of warfare in his brief fifteen years. The whole world had changed since the occasion in Whitehall when they'd gathered for the Villiers child's christening. The lighthearted youth was now a solemn young man. And William Villiers was dead. An image of a slaughtered Cavalier lying by his dying horse flashed into Allen's mind. Was that Leicester or Cropredy Bridge? No matter, the dead remained nameless. Someone else could mourn them. Allen shook himself out of his thoughts.

"My father is not coming," Charles offered, his words brief, not slowing his pace.

Allen had received no news in his dispatches of the king traveling to Barnstaple. "He was planning to advance here, sir?" he asked.

The prince nodded. "My cousins Rupert and Maurice both advised him so. They suggested he sail by boat from Bristol."

Allen continued his walk. The low sun cast deep shadows from the defensive earthworks; the once green pastures were now churned and muddy. Turning swiftly with the restless energy of youth, Charles gazed in the direction of Bristol, hand shading his eyes against the bright distant horizon.

"And now?" Allen prompted.

"The roads are too dangerous for him to leave Oxford. The Parliamentarian army lies in Somerset, between us." The prince paused and gazed east again, as if he expected Cromwell and the New Model Army to appear over the moors. Allen nodded. War advanced upon them, pushing through to England's westernmost reaches. "And so, I leave to join General Goring. His army is camped across the western counties, and he guarantees me a troop in Cornwall. I am back in the fight."

Edward's commander. But not Edward. He was not there. He was decaying in a stone vault in the country church of his forefathers.

Prince Charles continued his musings. "And Rupert says the same. He considers it no longer safe for me to lodge here. His dispatches urge me to move, and to keep moving."

Allen stared over to the rolling hills of Exmoor, merging like purple cloudbanks with the pearl-gray morning sky. A shaft of easterly sun illuminated a distant stream, shining ribbon-like from a deep crevice.

The prince followed his gaze. "You should accompany me. There is more to be won on the battlefield than ever you would find defending this garrison."

Allen continued walking with the prince. Better not to slow down, not to break the prince's train of thought. For so lay his own future, tied with that of the royal family.

"Have you heard from the king, sir?"

The prince nodded, his profile chiseled against the lightening sky. His mouth trembled. In that moment, he was just a boy, missing his father.

"I received a letter yesterday. He commands me never to yield. Never to comply with Parliament, even though I may think such an act would save his life."

Allen's heart sank. This language did not bode well for their future. The turning tide was now running at full ebb.

"He speaks of dying, Allen. He tells me that he praises God for my gallantry, for if I were to give in to the enemy, I would ensure his days be ended in a torturous frame of mind."

The prince stopped. The clatter and cries of the waking town swelled around them.

"And so I go to Cornwall, to Launceston, a flight, and to fight." Charles laughed without mirth. "There is little land left, Allen. I will have reached the western edge of our fair kingdom."

Allen nodded. "I remain here, my lord. Should Barnstaple become the front line, I will hold strong for you, for the king, and for all men in England who preserve the throne for your father and you. I would rather die defending Barnstaple than leave the town and live."

Prince Charles embraced him. The young man's bones were fragile under the greatcoat. He was just a lad.

"I trust you to keep Barnstaple safe. I may leave England, if this is the only hope to save our legacy. But England will never leave me."

"I'm not going with the prince."

This woman. Why did she always challenge him, cause him disquiet? Allen looked up from his desk, from the pile of dispatches that increased daily as the Royalists retreated and the Roundheads advanced.

"Frances, Barnstaple offers little safety. He leaves now, and offers you a way out of Devon. Just until we can reclaim the western counties."

"I have no interest in fleeing to Cornwall. Besides, they are all heathens west of the Tamar."

Allen tried another tactic. "You will leave. I will not be responsible for you."

"Fine. I will return to Lady Dalkeith and the princess. She has offered me a permanent place within her household."

God save him from this impossible woman.

"There are four thousand rebel clubmen between here and Exeter. They have no allegiance to king nor Parliament. They fight anyone who threatens their farms, their livestock. And I have no troops to spare to escort you. Do you really think you can ride across the moors safely?"

"Then I shall stay in Barnstaple." She leaned over the table and picked up a fistful of his papers. "Looks as though you may need some help organizing. And, if we are in for a blockade, I will be of more use here than trailing around Cornwall with the prince."

He tried one more approach.

"The citizens of Barnstaple are all likely to declare for Parliament the moment Fairfax's army reaches us. Will you do the same?"

"Never."

Allen gave up. "Then stay here, Mistress Petre, and make yourself useful. I have a war to fight. Do not look to me for protection."

"I never have."

Into the wet and miserable autumn, Allen received news that only served to strengthen his resolve and confirm that his fort was one of the last holdouts of the war.

Honiton, Crediton, Tiverton . . . all falling to Fairfax, all crumbling before the New Model Army. God knew Barnstaple was swelling daily as the country folk made their way to the safety of the town. If it wasn't the threat of the clubmen, it was Goring's army, out of control, raping and robbing their own countrymen. Billeted across all of North Devon, their ranks now overrun with French mercenaries, the disciplined army of Allen's time had deteriorated into a lawless rabble.

And then, he started hearing of the desertions. At first, a trickle. Word came of hangings in villages of those caught deserting, to send a message to the others. But then a rush, a torrent, men returning home. Allen remembered the trooper at Newbury. His own flight with Edward. Home.

Over dinner, which he had taken to sharing with Frances, he first voiced his thoughts aloud. She'd laid out a generous meal in the castle solar, a special effort to celebrate the Harvest Festival. Old traditions survived in the deep country.

"We may be the last left standing in North Devon." Allen took a deep draft from his goblet. The wine was good. Frances continued to magically find the best supplies. No doubt this had come onshore from a wrecker's haul at Clovelly.

"And you intend to defend the garrison against the might of Fairfax's army?" Frances put down a russet-colored apple she was coring, the first of the autumn crop from Barnstaple's orchards.

"I have no choice. The king and the prince are counting on me to hold Barnstaple. The city is overflowing with citizens taking refuge."

She handed him a slice of apple, which he absently accepted. The fruit was crisp, flavorful.

"And to what end will you hold Barnstaple?" she asked. "Until what happens, Sir Allen?"

"Until the prince returns with his army and reinforcements. We shall hold the west, and commence our attack east again."

"And so war continues," she sighed. "The ebb and flow of men, territory gained and lost, towns besieged and broken." Frances put down the rest of her apple. Allen's eyes lingered as the firelight shadows played across her face.

"War is not so black and white that winners and losers are determined overnight." He reached over and picked the fruit from her plate. "And, in the meantime, life continues."

The door flew open, and on a gust of cold wind, James strode into their quiet room.

"The Parliamentarians have taken Glamorgan. The Channel is now in their hands. We have no way to bring in supplies, coal, to sustain the townspeople." He threw his gloves down on the table and poured himself a goblet of wine, tossing the Rhenish back in one gulp.

Allen pushed back his chair. "Where did you hear this?"

"On every street corner. The townspeople are panicked. They see nothing but deprivation and starvation ahead." James turned to Frances. "Mistress Petre, I fear even your negotiation skills will fall short this time."

"We have to get more reinforcements, supplies. I cannot send to France; nothing is getting through anymore." Allen sank his head in his hands. "I do not know where to turn."

James sat next to him. "My ship—"

"Yes?"

"I must bring the vessel around from Torquay to the harbor here. And to equip it as a man-of-war."

Allen nodded. "I shall write again to Sir Edward Hyde."

"Tell him this." James jumped up and paced in the small room. By the flickering candlelight, he appeared possessed, fiendish in his intensity. "I want authority to seize upon any ship. A license to rob at sea. I must take any barge that stands in my way." He slammed his fist on the door, punctuating his sentences. "I want license to take everything. The enemy has stopped our ships. I will sink them all."

Allen shrugged. "I will do what I can. I will let him know that now we are in a blockade."

James snatched the quill from Allen. "Here. Let me."

He started scratching on a second piece of parchment, speaking aloud as he did so. "If I can get my ship and two more frigates, I can intercept the Bristol merchants who are supplying the Roundheads. Give me a commission for a man-of-war in the king's service, and I will make a prize of all the enemy's merchants. Give me the liberty to exact revenge on all these rascals, and it will be the most pleasing thing that can happen to me."

Allen stared into the single candle flame. Somewhere along the way, decency had been lost, and the brutality of war tamped all emotions. He welcomed the void again, the great and impenetrable emotional abyss that yawned beneath his feet. He did not care if James spewed anger and hate and retribution. He wished he could do the same. But he felt nothing. Nothing at all.

Frances leaned over and poured him another glass of wine. He caught a scent of rosemary from her hair, and for a moment, he was back in his mother's stillroom at the Tower, the aroma of crushed herbs permeating the air. A wisp of comfort in the remembering.

41

All things in present fighting posture be:
Yet in the promise we a prospect have
Of Victory swallowing up the empty grave;
Our foes all vanquished, Death itself lies dead

Luce Hutchinson
17th March 1646

In the rock-lined stillroom of Nottingham's fortress, Lucy crushed a dried rosemary twig between her fingers, the gray-green leaves crumbling into dust as she mixed an astringent paste. She paused, hand stilled as she considered the stone bowl.

Rosemary for remembrance.

Dust to dust.

The words crept into her mind, recalling the day her husband died and she'd fled to her stillroom in the Tower. Today, so many more to remember. Edward. William. The men of Nottingham. And now? Now, she looked after the scraped knees and elbows of her grandchildren, grazed as they played within the rough castle walls. Please God her nursing skills would be limited to these small limbs.

"You daydream, Mother?" John's voice broke her thoughts as he entered the chamber. "The peace must be soothing to you. Nottingham is quiet."

She dusted the powder from her fingers. "It is a relief to not hear the gunfire and cannon, John. And the children are happier now they can run outside in safety."

John crossed the stone floor. He idly picked up a bunch of lavender and smelled it.

"Remember the garden in Bartlett's Court?" he asked. "So many days I paced those paths, willing Luce to recover. I loved that garden, the chestnut trees, and the lavender beds."

Lucy nodded. "I preferred the garden to the house." She scooped the last of the rosemary from the smooth board and dropped the herb into the bowl. "Perhaps one day we can build such a garden together. At Owthorpe."

"Will you remain with us when all this has ended?" John stared intently at the dried flowers.

She waited patiently. He had something to tell her. To approach from an angle was always his way.

John continued, face still averted. "I know not what the situation will be with the outstanding warrants the king still owes you. Parliament will not be in a mood to favor his old allies. The courts will not consider your pleas worthy when thousands of men are clamoring for reparation. Would you consider staying with us? We do not want you to leave when the fighting ceases."

The warrants. Her husband's sacrifice for naught, another victim of the king. "What will the end be, John?"

He brushed the lavender with his finger, arranging the stalks so all were even. "I ponder the same question myself," he replied. "The king must realize that this war against his people is drawing to a close. There is to hand a time for peace, for men to come together and find a way forward. He must set the example by treating with Cromwell, by offering to surrender."

Lucy shook her head. "Surrender? Do you think men such as my sons will readily surrender after these years of war? You know Allen well. Is that truly your belief?" She bit back a sob, her throat raw with unshed tears.

In the silence that followed, all that could be heard was the distant cries and laughter of her grandchildren in the castle yard. John walked to Lucy, kneeling in front of her.

"I ask your blessing, Mother, and understanding for the work I have done to represent Parliament. I will protect you and provide for you as long as I shall live. If my actions in any way have directly placed Allen and James in danger, I would rather cut out my heart than cause you pain."

Lucy placed her hand on John's head, his hair soft to her touch. The tears spilled down her cheeks, hot in the cold air. This man was her son too, for all that he opposed in Allen was all that he sustained in Luce.

"God bless you and keep you, John." And may God bless and keep her sons, foremost.

Allen pulled another dispatch from the scuffed leather pouch. The garrison was quiet, holding its breath while the news trickled in, borne by fleeing men. No official messengers remained.

Torrington. Torrington fell, now. The foot soldiers who straggled into Barnstaple brought news of the rout. The rain-soaked wounded men of the wettest winter in memory told their mournful stories. The Royalist Horse quitted the place. Two hundred Cavaliers imprisoned in the church, massacred in an explosion of gunpowder and shot.

The Cornish Foot who fought for the king disappeared in the night.

Back to their own country.

Back home.

Fairfax. Allen pushed an untouched plate of food aside. 'Twas said Fairfax and his troop ate the Royalists' breakfast when they stormed Torrington. So rapid was his victory, the food was still warm. And the great panniers of stones that were constructed to block the streets? Held for a short while, and then destroyed.

Somewhere out there, General Fairfax watched Barnstaple.

He watched and waited and made his plans with Cromwell's New Model Army.

Goring abandoned his command at the end of November. Left to join the queen in France. Pled ill health caused his flight. His debauchery, more like.

Allen crumpled the parchment and flung it into the cold grate. And good riddance to that depraved bastard and his wretched army of French mercenaries who cared nothing for the honor of good Englishmen. Who fought not for justice or truth, but for the spoils of war. Who, if not paid, simply plundered. Who fled when they should stand and fight.

Another message. Another fallen town. Exeter was surrounded. They cried for his help, for him to remember his friends there. Send relief. Send five hundred troops. Else they shall be slaughtered in place.

Fair Leicester. Had their call for help gone unanswered, too?

Allen looked up as a hand touched his shoulder. The candle burned low, guttering in its dish, sending up a plume of smoke, signaling its end.

"You must eat," Frances insisted softly. "And rest." She held a plate of apples in her hand. Did she think to tempt him?

He turned from her touch and said nothing. Fair Leicester had once boasted the most fertile orchards in England. Before the burning. Before the destruction. Before the blood ran as water, soaking into the thirsty roots.

"I will leave it here for you." He heard her place the dish on the table. Felt a soft woolen Devon blanket draped around his shoulders. He sensed her presence next to him, sharing the bench. And then, quiet.

And still, the dispatches came. Days flowed, one to another, and the cold north winds worried at his bones. Allen hunkered closer to the fire, banked now to a glowing chunk of oak. God bless Frances, who had discovered the Parliamentarian estate of an absent Mr. Pottington a few miles from Barnstaple, a thousand acres of woodland ripe for felling. He activated fifty strong men, and within a few days, Barnstaple had replenished its fuel.

He sighed. That did not solve the longer-term blockade of food, and this latest news confirmed that James's ship had been captured before ever leaving harbor. There was no chance of getting any supplies by sea.

He broke the seal on another document. By a small window, Frances sat at the desk, adding accounts in a ledger. Allen watched her unnoticed for a while. Her hair fell across her face, her cap pushed back slightly as she leaned her head on her hand. He wanted to brush the strand from her cheek, relieve the tiredness in her shoulders. She sat that way for hours, patiently figuring how to turn the thin trickle of levies from the surrounding villages into funds to send to the king's armies.

"My God, they are coming." He rapidly read the letter. Frances looked up.

"Who?"

"Prince Charles. And the king. Both armies are on the move and heading across the moors toward us." Allen looked up and burst into laughter. "I know not who wrote this message—I do not recognize the name—but the tide is turning. Salvation approaches. Now we shall see the mettle of Fairfax and Cromwell." He waved the letter at Frances. "Send a notice to all the villages around. I require them to pay their weekly rates immediately for the provisions for His Highness's Army. In fact, I want three weeks, paid in advance, delivered in money or wheat." A surge of exhilaration ran through him. "And if any of these parishes shall fail in the payment by Monday next, they must expect to have a party of my troops sent to them for the bringing in of the same."

In his excitement, he drew Frances from her chair and whirled her around the room in an impromptu dance. Laughing, she kept up with him, and soon they were moving to imaginary music, their steps falling into place as if they had danced together all season. Faster and faster they spun, until at last, breathless, Frances pulled from Allen's arms, her hair mussed, her cheeks flushed. For a moment, they stared at each other, no more than a foot apart, until Frances smoothed her skirts and returned to the desk, her slim figure outlined against the window.

Outside, the rain spattered, the gray Devon clouds absorbing the last of the daylight. But, in this small chamber, Allen knew a warmth in his being that he had forgotten existed.

As so often they did, Allen's thoughts turned to Luce and his mother as he looked out from the fort's tower. Nothing approaching from the east. And yet on this March morning, unbeckoned came the memory of Richmond and racing against John through the park, coats flying behind them as they galloped, becoming fast friends through their love of racing and the outdoors. Those days were long gone.

He turned to the west. The fresh wind tugged at his hat, blowing cloud shadows across the rolling hills. Cloud shadows? Allen looked more closely. Dear God be praised, those were companies of men spreading across the greening Devon moors. The land above the pastures was unenclosed, and men walked freely over the earth.

"What do you see?" Frances's soft voice was tossed away by the wind, and he bent closely to her ear, throwing his arm around her shoulder and turning her.

"Look. Men, hundreds of them." She trembled and relaxed against him for a moment before she slipped away and clutched the rough stone parapet. "It must be the vanguard of the Western Army."

"What does this mean for us?" A gust blew her hair across her face, and she pushed it back with an impatient gesture he now knew well. "Look, a messenger breaks forth."

"It means we are able to fight again. We can take our five hundred men who are garrisoned here and advance toward Fairfax." Finally, time to act. Time to venture forth from this stale town. Time to return to the battlefields and finish this war, once and for all. "Let us go and greet the messenger, for there will be work to do to bring these additional men into the town and supply them."

The messenger was from Thomas Fairfax, General of the New Model Army. Dressed in a buff coat, the only mark distinguishing him from a Royalist a sprig of heather in his hat, the messenger remained at attention while Allen read the letter. James and Frances stood next to him, disbelieving, staring at the Parliamentarian envoy who had entered the garrison as if it were his own.

At first, the words did not register. Where was the king's army? This must be a jest, a joke perhaps from the prince, who was known to enjoy rough play. The messenger stood unmoving, unemotional, his eyes fixed ahead.

Allen looked down at the page again. "This cannot be true. Sir, tell me your name and rank and by what authority you deliver this news."

The messenger spoke, his eyes not meeting Allen's. "Colonel Frank Garten, sir. General Fairfax asked me to convey this to you personally." He handed Allen a bronze token, a seal engraved with a lion's head. Fairfax's crest.

James unsheathed his sword and stepped forward. "Tell me, you cur, tell me what news Fairfax delivers, and I will convey my response to him personally." The messenger did not flinch.

Allen put his hand on James's arm. "'Tis the end, Brother. The Western Army surrendered to Fairfax two days ago. And the prince has left for the Scilly Isles."

"I do not believe this. The prince would never leave," James roared, his face red with emotion.

"He has left. And the king goes to Newark. He marches north, not to the west." This false calmness concealed his inner turmoil. Allen did not know how much longer he could contain his feelings. He spoke almost to himself. "I promised the prince I would defend Barnstaple, and that I

345

would never desert. And yet, he has gone. The king turns tail. What choice does this leave me? For the sake of the people, I cannot condone the slaughter a siege would bring upon them." He looked again at Colonel Garten. "Does your general require a reply?"

The messenger nodded.

"Then tell him—"

"I would rather cut you to pieces with my own hand and sword than have you surrender this town, Allen," shouted James. "You have no honor, Brother, no guts. You are a coward to consider this is even an option."

Allen paused. "Tell your general that I am considering my position." Images of the blood-soaked streets of Leicester rained down on him. The screams of the people. The dead piled in the streets. The few left alive, mad-eyed and gibbering. He slumped onto the bench, and all around him crept the void. James paced to the window, to the fireplace, and to the window again.

Frances moved between them, passing them food and ale. He could not eat, but he could drink.

Five weeks since the message from Fairfax. Five weeks a blockade held Barnstaple hostage. He should be riding forth with his troops. The armies were on the move. Perhaps he could catch up with the king. Spring. April was here. Time to ride out to battle again. April. Oh God, Edward.

Easter Sunday. Where the congregation found the flowers to decorate their church, he knew not. He attended the service, in Edward's honor, the townspeople looking at him, murmuring. He knew they were waiting to declare for Fairfax.

Love one another as I have loved you.

When he arrived back at the garrison and discovered the small jug of primroses waiting on the table, he gave a great cry and swept it to the floor. Primroses such as those embroidered on Luce's bride ribbon—faded, barely legible, still worn close to his heart—the legacy that Edward had left him. Frances said nothing, just picked up the nosegay, mopped the water, and set the flowers down again on the table.

Five weeks. This was a blockade, not a siege; no artillery fired. No blood spilled. But starvation threatened. Where would this end? What honor would there be in surrendering?

"You can't go on, you know." Frances walked with him as he followed his old route along the town walls. The river ebbed fast, leaving bubbles in the mud. Gulls screeched overhead as they dove for the fish that the shallow waters gifted them. A fresh breeze from the sea lifted her hair, tied under a kerchief. Her cheeks were thinner now, no more the rosy Devon maiden's of two years' past. But her lips were still as full, still as succulent as June berries.

She followed him each morning, walking next to him. He tried outpacing her, seeking solitude, but she always kept up.

"What would you have me do?" he asked. To the south, permanently lay Fairfax's army. In the morning sun, their armor and guns glittered.

"Negotiate." She smiled. "Just as I did with the men of Exeter to gain supplies for the queen."

"James would rather die fighting. He will despise me for all time."

"James has his own demons to face."

Allen stopped. He could live with James's hatred if it meant saving the lives of a thousand others.

"I will not lay down arms. I will not be whipped into submission. I cannot dishonor my men by asking them to bend the knee to Fairfax."

"You will not have to." Frances took his arm and gently turned him back toward the fort. "I have thought about this long."

Luce watched Babs and her mother as they sewed by the solar window in the castle tower. She was too restless to pick up her work, too agitated to write in her notebooks.

She stood and walked around the room again.

"Luce, you pace like a Barbary in the Tower's menagerie," said Babs. "You make my head ache with your turning and returning."

"I am sorry," muttered Luce. "I am impatient for John."

"And I for George," responded her sister. "But that does not mean I wear a hole in the floor."

Luce stopped and ran to the window. "There. They return. I must know—"

"Wait here, Luce," her mother's voice stayed her. "Wait for them to come and tell us all they have witnessed. They will want to see to their horses and quench their thirst. The ride is long from Newark, and if they are here now, they must have left early this morning."

This waiting, always waiting. Luce thought she would scream with frustration. There must be news, they must come and tell her . . .

John entered the chamber first, followed by George. Luce and her sister and mother stood, silenced by their expressions. No word was spoken until Luce stepped forward.

"Is the deed done?"

John nodded. "It is done."

Gasps filled the room. Luce clutched at her mother's hand and pulled Babs close to her.

"The king?"

"He turned himself over to the Scots Army three days ago."

"Surrendered?" Luce needed to hear those words, needed that finality.

John shrugged. "I think, in his mind, there is no surrender. He seeks an agreement with them."

Her mother stepped forward. "And he stays with the Scots?"

"He considers them his allies."

Lucy nodded. "Of course he does. He was born in Scotland; his first years were there. He considers himself as much Scots as English. Of that I remember, when I knew his father, the old king." She shrugged her shoulders. "And yet, does he trust them?"

John shook his head. "I know not. All I can tell you is that our commissioners argued greatly with the Scots when they discovered the king sought their protection, and threatened them if they did not let our Parliament talk to the king. And then, perhaps to mollify us, the king ordered the surrender of Newark."

Luce caressed John's face. "You were there?"

He nodded. "George and I were the first in. We signed the order to ratify the terms."

Babs broke from Luce's side and ran to George. "Was it awful? Were the conditions—"

"Horrific." Even George's jovial spirit was quenched. Luce had never seen his face so solemn.

"What was Newark like, Husband? We have been besieged. We know the circumstance," Babs said.

George turned and stared at Babs; it was as if he looked straight through her. "You have never seen conditions such as these. There is plague in the city. There was no food. No clean water. No doctors, surgeons. No one to protect the dead from the starving dogs." He gave a great, shuddering sigh. "You need not know more."

John placed his arm around his brother.

"It is over, George. Newark was the last holdout. We have their surrender. The city is emptying even as we speak."

"Barnstaple? What has happened to Barnstaple, John?" Luce clasped her hands to her breast, knuckles white with anxiousness.

"I have no news. Nothing reaches us from the west."

"And the king?" asked her mother. "Where goes the king now?"

"He stays with the Scots," replied John. "We hear they take him to Newcastle."

"What does this mean, John?" Luce continued her pacing. "What is he thinking?"

"No man has ever been able to trust his thinking," he replied. "Some say he will abdicate in favor of Prince Charles. But others say he will not let his son fall into the hands of Parliament, and commands him to France. Always, he says one thing and does another."

"So, there is still much confusion." Luce turned to the window. "And where in this are James and Allen? What are their fortunes, so tied to this king and his vagaries?"

Her mother came to stand next to her.

"We can but watch and pray, my daughter," she replied. "Pray that these times of war are passed and that men fight now with words, not weapons."

42.

Where Love doth come,
If it comes powerfully, it leaves no room
For any other cares

Luce Hutchinson
16th April 1646

Fairfax accepted Allen's terms of surrender. April 14, 1646. One year to the day that Edward was interred at Lydiard. *Love one another.* The citizens of Barnstaple would not be slaughtered.

Allen read the document again, Frances next to him. She pushed back her hair, her fingers ink-stained. How many drafts he had dictated, she had countered. Finally, he'd agreed. If Exeter could surrender peacefully, and its men released with their pride intact, so should Barnstaple. Frances had told him that Lady Dalkeith was offered safe passage to any number of Royalist homes. Safe haven, protection for her and the little princess and her household until the king returned to Whitehall. She was taking Henrietta Anne to St. James's Palace, his cousin had written. A safe home.

His signature was all that was needed, now. Sir Thomas Fairfax, General of the Parliament's Army, had already scrawled his name in a large, confident hand across the page. Frances handed Allen the quill. He closed his eyes for a moment, tears blurring the lines, remembering other pleadings, where Edward had been the one who'd coached him and encouraged him to find his words.

He read the clauses aloud, for in the saying so, they became truth.

And, within the truth, arrived clarity of conscience. Frances took his hand, and he left his within hers.

Item. That all Officers and Soldiers, without exception, may march forth with their complete arms, flying colors, matches lighted, with their muskets laden, and twelve shots apiece in their bandaliers, to any garrison in England, where His Majesty shall be in person, and they shall have safe conduct and free lodgings in their march, and be not forced to march above ten miles a day.

They would march out of Barnstaple, colors flying, guns on their shoulders, free men.

Item. That in case they shall not be received by the king, they shall have free leave to pass quietly to their own homes.

He looked at Frances, and she returned his gaze, smiling her soft smile.

Pass quietly to their own homes.

Signed, Sir Allen Apsley. Governor of Barnstaple.

Allen stood with James in the garrison's armory as he buckled his sword. Around them, men hurried back and forth, carrying bundles and packages, checking weapons, stacking surplus muskets in a pile on the ground outside.

"You are certain of your decision, Brother?" Allen's heart was heavy, and his brother's jaunty attitude did nothing to allay his apprehension.

"I am joining the prince," replied James. "The king's future is uncertain. The prince's is not."

Allen nodded. "I understand." He stepped aside as two men lugging a cumbersome trunk of cartridges staggered between them. "Twelve each," he called. "Those are the terms of our surrender. Twelve shots each." They nodded and disappeared through to the yard.

"Still think you did right, Allen?" James drew his gun from its holster, peered down the barrel, and pushed it back again.

"I did what is best for all the men of this garrison. And the citizens of Barnstaple."

"Gave up."

Allen's temper flashed. "Surrendered. Rather than be slaughtered." He laid his hand on James's shoulder. "You know the prince leaves for France."

"Yes. I will throw my fortune in with his. Better that, than stay here."

"Do you have any words for our mother?" Allen swallowed. "I must tell her of your decision."

James tugged on his jacket and shoved his hat on his head. "Tell her I fight for my king and country. And that I may leave England, but England will not leave me."

Allen exhaled. "You've been planning this for a while. Those are the prince's words."

"Yes." James turned. "Good-bye, Brother."

"God go with you," Allen called after him. "God keep you safe."

In response, James lifted his hand and was gone.

And now, for the second good-bye. In its own way, just as difficult. Perhaps more so. He sought out Frances and found her in the stables. Dressed in her brown riding habit, she was loading a pack onto her mare. A pony was hitched to the ring next to her, laden with bundles.

Most of the horses were gone, for once the surrender had been signed, men had immediately started departing. Only he and a handful of others stayed until the end. His responsibility was not to leave before the fort emptied. In the far stall, Boreas shuffled and stamped his hoof. He was ready to leave, too.

"You go now." The words were a statement, more than a question.

"Yes." She did not face him, but pulled up on the girth, adjusting the leather strap tightly. He watched her capable hands tug on the buckle, adjust the saddle down on the mare's back.

"Who else travels with you to Exeter?" The clubmen still roamed the moors.

"I'll find someone."

He exploded. "You cannot do this. You cannot go riding about the countryside as if there is no danger, no vagrants, as if this is peacetime." He grabbed her wrist, turning her to face him. "I refuse to let you do this. Why did you think Lady Dalkeith would expect you to travel to her unaccompanied? Or do you return to your family? Do they send a troop for you?"

"I don't go to Lady Dalkeith. She is already on the move, and I hear now, not to St. James's. I would not be surprised if she heads for Dover, to take the princess across the Narrow Sea to the queen." She stared back at him and tugged her wrist from his grasp. "Where do you travel to?"

Allen stepped back. "Not to the king just yet. Nor to Prince Charles." He rubbed his face. God, he was so tired. *If not the king, then home,* the surrender said. Where was home? "Nottingham. I would go there and see my sisters, my mother."

Frances nodded. "They are for Parliament."

"Yes."

"What about your sisters' husbands? Will they welcome you? You choose their side now?"

"I don't know. I don't know what is left to choose." He looked down at her and shrugged. The abyss yawned at his feet again.

"Then you can escort me as far as Oxford. Lady Dalkeith has written me an introduction to Lady Villiers, her mother, who remains there. I am invited into her household. It is a start on whatever this next journey is."

Her words surprised Allen. "You go to my aunt?"

Frances nodded. "When the king returns to his court, there will be a need to organize and rebuild the structure and restore order. Much has been dismantled and destroyed these past years. The Villiers will be at the center of reconstruction. And Lady Dalkeith's niece, Barbara, the child William left behind, is in want of a household." She looked around the empty garrison, the last of the soldiers filing out across the drawbridge. "Will you ride with me? There is nothing left to stay for here."

Fairfax's army was true to the terms of the surrender, and as Allen and Frances rode from the fort, they were granted safe passage along the easterly way. The hatred in the townspeople's eyes could not be missed, however. Now that they were no longer under the Royalist rule, the people of Barnstaple were joyful to revert their allegiance to Parliament. Allen knew that if it were not for the Roundhead army, he would not be left unharmed.

Frances rode silently at his side, and they joined the last stragglers of the garrison riding east. He gazed after those who turned their horses' heads toward Cornwall and the prince, wondering where James was in the hundreds of troops riding south to the ports.

"It's not too late," said Frances softly. "You could still go after him."

Damn, she read his thoughts.

"Move on," he replied. "We should arrive in Exford before nightfall. The distance is short, but it will at least get us started on our journey."

She kicked her horse, which broke into a trot, the pack pony close behind. Two grooms followed, men Allen had promised a fair wage for an escort as far as Oxford.

The town gave way to countryside, and the rolling hills of Exmoor lay ahead. In the May sunshine, all looked peaceful and serene, but as they made their way through the village of Brayford, ruined cottages and trampled crops marked a swath where troops had plundered.

He was heartsick at the despair on villagers' faces. Not one was spared; all showed signs of violent occupation and deprivation. He pulled up next to Frances. Despite her fixed gaze ahead, tears rolled down her cheeks.

At a boundary marker high on Exmoor, they paused. This may have been where he'd passed the man with his son, an anonymous farmer returning to his home. Was he alive? Did he even now sit at his hearth and smoke his pipe, a rabbit stew bubbling over the fire? Or was he rotting in an open ditch, empty eyes turned to the sky, a victim of a vengeful mercenary? There was no predicting the outcome of this war, or this retreat.

The moors spread out before Allen, sunshine chasing rainclouds across a distant horizon. A west wind rustled the hedge, but no gunshot, no distant boom of cannons, no shouting of a surprise attack broke his thoughts. The silence would be the hardest to get used to. Just then, a lark ascended, its liquid notes riding on the breeze.

Frances circled her horse and kicked it forward. "We must keep moving, to reach Exford before nightfall." Without turning, she led the way across a worn track through the heather.

He nodded. The moment was over. The small party of travelers left Devon behind and crossed into Somerset.

Riding down from the high moors, they plunged into deep woodland that carpeted the fertile valley of the River Exe. Allen saw no beauty in these woods, though, for interspersed within the trees, small camps of soldiers were visible, smoke rising from their fires, men in ragged jackets with weapons worn boldly. He checked the carbine in Boreas's neck holster, for who knew who was friend or foe this day.

"The White Horse is a comfortable inn," he called to Frances. "It sits on the main coach road to Bristol. We should stop there."

She nodded and kicked her mare forward, and they crossed over the small stone bridge toward a large inn. The forecourt was a mass of men and horses, carriages and carts, and he despaired of how to find shelter for them. Frances dismounted and threw her reins to one of the grooms.

"Stay here."

Before he could protest, she disappeared into the inn, returning a few moments later with a boy running at her side.

"The rooms are all taken, five or six sharing. But we can have the ostler's lodging above the stables, here in this wing. And a pretty penny it cost me, too." She gestured to the boy. "Show my men where to feed and water our horses. Find them a place to lie down, and I'll give you twice more what I've paid you already."

Allen dismounted. Men shouted and argued, and women chattered shrilly. Half of Devon appeared to be standing outside this inn, waiting for coaches to take them to Bristol. It wasn't just the armies on the move. He followed Frances back into the taproom, the air smoky and thick after the freshness of the moors. A tiredness was creeping over him, a deep lethargy that went beyond the physical ache of his bones. Still, he must stay on guard.

"The landlord here is friendly to the cause," he muttered to Frances. "Word has it that the cellars have hidden many a Cavalier during the times North Devon's loyalties have shifted."

Frances shrugged. "He appears a neutral. My coin worked as well as anyone's." She took her pack and climbed a narrow staircase to the side of the bar, appearing moments later, her hair tied back and her skirt brushed from the dust of the ride.

Allen barely recalled eating, but he did drink several flagons of wine, and by the time darkness fell he stumbled up the staircase to the ostler's loft and sank gratefully onto the bed of straw. Before night closed over him, he thought Frances might have removed his boots. He cared not for the impropriety; she would soon be gone.

The moon woke him, a cold orb shining through the small opening above his head. The sound of the river rushing by the inn disoriented him for a moment, and he could not place where he was.

Exford. Barnstaple surrendered. James exiled. His troop disbanded. Twelve bullets, his sword, and a safe passage home.

Wherever home was.

The night grew darker, and the water gushed louder. Even the river was finding its passage to the ocean, seeking a destination.

And what was all this for? Now, the ghosts visited, thick and fast. Laughing William. Edward, joyful and full of life. Dancing at court. Swordplay. Tennis. Drinking games at Oxford. And debates long into the night.

But no longer. The war had taken them. He should have been proud. But he was desolate. There was no victory in death.

A great, wrenching sob exploded from his raw throat, and he doubled over, hugging his knees to prevent any more sounds escaping him. He shook, as if so bitterly cold that nothing would ever warm him again. And the black jaws of the void opened and waited for him.

"Cry, my love, cry," a woman's voice soothed him. Frances clasped his head to her breast, rocked him. "Cry for all that is lost, cry."

The tenderness in her voice broke him, broke the final resolve that had sustained him to defend the fort, write the terms of surrender, and leave.

The emptiness swallowed him whole. As a child, he sobbed for the unfairness of it all; as a man, he wept for that which was no more. Those laughing companions, his friends, his ambitions, his dreams. He wept for England, for the heart now torn from his land. He wept for the fear that lay ahead, the unknown that loomed greater than any battle foe.

Under the moon's lonely path across the window, he sobbed, while shadows traced across the floor, ignoring his pain, moving relentlessly forward. And as he cried, his shaking slowed. His tears ceased flowing. Now, he lay still as the grave, spent and silent as she stroked his hair. He lifted his head, close to hers, and reached for the sweetness of her lips. Wrapped in her arms, he felt life stir within him.

Hungry now, he leaned into her, yearning turning to desire, a longing she returned to him, nourishing him. He buried his hands in her soft hair, pulling the ribbons loose so her locks tumbled around him, scenting the air with honeysuckle and roses. She kissed him, and he drank desperately of her mouth, moving his lips to her neck, pulling her shift open, burying his head in her breasts. She held him tighter, embraced him as he laid her back on the straw.

Under the silver moon, he found light in her eyes, and as she gathered him between her legs and gave herself to him, he thought, perhaps this was home.

43

Return, return, my soul, to thy true rest,
As young benighted birds unto their nest;
There hide thyselves under the wings of Love
'Till the bright morning all thy clouds remove

Luce Hutchinson
6th May 1646

She was still sleeping when he trod softly down the ladder, the dawn relieving the moonlight for morning watch. Quiet were the stables, and as he walked into the fresh morning air, the river called to him.

He moved through the dewy grass to a rock and settled, its smoothness cool to his palms. The water tumbled down from the high moors surrounding Exford. He watched it foam over boulders, the quiet pools sheltered by rocks at the banks.

The river flowed south. This could be his life, he thought. The Exe's course should run north, for they were just five miles from the Channel, a simple route to the sea. Yet this river flowed south, to the unknown obstacles of bleak Dartmoor, through mysterious lands to an ocean more than fifty miles from here.

And along its journey, men built bridges and fords and placed water wheels in its way, and still the river flowed, its path carved by God, who only knew what lay ahead.

The water gushed bronze, tinted with the earth from the moors and minerals from the rocks it bathed. No red ran in this water, and he rubbed his eyes and opened them again to be sure. No blood swirled over the rocks, disclosing hidden currents.

He tossed a pebble into a tranquil pool, watching the ripples spread and the water close over the stone as if it had never existed.

He touched the little leather pouch around his neck that contained the bride ribbon.

He leadeth me beside the still waters.

When she caressed his shoulder, he was not surprised, for had she not always come when he needed her? He put his hand up and held hers, and she quietly sat next to him. For a long while, she watched the water, silent.

He had to speak now, else she would travel on like this river, for she was of the moors and rivulets of Devon, and she knew her way as instinctively as the water found the ocean.

"You will come with me and be my love? You will marry me, then?"

"Yes."

He turned back to the river, to the soothing waters, running constant, running true.

"I love you, Frances."

She smiled and brought his hand to her lips, her kiss soft.

"I have always loved you, Allen."

Lucy rode with John and Luce down the last hill to Owthorpe from Nottingham, a half-dozen guards flanking them ahead and behind. The countryside rolled before her, a green-and-gold mantle draped over the undulating earth. At first gaze, all was quiet, serene. Upon closer inspection, furrows told of where great troops of horse had gouged the earth, and the shattered door of a cottage showed a resistance beaten down.

"I wish to stop at the church," she told her daughter as they reined into the village. "You go to the house."

Luce nodded, and they parted at the church gate, John leaving two guards with Lucy.

Gathering her skirts, Lucy walked the straight grassy path alongside a quiet farm to the small stone church that stood alone in its graveyard, a spacious meadow to its west, a deep copse of woods to its south. Peace flowed into her soul, and when a lark rose from the green field, soaring into the air on the beat of its song, she embraced the liquid notes of joy.

"Wait here," she told the guards as she unlatched the rough-hewn door and saw the emptiness inside. "I shall be quite safe."

Clear glass let the sunshine pour into the chapel, where an uneven stone font revealed the age of the building. A few benches offered repose, and she sat upon one to the left of the aisle and let the peace of the church wash over her.

As she rested, the past came to visit, softly filling her mind and heart. The gentle sweet whispers of her beloved Anne, the ring of Theo's laughter, Edward's golden head illuminated in the summer sun, the warmth of Allen's embrace. The tears flowed now—a mother's tears, a lover's sobbing. For was it not a woman's lot to weep, to mourn for those lost, to grieve with those left behind?

In this peaceful place, there was room for the past to rest and hope to grow. She looked down at her hands, which had cured so many in her life. Perhaps her boys would return here and bring their wounded spirits to be healed by her. There was reason to stay, to watch her grandchildren thrive, to help her daughter rebuild her life.

Through the window, the lark reached its zenith before dropping back down to the ground to seek its nest. The little creature knew where her home was. As did Lucy.

Luce rode alongside John across the moat, her heart thumping. From here, the house looked as it had always stood—Owthorpe Manor, a testament to the protection the Hutchinsons had provided this village for centuries past. But small signs caused her stomach to churn. The gates were wrenched from the pillars and tossed into the long grass, and the trees felled, lying haphazard across the lawns as if a storm had strewn them in its wake.

As they reined their horses by the house, more fears. Windows broken, and the front doors yawned open, the splintered wood evidence that the locks had been smashed. All was quiet, save for the raucous crows on the roof, rising as they approached, settling again when they saw no danger.

John jumped down from his horse. Luce followed him.

"Stay, my love." He looked toward the guard they'd left at the gate.

"No. I wish to see for myself." Luce was not going to let him bear this pain alone.

Together, they stepped into the shadowy hall of their home and quickly stopped. Their furniture was gone, the tapestries, the paintings, no more. The walls were scarred, as if someone had taken an axe to the very spine of the house and struck it in a great rage. No doors were left hanging, and a great stench from the corner told her that men had desecrated this chamber as a privy. Sickness rose in her throat, but she took John's hand. *Stay strong for him.*

"Come, let us see what damage is done," she said. "Let us know the worst."

John looked at the wreckage of his home, the defilement left by the retreating Royalist troops.

"By God, they shall pay." His voice shook. "They will pay dearly for this carnage, this reign of pestilence."

Luce walked across the chamber, the shattered glass crunching under her boots. In the kitchen, the great oak table that she and her mother had worked on together was now splintered and broken, its legs missing. A half-burned chunk of it lay collapsed in the fireplace, where a cooking pot still hung from the iron. No chairs were left, nor plate on the board. The shelves were gone, and again, great gouges in the wall told the story of a hundred axe blows. A rotting dog carcass lay by the pantry, its putrid smell mingling with that of human excrement. All was despoiled.

Through their home they walked, each room bringing new horrors, deep sorrow. Even the chamber that the children had shared was filthy, its windows smashed and the delicate embroidered samplers torn from the walls and soiled with men's obscenity. A crow flapped onto the empty windowsill and filled the silent room with his harsh cawing. Once, Luce had sung lullabies to her babies here.

They made their way toward the stairs, the rail hanging to one side, wrenched from its sockets. Through the holes in the wall that were once the landing windows, Luce paused and looked out across the countryside, brilliant green in the June sunshine. The little village of Owthorpe clustered around the church, unchanged. To the east, a verdant meadow stretched to a distant wood, radiantly sunlit. From the shadows of their ruined home, the land dazzled her with promise. The acreage was flat, welcoming, unsullied.

A lark ascended on the wings of a warbling song as it fluttered into the sky. As she followed the tiny creature, it reached its apex and ceased singing, plunging down to the meadow. *A lark never descends to exactly where the nest is,* her mother had told her. *But watch carefully where the bird lands, for it is always close to home.* And so, they would rebuild, on new pastures, where her children would not suffer the taint of war.

A gentle breeze blew over her cheek as she gazed from the window. Two riders and a pack pony progressed through the village street. More travelers. The whole country was on the move as men and women returned to their homes. She saw them stop by the ruined gates and look up at the house. There was something familiar about the man, the white horse . . . and yet, who rode with him?

They looked once more up at the house and turned their horses away.

With a cry, Luce ran down the remaining stairs, clutching at the wall, scraping her hand on a splintered frame. She ran outside, into the brilliant sunlight, and shouted at the departing riders.

"Allen! Allen!" They had to hear her, must turn around. Hastened by her shouts, John ran to her.

The horses paused and circled, and Luce's brother and his companion rode back toward her.

His sister stood at the door of her ruined house, John next to her. They were here. But under what terrible blight.

"Come," Allen said to Frances. "Come."

They turned their horses' heads and rode back to the manor. Tethering them by the ruined pillars, they dismounted and walked across the grassy track over the moat. Allen kept his eyes fixed on Luce, knowing Frances was by his side.

Wordlessly, he walked into this sister's arms and held her within his embrace. Her slight figure was trembling. Pulling back, he held her at arm's length, staring into her face. Gently, he wiped the tears from her cheeks.

"Now, then," he said softly. "Why the tears to greet me? Are you so dispirited to see your brother that you cannot smile for him?"

Luce scrubbed at her face and shook her head.

"I thought you were—"

"Not I," he interjected quickly before she could say more. "Nor James. And Mother?"

"Safe." Luce glanced across the fields toward the church. "She paused to pray."

John stood silently by Luce's side, his eyes watchful. At last, he spoke. "You travel far, Brother. But the king is no longer at Newark. He journeys north, to Newcastle, with the Scots. You must ride hard to catch up. I suggest you start now."

Luce stood between them. Frances remained silent.

"I heard as much," said Allen. "I thank you for your advice." He looked at the ruined manor house. "I see the war came to your door, too."

John's face contorted. "The Royalists defiled my property, desecrated my home."

"Each village we passed on our journey was violated, John, by Cavalier and Roundhead alike." Allen spread his hands wide. "No one has been spared the ruin of war."

"And yet, you flee here, into the heart of Roundhead territory?"

"All of England is under Parliament's governance now, John." Allen shook his head, trying to dispel the fog of weariness that weighed so heavily on him. "You are the victors in this war."

"Yes. We won." John turned his back on Allen and stared at his ruined home. "Whatever winning means."

Allen met Luce's her worried eyes. "I think, John, the king has seen there is nothing won and all to lose. Perhaps now he will understand the passion that lives in his subjects' hearts and will negotiate terms that will satisfy all sides. Perchance there will not be Roundhead and Cavalier boundaries forever scarred on our land."

John did not move. There hinted a deep anger concealed behind his stiff back.

He gestured at his vandalized home. "You speak of appeasement, Brother. If your house stood in ruins, would you be reconciled? I know not where to find room in my heart for your kind." He turned back to Allen, put his arm around Luce. "Our family has been divided for five years. Our boundaries dwell in our hearts; they are not just seared upon our lands. If not within us, where is England's peace, now?"

Allen reached his hand out to John. "Peace lies with Edward and his brothers, and William. Peace lies with all the men who fought in this war, who set out spirited in their beliefs, only to have hope die with them on a battlefield."

His eye fell back on Luce, her attention caught by a movement by the church. A lonely figure was slowly walking through the gravestones, the breeze tugging on her long black skirts.

"Mother approaches," said Luce. "Would that she not find her children still at war."

John ignored her. "And you would change the course of the years, Allen? You still consider the king was justified in his actions?"

Allen shook his head. "There is no changing the past. But perhaps there is hope for the future."

He dropped his hand. John had not taken it. "You and me, Brother, we are no different than a thousand men across this land. We fought for our beliefs. And we lost all for our beliefs. Now has come the time for reconciliation."

"You put a lot of trust in men's honor," replied John. "And yet I have this to show for my politics." He gestured again to the ruined house.

Luce stepped forward from John's arm and took Allen's. "You have more than material evidence of your principles, John. You have the chance now to remedy the horror of war by structuring a peaceful settlement."

"Perhaps the time for violence is past." Allen smiled at his sister. Always, she turned to words, the power of language. "We who survive may take up the fight with our words and deeds, not weapons."

"And you think we will be the solution?" John searched his eyes, and Allen saw the weariness within—and deeper still, behind the mask, a hint of the void.

Across the field, leaving the church path, his mother paused for a moment and then gathered her skirts, her pace quickening.

He had to break through to John. Within a minute, she would be with them. He had to build a bridge across this chasm that divided them. "You speak for your people, John, your county, your constituents. I have the prince's ear, his father's trust. You are a confidante of Cromwell. Leveraging the Villiers influence, I can reach the king. Perhaps, together, we can engage in a settlement."

"Cromwell is an unforgiving man. He will not listen easily," replied John. "He is obstinate, even to the point of injuring himself to satisfy a point."

Allen nodded. "Then who better than you to deal with him? You are not one to shy away from the truth, however painful it may be. Your plain speaking will carry more weight than any courtier's flattery."

Luce slipped her hand in John's. "Cromwell has asked for your counsel in Parliament, John. We have spoken many times of our dreams for England when peace arrives. You could do more for your countrymen in Westminster than you think. The speeches you could make, the laws you could enact, now that the king must reconcile to ruling with Parliament."

"That would be a fair gain indeed, Luce." Allen shook his head. How could life change so swiftly? "I did not think I would see the day that John was appointed to Westminster with you at his side. Together you would be invincible."

Still, John hesitated. "The king has proven himself even more intractable. His refusal to accept any will but his own has sent thousands to their deaths. Why would you think we can effect change in a man who is eager to sacrifice the blood of his own people to support his beliefs? What guarantees that he will not betray us again?"

This man. Will he always throw up these obstacles? A gentle touch on Allen's arm, Frances cautioning patience. He tried for the last time.

"When the court gathers, the prince will return from France. The king loves his son. He will want to restore a peaceable kingdom for him to inherit. I trust that he will see that the way to achieve this will be to work with Parliament, be open to its requests, come together to build a government based on promises and assurances, not deceit and broken pledges." Allen looked across to the little village nestled in the land, its fields of ancient furrows that told the history of generations of farmers. "Surely, he will heed your argument, and conclude that peace and reconciliation is the future of our country."

"A peaceable kingdom," echoed John. "No poverty, crime, war. And the wolf shall live with the lamb. As king and Parliament may." He followed Allen's gaze to Lucy, now just a field away, walking swiftly toward them through the tall grass. "You sound like your sister. She has always put her faith in words." Slowly, he held out his hand.

Allen smiled. "We are not so different in our hearts, John." He took John's hand, its clasp familiar.

Frances slipped her hand in Allen's free one.

A rustle of skirts. The cherished scent of jasmine. His mother before him, her eyes alight with joy. She stood, half laughing, half crying, and he pulled her into his embrace, his tears mingling with hers.

"We are unharmed," he murmured. "James and me. The war is over."

Lucy caressed his cheek, soothing the fear that constantly escorted him, unwanted, uninvited.

"Who is this, Allen?" she asked. "Who travels with you?"

He grew calm, peaceful, and a river of emotion flowed into the void, filling the emptiness with serene waters. He said the words aloud for the first time. "This is Frances Petre. My betrothed."

"Then, welcome, Frances Petre," replied Lucy. "Welcome home."

For further reading, please enjoy this brief extract from *The Lady of the Tower.*

Orphaned Lucy St.John, described as "the most beautiful of all," defies English society by attracting the eye of the Earl of Suffolk. In 1609, the court of James I is a place of glittering pageantry and cutthroat ambition, when the most dangerous thing one can do is fall in love. Lucy's envious sister Barbara is determined to ruin her happiness and drives Lucy into exile from the court. Heartbroken, she has to find her own path through life, becoming mistress of the Tower of London and gaining a fortune through the patronage of the Duke of Buckingham. But with great wealth comes betrayal, leaving Lucy to fight for her survival—and her honor—in a world of deceit and debauchery.

Elizabeth St.John tells this dramatic story of love, betrayal, and loyalty through the eyes of her ancestor Lucy and her family's surviving diaries, letters and court papers.

The Lady of the Tower

The Lydiard Chronicles | 1603-1630

ELIZABETH ST.JOHN

PROLOGUE

God, who holds my fate in Thy hands, give me strength, I implore, for today I enter a prison like no other on this earth, and perhaps one that even Hell does not equal in its fiery despair. Give me fortitude to walk through those gates where so many traitors have gone before and never left. Give me compassion to hear the cries of forgotten men and not turn my head away. Give me, above all, Heavenly Father, courage to bear myself with dignity and Your grace when I am inwardly trembling with fear at the horrors that lie behind those walls.

Lucy
23 March 1617

Silver drizzle veiled the stone walls rising from the moat's stagnant water. To the north, the White Tower glistened but bade no welcome for all its shining. Gabled roofs with ornate chimneys pierced the mist and hid again, hinting at a house within the fortress. I was not comforted, for it reminded me that the kept must have their keepers.

Thunder resounded through the fog from water swirling around the center arches of the bridge, just upriver from our tethered barge. The first time I was rowed in a shuddering boat through the narrow span of columns was terrifying. "Shooting the bridge" the locals called it, the currents created by the arches manifesting river water into whirlpools. Recollections of impaled traitors' heads grinning from the pikes appeared before my closed eyes. What hell's gate was I approaching?

"Ho! Tie here!"

A clash of metal resounded as the pikemen stood to attention on the wharf. I pulled my mind back to the present.

"Aye, make way for the lady."

Roughened hands guided me from the rocking boat, and I carefully picked my way up the water steps. My heart beat faster as I gazed up at the sheer ramparts. They loomed over my head, broken only by a low arch with an iron portcullis. Blackened bars jutted forth, a reminder I entered a prison.

I shivered from the damp air, and not a little from apprehension, and stood still on the wharf. Behind me, the Thames ebbed now, and the ferrymen urgently called patrons to catch the running tide. In front, the moat lay impenetrably black and still. The cold seeped through the soles of my shoes, for in my anxiety I had forgotten my pattens. Out of the gloom, a man appeared beside me.

"Princess Elizabeth paused here," the Keeper spoke quietly, his words brushed by the lilt of an Irish accent. "She declared she was no traitor and refused to enter through that arch, for those who arrive through Traitors' Gate do not leave again."

The dark water gate, its walls defining the width of the ramparts above, did not welcome guests. I thought of the young princess defying her guards, perching on a wet stone on a rainy day similar to this, her own future cloudy with doubt and dread. I recalled the moment I heard I was to enter the Tower and how my stomach twisted with fear at the news.

"When I served her, none could see the frightened girl behind the majesty," he continued, "for we were all in love with her, each one of us outdoing the other in deeds and poetry to gain her favor."

The Keeper waved the bargeman away, and the boat was quickly untied and pushed from the wharf, the crew not looking back as they rowed rapidly upriver.

"Her 'adventurers,' she called us, and all through her life she played us one against many, declaring her affection and encouraging our competition—who could sail the farthest, dance the longest, fight the strongest." He pulled his black leather cloak closer against the cold. "She challenged us, and she baited us like dogs to a bear."

I looked at the Keeper, his faded blue seafarer's eyes gazing toward invisible horizons as he sailed into memories. Briefly, I glimpsed the queen's man in his prime, standing tall and strong, bronzed by foreign suns, his white beard a rich chestnut brown, his shoulders broad.

"Another woman whose own sister betrayed her, who knew not whom she could trust." My voice competed with the rushing water; there was no telling if he heard.

"All the princess recalled that sorry afternoon was her mother, who entered the gate at the king's command and never left." He turned away abruptly and hailed a guard standing by.

Just as I am commanded.

"Escort my lady to her lodging. Ensure my steward is there to greet her and introduces her to her household. I shall be at the armory."

He strode off, leaving me lonely on the wharf, my skirts heavy with the weight of the rainwater, thoughts swirling. I followed the guard along a narrow path to a bridge across the moat and toward the gabled house I'd glimpsed earlier.

Married to a man I trusted not, parted from family and friends, I entered the Tower of London. A bleak March morn in the year of our Lord 1617, and I was the new mistress of the prison.

Printed in Great Britain
by Amazon

17109798R00217